Passions in death

Robb, J. D.
08/27/2024

PASSIONS IN DEATH

Titles by J. D. Robb

Naked in Death

Glory in Death

Immortal in Death

Rapture in Death

Ceremony in Death

Vengeance in Death

Holiday in Death

Conspiracy in Death

Loyalty in Death

Witness in Death

Judgment in Death

Betrayal in Death

Seduction in Death

Reunion in Death

Purity in Death

Portrait in Death

Imitation in Death

Divided in Death

Visions in Death

Survivor in Death

Origin in Death

Memory in Death

Born in Death

Innocent in Death

Creation in Death

Strangers in Death

Salvation in Death

Promises in Death

Kindred in Death

Fantasy in Death

Indulgence in Death

Treachery in Death

New York to Dallas

Celebrity in Death

Delusion in Death

Calculated in Death

Thankless in Death

Concealed in Death

Festive in Death

Obsession in Death

Devoted in Death

Brotherhood in Death

Apprentice in Death

Echoes in Death

Secrets in Death

Dark in Death

Leverage in Death

Connections in Death

Vendetta in Death

Golden in Death

Shadows in Death

Faithless in Death

Forgotten in Death

Abandoned in Death

Desperation in Death

Encore in Death

Payback in Death

Random in Death

Passions in Death

Anthologies

Silent Night
(with Susan Plunkett, Dee Holmes, and Claire Cross)

Out of This World
(with Laurell K. Hamilton, Susan Krinard, and Maggie Shayne)

Remember When
(with Nora Roberts)

Bump in the Night
(with Mary Blayney, Ruth Ryan Langan, and Mary Kay McComas)

Dead of Night
(with Mary Blayney, Ruth Ryan Langan, and Mary Kay McComas)

Three in Death

Suite 606
(with Mary Blayney, Ruth Ryan Langan, and Mary Kay McComas)

In Death

The Lost
(with Patricia Gaffney, Mary Blayney, and Ruth Ryan Langan)

The Other Side
(with Mary Blayney, Patricia Gaffney, Ruth Ryan Langan, and Mary Kay McComas)

Time of Death

The Unquiet
(with Mary Blayney, Patricia Gaffney, Ruth Ryan Langan, and Mary Kay McComas)

Mirror, Mirror
(with Mary Blayney, Elaine Fox, Mary Kay McComas, and R. C. Ryan)

Down the Rabbit Hole
(with Mary Blayney, Elaine Fox, Mary Kay McComas, and R. C. Ryan)

PASSIONS IN DEATH

J. D. Robb

ST. MARTIN'S PRESS
NEW YORK

First published in the United States by St. Martin's Press,
an imprint of St. Martin's Publishing Group

PASSIONS IN DEATH. Copyright © 2024 by Nora Roberts. All rights reserved.
Printed in the United States of America. For information, address
St. Martin's Publishing Group, 120 Broadway, New York, NY 10271.

www.stmartins.com

The Library of Congress Cataloging-in-Publication Data is available upon request.

ISBN 978-1-250-28956-8 (hardcover)
ISBN 978-1-250-28957-5 (ebook)

Our books may be purchased in bulk for promotional, educational, or business use.
Please contact your local bookseller or the Macmillan Corporate and
Premium Sales Department at 1-800-221-7945, extension 5442, or by email at
MacmillanSpecialMarkets@macmillan.com.

First Edition: 2024

10 9 8 7 6 5 4 3 2 1

My fault, my failure, is not in the passions I have,
but in my lack of control of them.

—Jack Kerouac

The language of Friendship
is not words, but meanings.

—Henry David Thoreau

Chapter One

THE PARTY WAS A KILLER!

Erin Albright paused a moment in the madness to take it all in. The slash and crash of music designed to get your ass moving had those asses crowding the dance floor. Lights shifting from steamy red to electric blue to hot pink made it all so frigging sexy!

The bartender's generous pours on tonight's signature drink, Girl Power, didn't hurt a thing.

They'd chosen a Monday night at the Down and Dirty because they'd wanted the heat, the sexy, and an off night so they'd have plenty of room for the couple dozen friends they'd wanted to join in the celebration.

Plus, Monday nights at the D&D meant holo-bands, so people could jump on the stage and join right in.

And when they did, it added to the fun.

Shauna jumped up onstage—again—and someone made the mistake of giving her a mic. Shauna had a voice like a cat in heat, and she used it to screech out the lyrics to "Bang Me Hard."

God, could she possibly be more adorable?

And in five days, only five more days, Erin thought, on August 20, 2061, she'll be my wife, and I'll be hers.

Together forever.

At five-two, Shauna Hunnicut made Erin think of a sexy fairy, one with a wild tangle of red hair and big, beautiful blue eyes. And that smile? Another killer.

The hair had caught her eye that first time, and the eyes had dazzled. But oh, that smile. It had simply done her in from the get-go.

She'd walked into Fancy Feet for a pair of shoes, and walked out completely infatuated. She, the no-strings, live-life-for-today street artist had fallen, and hard, for the shoe store manager.

Who'd have thought that fifteen months, three weeks, and two days later, they'd promise each other lifetimes?

She couldn't wait to make that promise, to hear Shauna make it to her.

Shauna's friend Becca—her friend, too, now—grabbed Erin's hand.

"Gotta shake it, baby!"

She shook it with Becca on the dance floor, and like everyone else, joined in on the chorus.

"Bang me, bang me harder. Oh! Bang me, bang me harder. Oh. Oh. Oh!"

"This is so much fun!" Becca shouted, and shoved her swing of strawberry blond—now sweaty—hair back from her pretty face. "Why haven't I ever been here before?"

"Because it's a sex club and you're an upstanding young professional and executive at a stuffy Madison Avenue marketing firm?"

"Junior executive at a stuffy Madison Avenue marketing firm." Becca executed a spin. "Woo! And I might not be so upstanding after tonight! You and Shauna have to get married more often!"

"One and done for me." She looked back as Shauna wound up for the finish. "God, isn't she cute? Is anybody more adorable than my soon-to-be wife?"

"Loved her for years—in a straight-girl kind of way. I'm so happy for her. For you, too!" A little bit drunk, and sweaty with it, Becca wrapped her arms around Erin.

Cheers erupted. Erin added her own as Shauna threw her hands in the air.

"I'm going to go get my girl before she decides to do an encore."

Waving her own hands in the air, Erin wove her way through bodies to the stage. "Come down and dance with me, you sexy thing!"

"Anytime, anywhere." Face glowing, Shauna dropped down to her butt, then scooted the rest of the way off the stage. "This is so much fun!"

In her tiny blue dress and mile-high heels, she wrapped around Erin.

"You have the best ideas."

"My best idea ever was deciding to try on those wild pink shoes I saw in the window. Pink shoes led me to you. I love you, baby."

"I'm the luckiest woman in this club, in this city, possibly the world. Because I have you."

Swaying to the music, wrapped tight, they kissed. Soft, sweet, even as music boomed out a frantic beat.

Who knew, Erin thought again. Who knew she'd find the woman of her dreams—dreams she hadn't thought to dream? A woman who'd open her life to love, to plans, to the future.

Everything before Shauna had been the now. Always just the right now, forget tomorrow.

Now she loved, and wanted thousands of tomorrows.

So they danced, then danced some more as a couple, in groups. More cheers blasted as the next holo-band stripped down to G-strings. Becca rushed the stage, stripped off her short, slinky dress, and danced.

More cheers.

"We've corrupted her." Eyes full of delight, Shauna laughed. "She was the poster girl of straitlaced in high school. A complete doof. Now she's drunk and dancing in her underwear in a sex club."

"It's pretty underwear."

On another laugh, Shauna gave Erin another kiss. "Buy me a drink, gorgeous."

"You got it."

They made their way to the bar tended by the owner. Crack, a big, muscular, tattooed Black man, wore a leather vest over his bare chest. He shot them a wide grin.

"Another round, brides-to-be?"

"Girl Power!" Shauna shouted, pumping fists in the air.

"You got that going." He mixed drinks with his big, experienced hands. "Brought me a wild bunch tonight."

"More than a few out there would go for a handsome kick-ass dude like you," Erin told him.

"Got me a one-in-ten-million woman be waiting when I get home."

"Hey, I didn't know you had a serious going on."

"Ain't been in my place for a while, have you?"

"I guess not." Erin tipped her purple-streaked shaggy blond bob to Shauna's mass of red. "Because I've got my own one in ten million now."

"Aw." Shauna kissed her again. "But we're coming back, bunches, because I *love* this place. I thought we'd get all glammed up and go to an upscale bar and . . . I didn't mean your place isn't upscale."

He sent her a wicked flash of a grin. "Honey, it ain't the Down and Dirty for nothing. Now, if any of the chicks and slicks in my place hassle any of your group how you don't want to be hassled, you let me know and—"

"You'll crack their heads together," Erin finished. "It's how he got his name."

"For serious?"

Face fierce, Crack made a head-banging gesture with his hands.

"We don't be upscale, but we got standards." He slid the drinks toward them. "Drink up. This round's on me."

Shauna toasted him, then drank a third of the glass in one go. "God, this is so good, and I'm going to get so wasted. Let's dance some of this buzz off!"

Within twenty minutes, Shauna jumped back onstage to scream out another song, and this time stripped down like Becca.

Astonished in the best possible way, Erin watched her shimmy and shake. A couple others, inspired, climbed up to join in.

Erin checked the time and, pleased she'd estimated when the party would hit peak, sent a text, smiled at the response.

Then slipped away from the dance floor.

She'd planned this surprise, a winner, every detail, including that timing. Her accomplice would be waiting in the privacy room she'd rented.

She intended to make her bride's every dream come true, starting now.

The love of her life's dream? Hawaii.

She'd worked her ass off to sell enough paintings to afford the trip—something they'd started saving for, for later.

This time? Forget later. Now would shine.

She'd kept this secret for nearly three weeks—and that hadn't been easy for her. But she'd let Shauna think they'd hold off on that dream honeymoon for a year, maybe two, as they'd agreed.

Even her trusted accomplice—actually, her backup accomplice—didn't know. She'd just needed someone to smuggle in her overnight case holding the grass skirt, coconut bra, leis, and the crazy pink shoes that had started it all.

And those tickets to Maui.

Once she'd changed, she'd take the stage!

She headed toward the back. The privacy rooms weren't a hot ticket on a Monday night—she knew from previous experience. Dimmer lights, soundproofed doors offered an option for those who wanted a quick round between drinks.

She didn't regret that her days of those quick rounds had passed.

She'd already slipped her accomplice the swipe, so pressed the buzzer that would flicker the lights inside.

The door opened, and she entered the darkened room.

"Really appreciate this," she said as she walked in, then turned to close the door so the privacy locks clicked behind her. "She doesn't have a clue! Oh, she's going to go crazy! I'm going to need more light to—"

Something thin and sharp circled her neck, cutting off her air. Blood dribbled down her throat as it broke through the skin.

She flailed, tried to scream, struggled to drag the wire away. When her head slammed against the door, she saw stars.

As the wire cut deeper, the stars went out.

The communicator woke her out of a dead sleep. Lieutenant Eve Dallas cursed it, then pushed up in bed as her husband ordered lights at ten percent.

She shoved a hand through her short, choppy brown hair, nudged at the fat cat on her other side. Galahad just rolled.

"Dallas."

Dispatch, Dallas, Lieutenant Eve. Probable homicide. Nine-one-one caller requested you. Report to . . .

When she heard the address, Eve rolled over the cat and out of bed. "The Down and Dirty?"

Affirmative.

"Name of nine-one-one caller?"

Wilson Buckley, identified as the owner.

"I'm on my way, and will contact Detective Peabody. Dallas out."

"I'm with you," Roarke said, and had already pulled on jeans. "It's Crack's place. I'm with you." After a look at her face as she sprinted to her closet, he added, "If it had been Rochelle, he'd have contacted you directly."

"You're right. That sounds right." She grabbed what came to hand out of her closet. Black trousers, a white tee, a black jacket, belt, boots.

As she pulled on clothes, Roarke stepped in, already dressed, with her weapon harness.

"Thanks." She strapped it on. "Monday night—it's Monday night, right?"

"Just tipped over into Tuesday morning."

"Should be a slow night for the D&D. That's how I met him." She rushed out to snag her badge, her 'link, the communicator.

"DB across the street from his place. Nothing to do with his place, or him, but that's how I met him. Since you're coming, you drive. I'll contact Peabody, get her ass up and moving."

Other than herself, she trusted him most to drive like a wild thing all the way downtown.

As they jogged downstairs, she tried not to resent that he looked as if he'd had eight solid hours of sleep, probably with a massage beforehand. The impossibly blue eyes alert, that black silk mane of hair somehow perfect.

He wouldn't have given a moment's thought to the clothes he'd put on, and yet they looked exactly right on that tall, rangy frame.

It could be a pisser to wake up after less than an hour down beside an Irish god.

He'd already remoted her vehicle from the garage, so it waited outside the Irish god's castle.

After strapping into the passenger seat, she gave another finger swipe to her hair, then pressed the heels of her hands to her long, whiskey-colored eyes.

Everything felt like a pisser, she admitted as he all but flew down the long drive to the gates that opened on his approach.

Coffee would fix that.

She programmed two—strong and black—from the in-dash Auto-Chef.

At that first life-giving glug, some of the clouds lifted. She reminded herself she'd recently had a long weekend on Roarke's private island.

Just the two of them and sun, surf, sand, sex.

What did she have to bitch about?

Having a friend report a dead body at not quite one in the morning? Yeah, bitch-worthy, but that was the job.

Plus, she got to give her partner the same treatment.

She drank more coffee, let it perform its miracles, then contacted Peabody.

"Yeah, Peabody. What?"

"Jesus, block video. I don't need to see your tits."

"They're quite lovely," Roarke commented, and earned the hard eye from Eve.

"Oh, sorry, block video. We got caught up purging and packing for the Big Move. We practically just went down. Who's dead?"

"Don't know the who, but the where is the Down and Dirty."

Eve clearly heard McNab—EDD ace and the second half of Peabody's "we"—curse.

She supposed there were Friendship Rules just like there were Marriage Rules. She'd have two detectives on scene.

"Is Crack okay?"

"He called it in. Pull it together, get there."

She clicked off, gauged the speed and distance. She calculated even though Peabody and McNab lived downtown, Roarke would get there first.

"He doesn't have cams," Eve remembered. "No cams, in or out. God-damn it."

"It's a sex club, Eve. You'd thin out your clientele considerably with door or interior cams. And you didn't need them to deal with Casto when he attacked you at the D&D the night before our wedding."

He'd given her a shiner, though. She still resented it.

"I wonder how that corrupt asshole former cop likes prison."

Despite the speed, Roarke glanced at her, smiled. "I suspect not a bit."

"It's hard to see this being a fight gone south. Crack has a rep for deal-ing with trouble and troublemakers for a reason." Then she shook her head. "No point in thinking about who and why. Best to go in cold. But you know what part of the problem is?"

"You know too many people."

She shot him a hard look. "I was going to say that. How did you know I was going to say that?"

He didn't bother to glance over, but he did smile. "I know my cop's mind."

"Well, I do." She chugged down the rest of her coffee. "If I didn't know too many people, I'd still end up driving like a maniac to a crime scene at damn near one in the morning because that's the job, but I wouldn't know so many people somehow connected if I didn't know too many people in the first place."

She tipped her head back. "How did that happen?"

"Your magnetic, people-loving personality?"

"Oh, bite me."

"Didn't I do that earlier?"

He had, she recalled, and in just the right way.

"It's probably your fault. I don't know how exactly, but probably. And who hangs out at a downtown sex club on a Monday night?"

"People lovers?" he suggested.

"Somebody sure as hell didn't love somebody this Monday night."

She spotted the police cruiser, then the uniform on the door when Roarke pulled up.

A quick summer storm had rolled through about the time Roarke had been biting her in just the right way. Damp pavement and puddles gleamed in the streetlights. When she stepped out, the air steamed with August.

In the steam bath, the uniform's face gleamed like the puddles.

"Officer."

"Lieutenant. Sir, my partner's inside with the DB. We received the dispatch at zero hours, sixteen minutes, and arrived on scene approximately three minutes later. Female victim, discovered by one of the staff in a privacy room. From our visual it's apparently a strangulation. Roughly eighty people inside, including staff. About two dozen of those are part of a single party. The victim was with that party, identified by others as Erin Albright."

Pausing, the uniform used the back of her wrist to wipe a dribble of sweat from her temple.

"A hen party, sir. A girl party to celebrate an upcoming wedding. Albright was one of the brides. Crack—Mr. Buckley—"

"I know Crack," Eve interrupted.

"Then you know he got things under control quickly. Blocked off the room, blocked the exits, even before we got on scene. He has the other bride, Shauna Hunnicut, and a couple of her friends in his office. She's upset, sir, to put it mildly."

"Got it. My partner— Never mind, here she comes."

Peabody, in pink sneakers, khakis, with her red-streaked black hair bundled back in a short tail, hustled down the sidewalk. Beside her, Mc-Nab put on his usual show in red-and-blue-striped baggies, red airboots, and a blue tee that displayed a big red heart over his bony chest.

His forest of colorful hoops gleamed along his earlobe. His long—currently red-streaked—blond tail bounced at his back.

"Take the door from inside, Officer."

The uniform let out a sigh of relief. "Thanks, Lieutenant."

Eve turned to Peabody. "Female vic, found in one of the privacy rooms. About eighty people inside, a good chunk of those with a pre-wedding party deal. The girl thing."

"Golly, you had yours here."

"Under duress. The vic was one of the brides."

"Harsh," said McNab.

"Yeah, it qualifies. Crack has the other bride with a couple friends in his office. We're going to let her calm down some. McNab, since you're here, you can start getting statements, contacts and releasing. Start with anyone not connected to the party. Peabody, you start with partygoers, and I'll take the body."

"What about Crack?" Peabody asked.

"We'll talk to him. One of his people found the body, so we need that conversation. Then we'll take the other bride. You and McNab start clearing the place out. Roarke can assist me with the body. We've got no electronics except the door of the privacy room, and Roarke can take that. No cams," she muttered.

She glanced up at the glowing neon proclaiming DOWN AND DIRTY.

It probably would be.

Inside, the temperature dropped an easy ten degrees. No problem, she thought, separating those in the party group from those who'd come in for booze and boobs.

She supposed Crack had separated the brides' party—lots of weeping or the glazed eyes of the shocked—from the just happened to be theres. Plenty of irritation, fascination, boredom on that side.

The big man himself strode across the room, straight to Eve. He didn't look shocked, bored, or weepy. He looked furious.

"Somebody killed that girl in my place. You find who killed that girl. I knew that girl."

"Understood. We're going to do our job, starting right now. We're going to talk to you in a bit, and we need to talk to the person who found her."

"I've got him. He's pretty goddamn shook. I mixed her and Shauna drinks. I mixed Erin a fucking drink not two hours ago. And somebody killed that girl in my place."

"Crack, I need to go take care of her now."

He nodded, scrubbed his hands over his face. "I asked for you because I knew you'd take care of her. I knew all of you would take care of her. I'll show you where she is."

"Get started," Eve told Peabody and McNab, and followed him.

It brought on a flashback where the club blasted with music, lights flashing. Still-in-uniform Peabody gloriously drunk, pre-Oscar-win-and-bestseller-status Nadine Furst doing a striptease onstage. The shock of seeing the elegant Dr. Mira shaking her ass on the dance floor.

It would've been along those lines, Eve thought. Noisy, pretty drunk, happy women, shaking asses, bouncing around.

Why had one of the brides gone into a privacy room? Lured in, she wondered, as she herself had been by someone she'd considered—not a friend, in her case—but a colleague?

"Who rented the room?"

"She did—added it on when she booked the party like two, maybe three weeks ago. Between that," he decided. "Don't know why, but she said she had a surprise deal for Shauna, and not to tell anyone she had the room. I let her have it for the whole night. Mondays are slow."

And wouldn't you know it, she thought when they turned down the dim corridor. The same damn privacy room.

Crack handed her a swipe. "That's my master. Hers is in there, on the floor."

"You go take care of your people. We'll take care of her."

"I'm here when you want me."

She waited until he'd walked away, turned her recorder on, then swiped open the door.

The victim lay on her back, brown eyes staring at the ceiling. Blood from the neck wound had run down her throat to soak the bodice of a short, shiny green dress. One of her shoes had slipped off, and one arm lay outstretched. The swipe card swam in a pool of her blood just beyond her fingers.

One of those tiny, useless handbags lay open on her other side.

"Seal up," she told Roarke.

He'd already opened her field kit, and handed her the can of sealant. "You first."

"No jewelry," she noted as she coated her hands, her boots. "Somebody wanted us to say robbery. Somebody thinks we're stupid."

She handed him the sealant, took the field kit, then stepped around the blood to the body.

"She's got a fresh wound on her forehead, and blood on the inside of the door—that's going to be from that. So the killer was inside the room. Prepared to kill."

"Because?"

"I don't know why yet, but that's a thin wound on her neck, and a deep one. Piano wire, maybe. Some sort of garrote. You don't have that handy if you're looking to mug. You've got a sticker maybe, a stunner, a sap. Fresh manicure," she added as she crouched. "But two of her nails are broken, scratches on her neck where she tried to drag the wire away."

Eve lifted one of the victim's hands. "Skin and blood under the nails. That's going to be hers, too. Took her from behind, that's how you do it. Whip the wire around and pull, give her a good knock against the door to daze her. She'd have been drinking on top of it. Party time, happy time. So reflexes are slower than sober."

She glanced up at Roarke. "I hadn't been drinking when Casto went for me in here because, hey, getting married the next day. That was his mistake."

"In this room?"

"Yeah. Ten bucks says Peabody's going to talk about white saging it."

She took a sample of the matter under Erin's nails, sealed it, labeled it. Then pressed a finger to her Identi-pad.

"Victim is identified as Erin Albright, age twenty-seven, mixed-race female, resides on Twelfth Street—only a few blocks from here—with cohab Shauna Hunnicut."

She bagged both hands. "Maybe she got a piece of him. Doubtful, but maybe."

Before she reached in her kit for microgoggles, Roarke handed them to her.

Fitting them on, she leaned close to the neck wound. "Yeah, some sort of wire. Piano wire, steel guitar string, what's it—baling wire. Victim was garroted, with force."

She took out gauges. "Enough force the neck wound is a sixth of an inch deep at its deepest point. The forehead wound is fresh, a strike against the inside of the door, again with some force, but not a killing blow."

As she replaced gauges, took out others, she scanned the body. "The victim is five foot five. From the angle of the wound, the killer was several inches taller, pulling back and up on the wire. ME to confirm.

"Time of death, twenty-three-forty-six." Eve sat back on her heels. "Crack called it in at sixteen past midnight. Take a few minutes off for the one who found her to send up the alarm—and Crack's going to come back here and check to be sure. So nobody missed her for a good twenty minutes or more. That gave her killer some room. See what's in her purse, will you?"

He walked around the body, crouched down as Eve was. "Lip dye, breath mints, her ID, and . . . three swipes in a swipe case."

"No 'link, no cash or credits." Eve nodded. "Staging it."

Rising, she crossed over to open a black, top-handle case on the bed.

"Okay, this is weird. Is this a grass skirt?"

Roarke straightened and turned as she held it up.

"It certainly appears to be."

"And there's one of those boob deals out of half coconuts, those flower necklaces—two of them. A pair of pink heels, glittery, butterflies on the straps. Wait, something else. A card."

Eve loosened the flap, slid it out. "Got a scan of two tickets to Maui, leaving on Sunday. And the card reads: 'I want to spend a lifetime making your dreams come true. This is just the beginning. I love you, Erin.'"

She slipped the card and contents back in the envelope.

"She wanted the room so she could change into this getup. The shoes mean something—I'll find out what—but the rest is clear enough."

Frowning, she studied the black overnight.

"Why didn't he take the bag? Doesn't even open it to see what was in it? Because he already knew. Either he didn't care, or panicked after the kill and forgot."

She paced around the body and the blood. "How did he get in? Did she let him in? Why would she? A friend, a colleague. 'Great, you can help me change for the big surprise.'

"But I don't think so. I don't think so. Look at the position of the body, the blood on the door. He was in here, already in here. How did he get in here?"

"I took a look at the locks while you tended to her. I don't see any sign of tampering."

"If I'm wrong, he might have followed her, come in after. But not by force. She would've let him—or her—in, so that's trust. But the whole thing reads like her killer was already in the room."

"Someone had to bring the bag."

"Yeah, and if she didn't bring it in herself, her killer did. Something else to find out."

She pulled out her 'link. "I'll bring in the morgue and the sweepers. Then we'll start finding out."

Chapter Two

WHEN SHE WENT OUT, SHE SAW MCNAB HAD CLEARED MOST OF HIS SIDE.

"Some Monday night regulars," McNab told her. "They come in on a slow night for the boobies and brew, maybe try to get lucky. Crack verified. A table of tourists from Topeka, doing some club-hopping. Came in because of the name. They were pretty trashed, and their story checked. Working my way through, hit on a few hard cases, but nobody rings."

"All right. Finish it out."

She signaled Peabody.

As she walked to Eve, Peabody's sympathetic face went to cop face. "They're a mess, Dallas. They're all either friends of one bride or the other, most of them both. None of them, so far, knew anything about a privacy room, and nobody noticed the victim leaving the club area. Some of them, including the other bride, were onstage with the holo-band. A lot of them stripped down to their underwear—or less. According to the statements I've taken, they'd taken over the dance floor. Some not with the group came up, joined in. No problems. One guy even bought a round of drinks, but he left."

"When?"

"Closest we've got is about midnight, maybe a little before that. He got some 'link numbers. Wade—no last name. Tall, blond, tanned, built."

"TOD's twenty-three-forty-six, so that's cutting it close. But I want to know if he contacts any of them. I'll see if Crack knows him. Dead wagon and sweepers on the way. Why aren't any of them leaving?"

"Solidarity. They stay until they all can go. And they wait for Shauna. It's a nice group of women, Dallas."

"Nice people kill, too."

She crossed to the bar where Crack stood waiting.

Fury still vibrated. "Handing out Sober-Up, water, coffee."

"We'll clear them out as soon as we can."

"Shit, it ain't that, skinny white girl. We get trouble in here sometimes. I crack heads, kick some asses. You get people puking, passing out." He shrugged that off. "Had a guy last month—had to be ninety—shaking it like a kid out on the dance floor till he drops with a goddamn heart attack. Got the MTs in quick, but Siri—she's working her way through medical school—already had him back when they got here.

"Nobody ever died in my place. Nobody ever got murdered. I keep an eye, try to keep a good eye, but I didn't see her leave. Didn't notice how long she was gone. Mondays are slow, and we usually close down by one. Hell, I don't usually take the stick on Mondays, but I knew Erin, and I wanted to be here, make sure it went smooth for her. The way the girls were going, I figured we'd give them till two, so I texted Ro, just so she'd know I'd be home later than usual. I figured she'd be sleeping, but she was up. So I was texting with my lady, and I didn't keep a good eye."

"I'm going to tell you something while you make me some of that bullshit you call coffee in here."

"Don't drink that swill, girl. I got Pepsi."

"Better. I'm going to tell you whoever did this wouldn't have looked threatening, wouldn't have stood out to your good eye. My first instinct is Erin knew them."

Crack's gaze skimmed over the partygoers. "Not one of these girls. No fucking way."

"There's always a way, but I don't know yet. Who else knew about the room?"

"Just me, far as I know." He put a tube of Pepsi on the bar. "She was real insistent on that."

"You gave her the swipe."

"Yeah, she came in right around noon, picked it up. Said it was real cloak-and-dagger stuff. She was so fucking happy. The happy just bounced off her."

"Did she come alone?"

"Yeah, just Erin. And in and out, like she had an appointment."

"How about tonight? Did she come in by herself?"

"No, her and Shauna together, and a couple of others right behind them."

"Did she have a case, like a small overnight bag?" Eve held out her hands to indicate size. "A black case."

"I saw that, that case on the bed. No. She wasn't carrying it, or anything but that little purse."

"Did you notice her go out at any point?"

"Outside." He frowned, rubbed at his neck. "Don't think so. She and Shauna got here early, maybe nine-thirty. Most come in closer to ten, or some after."

"You had to take a break or two. You don't work the stick straight through."

"Took fifteen about ten-thirty maybe, gave it over to Renee. Shit, she's good on the bar, but doesn't have a sharp eye, not so much."

"I'd like to talk to her, and to the one who found Erin."

"That's Pete. I got him calmed down some. You want a room?"

"No, here's fine."

"I'll get Renee first, give him a little more calm time. Get you something?" he asked Roarke.

"I'm good. He'll carry this," Roarke added when Crack walked away. "Thinking he should've seen something."

"I can wish he had, but it's not on him."

A woman came out, dark skin, red lips, some fear in her eyes. And built, like all of the staff.

"I'm Renee. Crack said you needed to talk to me."

"You were tending bar when Crack took his break."

"Yeah, yeah." She pushed a hand over a cap of rainbow-colored hair. "He had me relieve him, I don't know, about ten-thirty. Thereabouts."

"Did you notice anyone leaving, or coming in when you were on the stick?"

"Um. Um."

"Those are lovely earrings," Roarke commented.

Some of the fear died away as she lifted a hand to one of the fist-sized silver stars. "Thanks. They're my favorite. Erin— Oh God."

Fear trickled back as she put a hand to those red lips.

"I didn't really know her, except tonight. I started working here a couple months ago, but Crack said we should make sure the brides got whatever they wanted. So she came up to the bar with her empty glass. She said like, hit me again, and how I should tell Shauna, if she asked, she went to the ladies'. And gave me a wink."

"Did she?"

"Yeah, I guess. But just a few minutes."

"When?"

"Um, right after I took the stick. I mixed her drink, had it waiting. She came back—just a few minutes—and—and—she looked so happy."

"Did you notice anyone come in during that time, when she came back?"

"No, but . . . Crack says to keep an eye, but—the ladies were having so much fun. Some of them onstage, half-naked, singing, dancing. On the floor, dancing with each other. I was watching them because they were having so much fun, and they weren't like our usuals."

"Did you see anyone with a black case, about this big? Black with a handle on the top?"

"No, ma'am, I sure didn't."

Considering the damp fear in those eyes, Eve let the *ma'am* slide.

"Okay. I appreciate it. I'd like to speak with Pete."

"He's with Crack, I'll tell Crack. Can I go home? It's just, my mom's watching my little boy, and I didn't want to tell her what happened. I get home by one on Mondays."

"Yeah, you can go.

"Door, back door," Eve murmured. "John's down that way. She could've let someone in the back, whoever brought the case. Doesn't want anyone looking for her. Give them the swipe so they can put the case in the room."

"And her killer goes straight there, inside."

"That's one way. Odds are good nobody sees them. After it's done, go out the same way. In and out the back. No cams to worry about."

"Why don't I go check the door?"

"Do that. I'll have the sweepers check for prints. They couldn't be stupid enough to leave any, but we'll check."

As Roarke headed off, Crack came out again, this time with a man in a tight, sleeveless black tee that showed off impressive biceps. Eve gauged him as early twenties, currently pale as a summer cloud. His curling mass of bronze hair framed a chiseled, square-jawed face.

He shook like a leaf in a windstorm.

"Pete, why don't you go around and sit down there by Dallas. Lieutenant Dallas," Crack corrected.

"Okay. Okay, but can you stick with me?"

Eve gave Crack a nod. With his arm around Pete's muscled shoulders, Crack led him around the bar.

"Why don't you tell me what happened?" Eve began.

"I found her. I served her drinks earlier. They had a table, and she and the other—the one getting married—they danced on the table. Then I found her."

"How long after you served the drinks before you found her?"

"Oh. I don't know exactly. An hour? Maybe more."

"It was just some after midnight when you took your break," Crack prompted.

"Right, right. Okay." Pressing his fingers to his eyes, Pete rubbed. "Crack said I could use one of the privacy rooms to crash for thirty. I'm taking some summer classes, going for my MBA. It's finals week, and I've been cramming it. I guess it showed. Sorry."

"Don't hand me that bullshit. He needed a break," Crack said to Eve. "I told him to take thirty, gave him a swipe. We only had the one room booked anyway."

"Got it. So shortly after midnight, you went back to crash for thirty."

"Yeah. Set the alarm on my 'link. I can show you."

"No need. And when you went into the privacy area?"

"Okay, I was walking by, and I saw the room—not mine, the one a couple up from it—wasn't locked. See, Crack wants the privacy rooms locked, occupied or not, right? We don't want anybody sliding in one of them without paying. Or if someone's using one, the door has to be secured or it's a violation."

"But this door wasn't secured."

"No. The green light was on—that's open. So I pushed the door open and—"

"You pushed the door open? It wasn't closed all the way."

"I . . ." Frowning, he rubbed his eyes again. "Um, wait. I was heading down, I saw the green light, and I . . . Yeah, yeah, I just pushed on the door. It wasn't all the way closed. I didn't say that before. I'm sorry. I'm really sorry. I didn't think of it. I—"

"Pete." Eve put a hand on the solid wall of his arm. "Take a breath. You're doing fine. You pushed open the door."

"I didn't tell the other cop that. I didn't think about it, but yeah. I just gave it a little nudge. And she was . . . God, God, there was so much blood. I've never seen that much blood, not for real."

His Adam's apple bobbed when he swallowed.

"And she was just lying there in all the blood. I couldn't stop staring, then things went sort of gray. I pulled the door closed. I didn't want any- one to see that. I'm always going to see that, all the blood, and her lying in it. I pulled the door closed, and I went and got Crack.

"I fucked up. I didn't handle it like I should. I left her lying in all the blood."

"You handled it exactly right," Eve corrected.

He gave her a pitifully hopeful look. "I did?"

"If you'd gone in, you'd have compromised the scene, made it harder for us to find who did that to her. You closed the door, and if you hadn't, maybe someone else would've gone in. You got help. You did exactly the right thing."

He covered his face with his hands. "I kind of knew her. She used to come in a couple times a month. Not lately, not for a while, I guess. But she used to, so I kind of knew her."

"How long have you worked here, Pete?"

"A few years. Almost three."

"So you've got a sense. Did you notice anybody paying too much at- tention to her?"

"Not the wrong kind. She—all of them—were really bashing it, so other customers watched some. And some of them got up and joined in. It's like contagious, you know? The energy. It seemed like the ladies in the group weren't interested in hooking up tonight, right?"

"Someone mentioned a man named Wade got some of their contacts."

"Yeah, well, Wade would."

He said it with his first shaky smile.

"He's a player," Crack told her. "Comes in most every week, targets some of the ladies. Goes smooth, not pushy."

"Got a last name? We need to check all the boxes."

"I can get it. He always runs a tab."

"Okay. Pete, when you went back for your break, when you pushed open the door, did you see anyone, or anything that seemed off besides the unsecured door?"

"I didn't see anything but her. Swear to God. All I could see was her."

"All right. If you think of anything else, you can contact me. You've been very helpful."

"You go on home now, Pete." Crack patted his back. "You take yourself another soother or whatever you need, and get some sleep."

"I'm afraid I'll see her in my sleep."

"You saw her dancing on the table," Eve reminded him. "Put that in front. See her like that."

"I'll try."

Crack waited until Pete walked out. "Gonna mess him up for a while, but he'll get through it. I'll get you Wade's name and all, but I'm saying he's a player, smooth with it, and sex is his game. Don't see him killing anybody."

"Have to check those boxes."

"Got that. You want Shauna now?"

"I'll go to her, but I want Peabody with me. One thing. You've got a back exit. People can get in that way. No security there?"

Crack shrugged. "We got no cover. Make the scratch on the drinks, privacy tables, and rooms. I don't care how people come in, as long as they cough up the scratch. When we've got live music and a slamming crowd, Big Tiny and I rotate off the door to bounce any assholes out. I don't bring him in on slow nights."

"One more. No monitor for unsecured privacy doors?"

Now he sighed. "I got the e's for that right under the bar, and another in my office. I missed it. Texting with Ro, maybe. If I'd caught it, I'd've gone back and spared that boy the trauma.

"You think he came in the back?"

"It's my most probable at this time."

"Fuck it. I guess I gotta break down and put a cam on the back door." He glanced over. "I guess he's the one to ask about it."

She turned, watched Roarke walk back to the bar.

"No tampering," he said, then looked at Crack. "My friend, I know you keep the doors unsecured during club hours, but Christ Jesus, you need better security than what you have when you're closed. A toddler could get through your locks."

"Nobody does 'cause they know who owns the place." His lips spread in a wide, fierce grin. "But we're going to do just that. How about you work something up for me?"

"I'll do that."

"No cams on the front. The bulk of our clientele's going to find some-place else to patronize we get cams on the front door."

"Why don't I work something up that won't show, even to that clientele."

"You got something like that?"

"He's got every-damn-thing," Eve said.

"You work it up. Want me to take you back to Shauna?"

"Give me a few."

When Eve rose, walked over to Peabody, Roarke sat.

"Any whiskey in stock that won't burn through my esophagus?"

Crack smiled again. "I got my private stash of the good stuff."

"I'll take three fingers of that, if you'll join me."

When McNab joined them, Crack lifted the bottle. "Whiskey? It's the good stuff."

McNab sent a longing look at the label. "It sure as hell is. The Scot in me says, 'Set me up, mate.' But I'm a cop on duty. I don't guess you've got any fizzies."

With an owlish stare, Crack took a sip of the good stuff. "Bony white boy, does this place look like a fizzy bar?"

"Ginger ale maybe?"

"I can get you that."

Crack started to pour one, then paused when the morgue team came in. "Hell. Fucking hell. Is she going to Morris, do you know?"

"Dallas would've asked for him." McNab took the glass.

"It's not right. None of this is right." Crack came around to sit. "She'll catch who did this."

Roarke nodded as Eve led the morgue team to the body. "She won't stop until she does. Get you a drink, Peabody?" he asked when she came over.

"Cold caffeine—not your coffee. I want to be able to keep my stomach lining intact. Dallas is having them take the victim out the back so her friends don't have to see. They won't budge until Shauna's released. McNab, Dallas wants you to direct the sweepers when they get here."

"On that. Totally on it, since here they come."

"Sit," Roarke said to Peabody as she downed that cold caffeine.

"Better not. Got another round to go."

She downed more when Eve came back into the club. Eve paused a moment, had a word with the head sweeper before signaling Peabody.

Crack pushed off the stool. "I'll take you back. Ginger ale," he added when she took a hard look at McNab's empty glass.

"Go home," she told Roarke.

He lifted his glass. "I'm enjoying some of the good stuff."

"Whatever. With me, Peabody."

The door behind the bar led to a half-assed kitchen where they generated half-assed bar snacks. Though it shined clean, she figured if she'd been trapped in a cave for a week with no food or water, she might have, just maybe might have, risked eating something not hermetically sealed from that space.

A short, skinny corridor led to another door where Crack stopped.

"I gave her a soother earlier. Can't say if it helped much."

When he opened the door, the three women huddled together on chairs he'd obviously brought in from the club froze.

Like hers, his office ran small, but he'd managed to wedge in two more chairs.

And like hers, his office space said business, not socializing. A desk, his data and communication center, a big desk chair for a big man, a mini-AC, and a speed bag.

She immediately wondered if she could put a speed bag in her office.

"This is Lieutenant Dallas and Detective Peabody." Crack eased over to take the middle woman's hands. "They're the best there is. I promise you that, Shauna. The best."

"Will they let me see her?" Her voice, like her eyes, was dull. "No one will let me see her."

"Ms. Hunnicut," Eve began, "the chief medical examiner is taking care of Erin now. There's no one who'll take better care of her. We'll arrange for you to see her tomorrow."

"I need to see her. I need to touch her. I don't understand."

"Shauna, you listen to Dallas and Peabody now. I'm going to be right outside, but you listen to them."

"Can we stay, please?" The woman on the right, a pretty strawberry blonde with red-rimmed, swollen green eyes, sent a pleading look toward Eve. "I'm Becca—Rebecca DiNuzio—and that's Angie Decker. We're friends, we're all friends. Can we stay with Shauna?"

"Yes." Eve nodded at Crack.

He gave Shauna's hands another squeeze. "I'm right outside."

A tear trickled down Shauna's cheek as Crack stepped out. "We're getting married in just a few days. On Saturday we're getting married. This can't be real."

"I'm very sorry for your loss," Eve said as she and Peabody sat. "I know this is a difficult time, but if we could ask you—the three of you—some questions, it'll help us find who did this to Erin."

"Someone killed her. They said she's dead, but I don't understand. Why would someone kill Erin?"

"That's what we need to find out. Can you tell me where you were, what you were doing about midnight?"

"Nobody was paying attention to the time."

"I kind of was." Angie, a stunning Black woman with razor-edged cheekbones and large, liquid brown eyes, slid a hand over Shauna's. "I have a job tomorrow. I'm a model and I have to report for hair and makeup at eight. I swore I wouldn't stay past one, so I was watching the time. And mostly drinking water.

"Shauna and Becca were both onstage. Chloe, too, and Margo about that time."

"I was singing and dancing onstage when she needed me."

"You didn't know. None of us knew. How could we, sweetheart? Lieutenant, Erin was my best friend in the world. I was standing up for her like Becca for Shauna."

Angie turned to Shauna. "You'd just come down, and you started looking for her. You asked me if I'd seen her, but I hadn't, not since we came back from the bathroom about an hour before."

"Sorry," Eve interrupted. "You and Erin went to the john about eleven?"

"More like ten-thirty. I saw her heading that way, so headed out and joined her. We made a deal about going to the ladies' in pairs or groups.

She thought I was being silly when I caught up with her, but that was the deal."

"What then?"

"Then?" Angie frowned. "Well, we used the bathroom, then she said she had a drink waiting at the bar, and she went to the bar. I took one of the tables."

She turned to Shauna again. "You asked if I'd seen her as soon as you came down from the stage. And right about then is when Crack came and told you. You were standing with me when he shut everything down and told us."

"None of you noticed her leaving the club area again?"

"We were all having fun, just crazy fun," Becca said. "I didn't even notice the time with Angie. God, I took off my dress! Then the music stopped, and I saw Crack and Angie holding on to Shauna."

"Was the rest of your group in the club area?"

"I don't know." Becca looked over at Angie. "I think so."

"Some of the rest of you must've used the restroom at some point."

"Oh, sure." Becca nodded at Peabody. "But, like Angie said, we had the buddy system rule. Nobody goes alone, two or more at once. We weren't the only ones in the club, and, well, it's the Down and Dirty, so buddy system."

"Why did she go without me?" More tears spilled as Shauna gripped Becca's hand. "Why did she go back there by herself?"

Angie sighed. "When I trailed her back to the ladies', she reminded me she used to be a kind of regular here."

"She'd booked a privacy room."

"What? But why?" Shauna stared at Eve. "Why would she do that?"

"Ms. Hunnicut, did Erin have a black overnight case?" Eve opened her hands to estimate size. "With a top handle?"

"Yeah, she did. Why?"

"Pink shoes? Heels, glittery, with butterflies on the straps?"

That question brought on a flood of tears. "It's how we met, how we met." When she broke down, Angie hugged her in, and Becca took over.

"Shauna manages Fancy Feet, a shoe boutique. Erin saw the shoes in the window. She had her first real art show coming up that weekend and went in to try them on."

"We connected." Shauna sobbed it. "We just connected. She said I should come to the show, and I did. She wore the shoes. We went out for a drink after, and just connected. I'd only been with men before, I'd never felt attracted to women. But we fell in love."

"You love who you love." Peabody spoke softly. "You love the person. The shoes were the start of it, for both of you. So they're important."

"But how did you know about the shoes?"

"She had the case in the privacy room, and the shoes in it."

"I don't understand, I don't understand."

"She also had a kind of costume, short grass skirt, leis, a card for you."

"I want the card. I need the card."

"We'll get it to you. She scanned two tickets to Hawaii. Maui."

"But—no." With the back of her hand, she swiped at tears. "That can't be right. That was just a silly wish of mine, and we talked about going someday. We'd save up for it. We wanted to get married now, so we'd save up for a honeymoon in Maui because we didn't want to wait to get married."

"I checked. She bought the tickets, booked a hotel, three weeks ago. Do you know where she might have gotten the money?"

"I . . ." Struggling, Shauna rubbed her hands over her face, but tears rolled through them. "Her parents, maybe. They're great, but I don't see how they could afford all that."

"She sold a painting? I bet she did," Becca put in. "You said she was spending a lot of time in the studio. She does mostly street art," Becca added. "But she shares a small studio with three other artists, and works through the— God, I can't think!"

"SoHo Arts." Shauna closed her eyes. "They held her first real show. Glenda, Glenda Frost runs it. She couldn't come tonight because she's in Italy."

"We'll check on that."

"She was going to surprise me with something I wanted. Now she's dead."

"She didn't bring the case with her tonight?"

"No, no, we came together. She didn't have it. Maybe she came by earlier and left it with Crack."

"No, she didn't. Who would she have trusted with it? Who would she have trusted with the case, with the surprise?"

"Any of us," Angie said. "Well, maybe not all of us, as some of us can't keep it zipped. She'd have trusted me, or Becca. I don't know why she didn't. She never said a thing to me."

"Or to me. You think . . ." Becca pressed her lips together. "You think whoever she did tell killed her. That doesn't make any sense."

"No one who knew her would do this. No one," Shauna insisted. "Everyone was happy for us. My parents were surprised, but once they met her, they loved her, too. Our families, our friends, they were all happy for us."

She dissolved into tears again. "I have to tell my family. I have to tell her family. I don't know how."

Peabody reached out. "We'll do that, Shauna."

"That wouldn't be right. You didn't know her. I have to tell them. I need to do that for her. It's all I can do for her now."

"We'll go with you, both of us." Angie looked at Becca.

"Absolutely."

"Ms. Hunnicut, you said you dated men prior to meeting Erin."

"So?" She shot a hot look at Eve out of drenched eyes.

"Did you have any bad breakups? Anyone you dated resent you stepping away? Or that you fell in love with a woman?"

"No." She leaned against Becca, closed her eyes again. "The last person I hung with before I met Shauna, we weren't serious that way. It was just convenient sex and someone to hang out with—go to dinner or the vids or whatever with."

"Could we have his name? It's routine," Eve stressed.

"Oh God, he's just a nice man, good in bed, and we made each other laugh. We're friends, just with, you know, benefits. He's coming—was coming—to the wedding. Marcus Stillwater. He's a publicist for Fordam Publishing."

"Who broke up with whom?"

"I guess I pulled the plug on the sex. Just a month or so after I met Erin, and realized I had feelings. I told him I met someone I thought I could get serious about. We didn't fight, he wasn't upset. We were friends before we started sleeping together. We were friends when we slept together. We're still friends."

"He met Erin then?"

"Sure. They liked each other."

"What about before him?"

She heaved out a breath. "Look, I wasn't promiscuous, but I dated a lot of men. I didn't have sex with all of them. But I'm twenty-six, I was a single woman in New York."

"No one's judging you. It's routine," Peabody told her. "Every detail can matter."

"All right. Okay." Shauna shoved at her hair again. "The guy I dated before Marcus, we were together a couple months. But it just didn't really work for me. It didn't click, so I broke it off. He wasn't happy about it, but I didn't break his heart, either."

"Name?"

"Jon Rierdon. He runs a home goods store on . . . I don't remember."

"That's good enough."

"Hell, how far back should I go? If I track back to high school, there's Greg."

Becca let out a quick laugh, then immediately winced. "I'm sorry, so sorry. I didn't mean to laugh. Greg, Shauna, and I all went to high school together. They were an item. Actually, The Item. The homecoming queen and the quarterback. Greg and I have been cohabs for over two years."

"We all scattered after college. Greg and I kept in touch off and on. Then Becca and I ran into each other on the street, just hey."

"It turned out we lived in the same neighborhood—Shauna had just moved to the city, and we ran into each other."

"There were two guys in college on the serious side," Shauna continued, "and a couple—no, three—between that and Jon. Nobody got their hearts broken."

"What about Erin? Exes."

"I know a couple, but we didn't go into all that much. We were together, and that's what mattered."

"Would you know?" Eve asked Angie.

"Yeah, probably. I could give you ones I do know, but another thing I know. Erin didn't love anyone she was with before. Liked, was attracted to, enjoyed. But she didn't love until Shauna."

"Names would help, just to eliminate. Then we'll let you go. If you think of anything else, or have any questions, you can contact me or Detective Peabody. It would also help if you give us access to where you lived with Erin."

"You can have it. I don't want to go back there, not yet." Her lips trembled. "Maybe not ever."

"You'll stay with me. I've got room." Angie took her hand again. "As long as you need."

Chapter Three

When Eve judged she'd gotten all she'd get from the three women, she let them go.

"Go home, hit the rack. We'll meet up at the vic's apartment at oh-eight hundred. See if Feeney can spare McNab to check out the e's."

"Can do." Peabody rubbed her tired eyes. "Are you heading out, too?"

"I want a word with the sweepers and Crack, then yeah."

As they stepped back into the club area, Eve looked around. The women, ringed around Shauna like a security team, filed out. "Nothing more we can do here tonight."

After consulting with the sweepers, she walked to the rear door, stepped out.

She scanned the short alley, where two white-suited sweepers filtered through the contents of the recycling bin.

So easy, Eve thought.

Just somebody turning into the alley on a hot, damp summer night, carrying a black case. Had she already given them the swipe?

Probably, she thought. Most likely, since she'd had company on that bathroom trip roughly an hour and fifteen minutes before TOD.

But why? If she'd wanted someone to bring it in that way, why not just go to the back door at some point, take the case? Thanks, pal.

Can't say, she concluded. But if that had been the plan, it hadn't worked.

Either way, she'd given that case and access to the privacy room to someone she knew. Trusted.

Either way, her killer had been in the room. Maybe they'd convinced her to let them go in with her. Or they'd waited for her in the room.

Eve stepped back in.

"Waiting inside. She couldn't say when, for sure, she'd be able to slip away unnoticed—as proven by Decker on the john trip. Can't ask somebody to wait in an alley indefinitely."

She walked down to the privacy room. Dim lights, soundproofing. Inside within seconds.

Still, risky.

She headed back to the club area, where only Crack and Roarke remained. They sat at the bar, and from the looks of it, had switched to water.

"The sweepers are nearly done," she told Crack. "Go home. They'll secure the place, seal it."

"How long you shutting me down? Not giving you shit about it," he added. "Just need to know."

"Keep it closed tomorrow. Give me another day on just the privacy room. If I hit on something that says longer, I'll let you know. But I don't see it."

"You gonna loop me in?"

"No."

When his eyes narrowed, she narrowed her own.

"Can't and won't. If we have questions you might be able to answer, we'll ask them. If we have information I think you can expand on, I'll ask. Otherwise, I can't and won't."

He stared down at his water, then looked at Roarke. "Hard-ass skinny white girl you hooked with."

"She is. And that's one of the reasons she'll find who killed your friend, and who used your place to do it."

"Guess I hear that." He rose. "You'll work that security bullshit up for me?"

"I will, yes."

"Well, fuck it. I guess I'm going home."

After watching him walk out, she turned to Roarke. "Well, fuck it. I guess we're going home, too."

He rose, took her hand. "You can tell me what you think on the way."

"Some I think, some I know," she said as they went out where the shallow puddles had dried. And the air felt as if it had absorbed every drop of wet. "I know the killer was in the room. I think already in it when she went in. I know the killer brought in the case. I think she found a way to slip them the swipe so they could. Since she picked it up about noon, that leaves plenty of time for the handoff. That says she knew her killer, and trusted them enough with her big secret surprise. Had to, as the case didn't have a lock."

She got in the car, stretched out her legs.

"I know the killer came prepared to kill, and I think they did it quickly from behind. Plus they weren't smart enough to take the case out with them and secure the door. Why leave the case, when that gives us something to work with? Why not secure the door so it takes longer to locate the body?"

"Panic?" Roarke suggested.

"That's my initial thinking, and if so, it's most likely a first kill. As far as we know—so that's not in the I Know column—none of her group arrived at the D&D with the case. But without cams, no way to be sure. Plus, she could've given the swipe to one of them earlier."

"They come in the back, put the case in the room, then join the party."

"Possible. But then why didn't Albright get the swipe back? Can't ask her, so possible. Maybe one of them had something going with the vic at some point. Now she's marrying someone else, taking them to Maui. That bitch! Or one of them wants to have a thing with Hunnicut, so wants Albright out of the way so they can move in and comfort the grieving bride."

"Extreme, but not unprecedented."

"Nope." She rolled her shoulders in an attempt to ease the stiffness. Had little success.

"I worked this case once—back with Feeney. A woman meets this guy at a party. They have some party talk. The guy intros her to his wife, and they all have some party talk. The woman decides the guy's her soul mate. Consults a psychic who, for fifty bucks, confirms same. Tells her the wife will leave suddenly and clear the field. Wanting to speed things along, *she* throws a party, invites them and about three dozen of her friends and acquaintances. She slips into the john behind the wife, where she bashes her over the head with—I'm not making this up—a frozen round of marble rye, then drowns her in a tub filled with scented water and floating candles."

"Inventive."

"Would've been more so if she hadn't stuck the bread back in the freezer. Parties are murder. Anyway, we got her."

Eve circled her head to release tension in her neck, with a little more success. "We'll get this one, too. Should've taken the case, ditched it and the contents somewhere."

"If it's one of the partygoers, it's possible she didn't want to be absent that long."

"Also possible. It would take a cold-ass mother to do the kill, then walk right back in and dance." She closed her eyes a minute, rolled her shoulders again. "But the world's got plenty of cold-ass mothers to go around."

When he drove through the gates, she let out one long, relieved breath.

"Hunnicut gave us access to their place. I sent Reo a warrant request just to back it up, but we'll hit that first thing. Hunnicut said nobody had keys except her and the vic."

"The killer could've made a copy along the way."

"Yeah, but why not just take hers once she's dead? They took her 'link, and that tells me they've had some communication on it that brings the killer into the light. Take her apartment key, or if they'd copied it, they don't wait for after the kill to get in, remove any communication. McNab will know if they did."

She got out of the car. "Peabody was basically asleep on her feet when I sent her home. Hell, I was getting there myself. Morning's soon enough."

As they went inside, she glanced at her wrist unit. "I can get a solid three hours down. That'll work. You'll get less."

He slipped an arm around her when they started up the stairs. "I re-scheduled my five A.M. I'll take the solid three with you."

She tipped her head toward his shoulder. "Slacker."

"The privilege of being the boss."

"Of everything. 'Cept me."

In the bedroom, she stripped off her jacket, her weapon harness, and, yawning, sat to pull off her boots. "I need to talk to the victim's parents. Maybe she told them about the big surprise. Shauna indicated they couldn't afford it, but maybe they helped. Then there's the artists she shared studio space with. Unless they were all at the party. Need to check that."

"You need to sleep first."

And as she stripped down, he pulled a sleep shirt over her head.

"I do. I really do. Move over, tubby." She nudged the sprawled cat over, then sprawled herself. Facedown.

Roarke slid in beside her, stroked a hand down her back. Since she went under before the second stroke, he set his internal alarm, and joined her.

She woke to the glorious scent of coffee. Opening one eye, she saw Roarke sitting on the side of the bed with a mug in his hand.

"Need that."

"I assumed you would."

She sat up, took the mug, gulped some down. "You're a pretty good deal."

"I'm an excellent deal."

Since she couldn't argue with that, she drank some more and studied him. Already dressed in one of his boss-of-the-universe suits—this one a medium gray, probably linen—with a deeper gray shirt and a perfectly knotted tie that blended the grays with a kind of—she guessed—maroon.

He looked as fresh as a man who'd just come off a relaxing weekend at some fancy spa. Plus, he smelled really good.

It could irritate, but she had coffee.

"How did you manage three hours down and get showered and dressed?"

"Efficiency. I was tempted to shower with my wife, but that would've led to other temptations. Neither of us have time for those temptations this morning."

"Really don't. So I'm taking this coffee while I go be efficient."

She drank more coffee as she went in to shower.

Between that and the beat of hot water pumping from multiple jets, her brain unclouded enough to let her go over her morning agenda.

Though she wished for time to set up her board and book in her home office, that had to wait. Apartment first, some conversations with neighbors. Have Peabody cross-check the partygoers with the other artists— and that might add in some visits and conversations.

The morgue. See what Morris could tell her.

Track down where Erin had gotten the costume, and see if that led anywhere. Talk to the parents and the traveling gallery owner.

But first, out of the shower, into the drying tube. Then more coffee.

She tossed on a robe the color of the sea surrounding Roarke's private island. When she stepped out, he sat, the stock junk on-screen and muted. Two domed plates sat on the table of the sitting area while the cat, on the opposite side of the room, gulped down his own breakfast.

Roarke set his tablet aside. "Work continues apace at the Great House Project."

"Just what does that mean? There's slow pace," she said as she crossed over and filled her mug with coffee from the pot on the table. "There's jogging pace, a run-like-hell pace. So what pace is apace when it's one weird word? Like afoot. Whose foot is it, and why?"

She started to lift the dome to see what he'd decided she'd have for breakfast and saw him smiling at her.

"What?"

"Starting the day with you is never boring."

He lifted the domes himself to reveal golden omelets, crisp bacon, summer berries, and flaky croissants.

Yeah, an excellent deal, even if he'd snuck spinach into the omelet.

"So does 'apace' mean ahead of schedule?"

"It does. Still a bit of time before everything's complete, but they can continue to move things into finished areas or where they're storing others in the garage. I thought we'd have the garden sculpture you wanted for Mavis and the lamp you wanted for Peabody delivered next week. That way, Peabody can find the place she wants for the lamp, and we can set up the sculpture where Mavis wants it."

"Fine, but that takes care of the whole 'we have to give you something for getting a house' thing, right?"

"It does. Though a bottle of wine when they have their housewarming, which they will, wouldn't be amiss."

"There's another." She pointed at him. "Apace, afoot, amiss. Why the extra letter? But anyway. Gifts? Check."

She made a check mark in the air, then attacked the omelet. Spinach, no surprise, but plenty of cheese to smooth that out.

"And yeah, they're going to want to have a party. Nobody ever learns."

"Someone could get bashed with a frozen round of marble rye."

"It's happened before," she said darkly. "It could happen again."

He leaned over, kissed her. "Never boring."

She switched to bacon. "Then Mavis is going to pop out Number Two. Except it's not popping. It's this whole weird, ungodly process."

"Which you shouldn't bring up over breakfast. Please God," he added fervently.

"And she's already said we have to be there again."

"Not over breakfast. In fact, never speak of it."

"Wait. Does that mean we have to have one of the girl parties, another shower thing?"

He took another bite of omelet. "Anticipating that question, I asked Peabody. She said no, as they have all the baby gear already."

"Thank Christ."

"But there should be a gift once Number Two arrives."

"Another gift." It never, ever ended! "For Mavis, for the kid?"

Roarke shot a warning stare at the cat, who'd finished his breakfast and tried a casual saunter toward theirs. "My information is a gift for Mavis would be thoughtful, one for the baby is required."

"Well, shit."

"The nursery is nearly done. Mavis and Leonardo decided on a magic theme."

"What, like rabbits coming out of hats?"

"Not stage magic, darling. A magical forest theme with elves and winged faeries, friendly dragons, that sort."

"Oh. Yeah, that sounds like them. But like what happens to get the kid out, I'm not thinking about it yet."

"Well now, I had a thought—on the gift, and it would cover all of it. Though Bella's getting a bed, and the crib and such will move to the nursery, the chair, the rainbow chair, isn't moving. It's Bella's, after all, and suits her new room. A magic forest chair would suit the nursery."

"Huh."

"The same sort of chair, but with the nursery theme."

"That really would cover it all. Let's do that."

"Mavis already has Leonardo working on the fabric design, as it's something she wants. And he's agreed to distract her there, run it by us, then tell her there's a bit of a backlog, but it'll be done by the time they bring the baby home."

"So another big secret surprise? Where did one of those just lead last night?"

"We'll keep privacy rooms and sex clubs off-limits."

"Fine." Then she shrugged. "It's a good idea."

"Peabody also mentioned a big-sister gift for Bella."

Eve's jaw literally dropped. "Oh man, come on!"

"I'm merely the messenger."

"I'll give Peabody a damn message." She pushed up and walked into her closet. "Do we have to do this every time Mavis decides to get knocked up? Because I'm telling you, she's not done!"

"Let's not think about that, either." As the cat rolled closer—a new tactic—Roarke pointed at him. "And don't you think about a second breakfast, mate."

In the closet, Eve thought about clothes. She hated thinking about clothes, but not as much as buying gifts.

She decided, instead of thinking, to follow Roarke's lead. Gray trousers, a gray linen jacket. It had navy buttons, and she supposed that was supposed to mean navy pants. But screw that. She took care of the navy with a sleeveless tee, the belt, and the boots.

Little thought required, so a win.

When she stepped out, carrying the jacket, she frowned at the table. "Where'd you put the stuff?"

"Inside the AutoChef panel."

Nodding, Eve strapped on her weapon. She glanced at the cat, the panel. "It might take him awhile, but he'll figure it out."

"Not if I put a bloody lock on it."

"Don't be too sure."

She tossed on the jacket, grabbed her badge and the rest. "Gotta go."

"As do I. I'll walk out with you."

"Don't you have a meeting?"

"I've a car and driver waiting. I'll take the first meeting in the car, then the rest in my office."

"A mobile meeting. Shows you're a very busy man."

"And that I am."

"No briefcase?"

"Already in the car. Summerset dealt with it."

At the mention of his majordomo, Eve gave a suspicious scan of the foyer. But he didn't lurk there.

"Well, good luck with your half a million meetings."

"I've only scheduled a quarter million today."

They stepped outside together. He took her face in his hands, kissed. "Take care of my cop."

"Can do. No privacy rooms or rounds of marble ryes for me all day."

Smiling, he skimmed a finger down the shallow dent in her chin. "And good luck with the rest of it."

She got in her car, and he in the back of the shiny black limo. It felt a little strange to drive out this way together, to find herself glancing back and imagining him running some important business meeting from the back of the shiny car.

They'd both left early enough to beat the hawking ad blimps. But not, she noted, the street traffic, the airtrams, or the bustle of working stiffs toward subway stations.

The limo peeled off toward his Midtown offices, and she continued downtown.

Plenty of people, she noted, crowding the corner carts for hot coffee, iced coffee, egg pockets, breakfast burritos. Pre-Roarke, she'd have been one of them. So yeah, an excellent deal.

A few blocks from her destination, the warrant came through.

"And that makes it nice and neat," she muttered.

Maybe more likely, she thought, if Albright had anything concerning the Maui trip tucked away, she'd have tucked it in the artist space.

But they had to check.

More, she wanted to see where and how the couple had lived. Private spaces told you things people often didn't.

She hunted for parking, lucked into a street spot under a block away. Then spotted Peabody and McNab hoofing their way toward her as she got out of the car.

Peabody's pink cowboy boots clomped; McNab's airboots with multicolored swirls pranced. His shirt somehow matched the boots, and his baggies shined neon blue.

At least Peabody wore sensible khakis and a blue—not neon—top under a tan blazer.

They held hands, but wisely uncoupled before they reached her.

"Warrant came through." She pointed down the block, then continued to walk. "McNab, I spotted door cams, so start with the security feed. Look for the black case. I don't expect to get that lucky, but let's cross it off. Also anyone entering from TOD to an hour after we released the party group. Then we'll want a search through any house e's for any reference to this surprise trip."

"All over it and back again."

"Anything hinky with the e's, we take them in. We're authorized."

She paused in front of the building for a longer look.

An old, faded brick, pre-Urbans, that had held its own during that violent era. No graffiti, sensible riot bars on the first-floor windows. Reasonable security. A four-decker, no retail space. Probably a walk-up, she thought, grandfathered in before mandatory elevators.

"They could both probably walk to work from here," Peabody commented. "I checked, and Albright usually set up about six blocks from here, and her studio space is just under four. Fancy Feet is one crosstown block and one short block north. Rent takes a bite, but with two incomes, manageable. Just."

"They'd save on transpo."

"Yeah, they moved in here together just about ten months ago. Both had studio apartments previously. Combining those rents, this place isn't much more. It's billed as a two-bedroom, but the second's smaller than your closet. I checked."

"Top floor, southwest corner. I checked," Eve said. "Let's go have a look." She walked up, mastered in.

The entrance area was smaller than her pre-Roarke closet, and barely fit the three of them.

Not altogether a walk-up, she realized, as it had one elevator. One dubious elevator.

She wouldn't have used it in any case.

Stairs, barely wide enough for two across, had a sturdy rail that looked fairly new.

No soundproofing, as she could hear voices—on-screens, in actuality, and the requisite crying baby—from behind doors painted what she thought of as apartment green.

It looked and smelled reasonably clean. No trash on the cheap laminate floors, no graffiti on the builder's-beige walls.

"Find the security hub or building super, McNab."

"Both basement level." He grinned. "I checked."

"Good to start off the day efficient. Let's move."

Chapter Four

As they started up the steps, Eve heard Peabody whisper, "Loose pants, loose pants."

At Eve's cool stare, Peabody shrugged. "It helps."

More noise on the second floor. Instead of a crying baby, a toddler wailed, "No! No! No!"

Eve knew it was a toddler, as it continued to wail as his mother carted him out of an apartment door. She knew it was the mother, as the woman with a messy tail of brown hair, an enormous bag on one shoulder, and a wailing kid on her opposite hip sent her an exhausted look.

"My mother told me being a mom's the best job ever," the woman said. "Every day's an adventure, she told me. She must just laugh and laugh."

She shifted the kid. "He knows," she said darkly now. "We didn't tell him, we didn't speak of it, but he knows we're going to the d-o-c for his c-h-e-c-k-u-p and his s-h-o-t."

"Aw." With a sympathetic smile, Peabody reached in her jacket pocket and pulled out some sort of cracker she palmed to show the mom. "Can he?"

"Ah . . ."

"We're cops." Peabody showed her badge with her other hand. "Peanut butter cracker. Still wrapped."

"Oh. Okay."

Peabody unwrapped the cracker, offered it.

The kid stopped wailing, squealed "Cookie," and grabbed it. Mouth full, he grinned.

"Bless you. A thousand blessings on you."

"No problem."

Continuing up, Eve shook her head. "You carry crackers in your pocket, Detective Loose Pants?"

"Peanut butter—for a boost when we miss lunch. Which we do. A lot."

"Now that you've done your good deed for the day, record on."

On the fourth floor, Eve turned to the apartment door. "Dallas, Lieutenant Eve, and Peabody, Detective Delia, entering residence of Shauna Hunnicut and Erin Albright, deceased."

She mastered in, and when they stepped inside, took a long, slow scan of the living area.

"A shoe store manager and a street artist. They missed their calling. They should've run a cleaning service."

The small space shined like diamonds. Multicolored diamonds, Eve decided. The sofa wore a sapphire-blue cover and showed off half a dozen pillows of varying sizes, shapes, and patterns that—somehow—worked. Mismatched tables, all painted in happy colors, a pair of small chairs, both covered in hot candy pink, a chest painted bright white covered with pink-and-blue flowers.

Art covered the walls. Cityscapes, still lifes, portraits.

A small round table painted the blue of the sofa and flanked by two metal chairs painted the hot candy pink held a clear vase filled with white flowers.

The two little front windows offered a view of the street below—which the victim had captured in one of the many paintings.

It struck Eve as not only amazingly clean, but girlie without the fuss and flounces.

"They were really happy here," Peabody commented. "You can see it, and feel it. And you know, the victim's work is really good. At least for me, it pulls me right in."

Because she agreed, Eve merely nodded as she looked over the tiny kitchen, separated from the rest by a short counter. They'd removed a couple of cabinet doors so their dishes and glassware showed.

"Gives it an illusion of space." Peabody wandered that way. "You have to be really organized and creative when you go with open cabinets. Looks like they were. A printout of their wedding e-vite on the fridge. I'd say Albright designed it. There's a lot of her here. I can see why Hunnicut needs some time before coming back."

"And that gives us room to go through the place."

Eve headed toward the hallway.

They'd set up the tiny bedroom Peabody spoke of as an office/art studio space.

It held a desk painted a kind of coral color holding a mini D and C, a little vase of flowers, and a photo of the two women, heads together, beaming smiles. At the window—about the same size and shape as Eve's skinny office window—stood an easel on a square of paint-splattered white cloth.

An unfinished painting stood on it—a crowded subway scene. Beside it, a makeshift table held a palette, brushes.

Peabody opened the closet. "Shoes! Glorious shoes! Hunnicut would get a discount. Man, they've got some beauties. Two sizes—six and a half, seven and a half. So they both stored shoes in here."

"Fascinating." Eve opened a cabinet painted black, with a skyline of New York under a full white moon.

"Painting supplies. We'll leave the e's for McNab, for now. Let's see the main bedroom."

The more generous space held a bed with a white duvet, deep blue shams, a bunch of fancy pillows. The wall behind the bed had a rainbow arching in a dreamy blue sky. The theme continued with a long dresser painted a pale, quiet green, the frame of the long oval mirror showing a blue a couple of notes up from the wall color.

Rather than curtains, the trim around the privacy-screened window had vining flowers trailing along the white.

"They wanted peaceful in here." Peabody sighed a little. "The whole place . . . they put a lot of time and thought and work into the whole place. It's really, really pretty."

Just two people, Eve thought, making their nest, living their life, looking toward a future that would never happen.

"Take the nightstands. I've got the closet."

Inside she found clothes organized in two sections—hers and hers. Below, a handmade pair of side-by-side drawers. Painted, of course, the frame the pale green, the drawers the dreamy blue.

They held carefully folded sweaters, sweatshirts, rolled belts, winter-weight socks and tights. Hers and hers again, she thought as she searched through.

On the side walls, handbags hung. She went through each.

No hidden cash, no secret messages.

Eve turned, faced the clothes. On each side, under clear protective wrap, hung their wedding dresses. No way to mistake that, she thought. One, strapless, had a short skirt, the kind that would flare out when you twirled. Albright's. The other had thin straps with a hint of sparkle, a longer, fuller skirt that fell from a nipped-in waist.

They'd both chosen white.

"Their wedding dresses," Peabody said from behind her. "That's so sad. Some sex toys in the nightstands, and each had a tablet. I tried the wedding date as passcode, and bang on both. And they both have folders on there for wedding plans, starting like three months ago. They were having it at Hunnicut's parents' place in Brooklyn—they have a yard. I've got the guest list—about seventy people. The caterer, photographer, the band, the florist, all of it. Each bride's parents were paying a third, and the brides a third. I'd say that shows family support."

"Money talks—but you can't always be sure it's telling you the truth. I've got the dresser. Take the bathroom.

"That'll be McNab," Eve said when she heard the knock. "Have him come back, give me a rundown, then he can take the e's."

She walked to the dresser with its perfume bottles, two little catchall bowls, currently catching hairpins in one, a broken earring in the other.

Another framed picture of both of them, ass to ass this time, in party dresses she'd seen in the closet.

She opened the first drawer as McNab bounced in.

"No case on the twenty-four hours of feed, LT. I've got the vic and her partner leaving together—wearing what they wore at the club—at about twenty-one-fifteen. The victim arrived home, alone, around two and a half hours before that. Hunnicut nearly an hour before that, also alone."

He looked around the room as he spoke. "This is nice. Anyway, one couple came in the building after TOD. The super ID'd them as tenants, a couple on the second floor. I stopped by on my way up here. Dinner, a show, then drinks with another couple. They've got the receipts."

"Okay. You can start on the e's in the second bedroom."

"On it. This is a really nice place," he said again as he went out.

The first drawer, a jewelry drawer with a sectioned insert. From the looks of it, they hadn't separated their own, but mixed them together in sections for bracelets, earrings, rings, necklaces.

But even she recognized two distinct styles. The bolder and the more conservative.

She took out two jeweler's boxes, opened the first. A white-gold band with beaded edges. The ring in the second box matched.

Yeah, Eve thought as she replaced them. It was fucking sad.

She replaced them, went drawer by drawer.

No secrets spilled out. And clearly each had her own side—two distinct styles again, which had her confirming her thought that the bold equaled the victim, the more conservative the fiancée.

She found a red, hinged-lid box on what she believed was Hunnicut's side, bottom drawer. A few more pieces of jewelry.

As she finished up, Peabody came back in. "Nothing but what you'd expect in a bathroom shared by two women. Some OTC meds, no illegals, makeup, hair and skin care, and so on."

"Nothing here, either. They didn't hide things from each other, not that I can see. Maybe that's why when she hid the trip from Hunnicut, she went over the top on it.

"Living room, kitchen."

She stopped at the second bedroom.

"Not finding anything that pops, Dallas," McNab told her. "They've got a joint account and split expenses down the middle. It looks like the victim did some moonlighting. I've got payments listed—fairly small ones—from Your Event Caterers, Lonestar Grill, Quick and Clean Maid Service. All cash deposits."

"Paid her under the table."

"I'd say affirmative. Also cash deposits from her sales—street sales. She kept good records. Some payments from sales through the gallery she worked with. Hunnicut's straight from the Fancy Feet place."

"No record of Albright buying those tickets, deposit for the room in Maui?"

McNab held up a finger. "I've got it, but she separated it from their joint. Sort of buried it. She got a solid payment from the gallery in SoHo. Almost twenty large—and a few days later, another for three, and she dumped them both in a different account, where she's also been slipping in some of the moonlighting cash—probably tips—for a couple months, along with what looks like some street sales. She had just over thirty-five in it—subheaded the file Shauna's Big Dream."

"Yeah, that fits."

"I've got her notes, her math here where she buried the transactions. She bought the tickets, booked the room, and earmarked some for food, drink, fun."

He glanced up. "She added some heart, smiley face, palm tree, and popping champagne emojis. Much love and happy all around."

"Okay. Take it in, dig some more on communications. Maybe Albright got some blowback, some threats, some something and deleted. Maybe she has emails with whoever brought in the case, and deleted. Have a look at the tablets for now, and we'll finish up."

It didn't take long to finish, not with a place so clean, neat, and relatively spare.

She ordered transpo for McNab to take the e's into Central, generated a receipt for them for Hunnicut.

When she reached the car with Peabody, Eve considered the time. "We've got plenty of room. We'll swing by the art studio, see if any artists are in residence. All of them live close, one in the same building, so we'll take them all if we can."

"I'm going to build a toy chest."

"What?"

"Bella already has one. I'll build one for Number Two, paint it. I'm no artist, but I can handle magic trees and some birds, I think I could handle a dragon. Maybe. That's the nursery theme."

"I know the nursery theme." Eve swung into traffic.

"Right. The chair. Leonardo's designing the fabric. Big secret, I'm zipped on it. Hey, I can try to do something that works with the chair. They seriously love the one you gave her for Bella—the chair."

"I know about the damn chair, Peabody. We're on a murder case."

"We're driving. Maybe a chest with doors on the front that open out. Or . . . make it like a treasure chest, and do a lift-out shelf. Or—"

"I'll stuff your dead, mangled body in the chest and drop it in the Hudson."

She pulled into a loading zone at the building, an old converted warehouse. After flipping on her On Duty light, she stepped out.

The street level held commercial spaces, including an art supply store, a tattoo parlor, and a vegan café.

Above, two levels of apartments. The studio space took half the fourth floor and an alternative health clinic the other half.

"Trina gets acupuncture in the Natural Health Clinic up there."

"Why?"

"Well, she's on her feet all day in the salon, or at Seventy-Five. She says it keeps her balanced."

"How does having somebody stick needles in you keep you balanced?"

"Oh, it's—"

"That was a question not looking for an answer." Eve walked to the residential door, buzzed the studio.

She gave it thirty seconds, was about to buzz Anton Carver—one of the artists—when the staticky voice answered.

"Jen?"

"Dallas," Eve answered. "Lieutenant Dallas and Detective Peabody, NYPSD."

"Ha ha."

"Not really." No scanner, Eve noted, no door cam. "We need to speak with Donna Fleschner, Anton—"

"You for Donna? Dallas and Peabody for me?" A snorting laugh came through the static. "Yeah, right. I'm usually up for pranks, but I'm working, so—"

"Buzz us in, Ms. Fleschner, or I'll master in."

"Shit, like I've got time for this!"

But the buzzer sounded, the locks clicked open.

Inside, the entrance proved narrow due to the big-ass cargo elevator.

Without a thought, Eve took the clanging metal stairs.

"Loose pants. Even looser pants."

The owner had soundproofed here, so the only noise came from boots on metal treads as they walked to the fourth floor.

Eve buzzed again at the wide double doors with a sign that read:

STARVING ARTISTS AT WORK

Half the door opened a crack, and a bright blue eye peered out. That eye popped wide as the woman behind the door said, "Holy shit! Not a prank. Holy shit!"

The door shut, chains rattled, then the door swung wide.

"Holy shit! It's Dallas and Peabody. Did Jen get you to come? My birthday's not until next month."

"No, she didn't. Can we come in?"

"Well, hell yeah! I never thought I'd actually meet Dallas and Peabody, in the flesh." Donna, currently goggling, had her multicolored streaky hair bundled back. She wore a white tank—as generously streaked with paint—and a pair of knee-length shorts on a lanky frame.

"After I saw the vid, I downloaded the first book—already read the second—can't wait for the vid. And I started following your cases. Wild stuff! Whoa, check it! You guys are mag cops. I mean so mag. I can't believe you're standing here. Shit, we don't have any coffee. I had to get my kick start at the cart this morning. I can go get . . ."

She finally ran down, then took a step back.

"You're standing there," she said. "Oh God, oh Jesus, do I know somebody who's dead?"

"I regret to inform you Erin Albright was killed early this morning."

Now, her face sheet white, she took two stumbling steps back. "No, that's no way. She and Shauna . . . They partied last night with a bunch of friends at the Down and Dirty. I know Crack, okay? I *know* that dude. You know him. No way that happens in his place."

"I'm afraid it did."

"But . . . no. She and Shauna, they're getting married in a few days. This can't be happening." She staggered back to the lump of couch in the center of the room. "Not Erin. This can't be happening to Erin."

"Would you like me to get you some water, Ms. Fleschner?"

Donna lifted shocked and swimming eyes to Peabody. "Please. We got a cooler back there. Please."

She covered her face with her hands, then dropped them.

"How?" she asked Eve. "Why? Oh fuck, just fuck. Where's Shauna? Oh Jesus, poor Shauna. They loved each other. You've got to know they loved each other. Shauna would never, ever hurt Erin."

"She's not a suspect. Why weren't you at the party last night?"

"I was in Baltimore. My sister had a baby, so I took a shuttle down when she was in labor the day before, with my mom. Quentin James MacAbee took his time arriving, like twenty hours or something."

Swiping at tears, she took the tube of water Peabody offered. She cracked it, drank, struggled to continue.

"Our mom's staying down there for like a week, but I was going to try and take the nine o'clock shuttle back last night. I missed it, then there were all these damn storms up and down the East Coast, and I didn't land in New York until around midnight."

She sniffled, drank some more.

"After all that, I just didn't have the juice to glamour up and hit the party. I just didn't have it in the tank. Maybe if I'd been there—"

"It wouldn't have mattered," Peabody said, and sat beside her.

Strong, ropey muscled arms, Eve thought. Tall enough. With an alibi easy to check.

"Can you give us the hospital or birthing center, and do you have your shuttle ticket receipt?"

"Yes. Lady Madonna Birthing Center in Baltimore. My sister's Alyce— with a *y*—Fleschner. I've got the receipts, going and coming, on my 'link."

She pulled it out of her pocket, swiped up the receipts before offering the 'link to Eve.

"I know you have to ask. You're mag cops, and you have to ask. I swear I'd cut off my fingers before I'd hurt Erin. I transitioned five years ago, and she was with me all the way. It hurt my mother, and I love my mother. She thought I was gay, and she accepted that without hesitation. But facing the reality that the son, Don, she loved was a woman inside? That hurt her. Erin was there for me, and for my mom, too. She helped me in so many ways I'll never be able to pay back."

Eve handed her the 'link. "She trusted you."

"Yes, of course. We trusted each other."

"So you knew about the trip?"

"The trip? What trip?"

"To Maui?"

"Maui? Sure, down the road. They needed to save . . ." She trailed off. "Wait. The paintings. She sold those paintings. Man, she worked so hard on those paintings. I'm telling her to take it easy, how she had a wedding coming, but she pushed on them. And damn, they were so good. She sold them, but she asked me to keep the sale on the down-low."

"She didn't tell you why?"

Swimming blue eyes met Eve's. "She didn't have to tell me anything.

She asked, that's all. Was she going to surprise Shauna with the big dream? At the party?"

"It appears so."

Tears rolled. "That's so like her. Just so Erin. She must've had something in her overnight. Leis or a pineapple or . . ." Donna covered her face again. "God. Erin."

"How do you know about the overnight case?"

"I was supposed to bring it. She brought it here a few days ago. When?" Now she pressed her hand to the side of her head as if to shove the memory through. "A week or two after the big sale. I don't know, last week? I think last week. She stowed it back in her supply area, and asked me to bring it in, to the party."

"But you didn't know what was in it?"

"I asked, like what's up, and she said she had a surprise for Erin. A surprise for everybody, so not to look, just to bring it to the party. She had a privacy room booked, and she'd give me the swipe when I got there so I could put it in the room."

After an uneven breath, Donna drank more water. "I tagged her from the shuttle station after I missed the nine o'clock. No, I still thought I could make it. I tagged her like about ten, when they started announcing more delays."

She swiped at her phone again to bring up the tags.

"Man, she looked so happy, and the place was already starting to rock. I told her I didn't know when the hell I'd get out of Baltimore, and I guess I was a little weepy with it. I really wanted to be there, and I was stuck. Then I remembered the overnight, and got weepier."

She wiped away more tears. "All about me, right? She said not to worry about the overnight, she had a backup handling it—just in case—since I had to go to Baltimore. To fly safe, how we'd party twice as hard at the wedding if I stayed stuck. She said, 'Love you, babe.' That's the last thing she said to me. 'Love you, babe.'"

"Who would have been her backup?"

"I don't know. Angie maybe, or Becca, or really most anybody at the party. I didn't ask. I was tired, feeling sorry for myself. Is it important? I can ask everybody."

"Yes, it's important. We've spoken with everyone who was there. Show us where she kept the case."

"Sure." Rising, Donna gestured toward an easel with a painting of an old man sitting on a bench, a spotted dog at his feet. "That's my area. Anton is over there. He does mostly commercial art—for hotels, office buildings. Roy's there. He's been doing a lot of mural work lately, but he still comes in a few times a week. And Erin's here."

Like the other stations, it had a worktable, a stool, shelves holding jars and tubes of paint, supplies. She'd stacked canvases, finished, half-finished, blank, against the wall. None sat on the easel.

"She hadn't started anything since the sale. And she had plenty finished to sell from her street spot. Plus, she'd do on-the-spot portraits—pencil sketches, charcoals, pastels. Tourists go for those."

As she spoke, Donna stroked a hand over the easel. "She put the case right there, bottom shelf."

"She didn't worry about your studio mates poking into it?" Peabody asked.

"Oh, no. Don't mess with anyone else's shit. Hard-and-fast rule. Plus, neither of them would've noticed it."

"Would she have asked either of them to bring it in for her?"

Donna shook her head at Eve. "I can't see that. We're friendly, and we're supportive of each other's work. But we're not real tight. And Roy, he works nights, waits tables at . . . ah, Cuchina—that's it. He's talking about quitting now that his mural work's taking off. And Anton—Anton's a talented artist, but just not the kind of guy you ask for a favor outside of the art.

"I don't understand why it matters."

"Every detail matters." Eve's eye landed on a canvas, a painting of an Italian place, a pizzeria. Bright colors, people sitting at booths and tables, drinking wine, eating a slice, a waitress in motion with a loaded pie on a tray. The long counter at the front window where people could sit on stools and watch New York go by.

A lone figure sat there, facing the window, a slice in one hand.

As she had when she'd first arrived in New York.

"I know that place," she murmured.

"Oh yeah, Polumbi's, one of our favorites. Great pizza. She really captured the vibe."

"Yeah, she did."

Pulling herself out, Eve turned to Donna again. "Who has access to the studio?"

"The four of us. Roy's got a serious girlfriend, so I guess she would. Shauna." Donna lifted her shoulders. "I can't think why anyone else would."

"All right. We appreciate your time and cooperation. If you think of anything else, contact me or Detective Peabody." Eve offered her a card. "Again, we're sorry for your loss."

"Can I—could I talk to Shauna?"

"I think talking to someone who was close to Erin would be good."

"You'll find out, won't you? It's not just a vid, is it? You'll find the bastard who did this to Erin."

Never make promises on an investigation, Eve reminded herself. But she said, "It's not just a vid."

As they started out, Peabody stopped, turned back. "I just wanted to say, I really like what you're working on. The man on the bench with the dog. It's restful. The man and the dog love each other. It just shows."

"Thank you." Donna's eyes filled again. "Thanks for that."

Eve started down the stairs. "She could've had somebody take that trip to and from Baltimore. She didn't," Eve added as Peabody started to speak. "But check her alibi—the birthing center, the shuttle station security feed. Let's cross her all the way off."

"Yeah, you're right. We need to check, but she didn't. She loved Albright. Like the man and the dog, it showed."

"Agreed. We'll do runs on the other two artists, confirm where they were from twenty-three hundred until midnight. But I think she knew Albright through and through. When she says Albright wouldn't have asked either of them, I lean that way."

"But we cross them all the way off."

"We do."

On the street, she considered the distance to the Down and Dirty. "Ten-minute walk from here to Crack's place. Plenty of time from when Fleschner tagged Albright from Baltimore for Albright to tag her backup if she hadn't already. They get here, swipe in—the swipes for this building and the studio were in Albright's purse, not the apartment. Killer goes to the club—probably back door again. She gives him the swipes—and thanks so much—he walks here, gets the case, walks back."

"She doesn't meet him at the back door the second time," Peabody began.

"Doesn't need to." Eve walked to the car. "Killer slips in the back, goes straight to the privacy room—she'd already given him that pass. Set down the case, and wait. When it's done, put the swipes back in her purse."

"Why leave the case? Leaving the case is stupid."

Drumming her fingers on the wheel, she waited for a break in traffic.

"Not much time to plan a murder, though, or come up with the weapon."

"I'm going to say they didn't need it. Maybe just waiting for an opening. Then a baby decides it's time to come out. Add storms along the East Coast, shuttle delays, and you've got one."

She swung into traffic. "This wasn't impulse. Maybe the time and place were. But somebody wanted Erin Albright dead."

Chapter Five

"ALIBI CHECKS." AS EVE DROVE, PEABODY VIEWED THE SECURITY FEED sent by the Baltimore station. "She's half-asleep in a chair in the terminal at twenty-three hundred, and I've got her boarding the shuttle a few minutes later. Considering the time she landed, and the distance from the station here to the studio, to her apartment, she couldn't have made it before midnight."

"Thoroughly crossed off. Cross-check the moonlighting gigs with the partygoers."

"I remember one had a catering business. Let me check my notes."

"Do that, and see if you can find her connection to the other two venues. Shauna would know, but I don't want to follow up with her yet."

"We should've asked Fleschner."

"Didn't want to do that until the thoroughly crossed-off. You can start on that angle while we check in with Morris."

"How many mornings do you figure we visit the morgue?"

"Too many."

After pushing through a tangled knot of traffic, Eve parked.

And with Peabody, started down the long white tunnel of the city's dead.

"I've got Tricia Pilly—the caterer. Maura Lang, bartender, the grill. And a Chassie Gordon, daughter of Blondina Gordon—owner of the maid service."

"Good. Find a seat, have conversations."

Eve continued on, then pushed open the doors of Morris's work home. Music played, something soft and bluesy, as he stood beside the body, his hands in the chest cavity.

Under his protective cape, he wore an oatmeal-colored suit with a pale blue shirt and a tie of a deeper shade of blue. He had his black hair in a long braid, starting high on his head and threaded with cord in the deep blue.

He lifted his long, dark eyes to Eve, and sighed.

"And so she'll be the center of a memorial instead of a bride."

"She trusted the wrong person. Don't know who yet, but it killed her. Piano wire?"

"I'd say yes. A pity something designed for beauty and enjoyment would be used to end a life."

"People are fucked up. They'll find a way to kill with pretty much anything."

"I once had a victim on my table killed with a binky."

"A what?"

"A baby's pacifier."

Even then, it took her a minute to identify what she thought of as a plug.

"Oh, yeah, yeah, I remember that. It wasn't my case, but I remember hearing about it. Father went nuts, forced it down the mother's throat so she choked on it. Why do they call it a binky?"

"I have no idea. Where's our Peabody?"

"Running down a few things. Never going to be able to trace piano wire."

"Wire used with considerable force, and as your on-scene speculated, from behind, drawing upward, then crossed in the back."

"Some sort of handles or grips on the ends."

"For this kind of force, yes. The skin under her nails is hers. The lab has the broken nails from the sweepers, but the trace under those will likely be hers. She dug at her own throat to try to drag the wire away. As deeply as it cut in, she wouldn't have fought for long."

No, Eve thought, studying the body. Not for long.

"No other defensive wounds?"

"None. The contusions here, here? From a blow to a solid surface—the door, as you've already concluded. And these? From the fall when she went down."

"He took the murder weapon with him. Stick it in a bag along with her 'link, the jewelry he took off her, any cash she had, stuff it in your pocket, walk out. Easy to dispose of in a recycler as you go. Smarter to do that a bit at a time, using multiples.

"Did he keep a trophy?" she wondered. "We'll find out."

"There are no indications of sexual abuse ante- or postmortem."

"No, the killer didn't care about that. This was personal, but not sexual. A straight kill, with a half-assed attempt to make it look like a robbery."

"Half-assed indeed," Morris agreed. "She'd consumed a considerable amount of alcohol—it was a party, after all. Her reflexes would have been slowed. She'd had some bar snacks. Pretzels, some nachos, and some pasta primavera earlier, about seven, given the TOD."

He walked over to wash his sealed hands.

"Otherwise, I find no signs of alcohol abuse, illegals use. The tox screen will confirm that. A healthy young woman, no body or face work, good muscle tone, and a small heart tattoo on her left buttocks."

He lifted his hands. "She can't tell me more."

"Then it'll have to be enough. Thanks. I'll tell Shauna and the victim's family to contact you about coming in."

"Good hunting," he called as she went out.

Spotting her, Peabody rose, but continued to talk on her 'link. "No, I appreciate the time, and I'd maybe contact Angie to see how Shauna's doing."

As Peabody finished up, Eve pushed open the outside door.

"Okay," Peabody began. "Statements are Albright was always open to off-the-books work if she didn't have something else going. So whenever one of the three venues we have needed more hands, they'd tag her. Usually she said yes. Which she did to a cleaning job yesterday morning. She worked with an Andrew Minor, from eight to about eleven-thirty. That's confirmed."

"Finished there, went by the D&D to pick up the swipe," Eve concluded.

"Yeah, she told Minor she had some errands. As it was rarely more than a hundred bucks, they paid her in cash. And she'd make that or more in tips with the bar and the catering deal. I hear personable, friendly, efficient, good worker from all of them. Oh, and Chassie isn't employed by her mother's company. She works at the Met—the museum—but will occasionally pitch in."

In the car, Peabody strapped in. "She and the victim went to high school together, and Albright worked part-time and a chunk of the summer with the cleaning service."

"Okay. We're going to head in. You can do the runs. Start with the other artists. Unlikely the killer would've stayed—had to get rid of the murder weapon, what he took off the body. But we'll run McNab's group, just to cover it."

"I'll get it rolling. You know, both Albright and Hunnicut have what feels like a tight circle of friends, and in both cases some of that going back to high school."

"Okay, and?"

"Well, a lot of people—probably most—scatter after high school. Different colleges, jobs, interests, locations. But these two found their tribe—or a member of their tribe—early and stuck. Stuck and expanded, then like blended tribes.

"It's like you and Mavis."

Though she saw where Peabody was going, Eve decided to make her work for it. "Mavis and I never planned to marry each other."

"Now that I think about it . . ." Peabody angled her head. "You'd make a cute couple. But what it is? The two of you recognized each other, on some level. So even though you busted her for street grifting way back, the two of you stuck. I met Mavis through you, and we have that hook, but we also have our own level of friendship. Same with the rest of the tribe."

Eve pulled into the garage at Central. "Now we have a tribe?"

"Sure. You, Mavis, me, Nadine, Reo, Mira, Trina—"

"Wait!" After she got out of the car, Eve slammed the door. "Don't I get a vote on tribe membership? I never voted for Trina."

"It's not a democracy, it's a tribe. Louise, Callendar, and Harvo are in there. We're connected, and we're connected inside the connection. We're all separate women with different backgrounds, personalities, and all that, but together? Tribe."

They crossed the garage to the elevators.

"It feels to me like Albright and Hunnicut worked the same way, so it's hard to see a member of their tribe having any part in the murder."

"So, you've never heard of intertribal warfare or treachery?"

Frowning, Peabody got on the elevator with Eve. "Okay, point, but wouldn't it be hard to keep that hidden? Hidden so well, nobody else in the tribe got a hint?"

"Peabody, if people weren't at least half-decent at wearing masks, we'd never have to investigate a homicide. We'd just scan the tribe, say, and point, 'You, you there with the murder face. You're under arrest.'

Then the judge and/or jury would take one look when he went to trial and it's: 'Murder Face is guilty on all counts.'"

"Murder Face," Peabody speculated as the elevator bumped to a stop. When the doors opened, two uniforms and a guy with clown-orange hair, blue baggies with rainbow suspenders, and a shirt that read WHEE!! stepped on.

"What's a murder face look like? Bared teeth? Slitty eyes?"

Clown Hair turned around, blew a small blue bubble with his gum. Obviously one of Feeney's, Eve thought.

"Is it a crime of passion or planned?"

"Planned."

"Ditch the teeth and slitty eyes. You'd go for something like . . ." He had bright green eyes, animated eyes that suddenly went blank.

Not flat like a cop's, Eve noted. But just dead. Like a shark's.

And she had to admit he pulled it off.

"Nah." One of the uniforms shook her head as the elevator stopped again and more cops filed on. "Me? I'd go for the friendly face." She burst out with a wide smile and eyes just over the edge of crazy. "Then it's 'Hey, pal,' right before you shove the knife in their throat."

The other uniform disagreed. "Not me. I'd go for the helpless, with mild distress. 'Oh, could you give me a hand? I can't quite—' Then you bash them over the head."

By the time the elevator stopped again, every cop in the car had an opinion on Murder Face.

Eve squeezed out and headed for the glides.

Peabody trotted after her.

"I never thought about how diverse and varied murder faces are."

"I'm sorry I brought it up."

"No, it's a good point. And it's not like I just look at the surface—I know better. But the friendships in this tribe just strike me as the real deal."

"Remember poisoned champagne, the devoted wife, the loving hus-band? That bond came off real."

"Well, yeah, but she was a professional. Actress, I mean. She knew how to put on the show."

"Any killer worth his salt knows how to put on the show. And what the fucking fuck does that mean? The salt? Why did I say that? That's what happens," she said darkly, "you get sucked into spouting those sayings that make no sense. Sucked in."

She jumped off the glide and arrowed toward Homicide.

One foot in the door, and Jenkinson's tie assaulted her with its multi-colored smiley-faced cartoon stars over a wild blue sky.

"Detective Sergeant."

"Yo, Loo!"

"Status."

"Rocking and a-rolling. Carmichael and Santiago caught one about an hour ago. Baxter and Trueheart"—he chin-pointed to where Baxter in his sharp suit worked his 'link, and the earnest-faced Trueheart his comp—"they're following up some leads."

In acknowledgment, Baxter tapped a finger to his temple in salute.

"Me and Reineke got a breather, so we dug out a cold one."

"No case, however cold, can outwit the badge," Reineke said.

"Let me know if you thaw it out. Runs, Peabody, and get an update from McNab."

She strode straight to her office, and straight to the AutoChef for cof-fee. Then with said coffee, took two quiet minutes at her skinny window with New York rocking and a-rolling below.

Peabody wasn't wrong about how the friendships and bonds of the group connection to the victim and Hunnicut felt genuine.

But feelings weren't facts. Resentments and worse could and did sim-mer well under the surface until something—anything—set them to boil.

At this point, evidence indicated—strongly—the victim knew her killer. A member of the tribe, as Peabody termed it? Maybe, maybe not. But someone known, someone trusted enough to do a favor and keep a secret.

And that, she thought, equaled: Advantage badge.

She sat at her desk and opened the murder book.

Another hit of coffee, and she began on her board.

Plenty of names and faces, she thought, and the bulk of them already eliminated due to their whereabouts at TOD.

But that didn't mean they had no connection to the murder. Advertent, or inadvertent.

Friendships were often complicated, she thought as she worked. And man, could she attest there. Then those connections within the larger group brought in different levels, different dynamics.

Friend A's great, Friend B says to Friend C. And Friend C agrees, but adds how it bugs the crap out of her when Friend A does X. And snickering in solidarity, Friend B agrees there. Right before she tags up Friend A and tells her how Friend C trashed her about X.

She'd heard that kind of bullshit plenty in school, in the Academy, and even on the job.

She sat, put her feet up, studied the board.

And in that big a group, wouldn't you have some overlap in relationships? Somebody slept with somebody else, who slept with another somebody.

She got up to pace, to consider the next step.

Peabody's pink boots clomped toward her office.

"The two other artists—both clear. Anton Carver was uptown at a swank dinner party. Lilibeth Warsaw, art patron, arranged it, and it checks out he was there until right about midnight. She had him taken home, her car, her driver. It all checks."

"All right."

"Roy Lutz was at a bar, Lower East. Its friends and family sort of opening. He'd painted the wall murals. About thirty people there, and I checked with several already, will swear he was there until nearly one this morning. And he had a date—the serious girlfriend—who swears they went to his place after. He was still sleeping when she left for work this morning about eight-thirty."

Eve just nodded, then stopped to study the board from a new angle.

"McNab's got nothing. Nothing deleted or hidden on any of the e's—except what he already found re the vic ordering the tickets, booking the hotel in Maui."

"Okay, as expected. Let's go talk to Hunnicut's exes. And we'll check, see when's the best time for a follow-up with her. Give me ten. I'm going to talk to the victim's family, make sure everything jibes there and nothing jumps out."

Eve spoke with the grieving parents. They hadn't known about the trip, the surprise. Knew no one who would harm their daughter—no enemies, no resentful exes. They added little to the investigation but the weight of their grief.

Eve carried it with her to the bullpen.

"With me, Peabody. In the field, Jenkinson. Albright's parents didn't know about the trip," Eve continued as she strode to the elevators. "Said they would have contributed to the cost of the tickets if they had. But she told them how she was going to reveal a big surprise, and would send them pictures."

"She wanted Shauna to know first," Peabody concluded. "It was Shauna's big dream, so Shauna first."

"That's my read."

Eve took one look at the packed elevator when the doors opened, turned on her heel, and headed for the glides.

"The father insists it had to be a mugging, a robbery, because no one who knew his daughter would kill her."

"It has to be easier believing that. If it can be easier."

"I'd say, right now, nothing makes it easier. Marcus Stillwater first," Eve said as they continued down. "Fordam Publishing's closest. His apartment's only a block or two from there."

"Stillwater—bootie buddy, right?"

"I guess that's one way of putting it."

"I never really had one of those. Did you?"

As they angled down the steps to the garage level, Eve glanced back. "Why would I want one of those?"

"Well, you know, for the easy, no-strings, no-worries sex with someone you know and like."

"And how often do you figure that really works out?"

Frowning, Peabody got in the car. "I don't know, since I never had a bootie buddy."

"I'd guess one in, oh, a hundred—at best. Sex gets complicated if it's more than a one-off." Eve swung out of the garage. "What do you do when your BB shows up at the door and you're naked with someone else? Or your BB decides they want more after all, or they want no more from you? Or you're the one who wants more than the buddy system and they don't? Maybe you get involved with somebody else, and your BB thinks, that's messing up my easy sex, and finds ways to screw with you?"

Peabody considered. "You know, I used to think it was too bad I never had a bootie buddy. Now I'm thinking I was lucky I didn't."

"Bounce naked on somebody, be ready for complications."

"I guess that's a good rule of thumb."

"Whose thumb?"

"I don't know," Peabody decided. "I really don't know."

"Then give me the rundown on Stillwater."

"Marcus Stillwater, age twenty-eight. Originally from Virginia, went to NYU. Employed at Fordam for six years. No marriages, no cohabs. Got a bump—indecent exposure, underage drinking, public lewdness.

All one incident. At age nineteen he and a couple pals got loaded at a party, and took a dare to run naked around the track. Got busted."

"Is that it?"

"On the criminal, yeah. Got degrees in communication and in public relations. One sib, female, age twenty-four, still lives in Virginia."

When she couldn't even find a loading zone on the street, Eve pulled into a shabby little lot, snarled at the obscene hourly price.

"Roarke should buy up all the parking lots in the entire city. He'd double his already ridiculous fortune."

"How do you know he hasn't?"

That gave her a moment's pause. "No. He'd do something like have the scanner read my plate. Wouldn't he? Or maybe he has, and he's messing with me. 'Well now, Lieutenant,'" she said in a reasonable approximation of an Irish accent as she got out of the car, "'you had only to ask.' Then he'd say something about how I actually own this one and that one, just to screw with my head."

Then she shook it off. "But no. Crap parking lots aren't challenging enough for him to bother with."

The heat had already set in so the air itself seemed to sweat. Sunlight bounced off steel and window glass and lasered the eyes, making her glad she'd somehow managed to hang on to her kick-ass sunshades.

When they reached the steel and glass that held Fordam, the wide auto doors slid open.

Inside the busy lobby, the temperature dropped easily thirty degrees.

"Why do they do that? Why do they take it down to meat locker?"

Now she found herself grateful for her jacket as they crossed the black-veined white tile floor.

People walked purposefully or wandered dressed in business suits, business casual, or tourist-special tees and shorts. The lobby, ringed with cafés, delis, and shops and centered with a burbling fountain, echoed with voices.

Eve cut across to the security station, palmed her badge. "Marcus Stillwater, Fordam Publishing."

"Got that for you," said the oddly cheerful blonde working the station. "If I could just scan your badge?" She aimed a handheld, then blinked—and her oddly cheerful smile bumped up a couple more degrees. "Welcome, Lieutenant, to Houston Street Tower. Fordam Publishing is on floors twenty-eight, twenty-nine, and thirty. We have Mr. Stillwater on twenty-nine. Bank B, elevators one through three. Please let me know if I can be of any further assistance."

"Okay."

"Maybe not all the parking lots in the city," Peabody speculated as they aimed for Bank B, "but it's a pretty good bet Roarke owns this building."

"Yeah, another way he screws with my head." She shoved her hands into her pockets as she waited for an elevator. "If he keeps it up, pretty soon I won't be able to bitch at any doorman, desk clerk, or security guard."

"He's diabolical."

Eve spared her a glance. "You think you're joking."

She got on the elevator, ordered twenty-nine. The elevator smelled, very lightly, of citrus. And though several people got on, got off, got on, on the journey to the twenty-ninth floor, the air maintained that faint, fresh scent.

Roarke class, she thought. It, too, was diabolical.

The lobby on twenty-nine featured pale gray floors, cream-toned walls, a ribbon of windows overlooking downtown, and a sleek black counter manned by two people.

Since one worked on a comp and spoke into a headset, Eve aimed for the other. A bright-eyed redhead who might have been old enough to buy a legal brew.

"Good morning, how can I help you today?"

"Marcus Stillwater."

"Let me check for you. Oh, I'm so sorry, Mr. Stillwater is currently in a meeting. Could I—"

Eve flashed her badge. "Maybe he could step out."

"Oh! Oh my goodness! Let me just—"

She jumped up and fled through a glass door to the right of the counter.

Watching her go, making damn good time on skinny red heels, Eve rocked back and forth on her sturdy boots. "What do you bet she, or somebody she knows well, had some trouble with the cops?"

"Not taking that bet. She flew like a bird."

"People never say she flew like a shuttle—faster than a bird. It's always a bird."

As she waited, Eve took a look around the small lobby. A little waiting area with dark gray seats, a couple of tall green plants in black pots, a scatter of strange, splashy art.

Two people in business suits came in, both with go-cups, and bounced numbers and statistics between them as they went through the glass door on the left of the counter.

A man came through the other door.

If he'd had a jacket and tie, he'd ditched them. His fitted dress shirt showed off good shoulders. He had a crop of loosely curled sun-streaked blond hair around a vid-star face.

Perfect proportions, a subtle tan, arctic blue eyes, and a smile as bright and warm as a summer sun.

He held out a hand. "Marcus Stillwater. I'm sorry, Dora didn't get your name."

"Lieutenant Dallas, Detective Peabody."

"Well, Lieutenant, Detective, I'm more than a little pressed today, but why don't we take a seat here for a few minutes?"

"Your office would be better. Have you spoken with Shauna Hunnicut this morning?"

His smile wavered a little. "No, as I said, I'm pressed today. Is she in trouble? I can't imagine it, not police trouble. Wait, wait. Last night was the party, wasn't it? Party at the D&D."

Now he shook his head, laughed. "Don't tell me Shauna did the crazy and needs bail. I'm going to say, good for her, and I can take care of that. I can send someone down asap to—wherever. What did she do?"

"Mr. Stillwater, it's best if we speak in your office."

Now the smile dropped completely and he gripped Eve's arm. "Is she hurt?"

"Sir—"

"For fuck's sake, tell me."

"She's not hurt, she doesn't need bail. Erin Albright was murdered last night."

Beneath the tan, he went pasty. "Is this some sort of a sick joke?"

"No. If we could continue this in your office?"

"I just—" He pushed a hand through his hair. "Hanna, let Bill and Tricia know I had an emergency."

He led the way through the door, and, Eve noted, a maze with a pecking order. Cubes, take a turn, desks, small meeting rooms, another turn, offices.

He stepped into one, waited, then closed the door behind Eve and Peabody.

"What happened? Tell me what happened. Sorry, sit. Should I tag Shauna? Don't tell me she's alone. I can—"

"Mr. Stillwater," Peabody interrupted, and gently touched his arm. "Why don't you sit down?"

He dropped down behind a cluttered desk. "I've been so busy, I don't even know if she'd tried to tag me. I turned off my 'link—no distractions. God. What happened? What happened to Erin?"

"She was strangled."

His hand lifted to his own throat. "Strangled? Jesus Christ. Where was Shauna? You said Shauna wasn't hurt."

"She wasn't. She wasn't with Erin at the time of the attack."

"But they were at the party. That was last night. I'm sure of it now. How—"

"Mr. Stillwater, where were you last night?"

The color that had begun to seep back into his face faded again. "Me? I—I'm a suspect."

"This is routine. It's helpful if you can provide that information."

"I need to take a breath. Breathe. Erin. They're getting married this weekend, did you know that? You must know that. Shauna and I have been friends for . . ."

He held out his hands, composed himself.

"Okay. Okay. We worked late—Bill, Tricia, Jorge, Liza, and me. Until, God, close to nine? Working on a major campaign. I think we logged out about nine, then everybody but Liza went for food and drinks—she's got kids at home, Liza does. Little kids. We went to—where the hell?"

Pausing, he pressed his fingers to his eyes. "Bojo's. We went to Bojo's, got something to eat, something to drink, went over the work, again. We were there until, I think, I think we were there until—had to be after eleven, maybe close to eleven-thirty. I walked home from there—turned off my 'link because Tricia was still batting ideas, and I know how that works. I wanted a decent night's sleep."

"What time did you get home?"

"I'm not sure. Bojo's is about ten blocks from my apartment."

"When's the last time you saw or spoke with Erin Albright?"

"Ah, maybe a couple weeks? I had drinks with them and Becca and Greg a couple weeks ago. They were full of wedding talk."

"When's the last time you had sex with Shauna?"

He leaned back in his chair, let out a long sigh. "Maybe a week or two before she fell for Erin. Was that a surprise for me? Yeah. She'd never dated a woman before. Did I expect it to last? Not really. But I was wrong. They had the deal, the real deal.

"Breathe," he reminded himself. "Shauna's my friend, my really good friend. I was happy for her, happy when I saw she had the real deal. And Erin, you had to like her."

Pausing, he scrubbed at his face again.

"She had so much—what's the word? Verve. I'd've tried to get along with her even if I didn't, for Shauna. But I did like her."

"Who didn't?"

He lifted his hands. "Honest to God, I don't know. I'd tell you in a heartbeat if I did."

"When did Erin tell you about the trip to Maui?"

He frowned. "Shauna's big dream thing? I guess I knew about that since Shauna and I became friends. The one-day-she'd-honeymoon-in-Maui thing. I know they were saving to go, delayed honeymoon. Next year, maybe the year after."

"Did you ever visit Erin's art studio?"

"Yeah, a few times. Shauna loved showing off Erin's work. It's good—at least to my eye. I actually bought one of her charcoal drawings for my apartment. And later, one of her paintings. I *liked* her, Lieutenant. I liked her.

"I really need to talk to Shauna, to go to Shauna."

"She's staying with Angie Decker."

"Angie . . . Right, right, I know Angie. Should I tag Angie? Is that better?"

"It might be." Eve got to her feet. "Thank you for your time, for your cooperation." Eve took out a card, laid it on his cluttered desk. "If you think of anything else, please contact either me or Detective Peabody."

"All right." He looked down at the card, then up at Eve. "They were getting married Saturday. Shauna asked if I'd help seat people. It doesn't feel real. It doesn't feel like it could be real."

"He felt real," Peabody said when they'd left.

"He did, but I've been in Bojo's. You could walk to the D&D inside fifteen minutes. Let's check the timing, Peabody. He's one of Shauna's good friends—why wouldn't Albright trust him? It also feels as if he'd be the perfect backup to Donna Fleschner."

Chapter Six

On the street, Eve strode toward the parking lot. Morning started to bleed into afternoon.

"Give me the rundown on the other ex who came up."

"Jon Rierdon. He manages City Style Home Goods. Ooooh. Thirty, single, one cohab that lasted about eighteen months. No criminal. New York native. Moonlights as a piano player at Swank—a piano bar downtown."

"Here's what we're going to do. You take Rierdon, I'm taking the player. Wade Rajinski—Crack got me his full name. Then together we'll follow up with Hunnicut."

"You don't want to go to a home goods store with me?"

"If I go with you, you'll drive me to kick your ass. I'm not in the mood."

"You're not in the mood to kick my ass?" Peabody did a quick dance shuffle. "It's my lucky day."

"I'm always in the mood to kick your ass. I'm not in the mood to be driven to do so by your drooling over light fixtures and table settings."

"That's fair," Peabody decided. "And bonus? I can drool without fear."

"Got cab fare?"

"Yeah, but I actually know this place. Just a couple stops on the subway from here."

"Fine. Tag me when you're done." Eve stopped at the lot, reconsidered. "I'm leaving the car here. Rajinski's place is walking distance, and so's his employment. Personal trainer and yoga instructor."

"I bet he's pretty. Stillwater was pretty."

"You're going to drive me to kick your ass after all."

"Nope. My ass is now a moving target."

As she hustled off, Eve called after her, "I've got really good aim." But she walked in the opposite direction.

She didn't mind the noonday heat, in fact preferred it to the fake, frigid air of the interiors. And she never really tired of walking New York.

Even when it was filled with wilting, sweaty tourists. Plenty of them trudged along the sidewalk, happy to spend their money on overpriced souvenirs and scratchy T-shirts from stalls or pose for pictures with their red, shiny faces in front of a shop or by a waiting Rapid Cab.

She'd never been a tourist here, she realized. No, not even when she'd had that first slice of New York pizza at the window counter. Nearly as far back as she could clearly remember, New York had been her destination, the badge her goal.

And when she'd finally been free to get there, New York was home. Her place, her city.

She walked it now surrounded by all the sounds and smells.

Honking horns, shouted insults, a distant siren, music thumping out of a car window, voices merging in a multitude of accents, languages.

Soy dogs on the boil, crap coffee, a tangy sauce from a plate on a table at a sidewalk café. A recycler overdue for pickup, some lunching lady's high-dollar perfume.

Every bit of it was just fine with her.

She didn't have to keep an eye out for street thieves—she had cop's eyes, so they stayed trained. But none crossed her path as she walked to Mind, Body, Spirit.

She went inside, where it felt like a brisk March wind had blown in. Fast, pulsing music blew in with it.

Lots of mirrors, she noted, and lots of shiny machines with people sweating and puffing on them. A good free-weight area with a couple of people pumping while admiring themselves in a mirrored wall.

Lunch-hour warriors maybe, she thought, and walked to the check-in desk.

The woman behind it had the proverbial brick shithouse build, and showed it off in skin shorts and a very inadequate sports bra. She had her hair done in many braids pulled up like a crown on the top of her head.

A pirate ship rippled across the rock-hard sea of her abs.

She folded small white towels and spoke on a headset.

"Hold on," she said, then glanced at Eve. "Just swipe your card, take any available locker."

"Not a member."

"Okay." She tapped the headset. "Get back to you." Then stepped over. "Help ya? A tour of the facilities, a day pass? Summer special on memberships through Labor Day."

Eve held up her badge. "Wade Rajinski?"

"Ha. Figured he'd run into cops one day. Second level. He should be finishing up his yoga class."

"Thanks." Then she leaned on the counter in a friendly way. "Why did you figure he'd run into the cops?"

The woman shrugged rock-hard shoulders, like boulders over the rock-hard ab sea.

"Too smooth, too shiny. Gotta be something under the smooth and shine, right? Total player with the ladies. Got dinged there a time or three."

"Dinged?"

"This one time, this woman came barreling in here. Wade, he's working with a client on the bench press and she flies right over. Me, I'm surprised we got any glass left in here the way she was shrieking about how he bounced off her and bounced right onto her sister."

"How'd he handle that?"

"Smooth." She glided a hand through the air. "Like butter. Gets somebody to spot his client, then takes her into the consult room. About ten minutes later, she comes out, all flushed up and starry-eyed. Walked out with a smile on her face, and Wade, he comes out and finishes up the training session like nothing ever happened.

"Smooth." She shrugged again. "We lose a client now and then because of it, but management likes him because for every one we lose, he pulls in three more. Guy's got a magic cock."

At Eve's lifted brows, the woman shrugged a third time. "Sure. I mean it's right there, just looking to oblige. I figure why not go ahead and use it if the mood strikes, before some woman gets pissed enough to whack it off. But me, I don't get emotional over a cock, right? Magic or not."

"Good policy."

With that insight, Eve wove through the machines and took a set of curved stairs to the second floor.

Through one set of glass doors, she saw about a dozen people wiggling hips more or less in unison, quick stepping to the right, then the left while an instructor faced them. One of those dance-the-pudge-away deals, she assumed. Since the instructor appeared to shout, and she imagined the music blasted, she gave the place credit for excellent soundproofing.

Inside the next room a woman in a white gi led another dozen or so—older, at or around the century mark to her eye—through some tai chi.

Rajinski held the third classroom. He wore black skin shorts and a black tank that showed off his attributes. It came as no surprise to her that twenty of the twenty-two students were female.

While she watched, he bent fluidly into a split-legged, seated forward fold, golden muscles damp and rippling, golden hair shining. Shifted fluidly into cobbler, and a flow into boat pose.

She couldn't fault his form as he finished up the floor poses and slid into savasana.

Keeping an eye, Eve pulled out her 'link and contacted Angie Decker.

On-screen, Angie's eyes welled with grief. "Lieutenant Dallas. Is there anything . . ."

"The investigation's ongoing. My partner and I are conducting interviews. I'd like to follow up with Ms. Hunnicut when it's convenient."

"We're at the—the morgue now. Shauna's with Erin's parents. Dr. Morris is very kind, just as you said."

"Yes, he is."

In the classroom, Rajinski and his students moved into a cross-legged position, eyes closed, hands palms up on knees.

"Becca and Greg just left. Becca's going to get some of Shauna's things, and Greg's picking up some food, I think. Shauna's going to stay with me until . . . Well, as long as she needs. I think—" Angie swiped at her eyes. "Actually, I think the sooner the better if you need to talk to her again. Get it over with, and we can be there with her."

"We'll come to your place, within the hour."

"All right. I'll tell her. We're all just . . . It feels like sleepwalking today. She's coming out now. I'll tell her."

Eve put the 'link away.

Inside, Rajinski put his hands in prayer, bowed. Most began to roll up their mats, but two women made a beeline for him.

Practice over, Eve thought, and went through the door.

Quiet music—bells, strings, flutes—played under the chatter of people getting ready to move on with their day. The room smelled of patchouli with just a hint of sweat.

The two women vied for Rajinski's attention with hair tossing, body brushing, arm stroking.

He managed to smile at both of them and give Eve the flirt eye as she crossed the room.

Smooth.

"Wade Rajinski."

"Yes." His eyes, a soft sea green, fixed on her as if only she existed. "Hello."

Eve held up her badge. "Lieutenant Dallas, NYPSD."

Curiosity crept into his gaze, his voice. "Really?"

"Yes, really. I'd like to speak with you regarding an investigation."

"Of course. Jin, Lea, you'll have to excuse me. You have a perfect day, and remember, five minutes of meditation before sleep quiets the busy mind."

They left, and Eve felt their looks of resentment burn into her back.

"Now, what can I do for you, Lieutenant? If you'd like to sit, we have a small water bar on the main level."

A water bar, she thought. Didn't it figure?

"This is fine. You were at the Down and Dirty last night?"

"Yes, I was, for about an hour. I enjoy its raw, real vibe."

"While there did you engage with Erin Albright and/or Shauna Hunnicut?"

"I *engaged* with a number of people—that's part of the vibe. But let me think."

He stepped over, took a rolled towel off a shelf, and dabbed at his face and neck. "Erin and Shauna, Erin and Shauna . . . Yes! I remember. The brides-to-be. Adorable, both of them. Their happiness just brimmed over. I enjoyed spending some time with their group. Such joy and energy."

"Had you met them, or any of their group, before last night?"

"Unfortunately no." His smile flashed. "But I hope to meet a few of them again."

"You won't meet Erin Albright again. She's in the morgue."

The towel paused in its dabbing. "I'm sorry, what?"

"Erin Albright was murdered last night, at the Down and Dirty."

"But that's—that's shocking. That's horrible." He tossed the towel in a wicker basket. "No, just no, the energy was joy, not violence. I have some sensitivity, and I'm sure I would've felt something so dark."

"Looks like you missed it. What time did you leave the club?"

"I'm not sure, but before midnight. Maybe eleven-forty-five, around. When did this horrible thing happen?"

"Why don't you tell me where you went, what you did after leaving the club?"

"Of course, if that's helpful. As I said, I enjoyed connecting with the women in the group, but— May I be frank?"

"You can be whoever you want if you answer the questions."

That little sarcasm slid right over his golden head. "A stop at the Down and Dirty usually results in a more intimate connection."

"You go to pick someone out to have sex."

"An intimacy of the moment," he corrected. "I like women. I like sex. I like sex with women, and that intimacy of the moment. Life is for living."

"Until you're murdered."

"Exactly. No, I mean, it's horrible, but that's my point. Live full while you can."

He looked blank a moment. "Where was I going with this? Oh yes, while I felt the possibility of a more intimate connection with some of the women in that group, the night was not the night for it. They were a group, they were celebrating. And while I feel marriage is a societal construct designed to restrict our natural freedom, they had joy. I took some contacts for a later connection, and left them to their joy."

"And what did you do, Wade, after that?"

"As I was still in the mood for the intimacy of the moment, I walked to Tango. It's not as raw and real as the Down and Dirty, but a little more polished, you could say. I felt a pull toward a lonely, lovely brunette, and bought her a drink. A Zombie. We talked—she'd had a recent bad breakup. We went back to her place and had that intimacy of the moment. Twice."

He smiled then. "She no longer felt lonely when I left—about two-thirty this morning."

"Did you get a name?"

"Of course." He actually looked insulted. "Daralee—isn't that charming? She moved to New York six years ago from Decatur, Georgia. Her accent was delightful."

"Last name?"

"We didn't find last names necessary, but I can give you her address and her 'link number."

"That'll work."

He held up a finger, crossed over to a small gym bag, and took out his 'link. "Here we are," he said, and read off the data.

"Okay. When you were at the Down and Dirty, did you notice anything that seemed off? Anyone who wasn't full of joy?"

"No. As I said, I have some sensitivity. I'm not a full sensitive, but I do have just a touch extra. I'm sure I would have noticed that. As right now, I feel this darkness inside."

He focused on her, eyes full of warmth, sympathy, understanding.

"You have such a demanding, stress-filled job where the dark lives. I offer private meditation practices. I'd love to work with you, give you some peace."

"Thanks. I have my own methods of working off stress."

A touch of humor now, and the sexy oozing through as he laid a hand on her arm. "I could help with that, too." He gave her biceps a quick squeeze, and his eyebrows lifted. "Slim as a willow, but muscles like stone. That's surprising."

"You'll be real surprised if you don't move your hand and I show you one of my ways to relieve stress."

He lifted his hand, held them both up, and added an easy smile. "I apologize. I'm a touchy-feely."

"Huh. I sensed that. I must have some sensitivity, too. Thanks for your time and cooperation."

"Lieutenant," he said as she started out, "I didn't get your first name."

"I don't find my first name necessary for this." With a mental eye roll, she kept going.

The brick shithouse now worked some poor schmuck through a circuit on the machines. She gave Eve a once-over. "Not flushed, not starry-eyed. Guess Wade struck out with you. But you didn't arrest him."

"Maybe next time." She paused a moment. "Has he ever been violent, overly pushy?"

"I gotta speak truth. Just no. You give him the back-off signal, he backs right off. There's plenty of others who want a ride on the magic cock, and he knows it. He's a dog, right, but he don't bite."

"Yeah, I got that."

Holding up a finger, Brick Shithouse turned to her client. "On the pad, Paulie. And give me twenty. I could help you bulk up," she said to Eve, "put some muscle on."

Amused, Eve stepped over to the weight rack, picked up a twenty-five, and did ten smooth biceps curls.

"My mistake."

"A lot of people make it." Eve replaced the weight and walked out.

As she walked back to the parking lot, Eve tagged Peabody.

"On my way back to the car."

"I'm just leaving—in a minute."

"Then meet me at Angie Decker's. They should be back from the morgue."

"I'll head there. Any luck with Rajinski?"

"Got an alibi to check, but it's going to. He's a horndog with not too many smarts and a magic cock. He's not our guy."

"How do you know about the magic cock?"

"I have it on good authority. And if you bought something in that place—and you did—I don't want to hear about it."

"I'll just say it didn't interfere with or affect my interview. I wouldn't mind hearing more about the magic cock."

"Get to Decker's."

She actively considered continuing the walk to Decker's, but had to admit she'd waste time. And it proved the right decision when she found a parking spot half a block from the building.

Pleased with her luck, she strolled down to a corner cart and ordered soy fries and a tube of Pepsi.

"You're eating." Peabody, huffing just a little, stopped beside her.

"I had to wait for you, so it passed the time."

"Veggie dog," Peabody ordered. "Mustard, Diet Pepsi. Rierdon didn't ring bells," she told Eve. "But he doesn't have an alibi. He's in a relationship—two months in—and the woman he's seeing teaches salsa on Monday nights. I confirmed. He grabbed takeaway, a gyro, on the way home, also confirmed. Got home about seven, had a beer."

She took the dog, paid. "Thanks. Ate the gyro," she continued, "watched some screen, had another beer, and crashed by eleven."

As they walked back, she munched on the dog. "He was up front. Shauna ended things before he was ready, so he was a little pissed and didn't want the whole we-can-be-friends deal Shauna did. Hasn't had a real relationship again until this one. He didn't know Erin Albright, but he'd heard through mutual friends that Shauna was involved there, then engaged there.

"One fry? Can I have one fry?"

Eve held out the scoop.

"Only one," Peabody repeated, like a mantra. "He said—and it came off true—knowing she switched teams made him feel better about the breakup. Then he heard about the murder right after he opened the store this morning, and remembered the name. He said he started to text Shauna, then didn't know what to say."

"We'll verify, but if he didn't know the victim, it's unlikely she'd bring him in on the big surprise."

Eve stopped outside the building, a nicely rehabbed white brick, mixed commercial and residential with a Greek place—coulda had a gyro—and an upscale hair and nail salon street level.

Eve walked to the maroon residential door, found Decker, and buzzed.

A male voice answered, "4202."

"Lieutenant Dallas, Detective Peabody."

"I'll buzz you in."

When the buzzer sounded, Eve stepped in, studied the pair of elevators in the tiny entrance. Then pushed open the stairway door.

"I should've had more than one fry."

"You can skip any cardio you planned for later."

Peabody brightened. "Good trade. And we've done some suspect eliminations."

"First-pass eliminations don't always stick."

"True, but these feel like they will."

"Stairway's clean," Eve commented. "And you hear that? The pretty much nothing? Solid soundproofing. Some baby's probably screaming somewhere in here, but we don't hear it. Solid building, nice neighborhood. Decker lives alone, she's still shy of thirty. She models, and also works for her family's business. They're plumbers."

"That explains it."

"Yeah, if you can fix a toilet on a weekend, you can charge two arms and one leg. One official cohab, male, lasted just over two years, ended last fall. If she's straight, it's unlikely she and the victim were involved in that way, but they might've been."

"Are you looking at her?"

"If Albright needed a backup, why not the person she chose to stand up for her at her wedding? Statements indicate she was in the club area at TOD. But it wouldn't take long to do the deed and get back. You'd need a way to ditch the weapon and the rest, but, if you planned it out, possible. She's tall enough, looks strong enough."

Eve paused on the third floor. "Say she and Erin had an on-and-off. Go back to booty buddies. Maybe even kept that on the down-low. Then Erin falls for Shauna. It doesn't pass or wear out like before. It sticks. Now they're getting married, and we cut to the classic 'If I can't have you, no one will.'"

Eve started up the next flight. "It's a theory."

"You wanted to follow up with her as much as Shauna."

"They were tight. She was trusted. Gotta look."

"Why didn't she kill Shauna—get rid of the obstacle?"

"What's that thing people say? How you always strangle the ones you love."

"I think it's 'hurt.'"

"I bet getting strangled hurts."

"Either way, I get it."

"Keep it in mind while we talk to them."

"I will. But now I wish I hadn't liked her right off. The way she and DiNuzio flanked Hunnicut, the way the three of them held together like a unit."

"And all that might be true. But somebody Albright knew and trusted killed her."

On four they walked to the apartment. Good locks, Eve noted, a door cam with intercom. The door opened before she could knock.

The male voice, she assumed. He came in just over six feet, about a hundred and seventy, a leanly muscled build in black pants, a pale-blue-and-gray pin-striped dress shirt open at the collar, rolled to the elbows.

Caucasian, and another vid-star handsome with a clean-shaven angular face, short, wavy brown hair and deep-set, deep brown eyes shadowed with fatigue.

"Lieutenant, Detective, please come in. I'm Greg, Greg Barney. We're . . . we're all in the living room."

He led them down a short entrance hall into a spacious living area with large windows offering a street view.

Shauna sat on a cream-colored couch, a rose-colored pillow pressed to her middle with one arm. Her other hand clung to Donna Fleschner's.

"They said I could come," Donna said quickly. "I wanted to come."

"That's fine," Eve told her.

Angie rose from the facing love seat, stepped to the side. "Please come in, sit down. I was going to make coffee, but no one wanted any. I can make coffee."

"We're fine."

As she crossed the room, Eve gauged the tableau. Stylish furniture—muted backdrop with bold splashes of color.

Some of the art on the wall had to be Erin Albright's; even Eve recognized the style.

Becca sat on the arm of the sofa on Shauna's other side.

Shauna, ghost pale, her red hair pulled back and rolled into a knot at the base of her neck. She wore a black dress, one a bit too big on her.

Greg stood, his hands going in and out of his pockets as if they didn't know where to settle.

"I went by the deli. I've got lunch meat and sides. Shauna, let me make you a sandwich."

"Not now, Greg. Not now."

"You need to eat," he insisted. "I got the pastrami you like. I'll make you a sandwich."

She just shook her head. "Maybe later."

Becca rose, went over to take his hand. "Sit, babe. Stop hovering and sit." She nudged him into a chair, then sat on that arm with a hand on his shoulder.

Shauna let out a long sigh. "Nobody knows exactly what to do right now. We all had something to do before. We needed to go see Erin. We went to see her in that place. And Erin's parents. We all went to see her, and Mr.—I mean Dr. . . . I can't remember his name, but he was very, very kind. But you know how people say at a funeral or memorial, how she looks like she's sleeping?"

Shauna's hollow, bruised eyes met Eve's. "It's not true. She didn't look like she does when she's asleep. It's not true."

"No," Eve said, "it's not."

"Erin's mom and dad—I thought they should plan the memorial. I thought that was the right thing. But they wanted me to have a part of that, and I asked if we could have our wedding flowers and some of the music. I thought Erin would want that. I don't know. Everybody thought so, too, but I don't know for sure. Do you think that's the right thing?"

"I think it's beautiful," Peabody said. "I think it's exactly the right thing."

"It feels like the right thing, but nothing really feels right. I can't imagine it ever will."

"Ms. Hunnicut—"

"Shauna."

"Shauna," Eve corrected. "You have a lot of support here, and that's going to be a tremendous help. But we're going to give you the name of a grief counselor."

"All right. But what if I don't want to let go of that? What if I don't want to stop the grief?"

"Then they—and your friends—will help you live with the grief. And when we find the person responsible, that will help you live with it."

"She'll still be gone."

"Nothing can change that. If you were gone, and Erin was here, what would she want?"

Shauna took a breath, straightened her shoulders. "She'd want you to find the son of a bitch."

Chapter Seven

"SHAUNA, CAN YOU THINK OF ANYONE ERIN WAS PREVIOUSLY INVOLVED with who might have harbored a grudge against her, or you?"

"I can't. I really can't." She looked toward Angie.

"No, I can't, either. Erin was what I think of as a flitter. She flitted, you know?"

"Did she flit with anyone who was there last night?"

Angie blew out a breath. "Well, yeah, some. Wanda Rogan, ChiChi Lopez. But not close to serious on anyone's part. Erin didn't do serious relationships. That's why Shauna was such a surprise. A really good one," she added.

Angie shifted toward Eve. "I met Shauna at Erin's art show, and I've known Erin for a long time, so I saw it. The spark. I even said something to her. I said something like: 'Erin, you're wearing your dream eyes, and isn't she straight?' And she sighed, she actually sighed like you do when you're just gone over someone, and said: 'Passion's passion, love's love.' I honestly thought she'd get her heart broken, and she told me if you don't risk heartbreak, you're not living. And she felt . . ." She trailed off as her voice thickened. "She felt like she'd finally started living."

"She said that?" Shauna murmured. "That very first night?"

"She did. Glenda and I talked about it. We worried."

"Glenda Frost?" Eve prompted. "The woman who runs the gallery?"

"Yeah. She loved Erin, as a person, as an artist. I let her know what happened, and she's heading back to New York today."

"Both she and Donna missed the party. Was anyone else a no-show?"

Shauna pressed a hand to her temple. "It's all such a blur."

"Kaydee couldn't make it." Becca spoke up. "She's an intern, doing an ER rotation. She tagged me about ten last night. Multi-vehicle accident, and they were taking the bulk of the injured."

"What hospital?"

"Midtown West."

"Anyone else?"

"No. Angie and I did the guest list," Becca said. "We shared the parties—this one and the shower last month—though Erin and Shauna did most of the planning for last night. But I did a head count once things got rolling. I'm kind of anal that way."

Greg looked up, smiled at her. "Only that way?"

She just laughed a little and poked him. "Maybe in a few others."

"Did anyone leave early? Anyone step out awhile and come back?"

"I didn't notice anyone. Angie?"

"No, not that I noticed, either. Bathroom breaks—but we went in twos or groups, like we already talked about. It's possible, I guess, but we weren't really that big a group. And between Becca and me, we know everyone. I'd swear there was no one there who'd do this."

Greg started to push up from his chair. "Shauna, let me get you some tea."

Becca nudged him back as Shauna shook her head. "Hovering," she murmured.

When he only lifted his hands in a helpless gesture, Eve continued.

"What about your previous relationships, Shauna? Besides Marcus Stillwater and Jon Rierdon."

"I talked to Marcus this morning." Tears swam into her eyes, but she didn't shed them. "He's coming over as soon as he can get away from work. This is taking over your apartment, Angie."

"Just stop. It's yours, too, as long as you need it."

"I have to find another place. I can't live there now."

"We'll deal with that later," Becca told her. "It's nothing to think about right now."

"I'll help you." Donna put an arm around her. "When you're ready."

"All right. Okay." Shauna took a moment to settle again. "I haven't talked to Jon in I don't know how long. We didn't have a big fight; it just wasn't working for me. Last time I saw him, it's been several years easy, I guess. At Jodi's party, right, Bec?"

"Yeah, he was there. He brought a smoker."

Shauna managed a smile. "She was, wasn't she? I came solo—I think that soothed his ego some. He has a pretty big one. Anyway, I dated some after Jon and before Erin, but nobody serious. And before Jon—are we going back that far?"

"Details matter."

"Well, there was Simon Pugh. I had such a crush on him. He didn't have one on me."

"I didn't like him," Becca muttered.

"Don't I know it. We dated for about three months. Me exclusively, him not so much. Then he dumped me."

"Wall Street guy," Becca filled in. "Full of himself. It was a meet-cute, shared cab."

"He was a little bit of a prick," Greg commented, and Shauna managed a weak smile.

"He really was. And I can't imagine he's given me a thought since he dumped me. I dated in college, but that was mostly party time and, we'll say, passions of the moment. If we're still going back?"

She gestured toward Greg. "High school."

"Shaunbar." He sent her a look of affection. "We were The Couple in high school."

"Good times."

"Good times," he agreed. "Then the emotional parting for college. You cried buckets."

"I did." The memory made her smile a little more. "Then I got over it."

"You did. And all of that netted me the grand prize."

"Aww," Becca cooed when he took her hand and kissed it. "We all knew each other in high school—I think I mentioned that. They were The Couple, and I was The Very Serious Student."

"Honor society, class valedictorian," Shauna continued. "Wheeze."

"Proudly. Then Shauna and I reconnected—or just really connected— and when Greg moved to New York, we had a kind of mini-reunion. That wasn't long before the cab ride with Snobby Simon. We had a double date. Well, Greg and I weren't really dating, more hanging. Now that I think about it, it was our mutual dislike of Simon Pugh that springboarded us into really dating."

"Do we have to thank him for it?" Greg wondered.

"Nah."

"You make me happy." Shauna spoke softly. "Seeing the two of you together always makes me happy."

"Where were you last night?' Eve asked Greg, and his eyes widened.

"Wow. I guess I walked into that one."

"Oh, Lieutenant, Greg would never—"

"It's okay, Shauna. Seriously, I get it. And thorough's important. I manage On Trend. A downtown men's shop. Since Becca was going out, I took closing last night. I'd say I was out of there about seven, seven-fifteen. I walked over to Tippler's, met a friend for a beer and some bar food. Clint

Wetz. He's with Jodi of the party fame. She'd have been at the party last night. I guess we were at Tippler's a couple hours. Clint called it because he had a breakfast meeting today, and since it was a nice night, I walked home."

"You bought me flowers," Becca reminded him. "Tiger lilies."

"Right, how could I forget? A stall still open on the way home. Came home, put them in some water. I figured to watch some screen, and crashed on the living room sofa. I don't know what time, but before eleven. I was streaming . . . what the hell was it?"

He shut his eyes as if to think back, then with a shake of his head, opened them again.

"Sorry, some science fiction thing, aliens. I just went out, and was out until Becca tagged me about Erin."

"He wanted to come." Becca rubbed Greg's shoulder. "But I said no. I didn't know how long we'd be, and I'd stay with Shauna, how she'd need him more today."

"Okay. Thanks, that covers it. We'll get out of your way. Detective Peabody will send you a list of grief counselors. When you've scheduled Erin's memorial service, please let us know."

"Isn't there something else?" Shauna asked. "Anything else?"

"Erin's our priority. You can be sure of that."

"I want you to tell me whenever you know something, or think something. I want you to ask me whatever you need to ask me whenever you need to ask. I want what Erin would want if she was sitting here and I was gone. I want you to catch the son of a bitch."

"That's what we're working for."

When they stepped out, Peabody glanced back. "Not everyone has that much real support. If she's lucky on any level, she's lucky there. The intern checks out," she added as they started down the stairs. "She was on until after one A.M. And Glenda Frost's shuttle should be landing in New York right about now. She booked the flight just after nine this morning."

"Do a deeper dive on no-alibi Rierdon. And we'll take a look at Rogan and Lopez. Could be one of them was more serious than Erin."

"I wonder how I'd feel if McNab hung around someone he'd flitted with."

"You flitted around with Charles and hang around with him now."

"Did not! I flitted around the flitting with Charles, but we didn't actively flit. Ever. Maybe I let McNab think we actively flitted, but he was being a jerk."

Then she shrugged. "And I was being a jerk, but we worked all that out. You actively flitted with Webster."

"One bang is not a flit. Add I didn't hang out with Webster. He was on the job, that's work."

"And now he's living off-planet with Darcia, and Charles and Louise are married. Life rocks and rolls."

"And some flit their way through it."

Eve stepped outside, put on her sunshades. "Greg Barney and Becca DiNuzio's address?"

Peabody pulled out her PPC to look it up. "Gotta take a look at half The Couple from high school."

"That's right. Shauna would trust him, no question. Can't say if Erin would have, but we'll take a look. No alibi for the time in question, so we look."

"And given his address, he could've made it work."

"Plug it in," Eve ordered, and got in the car.

"Plus, who's to say when he picked up the flowers, or where? I mean, that's a pretty good add, right? I bought flowers on the way home. But he could've bought them after he killed Albright, or earlier in the day."

Digging into it, Peabody sat back. "Say, on his lunch hour, and since he lives close to work, he runs them home."

"DiNuzio would've seen them when she got home, changed for party time."

"Right, right. But not if he tucked them away somewhere. Or brought them back to work in a bag, like they were something else."

"How long do flowers last without water?"

"You're crushing my buzz. Okay, so he could've bought them on the way home—the idea hits. Buy the flowers, establish my innocent steps. Or he buys them after the kill. Or! He buys them going to or from the art studio when he gets the case. Hell, he could've ordered them for evening delivery. How would we trace tiger lilies already in a vase?"

"While I appreciate your mind working in cynical ways, delivery would be stupid. If you can't find flowers—and it's New York, it's summer, you're going to find some stall with flowers—you pick up something else. Something for cash. Most likely, he bought them exactly as he said. Either because he's telling the truth all around, or because he wanted the little extra flourish as cover."

Peabody slumped a little. "Sure, if you want it to make more sense. We had The Couple in high school. Lauren Beals and Denny Parker. Why do I remember that? Is it sick I remember that?"

"Your call."

"It's a little bit sick," Peabody decided after some thought. "Not pathological though. Okay, so running through the theory that Greg Barney did the deed, motive. He still has it for Shauna, Becca's just the beard. She doesn't know. I'm sure of that one. He's hooked up with her so he stays close to Shauna. Then what! She's going for somebody else!"

"She's dated and had sex with somebody else—multiple somebodies."

"But now she's getting married."

"Point for you on that. There's the men's shop. And that puts his place between it and Crack's. A solid walk to the D&D, we're going to time that just to tie it down."

Peabody went back to her PPC. "And the bar where he met the friend? Two blocks north from . . . here."

Eve hit vertical and dropped into a second-level street slot.

Peabody swallowed her heart out of her throat, back into her chest. "You never warn me. You just never, ever warn me."

"Saves you anxiety time. Let's take a walk."

"Where do we start?"

"The bar." Eve jogged down the steps to street level. "Given the location, I'm betting Barney's at least a semi-regular. Meanwhile, pin down the friend, see if he verifies."

And, she thought as they walked in the steamy air, they needed to talk to Erin's friends and flit partners.

While Peabody worked her 'link, Eve imagined the walk after dark. Still traffic, sure, vehicles, pedestrians. But not as many people clipping or trudging along after dark. Cooler air, closed shops.

A block north, they hit a flower stall. And Peabody clicked off her 'link. "Checks out. They met where and when. Or by seven-thirty. The alibi says they left together around nine-thirty. Confirmed breakfast meeting this morning."

"We still start at the bar. Any of those tiger lilies?"

"Yeah, three bunches right there. Boy, they're really pretty."

"Keep walking."

"He probably got them there. Why wouldn't he? He'd walk right by them. So either a sweet gesture or a clever ploy. He did seem kind of sweet. Like stopping by a deli so there'd be something easy to eat. And I have to add Becca strikes me as a woman who'd know if she was just the beard."

"Maybe, but we play it out."

Since the bar was open, Eve walked in.

Tippler's smelled of beer and bar food—not unpleasantly. It had a decent crowd taking advantage of both.

Eve went to the bar, caught the attention of the bartender, a woman with a pink froth of hair and excellent breasts displayed in a low-cut, skintight black tee.

"What'll it be, ladies?"

Eve palmed the badge discreetly.

The bartender shook her head. "Should've caught that. What's the problem?"

"Who was on the stick last night, about seven-thirty to ten?"

"That would be me. Usually off at eight, but had to cover."

Now Eve held up a screen shot of Greg's ID picture.

"Greg? Come on, man, he can't be in cop trouble."

"Just verifying he was here last night."

"Yeah, with his pal what's-his-name. Give me a sec. Yeah, Clint. Couple of beers, loaded nachos. Their ladies were having a girl party. Greg comes in with his now and then. Pretty blond—that reddish blond type. They call it strawberry, but strawberries are red-red, so I don't get that."

Right there with you, Eve thought, but asked, "When did they leave?"

"Hell, hard to pin that down, but not late. I'm going to say before ten for sure. Friend wanted an early night. Greg toyed with hanging for one more beer, but decided to cash out and leave with the friend. Is that it?"

"That's it. Thanks."

"He's a good guy," the bartender added. "You can tell a good guy by how he treats his lady—or his guy, whichever. And he'll ask how you're doing and mean it. Tips decent."

"Good to know." Eve stepped away. "Time it," she told Peabody. "Steady walk, we pause at the stall, then steady walk to the apartment building."

"On your mark. He wouldn't have to dodge and weave so much on the walk at going on ten."

"It'll be close enough. We're going to take a look at the two women Erin flitted with who were at the party. Odds are she trusted them."

"Because she flitted with them?"

"Because she stayed friendly with them, friendly enough to invite them to the girl party. Pause."

Since they paused at the flower stall, Eve talked to the vendor.

"How late are you open?"

"Ten to ten, every day from May to October."

He hit mid-sixties, Eve thought, neat as a parlor in a short-sleeved shirt and well-pressed khakis. He wore a blue fielder's cap with a white daisy over a grizzled buzz cut, and metal-framed sunshades.

"You work the stall that late?"

"Oh, not me, honey." He smiled so sweetly, she didn't bite him for the *honey*. "My son comes on, takes over 'bout three most days. He brings a fresh supply in if we need it."

Once again, Eve showed Greg's ID shot. "You recognize him?"

"I sure do. He stops by, buys some of our pretties for his woman. Nice young fella."

"That's what we hear, thanks. That's about how long it should've taken him to buy flowers," Eve decided as they continued to walk.

They waited at the corner for the Walk signal.

"I'm starting to lose that buzz. Bartenders like him, flower vendors like him." Peabody shook her head. "All those women like him."

"And of course, likable people never kill anybody."

"Well, they shouldn't." They crossed the street in the pedestrian stream. "I could see it more if it had been in the moment. Like—crime of passion. It gets harder to see when you know it was planned out—and planned on a night when they were celebrating."

"Whoever killed her knew what was in the case. They'd have looked. Why wouldn't they? Definitely not trustworthy when you're going to gar-rote the bride. It's a fairly slick kill. Stupid part was wasting time taking the jewelry, leaving the case. No half-blind cop would look at the scene and think mugging. And he should've taken the case—in fact never picked up the case in the first place."

"Shit, when did he pick it up?"

"He's the backup—she told Donna she had backup, so he already knew about the case, the whole deal. Erin would have told him Donna had to be in Baltimore. Wouldn't surprise me if she dropped off the case to him herself. Or told him where to find a spare swipe. Then Donna heads out of town, Erin tags him. Plan B. It's his opening."

"If Donna's sister hadn't gone into labor—"

"She did. Fact. We stick with that, for now. Here's the building. Time."

"Twelve minutes, forty seconds, including the flower stop."

"If he'd rushed, he'd have cut that time. I don't think he'd need to."

She stood, studying the building. "What floor are they on?"

"Second."

"One of those post-Urban toss ups—no cams, crap security, sound-proofing's going to be crap, too. If he's smart, he makes some noise going in, maybe gets someone to notice. Gets in the apartment, takes care of the flowers, changes out of his work clothes. Checks what's on-screen. Turns it on. Not too loud, just loud enough. Get the case, the weapon, gloves, the swipe for the privacy room. If she'd let him in the back, she'd just take the case and go. So he's in the room. He'd dump the swipes to the studio—if he had them—in her purse after she's dead."

"You really like him for it."

"I'm just running it through. You want to be quiet leaving, you want to be sure you're not seen now. Gotta take your time—it's too early anyway. And you've gotta get your guts up. Yeah, you'd have to get your guts up."

Eve shook her head. "It's a hell of a lot over a high school deal. And that's what, nearly ten years back?"

"My buzz is dead on it."

"We'll finish it out. Time." Eve started to walk again. "On the street, you're just some guy carrying a case, and it's raining—more cover. Or just finished raining, depending. But it's damp, steamy. You're sweating. Could change your mind, just deliver the case. What's driving you, after ten fucking years?"

"Okay, so maybe the fire went out, after high school. Good times, fond memories, and all that. Reconnect, and maybe the spark with Becca was real, but as you go, that fire starts up again."

"How long have they been together, him and Becca?"

Peabody pulled out her notes. "Official cohabbing two years, three months."

"Long time to fake it." She shook her head. "But play it out. What killed the spark and started the fire? Shit, it's stupid." But she kept walking as the neighborhood got seedier. "No logic to it. Nearly there though, so we go around the block and into the back."

Once they had, Eve said, "Time."

"Sixteen minutes, twelve seconds."

"Have to give him opportunity. Definitely had opportunity, but motive is stupid weak, means is questionable."

Still, she broke the crime scene seal and mastered in.

Play it through.

"I'm going to say, coming in this way, getting into the privacy room quick and unseen, he's likely been here before. Scoped it out. He's already got the swipe."

With a nod of agreement, Eve shut her eyes. "Backtrack a minute. She's got a morning cleaning job, and she swings in here after that, before she heads home, or to the studio or wherever. Crack gives her the swipe—around noon, he said. She meets her backup, passes it off because Donna's in Baltimore and might not make it. Gives backup the swipe to the studio. And here comes opportunity."

"Why didn't she just bring the case herself, get the swipe, stow it?"

"She didn't or Crack would've noticed it, so . . . Had to be a time factor—time factor passing off the swipe to her backup."

Noontime, she thought. Lunch hour?

"We'll check on the timing, cleaning job, location. But this is how it went down. The backup, and let's keep Barney in the lead for now, comes in the back, goes straight to the privacy room."

In the silent club still smelling faintly of sweepers' dust, Eve started toward it. "Somebody sees him? Recognizes him? He can just scratch the kill, play up the secret. But nobody does."

She mimed swiping into the unsecured privacy room.

"It only takes a few seconds to come in, swipe in, get inside."

With Peabody, she stepped inside, closed the door.

"He doesn't think to secure it after the kill. Nervous, probably nervous, a little shock. This was likely a first kill.

"Can you do it, can you really do this?"

The room held little more than a bed. Blood had coagulated on the floor, and stained the air.

"She couldn't have given the backup a specific time," Peabody commented. "How could she know exactly when she'd be able to slip away without Shauna noticing?"

"Ballpark. She wants the party in full swing, wants this to be like the big deal that pumps it forward. Can't ask her, but he can't just drop it off because he has the swipe, and she needs it back. No other reason for her to want him to stay, or ask him to stay."

"No place to hide in here," Peabody pointed out. "She had to see him as soon as she opened the door."

"That's right. She's a little drunk, a lot happy, and probably doesn't think twice. Stand right there."

Eve stepped out, then in again. "She sees him, and happy, a little impaired, excited, says something. 'Oh, you're here. Thanks for doing this!' Turns, shuts the door. And he's on her. Get on me."

Peabody moved forward, cupped her hands around Eve's throat to mimic the garrote.

"Pain, shock. Drops her purse. She can't scream, but claws at the wire. Bam! He bashes her head against the door, and now she's blacking out, choking, terrified. Helpless. Struggling, but helpless. Goes down right here, loses a shoe."

After signaling Peabody back, Eve turned.

"He takes her 'link out of the purse. But he can't take just that, has to take it because there's communication on it, but he takes her jewelry, her cash, dumps the swipes. Takes the weapon and gets out the way he came."

"It didn't take long. Probably under five minutes. He may have waited for her longer," Peabody added, "but this part was really quick."

"Opportunity knocked." She opened the door again. "We'll head back to Central. See if you can reach Wanda Rogan, ChiChi Lopez, and bring them to us. I'll let Crack know he can open tomorrow—after he gets a crime scene cleaner in here."

"Greg Barney? Is he still top of the list?"

"We'll keep him up there with Rierdon, do those deeper dives. Motivation's weak and stupid on both, but with some, love can be both."

Chapter Eight

WHEN SHE GOT BACK TO HOMICIDE, SANTIAGO AND CARMICHAEL SAT AT their desks. Jenkinson, his tie, and Reineke didn't sit at theirs.

"They're following a lead on the cold one," Baxter told her.

"Good enough. Peabody, give the vic's two former flitters another push. If we can't get them in here, we'll go to them."

She went to her office, hit the AC for coffee. After taking her desk and writing up the interviews, she updated her board.

She stood studying it, then turned when Peabody came to her door.

"Rogan can be here in about thirty. I left another v-mail for Lopez."

"Let's take her in the lounge. We'll keep it friendly, sympathetic, so you take the lead. You interviewed her last night, so she's already got that connection."

"Check." Peabody glanced at the board. "A lot of overlap. Everyone on there's connected to either Albright or Hunnicut, or both. And a lot of them are linked to each other."

"Friendships can be incestuous."

"I guess you could think about it that way."

"Especially when you add the sexual component. The flitting, the banging, the one-offs. Before Albright, all of Hunnicut's flitting and banging partners were male. As far as we know, all of Albright's were female."

"I get that, but does it apply?"

"Everything applies at this stage, Peabody. The killer could be male, female, gay, straight, bi. But this was personal. The method, cruel and cowardly, but the location, the timing—even counting for opportunity knocking—it's deeply personal. Someone she knew and trusted, under a week before the wedding, when she's surrounded by friends, when she's planning to surprise the woman she loves by fulfilling a dream.

"It was fucking personal."

"A friend, a former lover. Someone on the board."

"Someone on the board," Eve agreed. "Or someone nobody's thought to mention yet. And I don't give that much weight. Dive into Rierdon. I'll take Barney."

"On it. I'll let you know when Rogan gets here."

Eve sat, started that dive.

Gregory Barney, age twenty-seven, New York native, New York resident. Parents: Cynthia and Walter Barney, married twenty-nine years—thirty in another month. He had two sibs, both female, both younger at twenty-five and twenty-three.

From what she read, he'd had a solid if average middle-class upbringing. No particular religious affiliations, no criminal but a standard arrest and release at a college protest when he'd been nineteen.

He'd played football in middle school, then in high school, but hadn't taken that with him to college. Solid grades but for some problems in advanced math classes.

She could relate.

He'd done four years at the University of Florida, switching his major after one semester from sociology to business management. He'd moved back to New York after graduation, lived with his parents for a few months while working in retail. Moved into Manhattan from Brooklyn. Got his own place, with a male roommate until he worked his way up to assistant manager, then took an apartment on his own.

He'd stuck, she noted, with On Trend, and that had worked out for him, as he'd gotten regular promotions and raises. For the past three years, he'd lived in his current apartment, and for some months over two, cohabbing with Becca DiNuzio.

No sign of gambling or wild purchases in his financials that she could see. He lived within his means—on the edge from time to time, but never over it.

He didn't own a vehicle or any real property, traveled once or twice a year—beaches and resorts.

Eve sat back. Average, she thought. Ordinary. Not that the average and ordinary type didn't kill. But trying to tie a murder to the average and ordinary over a high school romance just didn't play out.

Until she added the new and trusted factors. Which, she admitted, applied to nearly everyone currently on her board.

Peabody came back. "Wanda Rogan's here. I'll take her down to the lounge. I'll send you what I have on Jon Rierdon, but it's not much of anything."

"Yeah, I got the same on Barney." She pushed away from her desk. "We'll take her down, see if we get more than not much."

When Wanda rose from the waiting bench outside the bullpen, Eve judged her at about the same height as Erin. More muscular with a gym-fit body in wide-legged white pants, a crisp red shirt.

She had chocolate-brown hair liberally streaked with blond worn in a long fall of waves around a heart-shaped face dominated by large brown eyes. Under them spread the shadows of a hard night.

"Ms. Rogan, thank you for coming in. I'm Lieutenant Dallas."

"Yes, I know." Her voice brought on images of smoky rooms and saxophones. "I saw you last night. I don't know what I can do to help, but I want to help. I loved Erin, and over the last year, I grew to like Shauna so much."

"Understood. Why don't we talk in our lounge?" Eve gestured, led the way.

"I haven't contacted Shauna today. Didn't know if I should. I know she went with Angie, and I assume Becca's with her. I—I know Erin's family, but didn't want to intrude. I just don't know the right thing to do."

"I think offering comfort and support is always the right thing," Peabody told her. "That's what I felt from you and the others last night. An openness to offer comfort and support."

"We all know Erin and Shauna, and each other. Some better than others, but we all have that link. I still can't believe this happened, is happening."

"Why don't we have a seat?" Peabody chose a table. "Can we get you something to drink?"

"Don't risk the coffee," Eve told her. "You want something that comes in a tube."

"Is there iced tea?"

"Iced tea. Detective?"

"Water, thanks."

Since she wanted Peabody in the lead, Eve crossed over to Vending. And now had to face the damn machine.

"Don't fuck with me today," she muttered, and punched in her code.

"Welcome, Baxter, Detective David. Your code is verified and you are free to make your selections."

"Fine, whatever." She programmed for the iced tea, the water, and went for a Pepsi.

"Please be advised, your selections of Summer Time Iced Tea and Pepsi both contain artificial flavorings and chemical additives."

"Oh, bite me," Eve muttered as the machine listed them.

"Enjoy your selections, Baxter, Detective David. Your account has been charged."

"Great."

She walked back to the table where Peabody softballed the interview.

"So you and Erin met shortly after you moved to New York."

"That's right. I was just twenty. I came into a small inheritance—my great-grandfather—and dropped out of college, moved here. I was going to make my mark, and make it in New York. I rented a dump of a furnished apartment so small I had to crawl over the Murphy bed if I had it down to get to the bathroom. That didn't have a sink. The only sink was in the corner of the living room that claimed to be a kitchen. I loved it."

"You moved from Kansas."

"That's right, a little dot on the map in very rural Kansas. Not much opportunity to make my mark as a singer—the superstar I imagined. Add gay in a loving but very traditional family. I wanted bright lights, I wanted New York."

"Yeah, me, too. Free-Ager family."

"Really?"

"They're great, but I wanted New York, and they got behind me on it. How did you meet Erin?"

"About a year later—I was waitressing, going to auditions, discouraged. But I got a gig at a café in SoHo, and she was there. She bought me a drink after. She was a struggling artist, I was a struggling performer. Friendship came first."

Wanda cracked the tube, but didn't drink.

"I loved her art—I couldn't afford it, but I loved it. She did a painting of me onstage in this red dress I'd bought at a secondhand shop, and gave it to me for Christmas that year. I met Donna and Angie and Margo. It was so good to have a group, you know?"

"A tribe."

Lifting her hands, Wanda folded them together, gesturing with them toward Peabody as she smiled.

"Yes, exactly that. I hated waiting tables, but the gigs wouldn't pay the bills. Angie suggested I try selling real estate. So I took an online course, got my license. Now that pays the bills, and gives me enough flexibility to take more gigs."

She looked at Eve. "I know your husband—not personally, just know. I haven't sold him anything—I'm small-time. But anyone in my business knows Roarke. So I feel I know you, both of you, the same way. That's why as horrible as this is, I feel Erin's in good hands."

The big brown eyes went teary as she sipped her iced tea. "I need to believe that. I don't think I could get through this if I didn't."

"Losing a friend is crushing," Peabody said. "Were you and Erin ever more than that? Did you have a romantic relationship?"

"Oh, briefly, but I wouldn't say romantic. It was more, we're both at loose ends, we like each other, we're healthy young lesbians, so why not? And it was nice, but . . . I guess I brought some of my traditional background with me. We didn't really click that way. Sexually, sure, but the friendship meant more, on both sides. And I wanted—still want—what she had with Shauna. I want that real bond, that real love, that promise of forever. That wasn't Erin for me, or me for Erin. So friends it was."

"Did she trust you?" Eve asked.

"Yes." A slight frown crossed Wanda's face. "I mean, I hope so. I think she did. I certainly trusted her."

"With secrets?"

"If I had one, I'd trust her to keep it. If she had any and shared with me, I wouldn't tell you unless I thought it would help find who killed her. No, I'll tell you this one," Wanda corrected. "It can't hurt. They weren't going to have a band or a professional DJ at the wedding—they were saving for a big honeymoon down the road. Their parents would have kicked in, but they're not rolling in it, either, and had already contributed. Erin asked me if I'd sing, maybe talk some of the musicians I knew into coming—for the free food and drink. Just do one set maybe. Especially the first dance—they'd planned a recording for that. She was going to surprise Shauna."

Wanda dashed a tear away. "Then Shauna came to me with an almost identical request. Could I sing them down the aisle, maybe do the first dance. She didn't want me to work the whole wedding and reception, but wanted to surprise Erin."

She dug out a tissue. "God. I didn't tell either one of them about the other, and like I said, I know Erin's family. I know Shauna's now a little. I told them, so we put it together behind the scenes, you know?"

"That was a beautiful thing to do, each of them, the families, you." Reaching over, Peabody laid a hand on Wanda's.

"Did she tell you about the surprise for Erin she planned for last night?"

Drying her eyes, Wanda shook her head. "No. What surprise?"

"Did you know she'd sold some paintings recently? Studio work, not street."

"I don't think so. I mean not in the last few weeks. I've been slammed. Lucky enough to get some good evening and night gigs, showings and meetings at my day job. And we've been squeezing in rehearsals for the wedding. I haven't talked to Erin much in the last two or three weeks."

Now she blinked tears away, shoved back her hair. "And she and Shauna were busy with the wedding plans, plans for last night. What surprise?" she asked again.

"She took the money from the sale of the paintings, got a little boost from her moonlighting jobs. She bought tickets to Maui, booked a hotel."

Wanda stared at Eve before the tears rolled. "Oh, oh, that's so Erin. That's just so Erin."

"She had someone bring in her weekend case," Peabody continued. "She had a costume—grass skirt, coconut bra, leis."

Wanda pressed both hands to her mouth. "Even more like Erin. That's just what she'd do, just what she'd do. Big surprise, big fun, big splash.

Giving Shauna something she'd only dreamed of, and share it with all of us. That's who she was. That's Erin."

"Who would she have trusted to keep the secret, to bring in that case?"

"I—any of us, I think. Angie, Donna, me, a dozen others. Erin was so open. She trusted and loved her friends. Her tribe," she said to Peabody.

"But she didn't ask you."

"No. I would've done it. I would've been happy to. But, I guess, she'd already asked me for something, and . . . spread it out. I didn't think this could get harder, but now it is."

Struggling for composure, she turned to Eve. "Did you ask Angie? Angie's so efficient, she could've asked her. Except—"

"Except."

"Becca and Angie did the shower, and I know they helped at least some with the party last night. Spread it out," she repeated. "Donna—wait, Donna had to go to Baltimore. Her sister went into labor. Donna didn't make the party."

"Who else comes to mind?" Eve pressed.

"Honestly, they're first, or me, then it could be anyone. Well, I'd eliminate a couple who have a hard time not either blurting out a secret or who can't help but act like they have one. Why, is it important?"

"Everything's important," Eve told her.

They spent a little more time, pushing for details, for answers and memories, but couldn't pull out more.

When Peabody walked Wanda out, Eve sat another moment.

Not only did Wanda's statements ring true, she simply didn't ring.

Probably strong enough, Eve considered as she started back. Maybe tall enough in heels. But the rest? It didn't play through.

She met Peabody outside the bullpen.

"I bought it," Peabody said. "All of it."

"I'm not going to pay for it, but no, she just doesn't fit. She knew the victim for what, six, seven years. Tried on the sex, didn't click, stayed friends. Let's check out the sing-at-the-wedding deal, but that plays, and it weighs on the no side of things.

"Maybe she could've snuck the case in, maybe she's strong enough. The height's off, but heels would compensate. She'd still have to get back in the room, wait or follow the target in—and the crime scene reads already inside to me. Then do the kill, take the 'link, the jewelry, stow that where nobody notices."

"You're more looking at the exes, at least the ones we have."

"I'm more looking at somebody who came from outside. I want to go over McNab's interviews with the people there who weren't with the group. Whoever did this likely walked out that back door, but maybe someone left a table, didn't come back."

"I can go over that with him. Listen, Dallas, we're eliminating suspects from the group that was there. That's going to narrow it down. Unless it was some conspiracy and two or three of them planned this out together."

"No, two people can rarely keep a secret. Three? Forget it. And add murder? Not this one. Solo kill, solo planner, most probable. Known and trusted, and those are key factors. I'm going to write this up. You work with McNab, or if he's busy, take his interviews and do 'link follow-ups. Just take another pass."

She saw Jenkinson back at his desk, and the way he scowled at his desk screen concluded the lead hadn't panned out.

"You can clock out after you're done, Peabody. I'm going to head back to the D&D, talk to Crack, since he's too stubborn to hire a crime scene crew. His place, he deals with it. Then I'll track down ChiChi Lopez."

"Go now. I'll write it up. I had the lead," Peabody reminded her.

"Right, you did." She stuck a hand in her pocket. "Where'd I put the damn sunshades?"

"They're in your car."

"They're in the car. I want to take the gallery owner tomorrow morning. Glenda Frost. She's not a suspect, but she may know something."

"I can set that up."

"Do that, let me know. I'm in the field."

Since the elevator that opened as she passed disgorged cops, then stood empty, she chanced it and nipped inside.

She had a few floors of thinking time where she decided, on the Eve Dallas probability scale, it hit ninety-eight percent the killer brought the case in the back door and straight into the privacy room.

She'd go with a solid seventy-six the killer came from outside the group until she added the trust factor. There'd been a couple dozen people, give or take, the victim would've trusted in that group.

So lower that to sixty-five.

When the elevator began to stop and fill, stop and go, she pushed off for the glides and took her calculations with her.

She went back to ninety-eight percent the killer was already in the room when Erin Albright came in.

Back turned, head bashed against the door.

But that didn't change the in-or-out-of-the-group calculation.

The timing worked for Greg Barney—as did the lack of solid alibi.

Same with Jon Rierdon.

And they might find more.

Rierdon fell out with the trust factor. Why would Erin trust him? Unknown factor, but her gut took him well down on her list.

As for Barney? Why bring him into it when you had that group, that tribe?

Not bumping him down yet, she thought as she reached the garage level.

He and Becca, planning it together? Some resentments simmering all the way back to high school?

It happened, she decided, and drove out of the garage into traffic.

The wheeze and the rejected boyfriend. It could play. More logical to target Shauna herself, but . . . more painful to kill someone she loved, and leave her grieving.

She played with that angle, picked it apart, put it back together as she drove to the Down and Dirty.

A very doable walk, she thought again as she hunted up parking, from so many of the apartments, workplaces, hangouts of this intersecting group of friends.

Not surprising. Geography counted.

It counted again when she had to walk two and a half blocks from parking to the club.

The vibe started to change as it crept closer to the end of the workday, or passed that mark for some.

Not as many tourists on the street now, or at least not here where the sex clubs, the bars, the piercing and tat parlors ruled. She watched two women come out of one of those parlors. One had skin still pink under a vine of weird flowers now twining up her arm.

And her face as pale as chalk.

A trio of guys in work boots and sweaty shirts trooped into a bar. End-of-construction-day brews.

She spotted a junkie across the street, jittery as he hunted up an early score. And ignored him.

The neon on the D&D stayed dark and the front windows shaded.

She mastered in.

Rochelle Pickering, tall and built in worn jeans and a faded T-shirt, stood scrubbing at the bar. She'd bundled her black corkscrew hair under a floral do-rag.

She jolted when Eve stepped in, then blew out a breath.

"You startled me. I didn't expect anyone to come in."

"I didn't expect to find you cleaning the bar."

"Wilson won't let me near the room where it happened, so I'm helping this way. Nobody got to clean the place afterward last night. It's terrible, what happened. He's just sick about it."

She went back to scrubbing, putting some elbow grease into it as she spoke.

"He told me he knew her, that she came in off and on, and for a long time. And how they were having their bachelorette party here, she and her fiancée getting married in a few days. He's just heartsick, and won't have anyone deal with that room but himself."

"Sometimes it helps, to do it yourself."

"I know, and I'm hoping it does."

She put down the rag a moment, turned to Eve. "I was hoping to talk to you sometime—I wish it wasn't after this. But I wanted you to know how well Dorian's doing at An Didean. The counseling's helped her deal with everything that happened to her, back to her mother's emotional and physical abuse, through the nightmare of what was done to her at that vicious so-called Academy."

"Good."

"It's more than good, Dallas. She's got a lot more counseling in her future, but she's actually blossoming. She's so much smarter than her grades at her school before she ran away indicate. Her mother simply didn't allow her to blossom, and now she is. She's making friends—carefully, but making them. And the boy, Mouser—Tom? He's just a wonder. So damn entertaining, and not just smart, Dallas. Scary smart. He just latches on.

"You helped give them this chance, and I wanted you to know what it means."

"I'm glad to hear it. They both got knocked around more than any kid should. Roarke put you in charge of the school because he knew you'd find ways to not only give them a chance but convince them to take it.

"Seen much of Sebastian?"

Rochelle smiled. "I understand your issues with him, and why you have them. I don't disagree. He does check in with them from time to time, and

I promise you, they need that connection. He helped them—in his way, but he helped them."

"His way is . . . questionable."

"Agreed, but right now, with these two children, I'm seeing that blossoming. Without him, without you, without the school, I doubt they'd have survived long, much less bloomed."

Hard to argue, Eve thought, especially since she'd been through her own nightmare of a childhood, and had had no one but herself.

"Well, I'm glad to hear it. I'll check on Crack."

She went back, found him on his hands and knees, a bucket by his side, a scrub brush in his big hands.

Sweatpants, a ragged tee, and another do-rag—not floral, but ink black. He glanced up at Eve.

"That dust shit you cops use is bad enough, but the blood's worse. Been at this damn near an hour."

"Looks like you got it to me."

"Yeah, maybe." Still, he scrubbed a little more before he tossed the brush in the bucket. "I can still see her though. It'll take more than some scrubbing to wipe that away."

He rose, and she stepped aside to let him out, then followed him down to the men's john.

When he dumped the bucket in the sink, the water came out nearly clear. She imagined he'd dumped countless others running from red to pink.

"Maybe give it one more pass."

"Crack, let it be. You've done what had to be done. I'm betting that floor's cleaner now than it's been in years."

He smiled a little. "It's called the Down and Dirty. But I keep the floors clean enough. You got shit to tell me, skinny white girl?"

"I can tell you some shit, big, buff Black man. Buy me a Pepsi."

"I can do that."

He carted the bucket with him into the club area, then stopped and shook his head.

"Ro, you keep cleaning, none of my customers are gonna recognize the place, and walk right out again."

He crossed over, took the bucket and rag from her. "Sit on down here with Dallas. We've got us a private party."

But Rochelle shot him a worried look as he went in the back.

"He'll be fine," Eve told her. "He can open again tomorrow, and that'll help him get it back."

"I know you're right."

She took a stool when he came back.

"I'm having a drink," he said, and pointed at Rochelle. "You're having a drink. You still on duty?"

"I am."

"Girl." Shaking his head, he poured her a Pepsi on ice in a sparkling clean glass. Then pulled a bottle of wine from under the bar, poured a glass for Rochelle, tapped a beer for himself.

"Here's to fucking justice. You get it for her, Dallas. You get that fucking justice for Erin."

"Working on it."

"That's good enough for me. What do you know?"

"I know the person who was supposed to bring the case for her had to go to Baltimore. Her sister went into labor. It checks out. So Erin had to use a backup. I don't know who yet."

She ran through what she had, at least what she had that she felt she could share with him.

"That's more than I expected, less than I wished for. I wished you'd gotten the bastard, but I expected it would take you time. I expected not to know too much today."

"Do you really think one of her friends killed her?"

"Yeah." Eve nodded at Rochelle. "I do."

"Then that's what happened." Rochelle gave Eve a decisive nod. "When they killed my brother, you knew right away he hadn't overdosed, hadn't lied to me about being clean. And you found out who did that to him, and why."

She looked at Crack, laid a hand on his. "She'll do just that here, Wilson."

"I believe it. You held me like I was a baby when I cried over my sister. My baby girl's body. I've got every reason in the world to trust you with this. Erin died in my place, while I was right here where I am now. And that's hard for me to take. You're going to see who did it pays. I believe it."

"Anything that comes to mind. Anything you thought of, remembered, since last night? Dynamics," Eve added. "A look that didn't strike quite right. Someone slipping in and out. Anything."

He downed some beer. "I haven't thought about much else since, and I got nothing. Just nothing. Pisses me off I got nothing but a bunch of women blowing off steam, having a hell of a good time, cutting it loose. I thought about how Erin came in early for the swipe. She didn't tell me why, just she had something planned for Shauna, and could she have it now."

He shrugged. "I figured sure, why not?"

"Mondays are slow."

"Damn slow, and since she'd already booked it, I was going to keep it closed for her anyway. Tell you one thing." He pointed a finger at her. "Soon as Roarke gets me the plan for cameras and such, they're going in. Ain't letting this happen again. No use me asking you to give me five minutes with who did this before you lock them up, especially in front of my lady, who wouldn't like it. But I wish for that, too."

"A cracked head or punch in the face heals," Eve told him. "Life in a cage goes on and on." She pushed off her stool. "I've got somebody else to track down and talk to. Like I told you, you're cleared to open tomorrow."

"And we will."

"Good luck, Dallas," Rochelle called out.

"I'll take it," Eve said, and left.

Chapter Nine

A CHECK OF CHICHI LOPEZ'S RESIDENCE AND WORKPLACE TOLD EVE she'd have a five-block trip there from the D&D, and about seven to Delights, the strip joint where Lopez earned her living.

She considered the building traffic, the frustration of finding parking, and decided to walk it.

Adding the time to her considerations, and when she could reasonably expect to finish up, drive uptown and home, she tagged Roarke as she walked.

"Lieutenant, I see you're out and about."

"Yeah, I'm going to be late. I'm on my way to see a stripper."

"Anyone I know?"

She paused at the crosswalk with far too many others. "Just how many strippers are in your acquaintance?"

"Who counts? I'm just leaving the office. Why don't I join you?"

"I'm trying her residence first, so there may not be a show."

"I'll risk it. Give me your destinations, and I'll head your way. The car can drop me off, and we can drive home together. Maybe I'll talk you into letting me take you to dinner."

"A handful of blocks from Crack's," she began, and reeled off the addresses. "In that order."

"I'll find you."

Yeah, she thought as she shoved her 'link back in her pocket, he would. They'd found each other, after all, in a world of murder and mayhem.

She watched a couple of street LCs grab a cart meal before they started their nightly stroll. A woman in micro shorts and a sports bra stepped out on a third-floor fire escape and watered a wilting pot of flowers. A skinny white cat with black markings sat on the windowsill and watched her.

She passed a market with fruit stalls flanking the entrance. It smelled like summer.

A guy in a backward fielder's cap sold knockoff designer wrist units at a sidewalk table. He had a couple of tourists on the hook.

They'd be better off with a sundial, but you lived and you learned.

The after-work crowd began to flood the sidewalks, fast walking, talking on 'links, heading home or for drinks, an early meal. She passed a bar where happy hour spilled out to the sidewalk tables, and like the fire escape flowers, people wilted in the heat.

More poured up or down the steps at subway stations.

She turned a corner and watched a man in a business suit swooshing his way down the block on an airboard.

She caught snatches of conversation.

Frankie can fuck himself with a cactus.

We need to lock down that account.

My feet are killing me. Are you sure we're going the right way?

Then turned once more and stopped at the first address.

Surprised, she studied a townhome of painted white brick with a pot of flowers, not wilted, on the stoop.

Three tidy stories with solid security and windows shining clean, it nestled between another set of townhomes and a Mexican restaurant called Abuela's with sidewalk service under a red-and-white-striped awning.

ChiChi must be a hell of a stripper, Eve thought, and walked up to press the buzzer.

Though the entrance had an intercom, there was no answer, not even from an annoying program. She gave it one more buzz, and a woman stepped out of the next door, leading a little rat dog.

"She's not home."

Eve stepped down, walked over to the woman with battleship-gray hair worn in a top bun. She wore a flowered dress over a body whittled down, to Eve's eye, by a solid eight decades. She had a face of sharp bones, golden skin, lively dark eyes, and bold red lips.

Beside her the little rat dog sniffed at Eve's boots. Then yipped and yapped as if someone had kicked it in the ribs.

It bounced like a spring.

The woman snapped something at it in Spanish, and it sat, just staring at Eve with slightly crazed eyes.

"Do you know if Ms. Lopez would be at work?"

"Of course she's at work! We earn a living in our family. This is about poor Erin. A sweet girl, an artist." The woman crossed herself. "God has welcomed her into his arms, but too soon for those who knew and loved her."

Then she pointed a finger at Eve. "I know police when I see police. What do you want with our ChiChi? I'm her *abuela.*"

"You're her grandmother?"

"Didn't I say so? This is my place." She gestured to the restaurant. "The family business. But ChiChi, she has no skill for cooking, for this business. She has other skills."

The *abuela* smiled.

"Yes, ma'am. You knew Erin Albright?"

"A good friend of my granddaughter, a friend of our family. Our priest will dedicate a mass to her. Why do you need to talk to ChiChi?"

"It's routine, ma'am."

Now she wagged that finger back and forth. "The police say routine, but don't always mean it. So you talk to her, you go talk to ChiChi. There's evil in the world. It preys on the innocent and takes innocent lives. You know this already."

"I do."

"Then talk to ChiChi, but go find the evil. I have to walk my dog, then go to work."

"Yes, ma'am. Thank you."

She stepped aside so the woman could lead her dog to the sidewalk.

And continued on.

She considered the encounter fascinating, and telling. The stripper shared a wall with her grandmother, and right next to the family restaurant. And that family had known, and apparently liked, Erin Albright.

Would she have called on one of them for backup? Possible, she decided, and that opened up yet another avenue to explore.

When she reached Delights, it didn't surprise her to see Roarke standing outside, under the sign of a well-endowed woman in a G-string and pasties, head tossed back as if in orgasm as she rode a pole.

"And there she is," he said. "I was just about to tag you to see if I'd guessed correctly or had a bit of a walk coming."

"You guessed correctly. Lopez is at work. I talked to her grandmother, who lives in the townhouse next door. Do you know Abuela's, a Mexican place?"

"I do, yes. A very well-run restaurant. Her grandmother's then?"

"The family's anyway. The grandmother says ChiChi's talents lie in another direction. She knew the victim."

She scanned the exterior as she spoke. "More upscale than I expected. Not yours, is it?"

"Sadly no."

"You're faster. Check who owns the restaurant building, this one, and those townhouses."

He took out his PPC, and had the answer in seconds. "Aren't you the clever one. Lopez Family LLC owns those properties, and a few more besides—a few residential more."

"With all that, I guess ChiChi just likes getting naked. Let's go in."

Music thrummed. The lights held dim except on the circular stage, where a woman strolled and strutted in a three-piece suit and mile-high heels. She wore a fedora cocked on her head.

Eve recognized the woman she'd come to speak with.

Plush red seats circled the stage, and for this early in the evening, Eve found them surprisingly full.

More seats and booths lined the walls, and the bar in the rear did a brisk business. Servers in G-strings and pasties carried trays.

Some of them had bills tucked into the G-string.

A man in a corner booth enjoyed a lap dance, but his gaze stayed on the woman onstage rather than the one who serviced him.

She didn't seem to mind.

And Eve supposed ChiChi Lopez was something to see.

She'd stripped off her tie, shimmied/wiggled out of the suit jacket before doing a stylish turn on the pole. The vest came next, and more pole work.

Eve had to admit the woman was flexible, and had a style. Even while she stayed fully dressed, patrons tossed bills on the stage.

When the music hit a clash of brass, she tore open the breakaway dress shirt, revealing impressive breasts accented by tiny, sparkling pasties.

More money flew when she tossed a leg up the pole, executing a standing split. By the time she yanked off the breakaway pants, the crowd buzzed and cheered.

More cheers when she tossed away her hat, and black curls cascaded free.

Eve figured her pole work in the tiny spangles reached gymnast level, maybe contortionist.

Bumps, grinds, backbends, spins, and twirls, and Eve figured for about a ten-minute routine, she'd pulled in easily two hundred in tips. Maybe three. At roughly six in the evening.

"Entertaining," Roarke commented.

"Take off your clothes and people toss money at you. It's weird."

Since she'd already made security—the wide-shouldered man in the back in a black suit—she walked his way.

She held up her badge. "Lieutenant Dallas and civilian consultant, NYPSD. I need to speak with Ms. Lopez."

"About Erin? I'm ChiChi's cousin. Our *abuela* let me know you were coming. Have a seat—" He pointed to a booth. "Drinks on the house. I'll tell my cousin."

When he walked off, Eve shook her head. "More weird. His cousin gets naked onstage, and he doesn't blink."

"Just a job of work, Eve."

"A job of work where the audience is getting boners over your cousin."

"Plenty of women in here as well."

"They get the female equivalent of a boner."

She took a seat in the booth. "Stick with water, okay? We're on the job."

One of the nearly naked servers sidled up, gave Roarke a crystal clear eye fuck.

"Just water, please. Still."

"Whatever you want." She purred it. "I'm at your service."

"Jesus," Eve muttered as she hip-rocked away. "I'm sitting right here."

Roarke just smiled. "So tell me, why are we here about to interrogate a very talented stripper?"

"Interview. The stripper was at the party, and at one time got naked with the victim."

"I see."

"The victim had a friend lined up to bring the case—with the costume, the tickets—into the club. But that friend had to go to Baltimore—sister in labor, blah blah—that's confirmed, confirmed the friend never made the party at all. So Erin told the friend not to worry. She had backup."

"You're looking for the backup."

"I'm looking for the backup," she agreed, and gave him the bare bones while the nearly naked server brought their water, and they waited for ChiChi.

"A lot of legwork today," Roarke concluded.

"Yeah, some eliminations, some maybes, and now with the Lopez family, possibly some expansions. And here she comes."

ChiChi had changed into a black skin suit, cut nearly to her waist in the front. She'd left her hair down but had changed her stage heels for black sneakers.

There, Eve gave her points for sense.

She slid into the booth across from Eve and Roarke.

"Cops can make our clientele nervous."

"I wouldn't be here making your clientele nervous if you'd responded to my partner's v-mails."

"I didn't feel like it." She shrugged as the server brought her sparkling water. "I said everything I knew, which is nothing, last night. I lost a friend. I took a pill and went to bed, and stayed there until after noon. I had to tell my family, and they liked Erin a lot. Then I went to church with my *abuela*, and got ready for work."

"You work an early shift," Eve noted. "I'd think the later crowd would bring in more."

"I bring in more." She tossed her hair. "And I'm done by ten."

She shifted eyes very like her grandmother's to Roarke. "If you like redheads, Gia said to tell you she'd give you the first lap dance free."

"That's a lovely offer, but I prefer lanky brunettes."

"Your choice."

"You were involved with Erin at one time," Eve said.

"I wouldn't say involved. We took a spin a few times. I like sex—not a crime. I like sex with men, with women, also not a crime. I liked sex with Erin. We had some fun, but we weren't looking to pick out china patterns. She met Shauna, and we stopped taking spins."

"How did you feel about that?"

"How was I supposed to feel?" She tossed back her waterfall of hair, gave Eve a cool, patronizing smile. "Look around here. I could have my pick, but I keep sex and work separate. Maybe I didn't get what Erin's thing was with Shauna, but her life, right?

"Until it wasn't."

"Not a fan of Shauna's?"

"She's all right. If you go for boring and ordinary." With a shrug, she drank some water. "I just didn't get it, that's all. Why she wanted this shoe store manager, this dead ordinary person, and the whole marriage thing."

"Did she know how you felt about it?"

"She knew I thought she was making a mistake, sure. I mean, hell, how long do you have to be young, and she locks herself in with one person before she's thirty? I didn't get it."

"But you went last night."

"Sure, why not? It's a party, and she's a friend of mine. Was." She paused, drank again. "Was. And I thought, what the hell, they're having this deal at a place like the D&D? Maybe Shauna's not as dull as I figured. Anyway, she got trashed enough to get up there and strip down. No style to it, and not a lot of tits, but she was game. Gotta give her that."

"Have you spoken to anyone who was there last night since?"

"No. I didn't want to. I didn't want to go over and over it. What's the point? She meant something to me. I thought she was wasting her life, then all of a sudden, she doesn't have a life to waste."

"Have you ever been to her art studio?"

"Sure. We were friends, so sure. Hell, I posed for her in there, then we rolled around on the floor. Did the same with the big guy. Anton."

"Anton Carver? So you had sex with him?"

"One round, after he sketched me. A couple rounds since. Why not?"

"After Erin met Shauna?"

"Yeah, after. No big thing."

"Did you work here yesterday, before the party?"

"I take Mondays off."

"Why don't you run me through your day?"

"For fuck's sake." She set down her water with a pissy little slam. "Look, I have to get ready for my next act."

"Then make it quick."

"I slept in. I went over to the restaurant for lunch, hung out with the family awhile, then went home. I'm working on a fresh act. Worked on that, did some yoga, had some dinner, cleaned up, changed. I walked to the D&D, got there just before the storm hit. Maybe ten."

"Is that it?"

"That'll do for now. Thanks for your time."

"We got lawyers in the family. If you want more, go through them."

She pushed out of the booth and walked away.

"Interesting," Eve murmured, and pulled out a ten for the table.

"It was," Roarke agreed. "She's very angry."

"Tall and strong." Eve slid out of the booth, walked with Roarke to the door. "Enough to fit. Angry, and she doesn't like Shauna."

"More logical, wouldn't it be, to dispose of the one she doesn't like?"

"Not if you're looking for payback." Outside, Eve started back the way she'd come. "Erin cut off that part of their relationship, and she meant more than our stripper wants to admit. Revenge sex with Erin's studio mate, that's a tell."

"Revenge sex is a long way from murder."

"Dating's a long way from marriage. In a little over a year, Erin and Shauna went from one to the other. Nearly got there. Maybe you think, all right, it's just a phase. It won't last. She'll get tired of this ordinary person and we'll pick things up where we left off. Then they're doing that—what is it—china pattern thing, and it hits, it's not just a phase. You won't be picking things up where you left off. She's rejected you and chosen someone else."

"And you think her outline of her day gives her plenty of room."

"Plenty of room to get the case, the swipes. Possible she had a swipe to the studio—between sex rounds, posing. Plenty of room to get the case in there, then party, party, party. And try this."

She paused at the corner, glanced over at him. "She keeps the privacy room swipe, tells Erin how she'll help her change for the big surprise. Good friend, lending a hand, so she slips into the room and waits."

"Very cold and calculating. She seemed more hot and angry."

"Now," Eve agreed. "Now it's done, and she can't take it back." Eve gestured. "That's her place, grandmother next door, then the restaurant."

"And they also own the other townhouses there. Are you interested in tortillas for dinner?"

"I thought about it, get a look at her family at work, but no. If it's her, it's her, not likely them. Plus, they look packed, so not a good time to try to squeeze out any information.

"I'm parked a couple blocks from Crack's. I cleared him to open tomorrow. Rochelle was in there cleaning the bar. He did the crime scene himself. Wouldn't hire it out."

"It's his place. It's personal for him."

"It's all personal with this one. I was in the victim's studio today, and saw some of her work. It looked good to me. She'd done a painting of Polumbi's, the pizzeria where I had my first slice. Her artist friend—the one who was in Baltimore—said it was one of their hangouts. She got it, she really captured it. And she painted a figure at the window counter. It took me right back."

He took her hand, kissed it. "Why don't we go there now? I'll call ahead, get us a booth."

She started to say no, they should just go home. Her board, her book, the case.

"Yeah, let's do that. I could use that place, the pull back to that time, not to mention the pizza."

It worked its magic, the smells, the light, the energy. She sat so she faced the front, and the memory.

Roarke ordered a carafe of the house wine, and pizza.

"I did a lot of walking around New York today," she told him. "Downtown anyway. And it struck me how much it's mine. And that painting . . . I'd never felt what I felt when I sat on that stool at that counter looking out at the street. I never felt that freedom, and more, honest-to-God, like home. Mine. Never tasted anything half as wonderful as that first bite of pizza."

"Whenever I think of buying the place—" He held up a hand before she could object. "Whenever I do, I understand no, no, it would change what it is for you if it was ours in that way. But you should buy the painting."

"I should buy the painting?"

"If her parents, or whoever's in charge, will sell it. I'd buy it for you, but I think it's the same as buying this place. It wouldn't be the same. You should buy it for yourself."

She hadn't thought of it, but now . . .

"Maybe. I don't know if that's weird again."

"I don't think so." He poured their wine when the server brought the carafe.

"I'll think about it, but first we find who killed her so she'll never paint another. So far, I'm leaning toward exes. One of Erin's, two—possibly three—of Shauna's. You put an ex on somebody, no matter how it happens, there's a dig in there. A lot of times that dig keeps getting deeper instead of filling in."

He listened while she ran it through, and when the pizza arrived, put a slice on her plate, then his.

"You're leaning away from the bootie buddy."

"Leaning away, but not crossing off entirely. He doesn't feel right for it," she admitted. "But again, Erin got in his way. When and if Shauna wants to pick things up again, he's right there."

"Sex is powerful, but sex alone as a motive?"

"That's what we've got, so far. Weak, yeah."

She lifted the slice, took a bite. And yes, it took her back, back to where everything was new and bright and, most of all, free.

"But under sex is resentment, maybe a sense of betrayal. I sure as hell felt that from Lopez. 'You chose her over me? And now you ask me to help you give her this big deal? This dream? Screw that.'"

"And Shauna's exes."

"Starts the same. Rejection, betrayal. Then wait a damn minute, now she's with a woman? What does that make me? Was she faking it with me? Pretending? Using me? Asking him to help with the surprise, that's both insult and opportunity."

"But he doesn't target the one who rejected him."

"Maybe he still wants her. Maybe he wants to soothe his ego, maybe both. So remove the obstacle."

She ate more pizza. "Still weak, but it's what we've got. It's not money, it's not some deep secret, I don't find envy. What I find is personal. Sex, passion, rejection, betrayal. Add making a mistake—the way Lopez sees it. The timing, Roarke, days before the wedding, and at a party. That counts, too."

She picked up her wine. "Everyone I've looked at? No major criminal, clean finances, no signs of gambling, addictions. They're a tight group, close in proximity, a tribe. Peabody calls the women a tribe. I guess that makes the male portions just outside that, but they connect, too."

"Why don't I take a closer look at the financials? Of the victim, her fiancée, and your top suspects?"

"If you can't find anything there, it absolutely eliminates that as any sort of a motive."

"Plus, entertaining for me. You said her art was good."

"I thought so. So did Peabody. And apparently so does the woman who runs the gallery where she had a show, and sold the paintings that paid for Maui."

"Her art will likely be worth more now. Dead artist, it often follows."

Eve's eyes narrowed. "That's an angle. Some of this tribe has some of her art. And then the gallery. She didn't have a will. Most people her age, and in her financial bracket, don't bother. So do the paintings go to her parents—next of kin—or to Shauna?"

"Next of kin would be the legal answer, I'd think. Some sort of combination would likely be the emotional choice."

"Yeah, they'd probably work something out, and add some of her friends in, too."

She went back to pizza. "But how much could it come to? And still," she added, "people kill for less than whatever that may be. It's a good angle."

"Happy to oblige."

Like in the painting, a waitress walked by with a tray. People ate slices, wound pasta, drank wine.

"We need to find out who has any of her work. I know Angie Decker does. She's not hurting for cash—unless I didn't find that in her financials. There's art in the vic's place she shared with Shauna. I don't see

Shauna in this, but it's worth a look. Lopez posed for her, bound to have a piece or two. Stillwater told us he had a couple. And so did Wanda Rogan. And there were a hell of a lot of canvases in that studio—with crappy security. Someone could walk in, take their pick.

"This is an angle." And she felt the boost from it. "Maybe money after all. Or sex and money—always a top combo."

"I have a great deal of affection for both myself."

She gave him a "Ha! That's no secret. You may have reached your quota of sex already today, since that busty server eye-fucked you twice."

"And yet, I don't feel satisfied."

"You could've had a free lap dance with a redhead."

"And yet," he said again, "here I am, having pizza with my lanky brunette."

"If redheads are redheads," she wondered, "why aren't people with brown hair brownheads? Why brunettes?"

He lifted his wineglass. "A question for the ages."

"People with blond hair are blonds, with an *e* on the end if female for some stupid reason. You got black hair, they say black-haired. Who decided to make up a whole new word for brown hair?"

"I believe it's French."

"Should've figured." She shrugged it off. "Anyway. I don't get the lap dance thing. Paying somebody to sit on your lap and rub crotches. You can't put hands on her—gotta pay more in a privacy room there if the club has a license for it. You just sit there with your pants on while she grinds and rocks on you. So if you get off, you get off in your pants, and that's gotta be a damn mess."

Roarke took another slice of pizza. "Who else has such fascinating discussions over wine and pizza? I'll say I'm in general agreement re the worth of the lap dance, but to each their own."

"Whatever." She shrugged again, ate. "Lopez? She was born with those tits. Too much movement for otherwise."

Roarke eyed her over the slice. "Interesting comment. If I agree I might be accused of paying too much attention to those tits."

"Ace, if you weren't paying attention to that set, you're not the man I married."

"I'm very much the man you married."

Laughing, she took a bite of pizza.

Traffic—street and pedestrian—had calmed, at least some, by the time Roarke drove uptown. Eve used the time to update Peabody.

> Lopez goes on the list. Full report to follow, but she's angry, a hard-ass, and had plenty of time on Monday to collect the case, swipes, etc. My sense is she had stronger feelings for the victim than she admits, and more dislike for Hunnicut than she let show.

> New angle: Dead artist = steeper prices for paintings. Who gets the paintings in the gallery, in the studio, elsewhere? Who already owns her paintings? Who among those might have money issues we haven't uncovered?

> No will, so next of kin? But there are several pieces we saw in the shared apartment. So possession to Shauna there. Gallery might have some sort of contract. Need to find out.

> Contact Frost, find out what you can on that. If we need more, we bring her in tomorrow. Delay that. We'll go to the gallery tomorrow. Meanwhile, double verify her travel, in case.

I'm going to want a list of who bought or was gifted
any of her work. Let's play the angle out.

"It could go toward revenge, too," Eve said when she finished the text. "She tossed me aside, or she's the reason Shauna tossed her aside, I not only get rid of that bitch, I cash in on it. What does a struggling young artist give pals for birthdays, Christmas, all the damn gift-required shit we worship in our society?"

"A drawing, a painting, and likely something that has some meaning to the recipient."

"That's what I say. The amount of profit probably doesn't matter nearly as much as the satisfaction."

"And how do those just outside the tribe acquire them?"

"Maybe they buy. In Stillwater's case, he got to be friends with the victim, too—and he said he bought a couple. He stayed connected. Same with Barney, and he's added the Becca link to it. Rierdon? I'll find out."

"I've no doubt," he agreed, and drove through the gates.

She looked at the house that Roarke built as the quieting summer sun dropped in the west. Her home, she thought, inside the city that was her home.

Then she looked at him, the man who'd made home more than she'd ever known it could be.

"That was damn productive pizza."

Chapter Ten

Eve expected Summerset to have retired to his rooms for the evening, but he loomed.

She started to make a crack about vampires rising at sunset, but the cat padded over. Then stopped an inch from her boots.

Galahad hissed, arched his back, then on a throaty growl, sent Eve a hard, feline stare out of his bicolored eyes.

"What's your problem? The rat dog? Are you kidding me? Jesus, I never even touched that little rat dog."

In response, Galahad turned his back on her, stuck up his tail like an exclamation point, then stalked back to Summerset.

"I can't control every freaking dog in the city. Get over it, tubby."

Because she felt guilty, and that made her feel ridiculous, she stalked up the stairs without another word.

"He's a very proprietary cat," Summerset commented to Roarke.

"So it seems. I expect they'll both get over it. Go, relax. Enjoy your evening."

As Roarke started up, Summerset glanced down at the cat. "Now, now, the children are home safe, and all's well. No little rat dog could hold a candle to you."

Apparently mollified, Galahad trotted up the stairs.

"What an interesting family we make," Summerset murmured, and went back to his quarters to enjoy his evening.

In her office, stewing, Eve began to set up her board.

"The stripper's grandmother had one of those yappy dogs that looks like an overgrown rat."

"A Chihuahua?"

"Maybe. Whatever. It sniffed at my boots. I mean, for Christ's sake, a boot-sniffing rat dog is the least of my problems out in the field. For all I know at this point, the woman with the boot-sniffing rat dog may have a murderer for a granddaughter. But he doesn't think of that."

"I'm quite sure he doesn't, possibly due to the fact he's a cat."

Roarke watched the cat in question saunter in, ignore Eve, then take sprawling possession of her sleep chair.

He decided it was wiser not to mention it.

"I'll just start on those financials." And, he thought, retire from this particular field.

Eve finished the board, programmed coffee, sat at her desk to open her murder book.

The cat wasn't the only one capable of ignoring, with attitude.

Because she knew there was something there, she started a deeper run on ChiChi Lopez.

Her great-grandparents had crossed the border into the States—documentation vague on exactly when and where. But all four of their children had been born in the U.S. The younger two, including Anna Maria Lopez, née Delgato, had been born in New York.

The restaurant had started as a food truck, then two food trucks. Anna

Maria Delgato married Juan Lopez, and they had four kids while helping run the food trucks—now numbering three.

And their four kids had kids—a hell of a lot of kids, Eve noted. Among them, ChiChi, age twenty-nine.

Along the way, five years before ChiChi came along, they opened Abuela's. Six years later, they bought the building.

Nothing she found indicated anything but a large, hardworking, savvy family. No doubt if she dug into each one, she'd find some bumps, some issues, some problems, but unless she hit on something that applied to her investigation, she'd stay out of that rabbit hole.

She zeroed in on ChiChi.

Private school education, dance lessons. She unearthed several articles giving her raves for school musicals. Which explained the major in theater, at least at the start of her college career.

That switched to business major third year in.

Two dings for assault, charges dropped. Anger management required.

Worked as a server, then a line chef at the restaurant. And at twenty-one started as a dancer at the club. Worked her way up to headliner within a year.

And it paid, Eve noted. It paid damn well. From what she could see, Lopez reported her tips. Probably not all of them, but enough to keep the tax man from knocking on her door.

No cohabs, no marriages, no civil unions.

Picking through the finances, Eve noted she continued to take dance classes, spent a hell of a lot on clothes—most custom tailored—more on salons and spas.

She had weekly payments to a Dr. Rene Koons—a shrink on the Lower West Side. Another weekly to a Stefan Michael, a masseur.

And several payments over the last eight years to the gallery where Erin sold her work.

She glanced up when Roarke walked in.

"Lopez has two dings for assault—mandatory anger management fulfilled. She sees a shrink every week. Might still have those anger issues. Started off as a theater major in college, switched to business major halfway through. Kind of a star in school musicals prior, so maybe she couldn't cut it in a bigger pool of talent. And maybe some of the anger issues come from there. She's spent a good chunk of change at the gallery where Erin has some of her work."

"She invests well—smart investments. It's easy enough to find—through her insurance—how much of that chunk of change went for Erin's art. I'll look at it. For now, I can tell you she invests well, has no hidden accounts, is very careful with her accounting. She's in excellent financial shape."

Walking to her workstation, he programmed coffee for himself. "As are her siblings and parents. I can go back further if you like, but there's a pattern. Work hard, invest wisely, live within your means, but live well."

"The money—from the increase in art value—that would be a bonus, not the main driver. Feelings, passions, anger, sex—that would drive this. I keep coming back to that. What does a woman with a solid family, solid financials, living how she appears to want to live need weekly shrink sessions for? And why is she so pissed off?"

"I couldn't say, but I can see you have a thought on it."

"Because at the end of the day, she's alone. She comes from a family where people end up married and popping out more family, and she's alone. She's got an older brother, age thirty-one, married two years ago, already has a kid. Younger sister got married last May. She has no cohab on record. She may have wanted Erin Albright to fill that spot."

Pushing up, Eve paced. "She's got that nice house, nice neighborhood, and she lives alone in it. She clicks with Albright, the struggling artist. She could make life easier for her. Move in with me, don't worry about rent, concentrate on your art. Your art and me."

Pausing, she studied the board. "Lopez's family knew Albright, so Lopez brought her around."

"You're thinking for approval."

As usual, he followed her line of thinking.

"It's possible, more probable. I'd bet she didn't bring all her bed partners around to meet her *abuela*. She didn't like Hunnicut, and most of that, it strikes me, comes from jealousy. They both wanted Erin Albright, but Shauna Hunnicut got her."

"You sound half-convinced. Not all the way convinced."

"Half's about right. If she did it, what did she do with the murder weapon, the jewelry she took off the body, the 'link?"

"Little time to dispose of it all."

And that was the sticker, Eve admitted.

"Little, but not no time. Maybe fifteen minutes. But nobody noticed her missing for that long. So it's a stretch."

"An accomplice," Roarke suggested. "A family member or lover—or someone she promised sex to. Take the things to the back door, pass them off."

"Not impossible, so that makes it possible."

But, Eve wondered, could the person Erin trusted trust someone else that much?

"Yeah, possible. You could check the insurance, see how much she invested in the art. That could play in. She spent her hard-earned money to support the woman she wanted, and the woman didn't want her back. 'Let's just be friends' is the world's worst insult."

"And here I thought it was: 'It's not you, it's me.'"

"They're the same thing." She turned to him. "If I ever dumped you, it would totally be you and not me."

"I appreciate that, darling, and the same goes." Amused, he pulled her in for a quick kiss. "I'll go see about the art."

"Good. I'm going to take another look at Shauna's exes. Stillwater's out of it. His alibi's concrete, plus they didn't have the feelings, the passion. That was affection and convenience."

When she turned back to her command center, Galahad sat next to her comp. Looking, she realized, weirdly like the stuffed cat Roarke had once given her.

Walking back, she sat, gave him as hard a stare as he did her. "You know, you never freak when I come home with blood on my boots, with boots smelling like death."

He blinked his bicolored eyes once.

"Because that's the job. Well, when I'm investigating, I sometimes run into somebody's pet rat dog. And that's the job, too. Found you on the job, didn't I?"

She reached out, scratched him lightly between the ears. "The difference is, I brought you home."

He nuzzled his head under her hand, purred.

Feelings, she thought when he curled up on her command center as if to keep an eye on her.

Passions, anger, jealousy.

It fit here, and it fit in the murder of Erin Albright.

She opened the file on Rierdon. As she read, as she dug, she checked the time.

Not too late—though Roarke would probably disagree.

She contacted the mutual friend, Jodi, who'd been at the party, who threw her own parties. To remain a suspect, Rierdon had to have known about the bride party—the when and where.

But the conversation with Jodi, and the three-way conversation with her and her cohab, ended inconclusively.

Didn't recall mentioning it, but maybe.

So maybe, Eve thought. It didn't explain the swipes, the case, and those remained major sticking points. No reason she could come up with for Erin to have trusted him, asked him to do the favor.

More the opposite, she admitted.

Back to high school, she decided, and took a deeper dive on Greg Barney.

Nothing, she thought, just nothing popped. An ordinary guy, a regular guy. And sure, they killed, but nothing in his background, in his current living situation stood out.

Financially . . . Roarke would make sure, but financially, he looked clean. Ordinary again. No gallery purchases she found. Maybe he'd bought some of her sidewalk art, paid cash.

Maybe he had some through gifts, or through Becca DiNuzio. Would they bother with insurance for that?

Doubtful.

Still, she rose to pace and play with the angle.

Say they had a couple of pieces. And he could ask Shauna for another, in memory. Cash in when the value went up.

It had to be more than that, she decided. But didn't she have more? Sweethearts, parted by college, then reunited.

But one sweetheart is seeing someone else.

Let's just be friends.

So he turns to—settles for?—the other high school girl. That keeps him close to the tribe, close to Shauna.

But wouldn't tribes have their own rules, and wouldn't not screwing around with the person a tribe member is screwing around with be at the top?

How do you make a move on the old girlfriend when she's pals with your new girlfriend?

Very sticky ground, she concluded.

And how, she asked herself, would navigating that ground include murder?

On the other side of the scale, the victim would have trusted him. One of Shauna's oldest friends, someone not invited to the party. He lived and worked close. And would she believe as one of Shauna's oldest friends, he'd be happy with the surprise, happy to help pull it off?

Add no alibi. Just an ordinary guy, hanging out at home waiting for his girlfriend to come back from a girl party.

And see the flowers he picked up for her on his way home.

A non-alibi alibi, Eve considered. He'd been able to walk her through his steps—closing the shop, walking to the bar, having drinks with a pal, and so on.

She studied his photo on the board as Roarke came back in.

"He was pretty specific," Eve muttered. "I'm going to think about that. You could do that."

"I'm sure I could. Do what exactly?"

"Walk me through your day, times, people, meetings, meals. You keep a log in your head. Does he?"

"Who would that be?"

"Greg Barney, Shauna's high school guy, and her best friend's current cohab. He was pretty specific. Not like at nineteen-zero-two, I paused at the crosswalk. But close enough. But he didn't mention the flowers. DiNuzio reminded him about the flowers. An oversight, or a ploy? An oh yeah, right, I stopped for flowers. That way you're not absolutely specific."

She started pacing again. "Like you don't exactly remember the vid you were watching on-screen when you fell asleep on the sofa. Just some alien invasion thing. And that checks. *Duplicates*. Alien invasion deal available on the night in question. I bet if we checked that screen, that would've been playing at the time he said."

"You're looking at him now because he was able to walk you through his evening?"

"It's one factor. They were the big-deal couple—what did he say . . . Shaunbar. Some people never get over high school. Maybe he's one of them. Peabody was running through it today, mostly for the bullshit factor, but you know, it could play."

She paced some more. "But the thing is, Shauna's just not the type who'd jump back to him if he broke up with her best friend. That doesn't play for me. But would he know that? He should, but . . . Ego's blind."

"That's generally love."

"Works with ego, too. She'll be grieving, so she'll be vulnerable. He's right there to pick up deli meat and make her a sandwich."

"Is that a new euphemism?"

"No, that's literal. He was hovering—that's what Becca called it, and it's accurate. But shit, they all were in their way."

She shook her head. "I have to let this cook awhile. What did you find out about Lopez and the art?"

"That she has a considerable collection. Again, a wise investment. In that collection are fourteen Erin Albrights, currently insured for fifty-eight thousand."

"That's a lot by one artist, isn't it?"

"It is, but you have friendship, and you have, very likely, a taste for a certain style of art."

"I think it's a lot. I think it shows a focus on one artist, and one woman."

"The last she purchased, again through the gallery, about two weeks ago, for a bit over five thousand."

"She bought one of the paintings that paid for the Maui trip? Oh boy, that's just got to piss you off, doesn't it? You buy the painting, and she blows the money on somebody else's dream? You're partially paying for their honeymoon? And now she wants you not only to stand there and watch her big surprise, but help her with it? Fuck that."

Eve smiled. "Oh, that's a good one. That's very close to 'come into the box and let's chat' good."

"Meanwhile I took a good look at the victim's financials, and the fiancée's. As clean as it gets, and I hate to say boring. They had a joint account, which they both contributed to, and split the household expenses. They each had their own account, for personal expenses. Clothes, gifts, I suppose, salons, and so on. They both lived carefully.

"The victim opened a separate account three weeks ago."

"Yeah, the honeymoon fund," Eve confirmed. "McNab found that."

"And she used that fund to buy the tickets, for the deposit to book the room. There's enough left to cover the rest of the lodging, plus all the food, entertainment, souvenirs, etc."

He looked at the board, at the victim. "It was a lovely thing to do. To try to do."

"Did they insure the art in the apartment?"

"They carry the bare minimum renter's insurance."

"All right. I need to think about all this. The victim would have trusted both Lopez and Barney. I can stretch a motive on either of them. Still need to talk to the gallery manager."

"You'll think better on a decent night's sleep. You didn't get one last night."

"Give me another hour. I want to write this up, see if it makes any sense when I do. There was a meanness to this, Roarke, with the time and place. A meanness that says personal."

She pointed to the board. "It's going to be someone already on there, and so far, Lopez and Barney are who's standing out. But I don't want to miss someone else because I'm looking too hard at them."

"An hour," he said. "I'll play with more of the financials. It's not nearly as entertaining when it's all aboveboard."

"Yeah, the job's just made of fun."

"My part of it often is." He kissed her, then tapped the dent in her chin. "An hour."

She used every minute of it, but had to admit fatigue, both physical and mental, set in by the end.

So she didn't argue when Roarke, on the dot of the sixty-minute mark, stepped back in.

She shut down, stood up.

"Find anything interesting?"

"Financials are rarely so boring," he told her, and taking her hand, led her from the room. "Is Greg Barney still one of your top suspects?"

She shrugged. "He and Lopez are who I've got at this point."

"Which gives you two in under twenty-four hours," he reminded her. "In any case, financially, he's clean. Pays his taxes, his bills. Other than rent, his major outlay is clothing, with the bulk from the shop he manages, and dining. No investments, which is shortsighted of him, but he saves a bit.

"No art purchases," he added as they walked into the bedroom where the cat already claimed the bed. "No art insured. As he cohabs with Becca DiNuzio, I looked there."

"She was onstage dancing her half-naked ass off at TOD. But a cynical cop could theorize she and Barney were in on it together."

"I happen to know a cynical cop. Her financials, also clean and tidy, though she has some small investments—an also clean-and-tidy portfolio."

"Younger brother's a Wall Street guy."

"Who advises her wisely. She does have a gallery purchase. One Erin Albright, valued at twenty-five hundred, purchased about six months ago, and has insured a second—no purchase—for twelve hundred. Insured since the first week in January."

"Christmas gift, I bet."

"I'd agree."

"Not enough," Eve concluded. "Not enough for the dead-artist angle."

Stripped down to her underwear, she tried to think it through. Then just shook her head.

"Even the cynical cop has a hard time tying her into it. Why would she want Erin dead? I can't see it."

"Consider it time to turn it off, and see what comes to you in the morning."

She knew he had that right, but her mind wanted to circle. She considered him, standing there all lean and gorgeous in his boxers.

"Hard to turn it off. I need a distraction." She took three running steps and launched herself at him. Hooked her legs around his waist, her arms around his neck. "And here you are."

"Your distraction, is it?"

"You're so good at it." She captured his mouth with hers until her humming system smothered the fatigue. "See? I'm already distracted."

"I suppose I'd best finish the job then."

"Well, obviously."

All but nose-to-nose, she laughed as he carried her to the bed and dumped her on it.

With a low growl, Galahad rolled away and jumped down.

"Serves him right for getting pissy with me." Rearing up, she nipped at Roarke's chin. "All right, ace, you've got a job to do."

"And I do love my work."

Now he took her mouth in a slow, deep, dreamy kiss that not only sent her system humming but clouded her too-busy brain. She sighed into it. As his hands ran down her sides, her skin tingled.

"See, really good at it."

Everything in her went soft, and all the sharp edges of the day smoothed into quiet pleasure. As the half-moon peeked through the sky window over the bed, she combed her fingers through his hair, the thick mass of it, and down the firm muscles of his back.

She sighed again, lifting her arms as he drew her support tank up and over her head. His hands—they had magic in them—glided up her ribs, over her breasts, up to cup her face before gliding down again.

A gentle passion, lulling her into a dream state.

He loved seeing her like this, utterly relaxed, utterly open. All that fierce energy quelled into surrender, not just to him but to self.

He could give, and she could take, then give back in return.

It never ceased to enthrall him, this meeting of bodies, minds, hearts. No matter what troubled him, troubled her, no matter what horrors crept through the shadows of the world, they had this gift, this love, this passion. And the union it forged between them.

He rolled, reversing positions, and she came with him, her body fluid as wine. Her mouth sought his, and clung there while he peeled the simple white briefs down her narrow hips.

He rolled again, bodies tangling over the big bed, the smooth sheets. As warm skin edged toward hot, he closed his mouth over her breast, slid his hand between her legs.

When she cried out in release, he felt the orgasm rocket through that long, strong body. Even as she shuddered with it, he drove himself into her so dark delight layered over dark delight.

Not a distraction, an eruption with a change of tone both abrupt and glorious. She flew on it, stormed with it when he shoved her knees up to take more, give more.

And desperate for the more, she matched his speed, his urgency until everything went bright and hot and beautiful. Until more was impossible.

Until he said her name and emptied into her.

She lay under the weight of him, dazed and drowsy. She felt his heart pounding against hers, or hers pounded against his. She couldn't quite tell the difference.

The moon held a new place in the sky window, white and clear against the dark.

Her lips curved when he pressed his to the side of her neck.

"I believe I did my job."

"Damn good job. Kudos. Where does that come from? Kudos? What language is that?"

"Don't make me have to distract you again." He shifted her, nestled her in. "Give that mind of yours a rest."

"You don't have another distraction in you?"

"Well now, if that's a challenge—"

"No." She managed a sleepy laugh. "I'm tapped out." But she laid a hand on his cheek. "And the cat's back," she added when Galahad jumped on the bed again.

As she began to drift off, it occurred to her they had a really big bed, and she ended up sleeping in it night after night, wedged between Roarke and the cat.

And she liked it.

Chapter Eleven

It didn't surprise her to find herself within a dream. The dead woman preyed on her mind.

Maybe being murdered in the same room where she herself had been targeted for death played into it. Maybe dying right before her wedding as she herself might have played into it.

Whatever reason nudged at her subconscious, she stood in the Down and Dirty with the music pounding, the holo-band rocking. Onstage with them, Shauna Hunnicut and Nadine Furst, both half-naked, danced like lunatics.

There was Peabody, with her bowl cut, giggling like a drunk teenager, and Angie Decker laughing with Mira. Mavis, with no baby belly, standing on a table. Crack at the bar, grinning as he mixed a drink for Lopez.

All of this happened, she thought. Different times, but the same place, and now it blurred together into one wild and singular party.

"They're having so much fun." Erin stood beside her wearing the pink heels, the grass skirt, coconut bra. "Celebrating for us."

"I wasn't really into it," Eve said. "I was just coming around to under-standing I wanted the whole marriage thing. It still scared the crap out of me, but I wanted it. I just didn't know why I wanted it."

"I wasn't scared, and I wanted it more than I ever wanted anything. More than anything." Erin said it softly, like a sigh. "But we both loved, you and me. We loved somebody who loved us, and we both had friends who wanted to celebrate that. That's really mag."

Erin looked down at herself, brushed a hand over the grass skirt. "I never had a chance to put this on and make Shauna's dream come true. We never had a chance to put on our white dresses and make the prom-ises you made."

"No, you didn't. I'm sorry. I'm no expert," Eve added, "but I think you'd've made a solid life together."

"Who says you're no expert?" Erin did a little hula that made the grass skirt sway. "You know people. You get under the skin and know who they are."

"That's the job."

"Yeah. Your job, and you're trying to find out why I'm dead, and who killed me. I wish I could tell you, but this is just a dream."

"I know."

"You got lucky." The statement held no bitterness, just flat truth. "I sure as hell didn't. I'm glad you did, since you're trying to find out why and who. But you got lucky. He wanted you dead, that dirty cop, and if he'd gotten the full dose in you, if you'd been drinking like he figured, you'd be dead."

"I was getting married the next day. Maybe I didn't know completely why I was getting married the next day, but I wanted to stay sober."

"We were supposed to have a few more days before the white dresses. I was a little bit drunk."

They stood at the doorway of the privacy room now. For a moment Eve saw herself, fighting Casto off. He'd gotten some of the drug into her, and he'd blackened her eye, but she'd taken him down.

And the next day, a bright summer day, she'd married Roarke under an arbor of flowers. She'd carried petunias and made those promises to him. He'd made those promises to her.

They'd kept them for three years and counting.

"It's nice, isn't it, being married?"

She glanced over at Erin. "Most of the time, yeah. It's nice. And when it's not, you know it'll get back there."

"You trusted the bad cop, maybe not a hundred percent, but enough to be in there with him. But you knew how to fight. Me? I know how to paint, how to make art. I know how to tend bar and serve tables, how to clean an apartment. I don't know how to fight."

"You didn't have a chance to fight. And it wasn't personal with Casto. It was . . . business."

She saw Erin on the floor now, in her party dress stained with blood that had flowed from the necklace of blood around her throat.

"You never had a chance."

"I trusted the wrong person. So did Shauna. But I'm dead, and she still trusts the wrong person, right? She doesn't know she trusts the person who killed me."

"No," Eve said as the music and laughter banged her awake. "She doesn't."

When she woke, the man she'd married while she'd sported a black eye—mostly disguised with makeup—sat on the sofa, tablet in hand, cat across his lap.

The wall screen ran the stock report on mute as he sat in his sleek black suit with its gray pinstripes.

She smelled coffee, and wished someone would just pour some in her before she had to move.

The dream hadn't answered any questions, but it clarified, if it mattered, just how much the investigation brought back the incidents on the eve of her own wedding.

And what it meant to her to wake like this, on so many mornings, and see him there, sitting across the room.

"It shouldn't be possible," Roarke said without looking up, "but I can actually hear your brain waking up."

"It can get noisy in there."

"And often does." He looked over now, and the easy smile faded. "Did you dream?"

"Yeah. Not a nightmare, just a dream."

"That troubles you." Rising, he went to the AutoChef, programmed coffee. When he brought it to her, she sat up.

Instead of taking the coffee, she framed his face with her hands and kissed him. "It shows how smart I was and am to marry a man who'd know how much I need coffee and get me some."

"And how smart I was and am to have lured you with real coffee in the first place."

"Yeah, that was pretty smart." She took it now, drank. "Like that first bite of New York pizza, my first taste of real coffee was a revelation."

"And the dream? A revelation?"

"Not really. Maybe on a personal level a little. It blurred the murder party with the one at the D&D the night before we got married."

And because he remembered, very well, the bruises on her face, he stroked her cheek.

"That's hardly a wonder, considering."

"No, and it's stuck with me through this. The whole girl pre-wedding thing, the D&D, the same goddamn room. I got lucky; she didn't."

"It's never only luck with you, Eve. You have the training, the skills, the reflexes the victim couldn't have."

"I didn't trust Casto all the way. Enough to give him that shot at me, but not all the way. And . . ." She had to admit it. "I didn't like the way he was with Peabody. It bugged me the way he moved in on her. But she'd been my aide like five minutes, so I didn't push on that."

She shook her head, drank more coffee. "Anyway, everybody's all mixed and mingling together. Nadine, Peabody, Mavis, Mira, and all that along with the other group. And I'm standing there with the victim."

She told him.

"There's truth in there," he said. "Erin trusted the wrong person, and Shauna would trust the same one. Still trusts the same one."

"Which makes me wonder, should I worry about her now? Will that trust—or some detail or memory that cuts through it—make her a target?"

"It's easier to kill a second time, and yet, wouldn't that risk focusing the investigation even more narrowly?"

Too early in the day to hit him with how he thought like a cop. Plus, he'd brought her coffee.

"There was a lot of luck in that first kill. Planning, yeah, and I think the intent to kill Erin had been in the works awhile. But the opportunity, that just opened right up. And the victim, trusting, opened the door for her killer by handing over that opportunity."

"Right now, Shauna's surrounded by friends, family as well, I expect. Getting her alone with enough cover to get away with it? Opportunities would be severely limited."

"Yeah."

"But you'll worry." He tapped her head. "Because it's very noisy in there."

"Some. Thanks for the coffee."

She got out of bed and into the shower.

Surrounded by friends, Eve reminded herself. It would take more than luck for the killer, who was certainly among those friends, to get Shauna alone, kill her, and come up with cover.

She'd have to keep that worry in the back of her head, as she needed the rest to pinpoint the killer.

After a spin in the drying tube, she grabbed a robe—this one a pale lavender—and stepped out.

He had breakfast under domes, and the cat banished to the floor. Because he still worked on his tablet, she walked over, topped off his coffee, and poured herself another.

"What's going on with that?"

"Some of this, and some of that. Infrastructure improvement on your cop bar, Off Duty. We're so well under way that I imagine you can re-open by the holidays."

"I'm not opening anything. It'll have to open itself."

"Mmm-hmm."

Because his response made her think he had ideas, and she didn't want to spoil her breakfast, she ignored that.

"And some work on guest rooms on the Great House Project. Both sides. Some communications with Peabody's parents, who've let me know their housewarming gifts will be on the way by the end of the week."

"Partner's desk and blown-glass ceiling light. She's told me a half dozen times. More than." Eve lifted the domes.

Waffles! Never the wrong choice.

"They're coming, right? The Peabodys?"

"They are, but wanted the desk and light in place, as hopefully a surprise."

"Not big on surprises right now." She drowned her waffles in butter and syrup. "But I'll keep it zipped."

"They also have gifts for Mavis and Leonardo. A charming little child's picnic table with benches, and a lovely family sculpture—Mavis holding an infant, Leonardo holding Bella. A thank-you for opening their family to Peabody and McNab."

"Nice. Seriously on target. We've the gift thing covered, right?"

"We do, and they'll arrive well before move-in."

"Okay, good. The partner's desk deal. That would never work for us."

"I do on occasion use your auxiliary."

"On occasion, and for short duration. How could you buy the next quadrant of the universe if I'm sitting across from you digging for a murderer?"

"And how could you dig for a murderer if I'm sitting across from you negotiating the price of the next quadrant of the universe?"

"Exactly. But it'll work for Peabody and McNab. How do you negotiate buying a quadrant of the universe?"

"Skillfully. But this morning I settled for closing the deal on a small resort in Australia."

"Australia? What are you going to do with a resort in Australia?"

"Make some improvements, which will include a five-star luxury spa and a few private villas. It's been let go a bit."

"So you grabbed the opportunity."

"I did, yes. But I'll look into that quadrant for you first chance I have."

"Wouldn't surprise me." She polished off her waffles, rose to go to her closet.

"Why are there kangaroos there? It's not like you see them hopping around the Bronx."

"You don't often see elephants or lemurs there, either. I suppose things have their place."

"And crocodiles. They've got crocodiles down there. Who decided it was a good idea to make something that swims around waiting to eat you? Sharks. There's another one. What do they do but swim around, eat fish—or people when they get a chance—and make more sharks?"

"And people think New York's dangerous," she continued. "Then they're off swimming in some lagoon, la-la-la, and chomp. Or it's how much fun it is to hike in the woods, and bang, a snake bites your ass. You decide to vacation in some cabin, because peaceful and pretty vistas. And it's all fine until some bear mauls you to death."

Roarke listened with genuine fascination as she reeled off various deaths by nature.

"Sailing along in your big-ass yacht, drink too much, fall overboard.

And a shark bites off your leg. Take an African safari, and you're just asking to get eviscerated, dragged off into some jungle, and eaten. But people do it."

She stepped out in tan trousers, a white tee, carrying a navy jacket.

"People do it," she repeated, and walked over to hook on her weapon harness. "Then they come here, goggle at everything with their wallets all but hanging out, and when it's stolen, people back where they come from remind them, smugly, New York's a dangerous place. How they should've gone to Australia to see the cute kangaroos."

She loaded her pockets.

"And when they do, Marge is taking pictures of the cute kangaroos when one of the big bastards with the long claws hops up and slices Waldo open so his guts spill out on the ground."

"Remind me not to let you anywhere near the marketing for the resort."

She sent Roarke a dark, knowing look. "It could happen—the guts, not me and marketing. I've got to go meet Peabody at the art gallery."

Still fascinated, he rose. Then gripped her hips, kissed her. "I don't expect you to come across kangaroos or sharks and the rest, but see you take care of my cop nonetheless."

"I'll do that. Galahad's enjoying the syrup still on the plates."

Roarke glanced back, saw the cat licking his whiskers. "Bloody hell. You distracted me."

"Guess I'm good at it, too." She gave him another quick kiss. "See you later."

She'd distracted herself, she admitted as she jogged downstairs and out. With thoughts on predatory wildlife.

She'd rather face a gang of thugs hopped up on Zeus than a single kangaroo with six-inch claws.

Or however long they were.

She could probably take a kangaroo down with a solid stun, but for all she knew they traveled in packs or herds or whatever the hell.

And she had to get her brain off kangaroos.

She blamed Roarke and his Australian resort.

She hit traffic, which she preferred over predatory wildlife.

Since she had to deal with it, she used the extended drive time to think things through.

They weren't dealing with a lunatic—at least not someone overtly crazy. Not a serious calculator, either, because there had to be less risky ways to kill Erin Albright.

So target specific.

Motive? If Lopez, payback for rejection. If Barney, possibly still holding a flame for Shauna.

If someone else . . . so far the dead artist = paydirt didn't hold up well enough to rate high. But maybe she'd find out more from Glenda Frost.

While it remained true a decent percentage of the partygoers could have slipped away just long enough to kill, the question of motive, and removing the weapon and the rest from the scene, remained.

Motive first, she concluded, and the rest would come.

Where was the gain? What was the reason?

She added having a conversation with the other artist, Anton Carver, since Lopez had rolled around with him after Shauna came into the picture.

Maybe his alibi wasn't airtight. Or maybe he knew something. At least a different viewpoint on Lopez. A separate conversation with Becca DiNuzio, she decided. Another viewpoint on Barney.

She spotted Peabody at the entrance to the gallery with another woman. Pulling into a loading zone, she flipped on her On Duty light, waited for a break in the damn traffic. After nipping out of the car, she headed down the sidewalk.

Glenda Frost, her blond hair in a braided roll at the nape of her neck, wore a sleek black sleeveless dress with black pumps that added about four inches to her height. Black-framed sunshades guarded her eyes as she unlocked the gallery doors.

About five-three, she may have weighed in at a hundred pounds if you included the huge black bag hanging from her shoulder.

Even without the out-of-town alibi, her physicality would have ranked her low on Eve's list.

According to her data, Frost—forty-six, divorced, one offspring—had managed the art gallery for twelve years.

Polished, attractive, she wore silver hoops on her ears and a wide silver cuff, intricately carved, on her right wrist.

"Lieutenant Dallas," Peabody said, "Glenda Frost."

"Ms. Frost, thanks for meeting us."

"Whatever I can do to help." Her voice was as polished as the rest of her. "Erin wasn't just a talented young artist, she was a friend. Please come in."

She led the way, switching on lights that showcased art. It hung on the white walls, stood on pedestals and glossy white or black tables.

Some Eve understood, even liked. The portrait of a woman, her face a map of what was surely a century of life, the cobalt vase of bold orange flowers caught in a beam of sunlight.

Others baffled her. Red and blue dots on a white canvas, a carefully detailed bag of soy chips.

"The portrait there." Peabody gestured toward the old woman. "That's Erin's work, isn't it?"

"Yes. Very good eye, Detective. She finished that about three months ago, from a photograph of her great-grandmother."

"I think it's wonderful."

"So do I."

Glenda slipped off her sunshades, dropped them into her bag. She crossed the white floor to a black counter and stowed her bag behind it.

"She recently sold three pieces," Eve said.

"Yes, a triptych, moody still lifes, beautiful use of light and shadow. I saw them in progress, and told her I thought I had a buyer. My sister's an interior designer, and is working with a client I thought they'd be perfect for."

Glenda came back around the counter. "I took photos of the works in progress, showed my sister, who agreed. But there was a deadline, and Erin worked so hard to finish them. It was her biggest single sale. We were so happy."

"She also sold a single through you. About two weeks ago?"

"Yes, ChiChi bought one of Erin's we had on display. She's a collector. That's a smoke tree in full blossom. Erin painted it from one on the High Line, with a stormy sky behind, a flash of lightning in the clouds. Dramatic and detailed. We considered it an unexpected bonus so close to the wedding."

"Did she tell you what she intended to do with the money from those sales?"

"No. When I saw Shauna yesterday, she did." Pressing her lips together, Glenda looked back at the portrait. "It was so Erin, all of it. The trip, the surprise, the way she'd intended to announce it. Do you see the life in this portrait?"

Walking closer, Glenda gestured up at the old woman. "The light in the eyes, the humor in the curve of the mouth? I can see Erin in there, in her great-grandmother. That should've been her in another seven decades. Someone stole those years, that light, that life from her."

"You didn't make the party Monday night."

"No." Turning back, she faced Eve. "I'd arranged my travel and my schedule so I'd make the shower, and the wedding. I was coming back on Thursday—tomorrow—but . . ."

She let that trail off.

"The last time I saw her was in her studio. I helped her box the paintings, the ones for my sister's client, for transport."

"Was anyone else there?"

"Anton. He often works at night. He actually helped us carry the paintings down. It surprised me he interrupted his work to help, but, well, Erin's happiness could be infectious. And she was so damn happy."

"Any artist envy with the others who share the studio?"

"That wouldn't be uncommon." Idly, Glenda patted at the roll at the back of her neck. "Temperaments, egos. I've worked with artists for nearly twenty years. Some—many, in fact—can be challenging. But I didn't notice anything like that there.

"Roy—that's Roy Lutz—is focusing on his mural work, and that's a wise choice for him. My sister's commissioned him several times. Anton? He does mostly commercial art. Large pieces for offices and commercial spaces. He's quite good at what he does. He and Roy, opposites in style and personality. Roy's got a sweet nature, and Anton—you'd have to say a sour one. Donna? She and Erin were very close, and absolutely supportive of each other, in every way."

"Do you have access to the studio?" Eve asked her. "A swipe?"

"No. I wouldn't have any need for that. For the most part, I'd arrange to go by, see the work. Unannounced drop-bys interrupt the work. On commissions, occasionally the artist needs a little nudge, but you don't want to interfere with the process."

"Erin had a lot of her work stored at the studio. What happens to it now?"

"That depends on Shauna and Erin's family, as it does with what we have displayed here. If possible, I'd like to offer to do a showing. For the art, for the business of art. And for Erin, for Shauna and Erin's family."

"Regarding the business of the art, you think you'd be able to sell her work?"

Glenda glanced back at the portrait, smiled a little.

"I do. If I'm able to select the pieces, with the right display and marketing, I think her work would sell very well. That's my job," she added, "and also a tribute to a friend."

"Are you friends with all your artists?" Eve wondered.

"Absolutely not. But Erin was a friend. I met her when I browsed by the street art, something I often did and do. And I saw something in her work—that was, God, about five years ago. I bought two of her pieces—a cityscape at sunset, and one of a pub scene. Both underpriced, and I bargained her down from that just to see if I could. Then I gave her my card, told her to bring me what she thought were her two best pieces."

Glenda laughed even as her eyes went damp. "She told me I'd just bought them, but she had more. And that started our professional and personal relationship. I helped her. I like to think I helped her. Her work needed to ripen and mature, and she lacked business sense. I like to think I helped her."

"On the business of art," Eve began, "what's the price of the portrait up there?"

"Forty-seven hundred."

"And if you keep it on display, manage to have that showing?"

"I'd double it." She sighed. "That's the business of art."

Outside, Eve started toward the car.

"Double it," Peabody said. "That's a big jump."

"I'd say she knows how it works, what she can get. Friends or not, if she had a dead artist, she'd try for the posthumous showing. Likely, as manager, she gets a cut for finding an artist who sells, and maybe for putting on a showing."

Eve got in the car, tapped her fingers on the wheel. "She was out of town, but could, possibly, have worked with someone else to do the cash-in thing. But I don't see it. Unless she has a river of dead artists behind her, it doesn't follow."

"It doesn't make real good business sense, either," Peabody pointed out. "Find an artist, bring them along, then kill them to sell at a high price. You'd run out of artists sooner or later, or get a bad juju rep."

"Bad juju." Eve rolled her eyes, then pulled away from the curb. "And I hate to say you're not wrong about the juju. Check and see about posthumous showings and/or sales through the gallery. But it doesn't really follow.

"Let's talk to Anton Carver."

"He's got a tight alibi."

"Yeah, maybe we can loosen it. Or maybe he knows something. He was there when they took the art out of the studio. Maybe Erin got just happy enough to tell him she was going to book the trip. They're not particular friends—according to Donna—so he's not going to go blabbing to Shauna. She's happy, excited, wants to tell somebody. And he's right there."

"And if she did say something . . ."

"Maybe she said something to someone else, or he did," Eve finished. "Or maybe he or someone else who came in looked in the case she's stashed. It was all in there, the tickets, the costume, the note.

"Carver and Lopez had sex in the studio, at least once."

"Yeah, I saw that in your report. So maybe more than once. Maybe when the case was in there."

"She's pissed, and now more pissed. 'You don't want me, you're not going to have anyone.' Erin asks her to bring the case, and she takes that opportunity. Or Erin gets the case there another way, and Lopez, knowing what's coming, follows her to the room. Erin tells her, and she's 'Let me help you change.' She goes in first, or tells Erin to check the door, make sure it's secured. Kills her, tries to make it look like a robbery, leaves the door unsecured."

"The only person who knows who Erin told is Erin, and she's dead."

"That's how it stands. A tight group like that, your tribe deal. You'd think something like this big surprise would make the rounds."

"You knew Jenkinson was going for the DS exam, and we're a pretty tight group in the squad. You didn't tell anyone."

"Jenkinson told Reineke. Yeah, his partner," Eve added, and settled on the crappy lot to park. "And Reineke kept it in the vault. That's respect. But this is a surprise thing, not professional. People like being in the know, but so far, nobody's saying they knew."

"We've got Donna." Peabody got out of the car to walk. "She knew about the case, but not what it was for. I believed her on that."

"So did I. But Erin told her she had a backup, and that tells me she pulled somebody in when Donna went to Baltimore—so the day before the party. Or maybe knowing Donna might have to book it to Baltimore, she set up a backup in advance. A just in case."

"It was an important deal for her," Peabody commented. "I can see a just in case."

"Decker strikes me as the most logical, but she'd already put in time and trouble."

"And you—Erin—don't want to pile on. Lopez makes sense. In your report, it has Monday as her day off, so Erin would figure, hey, she's clear."

"On the other hand, why not ask someone outside the tribe, somebody who hasn't had dick to do with showers, wedding prep, drunk girl parties?"

"And that points, possibly, to Greg Barney."

"Shauna's best friend's cohab. Also logical. Lives and works easy walking to the D&D. Actually closer than Lopez. A longer hike to the studio for the case, but not a lot. Or she gets him the case and he stashes it."

"Motive being he still has a thing for Shaunbar."

"It's personal. Whoever killed her," Eve insisted, "it was personal. Sex, love, passion. Personal."

At the street door, Eve started to press the button for A. CARVER, then decided to master in.

"Second floor. Yay."

They trooped up the stairs.

"Even outside the tribe, they're an incestuous group. Shauna's high school guy hooked with her best friend—also from the same school. Lopez having sex with Erin, then with Carver. Barney having drinks with one of the other member's cohabs. The gallery manager's sister buying Erin's art for a client, commissioning the other artist—Lutz—to paint murals."

"Frost doesn't have that river of dead artists behind her, but she did have a couple of shows at the gallery for Anton Carver, four years ago, another two years ago. And Lutz's girlfriend sculpts. Frost carries some of her work."

"Incestuous," Eve repeated, and buzzed at the apartment door on the second floor.

It took a second buzz before Eve heard a very irritated male voice from behind the door.

"The fuck you want?"

"To speak with you, Mr. Carver. Lieutenant Dallas, Detective Peabody, NYPSD."

"You want to talk to me, come back when I've had more than three hours' sleep."

"We're here now. How about you open the door?"

"Unless you've got a warrant, I'm going back to bed. Knock off the buzzing."

"Would you like us to get one? Then have this conversation down at Central? Or would you like to open the door and get it over with quickly?"

"Fuck's sake. Cops are a pain in the ass."

"Yeah, that's why we make the crappy bucks. A woman's dead, Mr. Carver, a woman you knew, one you shared studio space with for more than three years. If you don't open the door, being a pain-in-the-ass cop, I'm going to start wondering why."

Chains rattled, bolts slid, locks thumped.

Chapter Twelve

THE MAN HAD SHOULDERS AS WIDE AS PARK AVENUE, AND STOOD AT about six-five, a tattooed cobra coiled, ready to strike, on his bare chest. Black sleep pants drooped at his hips.

The shoulders, bare chest, and all the rest were damn impressive.

He had brown hair falling in wild and disordered curls to those impressive shoulders. Big hands with a smear of bright yellow paint running down the side of his right index finger.

Hard, angry green eyes snarled out of a striking face that carried a couple days' worth of stubble.

He smelled like a man who needed a shower.

"I already talked to this one right here." He pointed the paint-smeared finger at Peabody. "I got dozens of people who'll tell you I wasn't anywhere near that damn sex club when somebody killed Erin."

"Then you shouldn't have any problem having a quick conversation. Want to have it out here?"

Carver gave a fulminating look at the door across the hall. "Biddy over there's probably got her eye to the Judas hole right now. That's right, you old bat!"

He stepped back, jerked a thumb. "Make it quick. I need my frigging beauty sleep."

He slammed the door behind them.

The apartment looked as though he'd had a weeklong party. Glasses, dishes, take-out bags, a pizza box, clothes all crowded tables, chairs, a lump of a sofa.

And art crowded the walls. Framed, unframed, some as big as the artist, others barely wider than his hand, hung everywhere in a riot of color and shape and texture.

Among them, Eve spotted one of Lopez. She sat on a backward chair wearing only a black top hat and sky-high red heels.

"You want to sit, find a spot on the floor. I'm not moving anything."

"Why don't you tell us the last time you saw or spoke with Erin Albright."

"Can't say. Don't pay attention."

"You helped her and Glenda Frost carry down some paintings."

"Yeah, yeah. Big sale for her. She goes all giddy. Decent work." He shrugged. "Pretty good work. She put in extra time on it, so we were in the studio some nights. She kept her mouth shut. I didn't have a problem with her."

"Did anyone come to see her—or you when you worked those nights?"

"Nobody came in. Nobody comes in when I'm working unless I ask them to."

"Did anyone contact her?"

"Can't say. Can't," he insisted. "When I'm working, I'm working. The rest of them, they'll stop, take tags, make them. I don't. And I don't pay attention unless they get loud with it. Then I tell them to knock it the hell off."

He shrugged. "Roy, he doesn't use the studio more than a few times a week, and he works days when he does. It's down to Donna and me now, so we'll need to get somebody else in there to make rent. Fucking landlord gouges you, but it's a good space."

"You don't seem very broken up about your colleague's murder."

"*Colleague*'s stretching it. We shared space. She was okay. I don't like people. They're not worth the time, the effort. But she was okay. Did decent work, kept to her area. Bubbled. I hate when people bubble, but she stayed in her space."

"She brought in a case."

"A case of what?"

"A black overnight case."

"What she kept in her area's no business of mine."

"I didn't say it was in her area."

He gave her an exasperated look. "If she brought something in, where else was she going to put it?"

"What did you talk about after you helped take the paintings down?"

He dug a hand through his mass of curls. "Jesus. I don't know. It was a major sale, okay? I said like congratulations or something. She came back up to clean her brushes, and she said thanks or whatever, and how she had big plans for the money."

"What plans?"

"I don't know. I didn't ask. Why would I care? Her money, her business."

"How often did ChiChi Lopez come in to see her?"

His gaze drifted to the painting. "Off and on, that I know of. Erin worked evenings mostly, until about a year ago. Worked the sidewalk most days. ChiChi came in now and then when I was in the studio. They had a thing going."

He slid his hands into the pockets of his sleep pants. "You don't have to like people to see what's going on with them. I don't do portraits often, because people, but an artist has to observe, has to see."

"You did ChiChi's portrait."

"Yeah. She's got a body on her, and a damn good face."

"You had a thing with her."

"Way short of a thing, and after she wasn't having one with Erin. You go bouncing on someone your studio mate's bouncing on, it's trouble. It's a bunch of talking and shit. Who needs that?"

"When did you do the portrait?"

"After I bounced on her a time or two."

"A time or two?"

"Three or four—who counts?"

"How did she feel about Erin and Shauna?"

"How the fuck would I—" He broke off, frowned. "Shauna's the redhead, right? The one Erin was going to make it legal with?"

"That's right."

"Great hair. Catches the eye."

"How did ChiChi feel about them, together, about to make it legal?"

"What do I care?"

"She never talked about it to you?"

"I don't know. Maybe. Shit."

He shoved at his hair again. "So she didn't like the redhead, figured she'd just screw with Erin, then dump her ass. Wanted to know how often the redhead came into the studio. I couldn't say, so I bounced on her to shut her up. Who needs the drama?"

Then he frowned. "You think ChiChi killed Erin?"

"Routine questions, Mr. Carver."

"She's got a mean streak in her. You can see it in her eyes, even the way she moves. Get her pissed enough, yeah, she could do it. But if she wanted the thing back with Erin, it makes more sense to do it to the redhead."

Then he shook his head. "Shit. Now I'm awake all the damn way. I might as well go to the studio. Nobody's going to be there. Is that it?"

"One more." Eve pulled out her 'link, brought up Greg Barney's photo. "Did he ever come to the studio?"

"I couldn't say. Not when I was working. Everybody's all-American. Good bone structure. Looks boring. Look, I'm sorry about Erin, right? She was okay. But none of this has anything to do with me."

"I guess it doesn't. Thanks for the time."

"Don't come looking for more of it." He opened the door. "But if you see the redhead, you can tell her I wouldn't mind painting her—from the back. The hair catches the eye."

"Right."

As they started down the steps, Peabody blew out a breath. "*Challenging* fits. He doesn't give a baby rat's ass about anybody."

"Run his alibi again. He's big, strong. Big and strong enough to have done it. I don't see him caring enough to kill anybody, but run it again."

"He liked her a little bit. As much as he seems capable."

"Yeah, a little bit. And he liked bouncing on Lopez. And Lopez bounced on him to try to get what she could out of him on Shauna. He's probably smart enough to know that, but liked the bounce. Was any of Erin's work on his walls, since you have a good eye?"

"My good eye says it was all his. But yeah, he'd know the business of art, he has access and could pick his way through the paintings she has in the studio. When he says her work's decent, that's high praise from him."

"Agreed. And if she told him she had plans for the money, maybe she—what he said—bubbled out the rest. Maybe she pissed him off about something. Maybe ChiChi talked him into helping her. It doesn't click nice and tight, but he's confirmed ChiChi didn't like the idea of Erin and Shauna together. She has a mean streak—I saw that myself. So we'll push some."

At the lot she got back in the car. "And if he never saw Barney in the studio, it doesn't mean Barney wasn't there. During the day, or when

Carver wasn't there. Harder to believe he never went in at least once or twice in the last year."

She pulled out of the lot. "We'll head into Central. I want some thinking time."

"Before thinking time, I need two minutes on the Great House Project. I've held it in," Peabody continued before Eve could respond. "I've shown heroic restraint. Pin-a-medal-on-me restraint."

Since Eve had expected that restraint to break long before now, and had mentally prepared herself for five minutes of house blathering, she shrugged.

"Two minutes. Mark."

"Okay, all the bathrooms are done, and they're all absolutely ult. I'm going to live in a space with three-and-a-half bathrooms. I can't believe it. Most of the lighting's in and just so mag. There's still some painting, then touch-up, and the built-ins in the craft room, and punch-out work, but Roarke says next month. We can live there. In September we'll be in. Mavis and Leonardo's isn't quite as far along, because it's a bigger space. But Roarke still says September."

"Security-wise, it wouldn't hurt for you and McNab to move in first."

"We thought about that, but decided we want to move in all together. Because it's special, for all of us. We can start moving stuff in though. Like Mavis's studio is set, and it's wow, just wow. Same with Leonardo's workspace, Bella's playroom's done, and the nursery is really coming along.

"I packed up and took over all my winter clothes. I have a place to keep off-season clothes!"

Peabody indulged in a quick passenger seat dance.

"And we all have stuff, you know, decor and stuff, stored in the garage just waiting. Plus, a lot of my fabrics, yarn, anything I don't have a project going with."

Peabody sighed as Eve pulled into the garage at Central. "Thanks for the two minutes. I just have one more thing."

"Make it fast." Eve got out of the car.

"It already feels like home. We don't have furniture in or a lot of personal items and the pretty things, but it already feels like home. And still, whenever I walk in, I can't believe it's real. That it's really happening. It's going to be our place. We'll live there and work there and sleep there and fight there, have sex there."

"Pee in your three-and-a-half bathrooms."

"Yes!" Throwing back her head, Peabody laughed. "It's everything I could want, so it doesn't seem really real. I'm going to take such good care of it."

"From what I've seen, you already are."

As the elevator door opened, Peabody's eyes filled.

"Time's up!" Eve stepped in. "Any blubbering, you take the stairs."

"I won't blubber." With some visible effort, Peabody blinked the tears back. "But thanks for saying that."

"Fact's fact. And murder's not only murder, but what we're paid to investigate. Add the fact's a fact that your paycheck's why you have boxes of stuff you bought to put all around the house currently stored in the garage."

"That's fact. And it's all perfect! Opening the boxes is going to be like Christmas squared."

"If you want to keep drawing that paycheck, you're going to sit your ass in your desk chair and see if Carver's alibi is as solid as it looks."

The doors opened; cops piled in.

"Metaphorically, my ass is already there," Peabody said. "I really think the alibi's going to hold."

"Check anyway." As the elevator continued up, Eve rocked back on her heels. "He's the type who'd bash somebody's head in if they pissed him off. In the moment, passion of the moment. It's hard to see him planning out something that required all the time, thought, risk—cold-blooded. But check anyway."

The elevator stopped again, and more cops pushed on. Eve started to push out for the glides when Mira stepped in.

"Hey, Dr. Mira."

"Peabody, good morning. And Eve."

She looked morning fresh among the uniforms in her white sheath with a short, elbow-length grass-green jacket. The sky-high pumps matched the jacket.

"Do you have any time free for a quick consult?" Eve asked. Mira time, she decided, might add more benefit than thinking time.

Mira glanced at her wrist unit. "As a matter of fact, I have some right now. I'll ride up to your office with you. How's the house coming, Peabody?"

"Oh, I was just telling Dallas." And Peabody told Mira, in detail.

Since she'd asked Mira for the consult, Eve didn't feel she could escape to the glides. So suffered the elevator's stops and starts, Peabody's house bubbling, and Mira's enthusiasm for the bubbling until they reached her level.

"Push on the alibi," Eve ordered.

She winced at Jenkinson's tie with a big, bug-eyed mouse the color of a tropical sea nibbling on cheese the color of spring daffodils.

He called out, "Hey, Dr. Mira. Got a second, boss?"

She risked her retinas and stepped to his desk.

"We want to follow up on a lead, on the cold one. It's warming up, but we need to talk to a possible source living in Boston. It's delicate, since she was married to the vic, and later married and divorced his best friend. Since the best friend's our prime suspect, we want to do it in person."

Eve considered the time, the budget. "How warm?"

"Getting pretty warm. I talked to Feeney—not his case, but he was LT back in the day—and he thinks we're on track. Running it through? Guy gets his head bashed in with a fireplace poker. Staged like a break-in, but that was bogus, sloppy. Only other person in the house, the wife. And she claims she had a headache, took some meds and a sleeping pill like nine o'clock. Found him dead downstairs in the morning. Before that, they're out to dinner and have a fight, she tells him she could kill him for that, and sails out.

"We got her going into their place—nice place, Upper East—twenty-thirty. Then the security system goes off-line just after twenty-three hundred. Vic hadn't come home by that time. Left the restaurant about fifteen after she did, and we can't trace his whereabouts."

"Why isn't it the wife?"

"She never broke, LT. Stuck with the story. And the ME said how she'd've needed a stool to have bashed him from the angle he was bashed, and maybe some Zeus to bash with that amount of force. Last thing, the security system went down by remote, outside. And she was in."

"Then why are you going to Boston? And why the best friend?"

"Three years later, she ends up married to the first husband's best friend. No evidence they did the hanky previous to the murder. They divorced like nine years ago, and she moved to Boston—and he got a pretty sweet settlement."

"So you're thinking the vic goes bitching to his best friend after the fight, the best friend decides to kill his ass, jams the security?"

"The best friend installed the system, so he'd have a leg up there. Vic and best pal go to college together, roomies, he's best man at the vic's wedding when the vic marries money. And a looker with money. Vic was pretty liquored up at TOD, so say best pal's 'Hey, I'll get you home,' does the deed, stages the break-in, then he's there to comfort the widow—who about a year after she got to be a widow, lent him money to start his own security business. He lived pretty high on her money. Still is."

Jenkinson lifted his hands. "Nothing to hang on him back when, Dallas, but you look at the pattern since, and it starts to smell. She was married to the guy for six years before she booted him. She may know something she doesn't know she knows. But it's delicate."

Since she trusted Jenkinson's instincts as much as her own, she gave the nod. "Go to Boston."

"Thanks."

Mira joined her in the walk to her office. "By my math, he's working a case that's eighteen years old."

"Guy got his head bashed in and nobody paid for it. That's first. Then? There's a different kind of satisfaction in taking someone down when they're sure they've gotten away with it."

"And you think they will, take the best friend down?"

"I think if Feeney says they're on the right track, he probably caught a whiff of what Jenkinson smells now when the case was fresh, but the investigator couldn't pin it. And what he just ran down for me? Yeah, it smells."

Mira looked toward the board when they stepped into Eve's office.

"Yours is fresh now."

"Yeah, and I can't pin it. Take the desk chair. I've got that tea stuff."

"I wouldn't mind some, along with your rundown."

"The victim, Erin Albright, garroted with piano wire at her pre-wedding girl party. Inside a privacy room, one she'd booked, at the Down and Dirty."

"At Crack's. That's difficult for him." Mira crossed her legs, watched Eve with her quiet blue eyes. "And you, as you were attacked there on the eve of your wedding."

"In the same privacy room. Adds to that." Eve offered the tea, took coffee for herself. "Her fiancée, another female, was also in attendance."

Eve gave the rundown.

"Someone she trusted, yes, almost certainly," Mira concluded. "She's young, in love, excited, and wants to give the woman she loves this gift in that time and place. In the company of friends who, she'd certainly believe, would share that joy in a dream fulfilled."

"Somebody didn't. Not a lot of time to plan if it came up when asked to deliver the case. I think wanting her dead preceded that."

"And the request opened the door," Mira finished. "There's no indication the victim felt threatened previously? Had a problematic relationship with anyone who had access?"

"ChiChi Lopez pops there." Eve tapped the photo on the board. "Sex, a few times, which by all appearances Lopez took more seriously than Albright, who cut off that aspect after she met Hunnicut. Lopez subsequently engaged in a sexual on-and-off relationship with Anton Carver, one of the victim's studio mates. This gives her easy access to the studio, and the case once it was there. She was at the party, could possibly have slipped away, murdered Albright, slipped back. Albright may have asked her to bring the case, which would give her access to the privacy room."

Eyes on the board, Eve drank some coffee. "She's got a mean streak in there, and doesn't much like Hunnicut."

"Personality or jealousy?"

"I'm going to say both. Plus, she got kicked out of bed, replaced. More, they're getting married, and she's supposed to act happy about that. The timing on it's tight but doable.

"Carver." Eve shook her head. "Access to the case, but he's so self-absorbed, why would he care? At the same time, he likes sex with Lopez, he strikes as almost permanently pissed off. His alibi seems solid, but Peabody's checking to make sure it holds. The vic had just sold three paintings—a what's it? Triptych. And another to Lopez—and though it's verified he seemed good with that, maybe he wasn't."

"So back to jealousy."

"Yeah. Jon Rierdon, one of Hunnicut's exes. She broke it off, before

Albright, and he wasn't happy about it. No alibi, but no way he had access to the studio, or that she would have trusted him with the case and delivery. Physically strong enough to have done it, and mutual friends may have mentioned the party—time and place—to him. Motive—back to jealousy and rejection—but I don't see the opportunity."

Now she tapped Greg Barney's ID shot. "Another ex, Hunnicut's, but going back to high school. All indications are they mutually parted at college time. Reconnected later, back in New York, but as friends. And he's cohabbing with Hunnicut's best friend. Also attended the same high school."

"You see trust there."

"I do. Yeah, she'd have trusted him. So opportunity—as he doesn't have a solid alibi. Means, he's physically capable. Motive? Does he still have feelings there? Maybe using her best friend to keep the connection tight, keep his pride. Maybe he didn't realize he had those feelings until she's about to marry somebody else.

"He wanted to make her a sandwich."

"A sandwich?"

"Make her a sandwich, get her tea." After a shrug, Eve stuck her hands in her pockets.

"Taking care of her. But they all wanted to take care of her—of Hunnicut. It's a tight group—Peabody says like a tribe. Everybody loves everybody. That's where Lopez stands out for me, because she doesn't. But Barney was the only male there at the follow-up when they're all there to take care of her."

"You're looking at trust, misplaced in that tight group, and jealousy, a rejection of intimacy and sex."

"That's what I've got. And where these two stand out. Lopez and Barney. Neither fit nice and snug. She doesn't bother to hide the resentment and a kind of disdain for Hunnicut. Previously, Hunnicut only dated men, so what the hell is this? Where did she come from, how does she rate? I'm sexier, got a better body. And she dumps me for her, then asks me for favors? I'm going to fuck it all up."

Eve nodded. "She's got that in her. Screw with me, I screw back harder. That's in there."

"And Greg Barney?"

"We were important in high school. The big-deal couple. Shaunbar. Now I'm hooked up with her best friend. It's not the same, it's not important. So I'm not important. Wants to get that back, and all of a sudden, she's with another woman? What does that make me? The only way to get that back is to take out the obstacle."

Frowning, she thought of Jenkinson's cold case. "And be there to comfort the not-quite-a-widow."

"There would be another obstacle there, wouldn't there? The best friend he's with. A tribe has codes."

"Yeah, it would take some time, some maneuvering. But it's already taken time. Since high school."

Eve tapped both ID shots. "These two stand out, but do they stand out because I don't have anyone else, or because one of them did it?"

"Killing her at that place and time indicates a deep need to punish, ruin, a willingness to take the opportunity and risk in order to prevent the marriage. It may have been the gift—the trip, the dream, that pushed the killer to take that risk."

"That's not much time to plan, to work out the timing, make or access the weapon. But yeah, that fits. They would've looked in the case, and the contents? A serious pisser."

"Misplaced trust, I agree. Someone harboring a resentment kept under control, concealed. And the gift, so very symbolic, ignited that resentment. It's personal," Mira added. "A very personal killing. A marriage thwarted—they will never take vows, never become wives. A honeymoon thwarted—they will never have that dream, one that includes, as honeymoons do, an emphasis on sex and intimacy."

Mira set her mug aside. "Though planned, as you said, for the method, for the timing, it was a moment of passion. Cold and hot blood running at the same time. They're not entitled to this, this won't happen. I won't allow it."

"Because she rejected me? Or because she's in my way?"

Mira smiled, rose. "That, I'm afraid, is for you, but whoever did this is very good at wearing a mask, and perhaps believing they don't wear one at all. They did what needed doing, no more, no less. The wedding—that insult—will now be a memorial. Which they'll no doubt attend. They may even grieve a little, but with no guilt."

"Masks slip."

"They do," Mira agreed. "You'll watch for that, and I believe you'll recognize what you see beneath it when it does. I have to go."

"Thanks for the time."

"If you want to talk any more of it through, just let me know."

Trust and sex, Eve thought as Mira's heels clicked down the hall. She got more coffee, took her desk chair, and studied the board.

Hot and cold blood running together to do what needed doing.

That, she found, was an interesting thought.

She heard Peabody coming, didn't bother to look around. "His alibi held."

"Yeah, no way Carver could've done it."

"No." Not enough cold blood there. "He's not in it. Let's see if we can talk to the two best friends again—DiNuzio for Hunnicut, Decker for Albright. But separately. Let's see if we can get them to come in—separately."

"Divide and conquer?"

Eyes on the board, Eve nodded. "Something like that. Makes it easier to get them to dish some dirt. Give me twenty, then let me know. We'll go to them if necessary, but I'd rather pull them in."

"Lounge or box?"

"Box. Let's keep it official, maybe a little intimidating."

"Got it."

Eve rose to rearrange her board.

Everybody wore a mask sometime, she thought. Even if for politeness, to spare hurt feelings. But put them in the box, push the right buttons, and that mask usually slipped.

You never knew what you might see or hear when it did.

Sitting again, she studied the new configuration of her board, one that put Lopez and Barney at the top, the victim in the center, and Shauna Hunnicut beside her.

Both victims—one with her life taken, one who would live her life with that loss inside her.

From there, other friends radiated with their connections highlighted. A lot of crisscrosses, she noted. Yes, a lot of intersects.

But some of those intersects had only started a year and change before, and others went deeper, longer.

The deepest and longest to Hunnicut: Barney and DiNuzio—as were their links to each other. Add Stillwater, but he was out of it, as was Rierdon.

The deepest and longest to Albright: Frost, Fleschner, Decker, Lopez.

Sitting back, boots up, she closed her eyes and let her mind circle.

Take DiNuzio and Decker first and see what, if anything, came out of it.

Another hit at Stillwater. Longtime booty buddy, and people said things in bed after sex they might not say otherwise.

Then Fleschner—devoted friend, absolute trust, first pick for helping with the surprise. Painting together, sharing that bond. What else might Albright have shared with her, or tossed off as an aside, an observation?

A tight group, sure, but even tight groups had their issues.

Push the right buttons, she thought, and maybe some of those issues spilled out.

She heard Peabody coming back. She opened her eyes, but left her boots up.

"That's your twenty, and DiNuzio's out running errands. She can come by in about thirty. Decker said she can come in when Shauna leaves to go with Erin's parents to make some arrangements. They've decided to have the memorial right away, like tomorrow."

"Quick."

"Yeah, they don't want it any closer to the wedding date. Decker needs a few hours."

"That works." Eve lowered her boots, swiveled around. "Here's how to play it."

Chapter Thirteen

When a case bogged down, backtrack and look for an area to shake something—anything—loose.

To Eve's mind, that began with the victim's tribe, who stood as witnesses and the suspect pool. Becca DiNuzio and Angie Decker, the brides' best friends, topped that list.

People knew things they didn't realize they knew, saw things they didn't register or remember without prompting.

Or, in her cop experience, did things only they truly understood, and hid those acts under the guise of innocence.

Becca DiNuzio spent her high school years outside the shiny circle of Shaunbar. Eve well understood standing outside that sort of circle as a teenager. While she hadn't wanted entrée—anything but, at that point in her life—she also understood many craved it.

Had there been envy, some resentment? Maybe some careless act or a few careless words that had rooted inside?

Now the one outside stood inside. Best friend of one, cohab of the other. But how did it feel to have the man she lived with "hover"—her own word—over his high school love? Had the close relationship of the two halves of Shaunbar stirred up that resentment?

Now Shauna's about to marry, and you're not. She's about to see a dream come true—and you're not.

Again, in her cop experience, people killed for less.

Opportunity? No. Other witness statements put Becca onstage at TOD. But connections crisscrossed. And there was Barney.

Albright asks DiNuzio to deliver the case. DiNuzio conspires with Barney to kill Albright.

In Interview A, Eve sat back.

"Bullshit. Smells like bullshit."

But she'd leave it open as a possibility.

More, she wanted Becca in the box to try to pry something—again, anything—she knew, had seen, sensed she didn't realize or understand.

She wanted a better handle of the group dynamics, the pecking order, the allegiances.

When the door opened, Eve closed the file, rose as Peabody escorted Becca in.

"Thanks for coming in," Eve began.

"No, it's fine. I want to help, and I was out and about anyway." With her strawberry blond hair pulled back in a tail, her blue eyes shadowed, Becca looked around the room. "Is this where you interrogate suspects?"

"Interview. It's an interview room. Please, have a seat. We'll try not to keep you long. We're going to record this."

"It helps keep the details straight," Peabody added. "Why don't I get you something to drink? I don't recommend the coffee."

"Oh, um, can I get a Coke? I could use the boost. None of us have been getting a lot of sleep."

"Sure. Pepsi, Lieutenant?"

"Yeah, thanks." Eve sat again as Peabody went out. "Record on. Dallas,

Lieutenant Eve, in Interview with Becca DiNuzio in regards to the investigation of the murder of Erin Albright."

"It sounds really official."

"It is. We're focused on finding who killed Erin."

With the intimidation factor firmly in place, she switched tactics.

"How is Shauna doing?"

"Actually a little better, I think, because she's mad. The mad's getting her through right now. But I worry about tomorrow. We're having Erin's memorial tomorrow."

"That's quick."

"I know, but Erin's family, and Shauna, too, wanted it as soon as possible. Because the wedding was supposed to be this weekend, and that's . . . It's hard. Erin's mom actually knows someone who works for a memorial service company, so they were able to schedule it right away."

Lifting her hands, she pressed her fingers to her eyes. "It's a lot."

"I understand. Peabody, Detective Delia, entering Interview. Is Shauna still staying at Angie's?"

"Thanks." She took the tube from Peabody, cracked it. "Yes. In fact, she doesn't want to go back to the apartment at all. Ever. Doesn't want the furniture or most of their things. One of my errands was to talk to her landlord to explain she'd sublet the apartment, and furnished, until the lease is up. She's going to find another place."

Eyes full of worry, she turned the tube around and around in her hands.

"I don't know if that's the right thing, but it's what she wants. And she's doing all that, deciding all this, while she's so upset, while she's grieving. I don't know if it's right."

"You're worried about her," Peabody said. "That's natural."

"I—I went by their place and got their wedding dresses." Becca took a deep gulp from the tube. "Took them to a consignment shop."

"That was hard for you," Peabody murmured.

"Oh God, it was awful. We helped them pick out those dresses. Me, Angie, Donna, Jodi. We made a party of it. But I think that was the right thing. I think that was right. How could she bear to look at them again?"

"She's lucky to have a friend like you," Eve put in.

"We're lucky to have each other. She'd be there for me if anything happened to Greg. God, I can't even imagine it, but I know she'd be there for me."

"Longtime friends. But no, not really," Eve corrected. "You weren't friends in high school. Not part of Shauna's—or Greg's—social circle."

"Me?" She laughed a little. "Hard no on that. They were gold, and I was the awkward wheeze who aced every test while always wearing the wrong clothes."

"High school's tough. It's so easy to get wounded at that age, and carry the scars with you after."

"I think I was too oblivious to get any serious wounds." With the faintest smile, she sipped some Coke. "A few scratches maybe. I had a couple friends—fellow wheezes and/or nerds. One joined the navy right after graduation, and I haven't seen her since. The other moved to London for a job about four years ago. We keep in touch when we can."

"But you weren't friends with Shauna or Greg?"

"No. I knew them—everybody did—and Shauna knew me, sort of, because we had a few classes together. We were lab partners on a chemistry assignment once. When we ran into each other again, I have to admit, I was surprised she remembered that, or me."

Smiling, Becca sipped more Coke. "Still a wheeze at the core, I guess, but I dress better now."

"And she and Greg? No rekindling of Shaunbar?"

"No. They'd both moved on. Lucky for me."

She fingered a gold chain with its pair of interlocking hearts around her neck.

"Still, I followed the code."

"The code?"

"You know, about dating a friend's ex. Even though we're talking some years. When Greg asked me out, I mumbled something about checking my schedule and getting back to him, and tagged Shauna to make sure it was okay with her."

"I take it, it was."

"She said she'd hoped we'd give it a try because she'd seen a spark. She's my best friend for a reason, Lieutenant. She's loving, kind. She's no pushover, but I've never known her to deliberately hurt anyone. Even back when she was high school royalty, she never punched down.

"I hate this happened. I can't understand how it could have."

"You're helping us find out how and why and who by being here," Peabody told her. "Shauna was all good with your relationship with Greg. What did you think when you met Erin?"

"Surprised—my first reaction—because this time I saw a spark where I absolutely didn't expect to. I said something to Shauna like did she know Erin had a crush on her, and it looked like she was crushing back. She started to brush it off, you know, then she blushed. The redhead's curse," she said, tapping her own hair. "She said, 'Well, maybe.' They just worked, fit together, made each other happy."

"How did your other mutual friends react, to Erin, to the relationship?" Eve asked.

"I guess there was some surprise, like my initial reaction. And I guess some figured it was just a phase, but that figuring didn't last long because it so clearly wasn't. Greg was a little weirded out."

"Weirded out," Eve prompted.

"Yeah, he's like WTF baffled. But he's a guy, and a guy she'd been with—her first been with—and reacted like a guy. I ran into Marcus—"

"Marcus Stillwater?"

"Yeah. We just ran into each other on the street, grabbed a drink, and he was a little bit baffled, too. Guys." She shrugged.

"Had she and Marcus ever been serious?"

"No, not on either side. Buds. Buds with bennies, but nothing more than that. And it didn't take long for him to make buds—no bennies, but good buds—with Erin. He tossed them a little engagement party at Tippler's. That's a bar some of us go to."

"It sounds like Shauna's circle absorbed Erin into it," Peabody commented.

"Yeah, you could say that. First, I guess, because Shauna loved her, but just as important because everyone just liked her. She was fun, talented, always up, you know? And it was so crystal how much she loved Shauna, how much she wanted to make Shauna happy, make a good life with her."

"You and Angie Decker seem like good friends," Eve said. "Did Erin's circle do the same, absorb Shauna?"

"I think so. I mean Angie, Donna, and Erin went back. I felt comfortable with them right out. I'd say we've gotten to be solid friends with helping plan the wedding, doing the shower, all of that. From what I know now, I'd say Angie and Donna, especially, had some worries Erin would get her heart broken. You know like some of Shauna's friends thinking Shauna was going through a phase. But it didn't last.

"And since you're talking circles, it's like the circle widened, or the circles interlinked. For me, the high school wheeze, having so many women friends is a personal miracle. And we sure as hell need each other right now."

"You're a diverse, interesting group," Eve commented, and opened the file as if referring to it. "We've talked to all of you now. Artists, managers, execs, businesswomen, professional mothers, medicals, chefs, a stripper with a family who owns restaurants and real estate."

She glanced up. "ChiChi Lopez and Erin were involved at one time."

"I'm not sure that's the word for it. Maybe buds with bennies again, at least on Erin's part. And like with Marcus and Shauna, the bennies stopped."

"And did ChiChi accept that as easily as Marcus did?"

Becca shifted, and hesitated for the first time. "I guess so. I don't know her as well as I do Marcus."

Eve offered an easy smile. "You're not as friendly."

"Not really. I mean, we get along fine. A bunch of us went to see her perform, and wow, that was an eye-opener." She popped her eyes wide to demonstrate. "I don't mean just the naked part, but she's got some moves."

Eve waited a beat. "But?"

"Okay, well, she's a little bit mean. Got a bite to her, and I try to avoid getting bitten, so we're not as friendly."

"Did she ever bite Shauna?" Peabody wondered.

"A few nips. Shauna let it go. I mean, she told me, and Shauna can bite back when she needs to. To tell the truth, I think ChiChi was a little jealous, and doesn't like Shauna very much. Or me, either."

She shrugged at that.

"I guess I don't know if she likes anybody much except Erin. Like Donna told me ChiChi said to her if she was going to transition, she should've paid for better boobs. That's just mean and—and ignorant. Donna said she said it like a joke, but it stung."

"But Erin trusted her."

"Sure. I don't think they were as tight as they were before, but I can't say for sure, since I didn't know them when they were, you know, buds with bennies. But friends were important to Erin—that's something else she and Shauna had in common. They kept their friends, they valued their friends."

"Becca, it's probable someone they considered a friend did this."

"I can't believe that. I guess I don't want to."

"When you were onstage with Shauna, when it was close to midnight and you were up there, did you notice anyone who wasn't in the club? See anyone slip out, like to use the bathroom?"

"I think about it and think about it. Every time I close my eyes I go right back there. I'd had a lot to drink, and believe me, I'd never pictured myself dancing half-naked in a sex club. It's just a blur."

"Did ChiChi get onstage?"

"No." Becca rolled her eyes. "A few people said she should. You know, like 'Show us how it's done!' But she just said how she got paid for that. I don't know if she even danced much on the floor. Dressed and everything, but I didn't really pay attention or hang out with her."

"Who did? Hang out with her?"

"Erin, I guess. Angie some. Oh wait, she did dance some. With that guy—the one who came in. Tall, blond, built. Sexy dance, but that was earlier. I didn't see Erin leave. I just didn't see."

She glanced at her wrist unit. "I'm really sorry, but I need to go. I still have some things to get done."

"We appreciate you coming in, talking to us."

"I don't know how it helps, but I hope it does. I don't want to believe it was one of us, but if it was, I want you to take them down."

Peabody rose as she did. "I'll walk you out."

"Interview end," Eve said, and opened the file to make notes.

Moments later, Peabody came back, sat. "We're not thinking she had any part of this."

"No. I played with the idea she held some resentment from high school, it sparked up when Shauna's getting married, getting everything she wants. But it doesn't hold. Add physically, she couldn't have pulled it off, and I don't see her conspiring with her cohab on it. Or with Lopez. She clearly doesn't like Lopez. Tried to, but doesn't."

"That was my take. But we got a couple things we didn't have."

"Yeah, Barney's WTF reaction. A different tone from Stillwater's, whether she saw it that way or not. The way she said it, Barney got a little pissy, Stillwater was surprised. And she put it down to: Guys."

"Some people try to see the best in people."

"Yeah, what's wrong with them?" At Peabody's laugh, Eve shook her head. "She's one of them. But she doesn't like Lopez."

"Didn't want to dis her," Peabody observed. "But we're cops, it's murder, and she felt like she had to say what she knew or felt. Mean streak, doesn't like Shauna, jealous. Lopez took some shots there."

"Yeah. Also took at least that one at Donna, which shows pattern rather than focus. We'll run Decker through it, see what meshes, what doesn't."

"We've got some time before she gets here. I'm going to grab something from Vending."

"Fine."

"Or." Peabody stretched the word out. "We could both get something from your AutoChef and not risk ptomaine."

"Fine. Bring it in here."

"Great. What do you want?"

"Whatever."

Peabody let out a wistful sigh. "I wish I could think whatever about food. My pants wouldn't just get loose, they'd fall off."

"Then, as you tripped over them and bashed your face, I'd have to arrest you for indecent exposure. After I took a vid for the bullpen's entertainment."

"I now see the wisdom in my non-whatever attitude regarding food. We'll have some pasta salad."

"How do you know my AC stocks pasta salad?"

"Due to my wise attitude toward food."

"Okay, grab the candy bar while you're at it."

"You have candy in the AC? What kind?"

Eve gave her a long look. "Shouldn't you know that?"

"I regret I did not, but I'm being careful about candy because loose pants."

"Never mind the candy."

Eve went back to her notes, but paused when Peabody went out.

Her partner could be the dreaded Candy Thief, but . . . she was being careful about candy these days. Didn't mean she didn't steal the candy bar Eve hid, then reward herself for loose pants.

Right now, there was an empty candy wrapper taped behind the drawing Nixie had given her. A deliberate smack at said Candy Thief.

And the emergency chocolate bar resided at the back of her bottom desk drawer, which took a tool and some work to remove completely.

She should check on that, just in case.

By the time Peabody came back with two servings of pasta salad, Eve was again deep in her notes.

"Really pretty pasta salad. Colorful."

Eve noted the color came not only from varicolored pasta, but also from vegetables.

Well, she'd said whatever, and she got it.

"The motive's not money," she began, and picked up her fork. "It's not going to be some deep secret, previous crime. It's sex, passion, jealousy, maybe ego. Some combination of those. Maybe all of them."

"If that's right, you could say killing Erin made Shauna the prize."

"Or killing Erin because you couldn't have her, now no one can."

Peabody ate, nodded. "Mean streak. Lopez."

"Or," Eve continued, "kill Erin because she took away what you wanted."

"Torch burning? Barney. I'd lean more there if he wasn't living with Becca DiNuzio."

Eve stabbed some pasta. "People get away with affairs right under the noses of spouses, cohabs, lovers. All the damn time. And this isn't even that."

"Unless maybe Shauna slipped? Maybe had one more round with the high school hero. Regrets it, tells no one. 'A terrible mistake,' she tells Barney. 'Never going to happen again.'"

"'I don't love you. I don't want you. I love Erin, and we've both be-trayed Becca.' He agrees, at least on the surface, accepts. But he believes if Erin's out of the picture, he can have her again. Maybe all the way, maybe on the side."

"If she did it once"—Peabody waved her fork—"she'll do it again."

"You can play it with Lopez, too. She comes to the studio, Erin slips, and the same basic scenario, without the best friend added on."

"It doesn't sound like what we know of either one of them, but people slip, people cheat. And if it happened early in their relationship, it's easy to buy. Like for Shauna, is Erin really just a phase? With Erin, is Shauna really what I want?"

Sitting back, Eve thought it through.

"Mira thinks it's possible the Maui trip was the trigger. The resent-ment, jealousy, even the thought of eliminating Erin was there, but the trip pushed the last button."

"Why?"

"Honeymoon. Not just the big dream, but honeymoon. Sex again."

Peabody pointed. "Not just sex, but dream sex. Sex in Hawaii. Ro-mance, blue water, moonlit walks on the beach."

Eve pointed back. "Dream sex. That's good. The killer knows they'll bang like hammers on their wedding night, but now? They'll do it in Maui. Dream sex, all romantic, passionate. Worse, Erin asks them to help make it happen, and in a big way. Asks close to the last minute because her first choice is stuck in Baltimore."

"She thinks she can take me for granted?" Peabody put on her mean face. "That bitch."

"It could play. Now, who has a garrote lying around, or the ability to put one together fast?"

"I'd go with the first. Already has it."

"Because they hope to find a way to use it, kill Erin, and not get caught for it."

"And she gives them the way."

Eve tolerated a small bit of broccoli with her pasta. "I come right back to the top two on the list, and it bugs the shit out of me they both work."

"What if they both work because they worked together?"

"I'm playing with that. She gets the case there, and gives him the swipe. That way, she's in the club at TOD, visible. And he waits inside the room."

"Hitch."

"Yeah, I know the hitches, but lay them out."

"Why would they trust each other? They're in separate circles, inter-linking but separate. If you're going to conspire to kill, you need more than motivation. You have to trust each other not to screw it up, or roll."

"True, but why do we so often catch people who conspire to murder?"

"Because they screw up or roll. But Becca's hooked with Barney, and doesn't have much to do with Lopez. They'd have to know each other enough to know they want the same thing. Different reasons maybe, but the same thing."

"Another hitch, unless we find he's spent some time in her club."

"And she could've vamped him. Hey." Inspired, Peabody waved her fork. "She could've vamped him because, first, good-looking guy, and because she knows his history with Shauna. Maybe they hatch it all to-gether, or she says if you don't do this—and you know you want to—I'll tell Becca you're having an affair with me."

"That's not bad. But the hatching had to happen fast, and be well timed and executed. That's where it stops me."

"Erin already had backup—that's what she told Donna. So that means more time."

"And that's where it opens for me, a little. Together or separately, they top the list. Rierdon's the only other one who comes close, and not close enough. No reason for Erin to have trusted him, or asked him to help her out. No reason for him to hook up with Barney on it, or Lopez if Erin tapped either of them."

"Plus, he's not as connected, and hasn't been since Shauna broke things off. Erin's not the reason she did. And he just didn't strike me, Dallas."

"They don't always," Eve muttered. "But he's not striking me, either. It's too personal for someone she dated for a few months a few years ago. He'd have pushed on her before, and she said he didn't."

She shoved the bowl aside. "We've got theories, angles, speculation. And nothing solid. We need some heat."

"Decker should be here soon. Maybe we'll get some."

Eve rose to pace. "The straight best friend, long-standing. Well-off enough to buy art, know its value. Dead artist value, but that angle's soft, and it just gets softer. It's not about money. Maybe money's an added benefit, but it's not the prime motive."

She grabbed her warming tube of Pepsi, drank as she paced.

"She's not in love with Erin, or Shauna. Was clearly seen in the club at the time of the attack. There's no motive there, and though I still wonder why Erin didn't ask her to help her out with the surprise, no opportunity. She's fit enough, tall enough to have done it, but that's not enough. She stays low on the list."

"Like Becca, she might give us a couple things we don't have, or confirm some of those speculations."

"Gotta try it. Most probable she knew Erin better than anyone. Given the length of the friendship, probably better and in more detail than Shauna. They only had a year."

"An intimate year," Peabody pointed out.

"Yeah, but it takes time for the rules to kick in, for people to see just who they're with, for the stories to come out."

"I guess McNab and I are still finding stuff out about each other. Not like secrets, just stuff, little bits of history and like that."

Still pacing, Eve rolled the empty tube.

"Yeah, it takes time, and they only had a year. Decker was there longer, and take out the sex, it removes a complication."

And that motive, Eve thought.

"Plus, I'm curious what she'll say about Barney and Lopez when it's just us, in here, no friends to hear her thoughts or feelings."

"She comes off a little more reserved in that area than Becca."

"Yeah, she does. We'll handle that. Let's clean this place up and get ready."

Chapter Fourteen

WHEN PEABODY ESCORTED ANGIE INTO INTERVIEW, EVE NOTED NOT only signs of fatigue but recent weeping. Careful makeup did a good job disguising both, but still they showed.

"Thanks for coming in," Eve began. "I know this is a difficult time. Please, have a seat."

Like Becca, Angie looked warily around the room. She sat, and when she spoke, even her voice sounded exhausted. "Am I a suspect?"

"No, you're not."

"Can I get you something to drink?" Peabody offered.

"Water. Just some water, thanks. Shauna's with Erin's family, finalizing some arrangements for tomorrow. I realized I'd felt I had to hold up for her, and it was the first time I'd been really alone since . . . since. So I fell to pieces. She was my closest friend. She was my sister. She was the one person who knew me all the way through and loved me anyway. And she's gone. She's gone."

202 J. D. Robb

Angie closed her eyes on tears that swirled in them. "So I was alone, and I fell to pieces."

Peabody laid a hand on her shoulder. "You needed to. I'll get your water. Lieutenant?"

"The same, thanks. Angie," she continued when Peabody stepped out, "we're doing everything we can to find the person responsible."

"I have to believe you are. I don't think I could stand it if I didn't."

"You can help us."

"I don't know how, but I'll try. Becca tagged me after you talked to her. She said you had a lot of questions, and she tried to answer. But she didn't think she helped."

"Every answer to every question helps."

Angie's eyes cleared as she looked at Eve. "I hadn't thought of that. I hadn't thought of it that way. Ask me anything."

"We're going to record this," Eve told her as Peabody came in with tubes of water. "Record on. Dallas, Lieutenant Eve, and Peabody, Detective Delia, in Interview with Angie Decker regarding the investigation into the murder of Erin Albright."

Angie shuddered once. "God, hearing it like that. Just hearing it. 'The murder of Erin Albright.'"

She let out a long breath. "Ask me anything," she repeated.

"Again, Angie, thanks for coming in. You helped plan the party at the Down and Dirty."

"Yes. Becca and I—Becca DiNuzio and I are—were going to stand up for Erin and Shauna at the wedding. We decided, when they asked us, we'd plan out the events together. The bridal shop trip, the bridal shower, the pre-wedding bash. Help with the invitations and so on."

"You and Erin were very close friends, but she didn't tell you about the trip to Maui?"

"No." After cracking the tube, Angie drank. "Erin loved surprises.

She loved the big reveal. I knew how much she'd wished she could take Shauna to Hawaii, since it was Shauna's dream honeymoon. But Shauna's very practical and Erin tries to be. Mostly succeeds, so they agreed they'd put it off, save until they could do it right. I had no idea she'd sold enough paintings to pull it off, or that she'd booked the trip."

Visibly, Angie struggled back more tears.

"She would have wanted to surprise me, too. Well, all of us. Shauna at the center, and the rest of us surrounding her. That's so Erin. The costume? God, that was Erin, too. Do it large or forget about it, make it fun or what's the point?"

She drank again.

"Do you know just one more sorrow in all this? That trip? Shauna's had that dream since she was a little girl. Now she'll never be able to go. It would break her heart all over again to go. So that dream's dead, too. Maybe that's a small, silly thing, but—"

"No, it's not," Peabody said. "It's not small or silly."

"She's holding up right now. She's so angry, and that's helping her hold up. I need to find my anger again, but right now? I'm too fucking tired to be angry."

"Shauna's staying with you."

"She doesn't want to go back to their apartment. I can't blame her, as I'm going to have a hard time going there myself. But I want to help Erin's family get her things. Becca's gotten some of Shauna's. Shauna's going to sublet it, look for another place. She can stay with me until."

"That's generous. You've only known her about a year."

"Erin loved her," Angie said simply. "And she loved Erin. She needs a safe place, and I have the room. Erin would expect it of me."

"Becca doesn't have the room?"

"Becca and Greg? No, not really. They'd squeeze her in, absolutely they'd do that. But I have the room—a dedicated guest room, and two baths. Shauna and I have gotten to be good friends over the last year or so, with the foundation we both loved Erin."

"Why do you think Erin asked Donna to bring the case to the D&D, and not you?"

"There's a question I've asked myself over and over since we found out about the case, and I realized you think whoever did bring it killed her. If she'd have asked me . . ."

Angie shook her head. "No point going there. I think she asked Donna because they saw each other nearly every day, shared the studio space, and that's where Erin brought the case so Shauna didn't stumble over the surprise. And Donna thought she had a few days after the wedding before her sister had the baby."

"Seems like babies come when they want to," Peabody commented.

"Yeah." As Becca had, Angie turned the tube around and around. "Donna started worrying there when her sister let her know at the last visit, the midwife said it could be any day."

"Oh?" This was fresh, Eve thought. "When was that?"

"I . . . I'm not sure. No, wait. It had to be last Friday. I happened to talk to Donna right after she got the news from her sister. I remember because she was so excited about the baby, but really worried about the party, and said she had to let Erin know."

Angie lifted her hands. "At the time I thought she overreacted—and she can do that," Angie added with a smile. "But I didn't know she was supposed to bring the overnight case in for Erin."

"You don't seem surprised or shaken by the fact we believe one of your group killed Erin."

Angie met Eve's gaze levelly. "I suppose because I have to believe that, too. At first I had to think it was someone else, in the club, working at the club. But what sense is there in that? Someone gets in that room with her, kills her that way, and for what? The hardly anything she had of value? Some stranger just happens to get into that room when she's in there, or going in?"

"Yet your group agreed to go to the restroom in pairs or groups," Peabody pointed out.

"So nobody'd get hit on, or cornered. But that's not what happened to Erin. You didn't say anything about her trying to fight off something like that."

"You've thought about this a lot," Eve said.

"I have. I knew her as through and through as she knew me. She wouldn't have let anyone in that room she didn't know. If someone pushed their way in, she'd have fought or tried to. So it had to be someone she knew, and she didn't get a chance to fight."

Angie pressed her lips together, and her voice went raw. "She didn't have a chance. That's so much worse than a stranger, so much worse. And I want you to *bury* them."

She shuddered again, then her shoulders stilled, straightened. "And there it is. There's the anger. Welcome back."

"Who?"

Angie's eyes, dark and hot now, met Eve's. "If I had even the faintest glimmer of an idea, I'd tell you. She was—she was my person, Lieutenant. The person who meant more to me than anyone in the world."

"All right. Who do you think she would have asked after Donna went to Baltimore—or maybe after Donna let her know she might have to go and miss the party?"

"I'm stuck there, too. I think she didn't ask me or Becca—and those would be my first guesses—because she didn't want to load on. And in Becca's case, maybe because Becca might slip—not tell Shauna, but tell me because we were planning it all, or say something to Greg the way you do with a partner. Becca would be the first to tell you she's not always an impenetrable vault with secrets and surprises. But any of us, really."

"All right, try this. Who wouldn't she ask—most likely," Eve added.

"Oh, well. Glenda, because Glenda would be in Europe. Probably not Jodi, as Jodi's so damn busy. Wanda's unlikely because also busy. Kaydee because of just what happened—ER doctors have to handle emergencies."

She named a few more. Moved across town, crazy workload, not altogether reliable.

"I don't know all of Shauna's friends well enough to say either way. Erin got to know some of them better than I did over the past year."

"You've still formed a pretty tight group," Peabody commented.

"Yes, we have. I like these women, and it's hard to think one of them did this."

"Wanda and Erin had a sexual relationship."

"They did, briefly and nothing serious on either side. And honestly, I can't see Erin asking her for something like this when she knows Wanda's crowded schedule."

"She also had a sexual relationship with ChiChi Lopez."

"Yes." Angie drank more water. "Yes, she did. Erin certainly wasn't serious about it. I've never known her to be really serious before Shauna."

"Was ChiChi serious?"

Angie set down the tube, folded her hands together on the table. "It's hard to say what ChiChi takes seriously. You want to know if Erin might have asked her, and I suppose it's possible."

"They maintained a friendship?"

"Yes."

"Do you consider Lopez a friend?"

"Erin did." Angie unclasped her hands. "ChiChi is . . . can be difficult. We have certain things in common. We both grew up with certain advantages—a successful family who provided emotional and financial safety nets. ChiChi has a very loving relationship with her family, as I do with mine. She has a solid work ethic, and I like to think I do as well."

Eve smiled. "But?"

"All right, every answer to every question helps. ChiChi's either wired to or really just enjoys shooting out sharp little arrows. She's judgmental, and can be harsh—deliberately harsh. She'd sometimes take shots at Donna because Donna and Erin were close. Donna wouldn't tell Erin."

"But she'd tell you?"

"She would, because ChiChi often took shots at me for the same reason. I could and did ignore them. Donna's more tender."

"So, territorial."

"Yes, that's a good term. And ego. 'I need to be the center of your world. Look at me.'"

"She couldn't have been thrilled about Shauna."

"No. She put on a good act, but no. At the same time, she had strong, proprietary feelings for Erin. I sincerely can't see her hurting Erin like this. If it had been Shauna in that room? I could see it—what's it called? Crime of passion. I could see her hurting Shauna."

"Did you see her, or anyone, slip out of the room between eleven-thirty and eleven-forty-five?"

"Something else I've thought about countless times. I just didn't notice. Becca and Shauna were putting on a hell of a show. Jodi was up there, at least for a while, and a few others. But it was Becca and Shauna. So out of character for both of them, so just more entertaining. I was in the crowd of us, sort of half dancing, but mostly watching them and making noise. I figured Erin was, too."

She looked down at the table. "I didn't really think about it, and was congratulating myself for having helped plan the party that would be the queen of parties for months."

"How about people outside the group of women she might have asked?"

"Oh." Frowning, Angie narrowed her eyes. "I didn't think of that. I don't see her asking her other studio mates. Anton's a bit of a prick, and Roy's rarely around. She—we, really—got to be good friends with Marcus—Marcus Stillwater. He loves Shauna, and he clearly came to love

Erin. Shauna and Marcus go back. I could see her asking him, but again, sincerely, can't see him hurting Erin. Or anyone."

She paused a moment, rubbed her temple as she thought.

"There's their across-the-hall neighbors. The—God, need a second. Burgers. Yeah, the Burgers. Erin gave their kid a few art lessons—gratis. But I don't really see that, and why would either of them kill her? There's Clint—he's with Jodi, and Erin knew him better than I did, but I can't see why she'd ask him. And there's Greg—you met him. Becca's guy—who dated Shauna back in high school. Like Marcus, I can see Erin asking him, but can't see him hurting her."

"Becca mentioned both Marcus and Greg were surprised when Shauna and Erin got together."

"Oh? Well, I'm not surprised they were surprised. I was, too. But more worried, actually. That Erin would get her heart broken. Not that Shauna would do that deliberately, but that Erin was more of a fling for her.

"I realized differently pretty quick. So did everyone."

"You never had a sexual or romantic relationship with Erin?"

"No. I like men for that."

"So did Shauna."

Angie let out a half laugh. "That's true. I'll say Erin and I never had that feeling between us—and a friendship that was so strong. I haven't met a woman who's brought me that feeling. That would be one of the reasons I worried this was a fling for Shauna."

"Would you say there are any of those feelings with either Marcus or Greg for Shauna?"

"Marcus and Shauna—that was never romance. It was no-strings, no-worries friend sex. I'd like to find a friend like that myself. Greg's got Becca, and from my viewpoint, they really work. I can't imagine him still having feelings like that for Shauna. It's more brotherly, from what I see. Sort of big brother, though they're the same age."

"Becca mentioned you all went to see Lopez perform at her club."

"Yeah, we did, last fall maybe. I think about then."

"How many of these men were in that group?"

"Oh, well, let me think. Not Marcus. Greg was, and Jodi's guy, and a few others who are in relationships."

She shut her eyes, thought, then named four other men.

"I think that's it."

"Did Lopez join the group after her performance?"

"For a while—she had another couple acts, but she came out awhile. I remember somebody said something about how she was mega flexible, and right in front of Shauna, she rubbed against Erin and said how Erin always liked that about her."

Scowling, Angie nudged the tube of water aside. "It was crude and uncalled for. But Shauna? She just laughed, then bent her leg up behind her—grabbed her ankle and bent her leg up over her head. And said like 'Me, too.'"

The scowl turned into a smile. "I fell in love with her for that. I liked she set a tone. 'You don't bother me, sister.' And I'm afraid I'm giving you the wrong impression, because ChiChi often rubs me wrong. It's a personality thing. But again, there's no way I can see her hurting Erin. As much as she's capable, she loves Erin. Loved her."

"Understood. You've been helpful, Angie. We appreciate you coming in, taking the time."

"I feel . . . After saying all this, talking like this, it had to be a stranger after all. It doesn't make sense. But neither does it being one of us." She sighed. "And there goes the anger."

"Save it for when we find who killed her. Detective Peabody and I will attend the memorial tomorrow if at all possible."

"That would be good. I think it would be good for everyone to see you there, to know it matters—Erin matters—to you."

"She does. Interview end. Detective Peabody will show you out."

As before, Eve stayed where she was, added to her notes. Then rose when Peabody came back.

"Let's log and file the recordings."

"Sometimes you're too close to see."

"Yeah," Eve agreed. "Neither of them can see one of them putting that wire around Erin Albright's neck. Neither of them much like Lopez—personality thing—but they can't see her doing it."

"You do?"

"I can see it. Doesn't mean she did it, but I can see it. And she slides into Mira's quick profile neat enough. We're going to do a run on all the names she gave us—the men who went with the group to the club. That connects to Lopez."

As they started out, Peabody shook her head. "That snark at the club—about Erin liking the flexible? Nasty, and designed to cut Shauna, to piss her off not just at Lopez but at Erin."

"Didn't work."

"Probably did a little, but she deflected. I haven't even met Lopez yet, and I already don't like her much."

"You should have a chance tomorrow. She'll probably be there. And whether or not it's her, the killer's likely to be there."

She checked the time. "Look, I'll do the runs, write this up. You go by the shoe store. Let's see if Lopez ever came in—or anyone else in the group—and gave Shauna any trouble. I can't see her not telling Becca if so, but maybe not."

"You're sending me to a shoe store! Solo!"

"I'm saving myself the aggravation of watching you drool on shoes before I have to kick my own footwear up your ass."

"I'll take care of the recordings, and maybe see how close McNab is to closing down. He doesn't mind when I drool."

"Just get it done. I think we have enough to justify another conversation with Lopez. After the memorial. Before, I think we talk to Stillwater again, and to Barney."

"The first as a wit—observations, impressions—the second as suspect?"

"In that order, yeah."

Eve turned into her office. With coffee, she sat first to write up the report—and decided what the hell, to copy Mira.

If/when you have a chance, I'd like your opinion. Both recordings are logged and filed. The victim's memorial is tomorrow, and I expect to have more observations and conduct more interviews.

Appreciate any time you have. Dallas

Fishing, Eve thought as she started the runs. But if she put any credence in Angie's opinion of who Erin might have asked—and she did—the pool had shrunk somewhat.

She had a friendship like theirs—the through and through sort. Mavis could have answered that question on the mark. Peabody, too, she decided. Partnership, when it worked, held intimacy.

God knew Roarke had that through and through, and still there were things Mavis knew he didn't. Not secrets, but as Peabody had said, just things from before that hadn't come up.

She remembered asking him once why he didn't have a big-ass boat, since he had every-damn-thing. And he'd told her about a storm at sea during his smuggling days.

She hadn't known because it had never come up before.

But credence or not, she did the runs, as it was possible the killer had a partner.

Once done, she decided to either close that door or open it a crack wider and contacted all four.

Routine inquiry, blah blah.

Two served as each other's alibi. Poker game, monthly deal—with three others. Broke up at midnight.

Easily checked and verified, so she did.

The third worked the night shift as an MT—also easily checked and verified.

The last, no longer with the woman he'd been with at the club, claimed to be home, in bed. But not alone.

Eve checked and verified.

Smaller pool, Eve thought as she rose. Her gut told her Lopez and Barney remained most likely. And so had Angie Decker's take on her friend.

She headed down to the garage and decided she'd swing by the victim's apartment, see if she could talk to those neighbors. Impressions again of who visited, how often.

She didn't have far to go, but the traffic made it feel a lot farther. She found parking, considered it a bonus, and walked through the hot August evening toward the apartment building.

A lot of sweaty people had ended their workday, headed for happy hour or home, an after-work appointment, an early vid with a friend. She hoped the Burgers had ended their workday and chosen home.

She mastered into the building and headed up.

Plenty in the building, from the sound of it, had chosen home. No baby screaming this time, but an older kid's maniacal laughter that reminded her of Bella.

And reminded her about the damn chair she had to make sure about before Mavis's second kid came along.

When the hell was that, and how could she get out of witnessing another birth and having those images burned freshly in her brain?

"Don't think about it," she muttered, and came out on the fourth floor.

Since she heard another kid proclaiming loudly that she pooped in the toilet, which was followed by adult cheers and applause, she figured her luck was in.

The woman who answered the buzz had short blond hair, wore a black linen dress that had wilted some, and had bare feet. Eve could smell whatever was for dinner—and decided Chinese takeout.

"Can I help you?"

Eve held up her badge; before she could speak, the woman glanced back.

"Allen, I need to step into the hall with the p-o-l-i-c-e." She eased the door shut but for a crack. "This is about Erin. We're sick about it. I don't want our daughters to hear yet. They're too young."

"Daddy, wipe my butt!"

"Potty training," Ms. Burger said. "She's very proud. So are we."

"Okay."

"It's just awful. She was a sweetheart. Both of them. Erin gave Trixie art lessons." Burger smiled. "Our older girl. She's six. It was so sweet of Erin to take the time."

"Since you live across the hall, you might have noticed visitors."

"Some, sure. They had a lot of friends. No loud parties, which we appreciate. I mean we could hear some—the soundproofing doesn't exist here—but they weren't obnoxious."

"This is just a routine inquiry. Can I show you some photos? Just to get a sense who visited, how often?"

"Sure. Oh yes." Burger studied Angie's ID shot. "What's her name? Andi—no, Angie. Angie and the other—pretty hair. Becca! They were here a lot, especially in the last few months. Helping with the wedding."

She stopped, teared up a little. "Oh, it's so awful. I haven't seen Shauna since it happened, but I just want to hug her. Becca's been by—she told me what happened—to get some of her things. And the—God—their wedding dresses."

"Yes. How about this one?"

Burger studied Lopez. "I think so, yes. Not like the other two. But I re-member riding up on the elevator with her." She shrugged. "A little snooty, which Erin and Shauna aren't."

Eve went through the photos, got positives, negatives, then brought up Barney's.

"Sure, sure. Sometimes with the one with the pretty hair—Becca. I think they're together. Sometimes by himself. Sharp dresser, that one. I remember. I rode up with him and Shauna just last week, I think."

"The two of them?"

"Yes. I guess we all got off work at about the same time. Her work's not far from here. I guess it was about twenty minutes later when they went out again. I rode down with them—she'd changed her clothes. It was my turn to do the laundry, so I ended up riding down with them after I changed mine. We laughed about it.

"I was heading down to the laundry, and they were heading out to meet their cohabs for dinner. I said I'd rather go to dinner with them, something like that. Seems to me he'd walk home with her now and then. I think Erin said they'd been friends since high school. That's sweet."

"Yeah, well, thanks. I'm sorry to interrupt your evening."

"It's no problem at all. I really liked her. Both of them. Just the kind of neighbors you want. I hope you find who did this."

Eve waited until she'd gone in, then turned to look across the hall. She'd heard movement in there, and debated going in or just waiting.

She didn't have to decide, as the door opened.

Greg Barney stepped out carrying a large, lidded box.

He jolted, blinked, then let out a breath. "Jesus, you startled me. Did you need to go inside again? We thought you were done, but I can let you in."

"That's all right, just a routine check on my way home. What's in the box?"

"Oh, stuff from the friggie, the AC. Becca thought of it—she thinks of things. Since Shauna doesn't want to come back, Becca said we should clear those out. Not that much in there, really."

He glanced back. "It doesn't even feel like their place anymore. It already feels empty, even though the furniture's there, and dishes and all that. Becca's been coming by to get things for Shauna. And Angie's going to help Erin's family get her things."

He looked back at Eve. "The memorial's tomorrow."

"Yes, I know. Shauna's lucky to have friends who'd do this sort of thing for her."

"It's nothing. A quick stop after work. She doesn't even want this." He shifted the box. "Becca said just take it to our place. We can do the food bank thing or something. It's not that much."

He shifted his feet, shifted the box.

"But, um, there's some perishables from the friggie, so—"

"I'll ride down with you."

And wished she'd had a warrant or probable cause to look in the damn box.

"How's Shauna doing?" she asked as they waited for the elevator.

"She's fragile right now, maybe still in shock. Hardly eating, not really sleeping. But she's stronger than people think."

"People?"

"She's little, you know. Petite." He got in the elevator car, pressed for the lobby. "So people think she's delicate. She's going through a lot right now, but she'll be okay."

"You're there to help her."

"Absolutely. Are you making any progress? I know it hasn't been very long."

"I think so, yes. We're following leads."

"That's good news." He shifted the box again. "It had to be somebody in the club, some lowlife, right? I wish they hadn't gone to a place like that. A group of women going to a place like that. I don't mean to be critical, but it just seems like a bad choice. And it was, as it turns out. It was."

He waited for Eve to step out in the lobby, then tried to juggle the box to get the door.

"I've got it."

"Thanks. Not heavy, but awkward. I guess you deal with this all the time. I mean, it's a job. For us, it's trauma, tragedy. I hope you find that lowlife so Shauna can start putting this behind her. Maybe somebody who works there. That seems the most logical, doesn't it? Somebody who works in a place like that."

"We're looking at all possibilities. Do you need a ride? I'm parked right down there."

"Oh, no, thanks. Not going far, and it's really not heavy. Have a good evening."

She watched him walk away.

The helpful friend, she thought. The very nervous helpful friend trying to dig out information on the investigation.

And he had something in that damn box that wasn't out of the AC or friggie.

Something to think about.

And since the shoe place was only a handful of blocks, she'd think about it and walk down there.

Chapter Fifteen

Before she reached the intersection, her 'link signaled. She saw Roarke on the display, then his face on-screen. Those brilliant blue eyes smiled at her.

"Lieutenant."

"Civilian."

"Out and about again, are you? As I am. A meeting downtown that ran over. Where might you be?"

"Heading to a shoe store downtown."

"Before I have a slight stroke due to shock, I'll assume this is field-work."

"Your brain's safe. I had another stop in the area." She joined the river of pedestrians crossing at the Walk signal. "Peabody's probably already there, but I'm this close anyway now."

"Give me the address. I'll meet you and catch a ride home."

She gave it to him. "Should be a quick stop."

"I'll be quick as well, as I'm also close."

She slid the 'link back in her pocket, discovered her sunshades, and put them on. On her right, a maxibus wheezed its way to a stop. People flooded off like refugees.

A trio of teenage boys, all in identical black baggies, strutted out of the flood and into a gaming store.

A woman with blond hair down to her ass sashayed—the only word for it. She wore purple micro shorts, a matching tank, and sandals with a three-inch platform that showed off purple toenails.

She carried a big flowered bag on her shoulder. A tiny, pointy-eared dog peeked out of it and goggled at Eve.

Thinking of Galahad, she gave the purse-dog a wide berth.

Two women headed up the block, both of them hauling shopping bags with the Fancy Feet logo. As they passed her, she heard one of them say:

"There's nothing like hitting an end-of-season sale!"

Why were there seasons for sales? Eve wondered. If the season was ending, did you have to wait until the next year to wear what you bought at the end of the season? Then you'd probably hit the preseason sales and end up with a closet full of pre stuff and end-of stuff before you bought in-season stuff.

A sickness, she decided. It was all a sickness.

Pleased to be healthy in that regard, she paused at the store, studied the signs announcing that end-of-season sale.

UP TO 50 % OFF!

LIMITED SIZES!

END YOUR SUMMER ON FASHIONABLE FEET!

Fashionable feet apparently meant sandals—platform, heeled, flats. Or open-toed shoes. Open-toed boots, which made virtually no sense whatsoever to her mind. A lot of candy colors, or more inexplicably to her, the clear ones that exposed your entire foot.

But as she opened the door to mild chaos, she decided the marketing just worked.

At least a dozen people sat on tiny scoop chairs or narrow benches, both with piles of shoes scattered like shrapnel. More crowded the shelves and racks while clerks hustled to bring more boxes out, take more boxes away.

The noise level reached awesome.

She spotted Peabody and McNab toward the back with a mid-twenties Asian woman in New York black and those weird clear, open-toed boots. She began to weave and dodge her way back.

Peabody saw her coming. "Oh, hey. Lieutenant Dallas, this is Mae-Lu, the assistant manager. Mae-Lu was about to tell us about an encounter with Ms. Lopez."

"Truth," Mae-Lu said, and spoke in a voice that rang with Queens. "So she comes in—the one in the picture they showed me, yeah? This is like back last fall before I got promoted, and we weren't swamped like today, yeah? We had some customers, but Roxy had them and I was free, so I asked if I could show her something, and she gives a look that's all: As if, and says she wants the manager."

"Did she ask for her by name?" Eve wondered.

"Nope, just 'the manager,' and I thought how uh-oh, she's one of those, come in to bitch about something. So I went in the back where Shauna was handling some things, and told her. She comes out, and she says like: 'Oh, hi, ChiChi'—I remember the name because my aunt has a cat named ChiChi. Anyway, the woman says how she wants to look at some shoes, which I could've helped her with, yeah? But Shauna takes care of her."

"So she bought shoes?"

Mae-Lu shifted on her invisible open-toed boots, then set a fist on her cocked hip.

"Nope, here's the thing. I got busy with a customer, then I noticed how the ChiChi woman's sitting there, with a bunch of shoes and boxes all around—that happens—but she's being bitchy about it, and she's got Shauna down on the floor, putting her shoes on like she's freaking Cinderella, yeah?

"We weren't all that busy, like I said, but I bet I served three customers while this one's sending Shauna back and forth. So when I'm free again, I go over and ask if I can take some of the shoes back for Shauna, and Ms. Cinderella gives me that look again, and she says how a manager should be able to manage."

Expressively, Mae-Lu rolled her gorgeous onyx eyes.

"Then she puts her own shoes back on and says how there's nothing in this store worth having. And gives Shauna that nasty look and says: 'Nothing at all.' Then she walked out like the queen or whatever. I said something like, you know, 'Whew, rude much,' but Shauna's all 'It's no big.'"

Mae-Lu shrugged. "That's why she's the manager, yeah. She rolls. Anyway. We put all the shoes away, and I can see she's a little steamed, a little upset, but she just goes back to work, yeah? Shauna's totally professional, and really nice, too. She put me up for promotion. I'm really, really sorry about what happened to her fiancée."

Those onyx eyes went damp. "She'd come in once in a while—Erin. Everybody liked her."

"Did ChiChi ever come in again?"

"Not while I was working, and I'd probably have heard if she did from one of the other staff. Because, whoa, talk about 'tude. And not the good kind, yeah?"

"Yeah, thanks."

"Um, if you talk to Shauna, just tell her we're all really sorry. And we're going to cover things here, yeah? Not to worry about any of it. I need to get back to it. Our big sales rock it out."

"Go ahead. Thanks again." She turned to Peabody. "Let's step outside."

And out of the mayhem to where Roarke in his perfect suit stood on the sidewalk perusing the shoes on display.

"Hello, Peabody, Ian. Lieutenant. Quite a busy hive in there, I see."

"It's all that," Peabody agreed. "A really good sale."

"Don't even think about it," Eve said.

"Hard not to. I didn't expect you guys."

"I decided to go by, talk to the neighbor. I'm parked there." Eve pointed. "Walk and talk."

Though Peabody gave the store a wistful glance, she fell in line. Roarke strolled behind them with McNab prancing by his side. Eve heard them launch into some e-geek thing about the Great House Project, and tuned them out.

"I talked to Ms. Burger—she recognized several photos."

"Friends drop by, come around, pop in."

"These did. Including Lopez—Burger deemed her snooty."

"She's not wrong."

"She states that Barney sometimes came in with Shauna, like after work. Sometimes came with Becca, but sometimes alone. And he came out of the apartment while I was there, carrying a box. Pretty good-sized box."

"Of what?"

"Since I didn't have a warrant, I can't verify. He said, at Becca's suggestion, he came over to clear out the friggie and the AC."

"Oh, well, that makes sense."

"It does. He literally jolted when he saw me in the hallway. He was nervous."

Beside Eve, Peabody weaved through pedestrians. "I gotta say, cops can do that to people. You really can do that to people."

"Proudly. He asked about the case, also not out of line, but pushed, a couple times, that it had to be some lowlife—his word—on the staff, or in the club outside the group.

"Not like Decker," Eve continued. "Not that tone. Hers was rooted in hope and grief. His was like he wanted to nudge me there or find out if that's where we focused."

"You're leaning toward him."

"Lopez is still in the running. Going into her rival's workplace, taking that time, wasting Shauna's time, and trying to humiliate her. And risking Shauna would complain about it to Erin."

When they reached the car, Eve stopped. "Lopez didn't just get replaced in bed, she got outdone. Her type can't stand for that. She had to know she risked getting cut out completely with that stunt, but she did it anyway."

"Lack of control."

"Yeah, and that need to humiliate, to take the power. And Barney's the hoverer. He made noises about how they should never have had the party in a place like the D&D. He didn't come out and say Erin was asking for it, but it was implied."

"I'm starting not to like him, either."

"And he had something in that box. Something he took out of there that wasn't from the AC or friggie. The way he looked, the way he held it."

Eve looked back toward the apartment building. Can't verify, she thought. But know it.

"I need to sort through this. Pile in. We'll give you a lift."

"We're actually going to the house. You can just drop us off," Peabody said when she read Eve's face. "I mean, Mavis's gang is there, and they'd be sad to miss you, but you could just drop us off."

"Ten minutes." She shot Roarke a look. "Ten."

"Your call, darling. Why don't I drive? Ian, we'll just take a very quick look at the comm system while we're there."

"Mag. Clicking in the house-to-house would be handy." He piled in.

"She-Body, you sure you don't want them to drop us at the apartment? Grab a couple of the boxes?"

"Well . . ."

In the front seat, Eve felt more time ticking away. "Fine. Fine. We'll go by there, wait, and take you to the house."

"We'll be fast," Peabody promised.

"Yeah, yeah." She ignored Roarke's amused look, and put her mind back in work mode as he drove. "I want to talk to Stillwater again. He's not on the list, but he's in the group. He'll have impressions. It's a stupid murder. It gains nothing. And it's not the batshit kind, either. There's motive in there, specific target, but where's the gain?"

"Shauna can't marry a dead woman," Peabody pointed out.

"Yeah, and that's it. That's what we've got."

Roarke slid into a parking space outside the apartment building.

"How do you do that?" Eve demanded. "How do you just find parking right where we're going? What, do you bribe the parking gods?"

"Every chance I get."

"We'll be fast," Peabody promised as she and McNab climbed out. "We'll be lightning."

Eve watched them dash, hands linked, to the building.

"Friendships probe around, find the guilt, until you're waiting outside an apartment in a parked car."

Roarke patted her hand. "It won't take long. And consider this. Friendships, healthy or unhealthy, are very much a part of your investigation."

"They crisscross all over. But no one I've talked to, once I dig down a little, much liked Lopez. Erin must have. If it had just been sex, she'd have eased away over the last year. But she didn't. Everybody seems to like Barney, Mr. Helpful who hovers."

"From the sound of it, you don't."

"He was nervous," she muttered. "Why was he nervous? Okay, first, seeing me in the hall—a jolt. Not expected. But after."

"And you think there was something else in the box."

"I do. But I can't imagine what. We went through the place, and there was nothing incriminating. But he was nervous."

They weren't lightning, but fast enough as they came out, each carrying a box, lidded, as Barney had. Eve noted theirs were sealed and labeled as, from behind the wheel, Roarke popped the trunk.

"Big thanks," Peabody said as she slid back in the car. "Getting stuff over there this way's going to make the final move a lot easier, and we can put in more time helping next door."

"Don't want Mavis carting too much," McNab added. "And when August isn't there, somebody's gotta keep an eye on Bella."

Friendships, Eve thought again, they sucked you right in.

"Mavis tagged us as we were heading up," Peabody said. "Wanted to know if we'd make it tonight. She's juiced you're coming by. I told her you couldn't stay long. She gets it."

Well, that was something anyway.

The gates opened as they drove up, and there was the family, sitting in the brightly colored chairs on the big front porch. Bella, hair in two high tails on either side of her head, in bibbed shorts as blue as her eyes, popped out of her kid-sized chair.

Mavis didn't pop, but sort of levered herself up. Eve didn't know how—it hadn't been that long—but the belly under the snug green tee was bigger than ever.

The tee matched the color of the explosive topknot of hair and the swirls all over the white tennis shoes.

Leonardo, the gentle giant, took Mavis's hand and stood with her in a flowing sleeveless shirt and baggies that cropped at his ankles.

The minute Eve opened the car door, Bella shot off the porch.

"Das here! Das, Ork, Peadoby, Nab. Friends!"

That seemed to be the theme of the day, Eve decided as she caught the flying blond rocket.

"Hi, hi, hi!" Bella beamed and gave Eve an enthusiastic and sloppy kiss.

"I've got this, Peabody." Roarke lifted a box from the trunk.

"Thanks. You can just take it around to our side."

"We'll drop them off, take a look at the comm system," McNab told her. "We'll be lightning," he said to Eve.

She carted the now babbling Bella to the porch.

"I know you can't stay—bummer." She embraced Eve, sandwiching both the kid and the one yet to come between them. "But I made lemonade! I mean made-made from the recipe Summerset gave me. Who knew? And I totally, abso didn't screw it up, did I, moonpie?"

"It's delicious."

The pitcher, glasses, an ice bucket sat on a tray on a table.

"Sounds good."

"Das pray!"

Eve could only stare. "She wants me to pray? For what?"

"Bella." Mavis laughed as Leonardo poured out lemonade. "Pl-pl-pl."

"Pl-pl-pl-ay. Das play."

"Can't do that, either." Even if she knew how. "I have to go to work in a minute."

"Aww."

"Maybe just come inside a minute. See what you think. Let's show Dallas, baby girl of mine."

"See, see!" Bella scrambled down, and when Mavis opened the door, shot inside.

Lemonade in hand, Eve followed.

In the entrance the walls were . . . what were they? Eve wondered. Orange. But not like an actual orange or a pumpkin, but a deeper, maybe a softer tone that somehow worked against the thick, dark millwork.

Overhead, a many-armed light hung from a ceiling medallion. Most of the floor lay under some sort of protective paper, but what she could see gleamed.

"I love the light!"

Mavis grinned at Peabody. "I know! They just got it up today. They're nearly done in here."

The entrance gave way to the living area, walls the same color, evening sun still streaming in the windows. The fireplace, with its thick, carved frame, looked old, important. For the built-ins that flanked it, she'd chosen green—deep and soft again.

"I've got to have color. Just have to have it."

"I see that. And it works."

Rather than detracting from the old and important, the colors just enhanced that focus.

"It feels like home." Leonardo looked around with an expression of utter contentment. "Even without furniture, it's already home."

Eve remembered Peabody had said exactly the same.

"Roarke said we can start moving in furniture next week, in here for sure, which is beyond mag. And over in the parlor or sitting room. Over here."

Stroking her baby belly, she crossed the hall to a smaller space done in a rich, saturated blue.

"I think more like a den or whatever because the sofa I got for here says take a nap, and you can close the room off with the pocket doors."

"The lighting's really good," Peabody observed. "It's all coordinated but not matchy. It's modern, but it slides into the old with just the right tension."

"I had a lot of help. You, Leonardo, Roarke."

"It looks good," Eve said. "Really good. It looks like the three of you."

"Anybody home?" McNab's voice came through a speaker somewhere.

"They made it work!" Baby belly jiggled and swayed as Mavis bounced. She dashed over to a switch on the wall. "We're here! You fixed it! Big slooch!"

"Hi, hi, hi," Bella shouted. "Hi, Nab."

"Hey, Bellamini. Be right over."

Still bouncing, Mavis turned back. "McNab wanted to add that feature. The house-to-house dealie." She patted her mountain of belly. "He said they want to be on alert when Number Two decides it's time."

"Then for sure," Peabody agreed, and scooped Bella up. "And down the road, it's just convenience."

"Added security." Mavis rolled her eyes, but smiled. "I know you guys."

When Roarke and McNab came in, Bella deserted Peabody to launch at him.

"There's that pretty girl."

"Ork pretty," she said, and batted her eyes.

He laughed with her, then looked up. "Lights look just right, and I'll say the same about what I saw installed at your place, Peabody. Well done, all."

"Well done, all," Bella echoed, and batted her lashes again.

"Agreed, but we've got to go."

"Thanks for the lift," Peabody said. "Mega thanks."

"No problem."

"Come back." Mavis sandwiched again, fiercely. "When you've got real time. There's a lot more done, both sides, and too totally awesome. I want the Dallas seal of approval."

"You've already got it, but yeah, when I've got real time. And you rocked the lemonade," she said, and handed the glass back to her.

"I really did! Tell Summerset!"

"Somebody will."

"Here now, Bella, go to your da. We'll see you again soon."

"Bye, bye, bye. Bye-bye, Ork, bye-bye Das." She blew kisses from Leonardo's hip as they started out.

"There now." Roarke got behind the wheel. "That didn't take much time."

"Not much."

She glanced back. The whole group stood on the porch. Like family. Friends. All those connections crisscrossing.

"They're going to be stupid happy. They already are, but even more stupid happy. The house-to-house? Good idea."

"I didn't initially suggest it. Some might find it intrusive. They don't."

"They've merged. Yeah, they'll have their separate spaces, separate lives, and all that. But they've merged."

"And it's been lovely to watch. You're tense."

"Am I?" She circled her shoulders, felt the twinges. "Maybe some." She remembered she'd thought about a swim, but friendship had eaten that time away on her mental schedule.

"Tell me about today. It'll relax you to talk it out."

"It will. Is that weird?"

"It's you, Lieutenant. And when we're home, we'll add a glass of wine, a meal."

"I had pasta salad for lunch."

He glanced over. "Voluntarily?"

"Peabody did it. And considering how much hiking we've done around New York the past couple days, probably a good thing."

"Eating lunch isn't a sign of weakness."

"No, I just don't think about it most days. We stuffed a lot of walking and talking in this one," she said, and told him.

By the time they drove through their own gates, she had relaxed, at least a little.

"Wine wouldn't hurt," she decided. "I need to rearrange my board, write some things up, and I want to talk to Marcus Stillwater. But wine wouldn't hurt."

He took her hand as they walked to the house. "Any contact with dogs today?"

"None. I should be safe."

And when they walked in, the cat, sitting beside Summerset, padded over to ribbon through her legs.

"Late," Summerset noted, "but unbloodied."

"We ended up taking Peabody and McNab to the house," Roarke told him.

"Ah, and it's coming along beautifully, I thought. I had a tour today when I took over some lemons."

Instead of a snide remark, Eve felt obliged to tell him, "She did the lemonade. It worked."

"She's a quick study, Mavis."

Leaving it there, Eve started up the stairs.

"She feels pressed," Roarke observed, "but she made time for them."

"Love always finds a way. There's some nice barbecued chicken. It would go well with the fries the Lieutenant is so fond of."

"Then I'll see to it. Thanks."

He went up to find her already shed of her jacket and at her board.

"Want to do this first, want the visual. Then I want to contact Stillwater. Then—"

"Wine and a meal before the rest."

It seemed fair enough.

"Give me twenty."

"Twenty it is." And he went into his own office.

Once she had the visual, she stepped back, nodded.

She leaned where she leaned, she admitted. But she'd get Stillwater's take. Then see what she'd see at the memorial.

She needed a lot more than leaning.

At her command center, she tried Stillwater.

He answered right away.

"Lieutenant, is it done?"

"If you mean have we made an arrest, no."

His eyes went from hopeful to deflated. "I guess I hoped, when I saw your name on the display. I just left Angie's. We finally talked Shauna into eating something, and lying down awhile. Rough day for her."

"I'm sure it was. Who else was there?"

"At Angie's? I started to say the usual suspects, but that sounds really wrong given the circumstances. Angie, of course, Becca, Greg, Donna. Donna left when I did."

"I ran into Greg at Shauna's apartment building."

"Oh? He didn't mention it. I think he went by to clear out food. Shauna doesn't want to go back. I can't blame her."

She could see what she took to be his apartment behind him.

Pale gray wall, enormous screen flanked by darker gray shelves.

Like Roarke, he had real books.

"Mr. Stillwater—"

"Marcus. It's Marcus."

"Marcus, do you know ChiChi Lopez?"

"Sure, a little. Not really well. The family restaurant's great."

"Ever been to the club where she performs? Delights?"

"I actually haven't. I'm more hands-on getting a woman naked, I guess, but I've heard she's talented."

"Right. At the moment I'm asking for impressions. We can start with her."

"Okay, but like I said, I don't know her all that well. Sexy, confident, a little . . . *hard* isn't exactly the word. *Edgy* might be better."

"And her relationship with Erin?"

"That ended with Shauna—the sex part of it. Not that they didn't have a friendship after, or I guess I wouldn't have met her at all."

"Impressions again. How did she feel about Shauna, Shauna and Erin?"

"Impressions? Not especially warm." He hesitated, moving around as he did so she caught more pieces of his living space.

And what she believed was an Erin Albright cityscape.

"Okay, she didn't like Shauna. At least Shauna told me she didn't, and Shauna didn't much like her back. I think she told me rather than Becca or Erin because, well, I'm not one of the girls. Shauna didn't want to make waves. ChiChi was Erin's friend, and she didn't want to cause trouble between them."

He shrugged. "I figured the same. Why muck things up? And told her I thought it would smooth out as time went. You don't think ChiChi—"

"I'm just gathering impressions. What about Greg Barney?"

"I know him better. Nice guy. We don't hang much, but he's a nice guy. Really into fashion, schedules, but that's what he does. He and Becca have a good rhythm. He's like a big brother with Shauna, from my POV. Sometimes it crowded her—she told me—but he meant well. They had a thing back in high school."

"I'm aware."

"But there wasn't any animosity, not that I ever saw, or she ever told me. I think she would have. She and Becca are really tight. More good rhythm. That wouldn't happen if there were old scars, you know what I mean? So no scars, my impression, but a bond, between all three."

"He's aware you and Shauna had a sexual relationship?"

"Sure." Now he sat in a black scoop chair. "He didn't have a problem with it—not that I could tell anyway. Even when Shauna and I weren't planning on having sex, the four of us went out sometimes. To dinner, a club, just for drinks. He treated her more like a sister than an ex."

"Okay."

She took him through others in the group, to round it out. And decided he was observant, fairly insightful.

"I appreciate the time," she said when Roarke came in and walked to the wine cabinet. "It helps to get different perspectives on Erin's circle of friends."

"She had a wide one, and a good one, I think. I expect all of them will be at the memorial tomorrow. Shauna's going in with her parents and

Erin's. I'm going to try to go in with Angie and Donna if I can juggle some things."

"Detective Peabody and I plan to come, pay our respects. Again, thanks for your time."

"Anything that helps, just let me know. She was my friend, too."

"I know, and I will. Goodbye."

Eve clicked off, sat back.

"Was that helpful?"

"Maybe. Maybe."

He opened a chilled bottle of sauvignon blanc. "You think you know."

"What I think I know toggles, but it's started to settle. I want my own impressions tomorrow at the memorial. Either way, it's a stupid fucking murder."

He poured two glasses, brought one to her. "Have some wine. Pace about with it as you need to. I'll see to dinner."

"There were vegetables in the pasta salad."

"I'll keep that in mind."

He went into the kitchen, followed by the hopeful cat.

Eve pushed up, and drank some wine.

And paced about.

Chapter Sixteen

SHE KEPT PACING WHEN HE BROUGHT IN PLATES.

"It's mean."

"Murder?" He set the plates on the table by the balcony doors. As they both enjoyed the air, he opened them before turning to her. "It is, yes."

"Sure, but sometimes it's clean in a straightforward way, or crazy, impulsive, or purposeful. This is mean and stupid and personal."

"Murder offends you." Roarke brought the wine to the table. "It often makes you sad or angry—or both. This one also annoys you."

She frowned at her board. "Guess it does."

"You feel for the victim, always. You're their agent of justice."

"Eve Dallas, Agent of Justice." On a half laugh, she rolled her eyes.

"It has a ring. You feel for those left behind, always. And when you look at that board, you know one of those claiming that loss took her life."

"Yeah, but that happens." Frustrated, and yes, annoyed, she shoved her hands in her pockets. "It happens more often than not."

"And all that you handle, day after day. But for this you see that mean stupidity, a friend killing a friend and bringing grief to so many others they claim as friends, so many others who were on the verge of celebrating that victim starting a new phase of her life."

She did see it. She did feel it. And yeah, she admitted, it seriously annoyed.

"That was the point, or part of it. Ending it before it began. When Casto came for me, in that same room at the same sort of deal, he didn't care about any of that. He just needed to end me because I was too close to exposing him. That makes sense. It's not stupid. It was logical."

She gestured to the board with her wineglass. "This one cared about all of that."

"Come eat now. You're frustrating yourself."

"I probably am." She walked over, angled her head at the plates. Chicken glossy with sauce, a heap of fries, and the purple carrots she actually liked, mostly because purple. "That looks really good."

She set down her wine, stepped over, and kissed him.

"That's because I kicked Casto's ass that night so now we can sit here and eat what looks really good."

She took her seat, snagged a fry. "Looks aren't deceiving here. Frustrating myself some," she admitted. "I liked it better when the dead artist's paintings' value seemed like a viable angle."

"Because murder for monetary gain at least has some logic."

"Yeah, it would still be mean and stupid and a little sloppy, but you could see the logic. But that's not it. Maybe, on some level, it adds a benefit because just about everyone on the board has at least one of her paintings. It's just not the reason."

She sampled the chicken, found whatever coated it had an excellent tang. When Roarke topped off her wine, she decided that was fine. She was just circling anyway.

Set it aside, she told herself. Let it circle, but set it aside.

"Why were you downtown?"

"A meeting at your Off Duty club."

"You get a charge out of that, don't you? Saying it's my club."

"As it is yours, and yes, I do. You already have tenants applying for Stone's apartment above."

"That asshole. Do I?"

"You do. Once we do some vetting, you can choose."

"I can vet. I'm a cop."

"That you are." He smiled, a man who already knew the answer to the question. "Would you like to?"

"Absolutely completely not."

"We'll be interviewing for managers, bartenders, kitchen and wait-staff, and so on in another couple of months. Would you like to take lead on that?"

"Stop it." Laughing, she went for a carrot. "I'm giving all that to you, like a present, because you like it."

"Why, thank you, darling."

"You're welcome." As she ate, thunder rumbled in the distance.

She remembered it had stormed the night of Erin Albright's murder. While the group had partied and danced and drank, the storm had rolled in, and rolled out again.

"You're doing that security for the D&D."

"We are. We should have a system up and running inside a week. You're wondering how different this would be if he'd already had one."

"People find a way around them if they're smart enough, motivated enough. But yeah. He'll show at the memorial tomorrow, with Rochelle. It's personal to him, too."

"His place."

"There's that. And he knew her. He liked her. People tended to like her," she added. "Her across-the-hall neighbors liked her. She gave art lessons to one of their kids, wouldn't take payment. They had parties, but not loud and obnoxious. When you buy that building in your quest to own every inch of New York, add soundproofing."

"I'll make a note. You have a good picture of her."

"Yeah, I do. I have a decent picture of all of them. Still, people have, like, undercurrents. I'm looking at Mavis and her place, right? There she is, green hair—and who knows what it'll be the next time I see her? That doesn't surprise me."

She lifted her wine, drank.

"Even knowing she's going to pop out another kid doesn't surprise me. Her, well, road, shifted with Leonardo. That doesn't change basic Mavis, but it . . ."

"Expanded her."

"Yeah, and literally when you consider Number Two. The color in those rooms, not a surprise. But the way it works, the way the whole place works, the gardening thing, Jesus, making lemonade from actual lemons, all that can still surprise me until I step back and realize all that was always there. She just didn't have the way, the means, the people to do it.

"She's still Mavis, but that road shifted, and she's taking it."

"You shifted mine."

She looked back at him. "Guess I did. That goes both ways. So we're sitting here, having dinner. The cat's across the room sleeping because you gave him some of that cat candy he likes. We got a breeze coming in because that and the thunder say a storm's coming. And a handful of years ago, I'd never have pictured this.

"You, either."

"No. I didn't have a glimmer. Not until I picked up that gray button that came off your unfortunate suit and slipped it into my pocket. Even then, just a glimmer."

"You sent me coffee, and maybe I had a glimmer. I just didn't get it.

But here we are. Still, under it, through it, we are what we are. I'm still a murder cop, you're still a gazillionaire."

"It works for us, who we are."

"Good thing, or I wouldn't be eating these fries made from actual potatoes." She studied him as she ate one. "Do you still have that button?"

He reached into his pocket, took it out.

She shook her head; her heart simply soared. "Sap."

"In this area," he said easily. "But smart enough to get through those initial and formidable defenses of yours with coffee."

"Yeah, that was pretty damn smart." She ate a fry made from an actual potato as she studied that incredible face again. "If I'd gone for somebody else, would you have killed me?"

Brows lifted, he picked up his wine. "Now, there's a sharp turn." He looked over at her board. "No. I might have bought up the world's supply of coffee, then convinced you of your mistake. Or, alternately, found a way to . . . disqualify my rival."

"Disqualify?"

"One way or the other, short of murder," he added. "You being a murder cop would have discouraged me on that tactic. And you?"

"Me? Oh, if you'd lured me in with your seductive coffee, then dumped me? Murder cops know a lot of ways to kill without leaving a trace. But short of that? I'd have just hounded you on your shady past until I got you tossed in a cage."

She angled around to look at the board. "Somebody on there didn't stop short."

"Killing the rival, or the one who rejected them?"

"Not completely sure. But I know Lopez took the time to go into that shoe store to fuck with Shauna. I've got no doubts she tried to put the moves on Erin within the last year. I'd've put some money on her for it."

"Now?"

"Holding that bet because Barney had something besides what came out of the friggie and AC in that box. He was nervous, stayed nervous, and pushed for information on the case. Trying to size me up on it."

She shifted back. "He took something, maybe just some little thing. And that's stupid, like the murder was stupid. He's got a thing for Shauna. It doesn't come off sexual, even romantic, but it's a thing."

"You're changing your bet."

"Not yet." She polished off the fries. "Not yet, because either one of them could've done it. And both of them wanted to."

"A partnership?"

"I've played with that. May play some more, but it doesn't hold for me. It . . . wobbles," she decided. "I can't see them hooking up, not for this, not for anything."

Shrugging, she picked up her wine again, did a half toast. "I'll know more tomorrow when I see them at the memorial."

As she drank, lightning cracked the sky. Rain poured out.

"Here it comes," she said. Then she rose. "I've got the dishes."

"Is there anything I can do to help you? Runs? Finances?"

"Not really, no." She walked to the window to watch the rain, to feel the whip of the wind. "I need to write it up—and I'm going to copy Mira. Maybe writing it up will click something into place."

When he joined her at the open doors, she leaned against him. Just two people, she thought, watching a storm blow its raging way over their city.

"I need to see them all together tomorrow. Together over death, how they react, how they interplay. I've got some of their impressions of each other, a lot of the dynamics. I need to see how it all plays out."

She looked up at him. "What have you got going?"

"Oh, a bit of this, a bit of that. I'll entertain myself well enough."

"How about you give it an hour, then we entertain ourselves with a vid?"

Watching the storm, he stroked a hand down her hair. "A vid, is it?"

"If something doesn't click, I'm just going to keep circling."

"A vid works for me. So does an hour."

She watched the storm another moment. "A good thing I lost that button."

"And I intuited you could be won over by coffee."

"Yeah. Anyway, I've got the dishes."

Though she didn't feel she made any progress or opened new avenues, Eve took the hour.

They settled into their usual vid spot, the sofa in the bedroom. The action and complexity of the vid took her out of the investigation for a while. As did the slow, lazy sex that followed.

She slept peacefully, curled between Roarke and the cat.

Until she didn't.

Back in the club, with Crack at the bar and the holo-band playing wild. Her friends, Erin Albright's friends, mixed and merged into one colorful, drunk, girl party.

Why was she back here? Eve wondered. Nothing new here.

She'd stayed sober, she thought. Getting married tomorrow.

"I guess I should've stayed sober, too." Beside her, Erin looked over the people, the color, the movement as Eve did. "But we weren't getting married until the weekend. And we were all having so much fun."

"You couldn't have known what was coming."

"You didn't know, either."

"Yeah, true enough. But even if you'd been cold sober, you're not trained. An ambush like that, from behind? You didn't have a chance."

"I love her so much." Tears gathered in Erin's eyes as she watched Shauna dance onstage. "She'll never go to Maui now. It's ruined for her. They killed me, sure. But they killed something in her, too."

"Might've been the point."

"If I had it to do over, I'd know who to trust and who not to."

"You don't, and you didn't. Why the hell am I back here?"

"Don't ask me. I'm dead."

Looking for something she missed? What the hell could she have missed in that small room?

But she followed the dream, walked out of the club area, down the hallway, and turned into the privacy room.

Casto jumped her, the syringe full of the drug Immortality in his hand. To protect himself, he'd take her down. He'd take her out.

He managed to get a trace in her, but as she told him, she hadn't been drinking. She was getting married in the morning!

He hurt her, blackened her eye, pounded her ribs, but that training, her determination to survive, met his head-on.

And she took him down.

A little woozy from that trace, she cuffed him. She started to stumble her way to the door.

The wire went around her neck, biting into her skin. Blood trickled warm down her throat as she gasped for air.

Unlike Erin, she didn't claw at the wire, but threw her body back against the attacker, added an elbow jab.

For a second, just an instant, the wire loosened. But as it tightened again, she felt herself weaken. Pain, cutting pain. No air, her mind starting to slip into the gray.

She thought of Roarke, waiting for her. Thought of the people in the club celebrating both of them. Thought of the life she'd never know.

Roarke pulled her up.

"You wake up now. You wake up, damn it, and breathe. Eve, *breathe*!"

She sucked in air like a drowning woman, let it out with a shudder. Still on the edge of the dream, she lifted a hand to her throat.

No wire cutting into her, no blood sliding down.

"Jesus, Jesus, that was too fucking real."

With his arms around her, with the cat butting his head against her hip, she dropped her head on Roarke's shoulder.

"I'm okay. It's okay. It was just so real."

Galahad stopped butting his head against her and leaned heavy against her back.

"You were choking. You didn't seem to breathe." He drew her back as he called for lights at ten percent. "Ah God, you're so pale."

"Shook me up a little."

More than a little, she thought as she struggled to even her breathing. She'd felt the pain, she'd felt the panic.

"Thanks for pulling me out." She reached around, stroked a hand over the cat. "You, too. I was back at the D&D, then I went into the room, fought with Casto—that prick. Had him down, had him cuffed. Then behind me, somebody, the garrote around my neck. I was dizzy and I was losing. I was dying."

Eve wrapped around him in turn. "But there you were, pulling me back."

"I don't know how long you were struggling to breathe. I'd just walked in from a meeting. You're still shaking a bit."

"That might be you."

"I might be at that. Sit a minute more. I'll get you coffee."

She sat, watching him in the dim light. The sleek suit, the flow of his hair, the grace in his movements despite the shock.

He programmed coffee for both of them, walked back, and handed her a mug.

"It's nice being married," she said. "I didn't know if it could work with us, didn't see how it could. But here we are, and it's nice being married."

"You're well stuck with me."

"Both ways." She gulped down some coffee, felt alive again. "Really sorry for the scare. I don't know what the hell that was about. Going back there doesn't do any good."

"You lived; she didn't. You relate to her because of the circumstances."

"I guess I do. We're nothing alike, except for the circumstances. But dwelling on those parallels is stupid and unproductive."

"I disagree." He smoothed her hair, then laid a hand on her cheek as color came back into it. "It helps you see her, and you need to see the victim."

"It's screwing with my objectivity. It puts a shadow over it."

"If you didn't use those shadows, Lieutenant, you wouldn't be the cop you are. But Christ knows there are times I wish it didn't get inside you as it does."

Then he sighed. "And yet that's what makes you who you are. So I'm well stuck as well, aren't I?"

"Looks that way to me. What the hell time is it?"

"It was half-five when I finished the meeting, so just shy of six."

"Okay, all right. Boy, am I awake, so I'm going to grab a workout, smooth myself out some."

"You should try this new program, an urban obstacle course. Program New York Challenge. It earned the title."

He cupped her cheek. "We'll see if you're up to it."

She decided it sounded perfect.

The program proved it earned the title, and she proved she was up to it. Inside of three minutes she broke a sweat as she ran, climbed, belayed, tunnel crawled, dodged, jumped, and swung her way through Midtown.

She capped that off with ten laps in the pool, and felt normal again as she rode back upstairs.

In the bedroom, Roarke and the cat sat on the sofa. The screen scrolled with stock reports. And all was right in her personal world.

"You were right about the program—it's a killer. I was up to it."

"You look yourself again," he noted.

"It pumped me up."

She programmed coffee, took it with her to shower.

When she came out, he had two domed plates on the table. Galahad sulked on the foot of the bed.

Roarke smiled at her as he removed the domes. "It seemed like a pancake kind of day."

Pampering her, she thought, when she'd scared them both.

"It should always be a pancake kind of day."

"You have the memorial later."

"Yeah, and you're fortifying me, but not with spinach. They're not cakes," she said as she sat beside him. "And don't they make them on a griddle sort of thing? But they call them pancakes anyway."

She drowned them in syrup. And after the first bite, didn't care what the hell they called them. She called them good.

"What did you give the cat for helping pull me back?"

"He enjoyed some smoked tuna for breakfast."

"And still he's pissed because he's not getting pancakes, too." She took another bite. "It is nice to be married. It's stupid for me to keep thinking Erin Albright didn't get the chance to find out if it would've been nice for her."

"It's not stupid." Touched, Roarke kissed her fingers. "It's compassionate, and how does that compassion interfere with your cop brain? Not a bit, darling Eve. Not at all."

"Maybe not."

"You have to know your victim. It's always how it works for you. Know the victim, find the killer. It's fascinating to me. Endlessly."

"Maybe. Maybe. They made stupid, rookie mistakes. They shouldn't have brought the case in—or if that was cover in the event they got spotted, they should've taken it with them when they left.

"Luck," Eve continued, "pure idiot luck they didn't get spotted, that they got in and out without being seen. And they stage a half-assed robbery. Stupid. But they had to take her 'link. There had to be communications on there. If I had enough, I could get a warrant for the suspects' e's. But I don't."

"The unregistered could deal with that easily enough," he reminded her.

Frowning, she drank more coffee. "If I felt there was any chance another life was in danger, I'd be tempted there. But I don't. The job's done. Erin was the target. Shauna's hurt is either a by-product or an added benefit. But there's nothing to indicate anyone else is in danger."

"If you change your mind, it's available."

She polished off the pancakes, rose.

"I'm going to a memorial. I'm wearing black."

"Understood."

"Just wanted to get that out of the way."

"We're due for a bit of a break with the heat, but you might want to go with linen."

She made some noncommittal sound as she went into her closet. She wasn't always a hundred percent sure which was linen.

Black tee, black jacket, black trousers and boots, belt. Easy as it got, she decided. And if the jacket and trousers weren't linen, they were lightweight.

She came out for her weapon harness.

"I like color," she began. "I do like color, but if they'd never invented it, getting dressed in the morning would be a hell of a lot easier. Creepy," she realized as she strapped her weapon on. "It would probably be creepy, and make it harder to identify a fleeing suspect."

"Boring, and creepy. That said, you look respectful and formidable in your full black."

"I want to intimidate the hell out of my top two suspects."

"My money's on you, always."

Rising, he walked to her, kissed her. "Take care of my formidable cop."

"Plan to." She kissed him again, added a quick, hard hug. "Yeah, it's nice being married. See you later."

She started out. And it flashed into her brain, just leaped inside and stuck. She turned around and went back.

"It wasn't a mistake. It wasn't a goddamn mistake. It was deliberate."

"The case?"

God, it was amazing to have someone who got her, who got *it*.

"The case, yeah, the frigging case, and what was in it. Not a mistake to leave it there, a deliberate shot. At Shauna. The big dream, forever ruined. Her dream, and one Erin wanted to give her, was going to give her."

Eve started to pace. "The killer doesn't have to take the case, the tickets, the costume, those pink shoes to the D&D, but they do. Okay, maybe cover—that's a benefit. 'Oh, it's a surprise. Shh.' But they left them for a purpose.

"To destroy the dream."

"That's damn right—not stupid after all. Mean, vindictive, and purposeful."

Behind them, a dome crashed to the floor. Roarke turned to see the cat busily licking syrup from a plate.

"Bloody hell."

"Knock it off," Eve snapped. "Down. Now!"

When the cat leaped down, slunk away, Roarke snarled.

"Now I'm insulted. That fecking cat. That's insulting he cowers off when you tell him to."

"Never mind that. It's a twofer. Erin's dead, but Shauna not only loses her, she loses this dream she's had. Not only loses it, but knows she was just this close to having it. Now it's gone, it's all gone. It was fucking deliberate, Roarke. I didn't see it was on purpose."

"You do now, don't you? And I say you're right on it. It makes a miserable sort of sense, doesn't it then? Punish them both."

"Not a mistake," Eve said again, "so smarter than I gave them credit for initially. The half-assed robbery? No real choice. Have to ditch the 'link. Something on there that relates, so have to get it gone—and the rest is window dressing."

On her next pass, she scooped up the dome, tossed it back on the table.

"A first kill—I'm sure of that, the first kill. But not as stupid as I figured. Impulse maybe—opportunity knocked, but always planned out. Always with the purpose of taking a slap at Shauna along with it. She had to pay, too."

"Does it tell you who? As, not being a cop, I don't see."

"I am a cop, and I'm not sure. It works for both Lopez and Barney. In a twisted, selfish, bitchy way. But it changes things up a little. Looks like that dream wasn't a waste of time after all."

"I'd so much rather you come to these conclusions without scaring the life out of me."

She stepped to him, kissed him one more time. "I'll see what I can do going forward. The cat made a mess out of the table. See you later."

"Good hunting," Roarke said, and looked back at the table.

She wasn't wrong there, he noted.

"Bugger it," he decided.

He'd apologize to Summerset later.

Chapter Seventeen

SHE LET IT ROLL AND CIRCLE AND BACKTRACK AS SHE DROVE DOWNTOWN. It mattered, she thought. Not only because every detail mattered, but because—if she'd hit it right—it widened the motive.

Still a stupid murder, but not as stupid if it accomplished two for one.

Take a life, destroy a dream.

For Lopez, take the life of the one who rejected you and destroy the dream of the one she chose instead.

For Barney, take the life of the one who—even years later—replaced you, and destroy the dream of the one who moved on from you.

It felt stronger with Lopez, she decided—and it had been a downright mean murder: the time, the place.

But Barney had put something in that damn box. Nerves, a trace of guilt. She wasn't wrong there.

Erin could have given the swipe and the case to either of them.

The killer came in the back, almost certainly. Nothing to stop Lopez from sliding in back there, putting the case in the room, then joining the party. In fact, wouldn't that be exactly what Erin would've requested?

And nothing to stop Barney—except the risk of being seen—from using the swipe, going in, waiting.

She could see it both ways, and found that incredibly irritating.

When she pulled into Central, she considered tagging Mira. Not yet, she decided, no point yet. Speculation, and lots of it, but not yet.

She'd wait until she got a better feel at the memorial.

The elevator hadn't cleared the garage levels when the doors opened. Two uniforms who didn't look old enough for a legal drink walked an obviously jonesing junkie inside.

He had wild red hair, wilder blue eyes and smelled like a dumpster that hadn't been unloaded in a week, then had its contents pissed on by a group of drunks.

"Oh, come on, man" was all Eve could think of.

"Sorry, Lieutenant."

The wild blue eyes wheeled at Eve. "I'm the captain. I outrank you. I'm the captain. I just need a taste. Just gimme a taste!"

As he wailed it, the second cop sighed. "Just settle down, Jack. Stronger than he looks. He tried to throw some schmuck through the window of a twenty-four/seven."

When the door opened again, Eve started to step out—away from the smell. Jack the junkie wrenched away from the uniforms and launched himself at Eve like a cannonball.

"I'm the captain!" He screamed it as they both flew through the elevator doors.

Her hip struck the floor hard enough to sing, but she rolled clear. With his hands cuffed, Jack just slid, face and body. When he tried to scramble up, Eve simply stuck out a leg, tripped him, and sent him sliding again.

"Sorry! Sorry, Lieutenant!"

The uniforms grabbed him from both sides, hauled him up.

"Jesus Christ, Officers! Maintain control of your prisoner."

"He's slippery. I mean literally, sir. Greased-pig slippery. Do you need medical?"

"No, I don't need frigging medical. Maybe the fume tube, but not medical."

As Jack began to shake, sob, laugh, she decided a dressing-down, deserved, would only delay the process.

"He needs medical and the tank. Get medical to meet you at Processing, for God's sake. His system's wrecked, he needs Psych, and now his nose is bleeding. In your charge," she snapped, and made her way to the glides.

How the hell did two rookies get tossed out on the street together? she wondered. They damn sure needed a trainer.

She sniffed at her shirt, just in case that brief contact had contaminated her clothes.

Seemed clear enough.

By the time she made it to Homicide, she was more than ready for another damn coffee.

She walked in to see Jenkinson wearing the same mouse tie as the day before.

"What, you got two of them?"

"Huh? Hey, morning, boss. Reineke's hitting the break room for coffee. We got his ass. The best friend. Fucker killed his friend, for nothing."

The cold case, she remembered. The trip to Boston she'd authorized.

"Got him as in he's in a cage?"

"Oh yeah. Boston gave us the lever, Dallas. Once we got a face-to-face sit-down with the widow, she opened up about some of the inconsistences in the bastard's statements. How she didn't think of all that when it happened, but later."

Reineke came out of the break room with two mugs of cop coffee.

"But she didn't believe he'd do anything to hurt her husband, them being such good pals and all." Reineke picked up the report, handed Jenkinson a mug. "How broken up he'd been."

"How he'd been there for her," Jenkinson continued. "Helped her plan the memorial. How he'd come up with flowers to try to cheer her up."

"How they'd sit and talk for hours about the dead guy, and cry on each other's shoulder." Sipping coffee, Reineke sat on the corner of his partner's desk. "And he never made a move on her, just comforted, supported."

"Add she felt guilty because they'd had a fight," Eve assumed.

"Oh yeah. He'd say how the dead guy loved her, and knew she loved him. Married people have fights."

Jenkinson gestured with his mug. "Wove in there how he felt so sorry he'd let the dead guy walk home when he'd had so much to drink. How he'd live the rest of his life wishing he'd talked him into staying the night."

"Then she'd automatically tell him how it wasn't his fault."

Jenkinson nodded at Eve. "Got that in one. He gives it some time, then he takes her out—just friends. She's got the money, and the society rung, so it's fancy parties and the gala shit."

"And it's 'Oh, you don't have to, no, you shouldn't,' when she insists on buying him a tux and shit like that." Reineke shook his head. "Playing the long game. Takes his time, rakes some fancy stuff in before he makes any move on her."

"She falls for it," Jenkinson said. "She's ripe for it, and he sweet-talks her, romances her, though she's paying the freight. Even after she marries him, everything stays nice and sweet awhile."

"Then he starts pushing for more," Reineke added. "More trips, a boat, buys himself big-dollar crap with her money, and gets pissy when she draws some lines."

"He starts making mistakes." Jenkinson looked at his partner. "They always do. Saying the wrong thing if they're arguing. Like how miserable she made the dead guy, how he wanted a divorce. And the kicker?"

"How the night it happened, dead guy wanted to stay with the best friend, but friend made him go home to his bitchy wife."

"Inconsistencies," Eve concluded.

"She starts thinking about that, and how the dead guy used to say best pal used to whine about money, how his good friend had more than he needed. How he'd made some loans the pal never paid back."

"'You got that rich wife in your pocket.'" Reineke nodded. "She remembered her dead husband telling her the friend said shit like that. How he'd know how to live, and how to help out his pals if he had a rich wife."

"Bloom went off the rose." Jenkinson fluttered his mouse tie. "Took awhile, but that rose lost its bloom. Best pal, talking trash about the dead guy, drawing out money until she blocked him off her portfolio."

"She said he started to scare her, so she filed for divorce and, the house being hers, locked him out."

"He got back in," Jenkinson said. "Knew the security, how to get around it, since he'd installed. And that made her start thinking. Thinking hard enough she had the security switched out, closed up the house, and moved her ass to Boston. She's got people there."

"She didn't go to the cops with the inconsistencies, this feeling she had?"

"Nope, LT, she didn't." Jenkinson shrugged. "She told us she couldn't make herself really believe he'd do something like that. Accepted he'd married her for her money, but couldn't swallow he'd kill, not all-the-way-down swallow."

"After we had a talk with her, we had a talk with him, let him know we'd reopened the investigation, and were doing interviews again."

"That fucker's face." With a broad smile, Jenkinson shook his head. "It was all right there on his face. He'd gotten away with it. He'd gotten what he wanted and never paid nothing. But now here we come sniffing."

"And he started sweating. Got his story mixed up—claimed, hell, who could remember. But he kept tripping up. So we brought him down here. Formal interview. Took us awhile."

"Took us awhile, but we got him. Guilt was eating at him some maybe or we stirred it up enough to make him break."

"Or we're just damn good at what we do."

Reineke grinned, slapped high fives. "We are that. We got him, eighteen years later, but we got him."

"Good work. Have you notified the widow?"

"Going to wait until like after nine. Like civilized," Jenkinson said. "I think she knows. Damn clear she divorced him because she worried or wondered. Then when we showed up at the door, she knew."

"Close it off. Good work," she repeated, then turned to her office as Peabody came in, pink boots clomping.

She had her hair in a high-flippy tail. Eve decided it could be worse. Those streaks in it could be pink instead of red. Obviously, she'd considered the memorial, and had gone with black pants and jacket even if the shirt was a pale blue.

"Morning, all."

"My office," Eve said, and headed for it.

"Sure. Let me just stow my stuff." After Peabody pushed her bag into a desk drawer, she trotted after Eve. "Did something break?"

"No, no break." Eve programmed two coffees—one black, one regular—as she studied the board once more. "Just a shift in motive, maybe. One that clicks for me."

Over coffee, she laid it out for Peabody.

"I can see it. Easier to fix Lopez in that box than Barney. She'd have no trouble destroying Shauna's dream trip, her wedding, or anything else. Harder for me to see Barney. Long friendship, partnered up with her best friend."

"Jenkinson and Reineke just closed a cold case. Murder by best friend. He wanted a shot at the wife, and eventually got it. Couldn't keep her though. Guy bashed his friend's head in hoping he could hook up with the guy's wife—and her money. Maybe Barney wants to hook up with Shauna again."

Peabody frowned. "Maybe he's even—carefully—suggested it, or made a little move."

"Now you're following. Tested the waters, perhaps. That's a hard no, and you have the rejection angle right there again."

"Okay, with that, I can see either one of them. Which one? You usually know, or at least have a strong sense once we get to this point."

"If I bet on the job?" Eve tapped an ID shot.

"Really? Damn it, I was betting on Lopez."

"Also a viable bet."

"Then why Barney over her?"

"You didn't see his face," Eve murmured. "You didn't see his face when he came out of the apartment carrying that box. I'd probably go with Lopez if I hadn't seen his face."

Eve moved to her skinny window, stared outside. "She says she doesn't want to go back there, and if he takes her at her word, maybe he takes something he wants."

"If it was valuable—"

"No, nothing of value. Sentiment, more likely. Something Shauna won't think about asking for. Or if she does, they can't find it. Just a little something. Because she's his. His ex-girlfriend, his friend, his to hover over, to walk home from work. His."

"Okay. You're convincing me."

Eve shook her head. "I could make pretty much the same case with Lopez. We're going to get Shauna's permission to go through the apartment again this morning before we go to the memorial. Maybe we'll see—or not see—what he took out in that box."

"Anything I can dig into until?"

"Just take another pass through both of their data. I'm going to do the same. A first kill," Eve muttered. "It looks and feels like a first kill. And it looks and feels to me like the wedding—only days away—was the real trigger, with the honeymoon deal cementing time and place, and the willingness to risk exposure."

She paused by the board again. "We need to have another conversation with Becca. Just like with the cold case Jenkinson and Reineke just closed, she might have seen, heard, sensed something, but dismissed it. She wouldn't believe the guy she's in love with could or would kill."

"And for what?" Peabody added.

"We'll get the what once we get the who."

Eve sat back at her desk to pore through what she'd already pored through multiple times. But she couldn't shake the feeling, or maybe just the hope, that something in that background data would bring a spark.

Lopez, a woman born in privilege thanks to the hard work and enterprise of those who'd come before her. Still, her work ethic stayed strong. Her choice of career put her, and her body, in the spotlight.

She didn't strip for the money, to pay the bills, to put food on the table. She stripped for style, for the attention, and because she was good at it.

But the money wasn't nothing.

A relatively diverse family, though the majority married within their culture of origin. Those who hadn't appeared to enjoy the same tight family and financial ties. A sprinkle of same-sex marriages over the decades, also by all indications accepted.

A very large family, so it didn't surprise her to see a handful of criminal bumps, a few relations who'd done some time—either in prison or in rehab.

Nothing that stuck out to her, let her see some pattern.

A well-off woman closing in on thirty who'd had no legal cohabs, no marriages, no offspring. One who worked diligently at her chosen profession. And had a mean streak.

"Leave out the well-off and that could describe me a few years ago."

She sat back, added a big, tight, supportive family as another difference.

A planner, Eve thought. She'd have to be to select costumes, work out choreography, handle her part of the real estate arm. Passionate—a temper, the mean streak, the use of sex as either revenge or solace.

Add the ego, the bitchiness.

"You fit, Lopez. You slide in smooth enough."

She toggled over to Barney, and thought the same thing as she reexamined his background.

Not as privileged financially, not as big a family, but a good-looking white male, just shy of thirty. That brought a built-in sense of privilege.

A better-than-average student, part-time work during the school summers and breaks. Responsible. Football quarterback, team captain, lettered in high school there. And of course, stood as the male half of Shaunbar.

Two sisters, younger, parents that had each been married once, and stayed married for thirty-one years and counting. Two uncles on the paternal side, one aunt on the maternal, and a total of six cousins.

No, not as tight, Eve thought, as the family had scattered in the last couple of generations.

One same-sex marriage and one divorce, one charge of simple assault among the cousins. None currently lived in New York.

Since he'd majored in business management, had taken leadership courses, she assumed he'd reached his career goal.

No marriages, the single—and current—cohab, no offspring.

Another planner—couldn't manage and lead successfully otherwise. Passionate enough to make captain of the team, pursue a singular career goal and achieve it.

Ego, yeah. Mean streak? None that showed.

She glanced at the board, at his good-looking, all-American face.

"I'm betting you just hide it better than Lopez. She doesn't give a shit who sees hers. You would."

Enough, she thought, and closed the files, enough circling.

She contacted Shauna.

"Lieutenant, did you find them?"

"I don't have any information for you at this time. I'm sorry." When Eve looked at her, she saw what she often thought of as survivor's exhaustion.

"I keep hoping . . ."

"We're actively investigating, I promise you. I know this is a hard day, and I'm sorry to intrude on it. Detective Peabody and I would like your permission to go through your apartment again."

"The apartment?" With dull blue eyes, Shauna just stared. "I don't understand."

"We'd like to take one more look, to be absolutely thorough."

"I haven't been back. I'm not going to, but Becca brought some of my things. Clothes and things. Um, Greg cleared out the food we had so it wouldn't spoil. Erin's family . . . they're going to get her things after today. After the memorial. Angie and Donna are going to help them."

She passed a hand over her face. "I don't know what I'd have done without them the last few days. Or Becca, Greg, Marcus. I don't know what I'd do."

She closed her eyes. "I don't know what I will do."

"I hope you'll arrange for the grief counseling."

"I need to get through today. You can go in the apartment. I don't care about the apartment."

"All right, we'll go through this morning before the memorial. We'd like to come to pay our respects."

"That's kind of you. Greg says I should take a soother before, but I'm not going to. I'm saying I did so he stops worrying, but I won't. I need to feel it, all of it."

You will, Eve thought after she clicked off. You'll feel it all.

To take just another minute, she got coffee, stood at her window. It wouldn't help Shauna, not today, to know how many other people out there felt that exhaustion, felt that grief, felt it all.

Taking a soother (hovering?) wasn't bad advice, but she understood the need to feel it all. She felt it now, let herself feel it, because it helped push her to do the job she'd sworn to do.

She couldn't protect Erin Albright—it was too late for that. But she could and would serve her.

She walked out into the bullpen, saw all her detectives at their desks, all doing the work. Eventually they'd be called out into the field, to another scene, another body.

And they'd serve the dead, as always.

"Peabody, with me."

"Shauna's first?" Peabody asked when she caught up.

"Yeah. She knew Barney cleaned out the food, so that wasn't on the sly. Erin's family is getting her things out after the memorial. Angie and Donna are helping them. Barney's pushing Shauna to take a soother before the memorial. She's going to tell him she did so he lays off."

"You're leaning toward him again, and damn it, I'm nearly all in on Lopez."

"You first."

"Okay. Some of it's personality. She's got a hard edge to her, and she gets what she wants. She works for it, but she gets it. She's used to getting it, and being the one who says yes or no. Erin said no to her. And if she has—or had—real feelings for Erin, say more than just sex, but feelings, how would she handle that?"

"All right, decent question, decent point."

"When it's just sex, it's easier to move on, right?"

"How good is the sex?" one of the cops who'd shuffled on wanted to know.

"Also a decent question, decent point. I'm going to surmise, pretty damn good."

"Not a snap to move on from pretty damn good sex. And you start thinking it was better than maybe it was anyway. Ask me about my ex-wife."

"That's okay," Eve told him. "You can keep that one to yourself."

"I still say it's easier to move on from just sex than sex with an emotional element mixed in," Peabody insisted. "Especially if you don't usually feel, maybe never feel, that emotional element."

"I had that element." The cop, a grizzled detective with tired eyes, shook his head. "Started out one way, then hit the other end of that scale at the end. You get pushed to move on, it pisses you off."

"That." Peabody pointed at him. "That's what I'm saying. Erin forced Lopez to move on, and those feelings took that dive. So she killed her, and set it up to screw over Shauna's big dream."

"A reasonable scenario," Eve agreed, and when the doors opened to let their elevator companion off, she asked, "You didn't kill your ex-wife, did you?"

"Nah. Had a kid who'd've been pretty pissed off at me if I had. Me, I just imagine her miserable, and that keeps a spring in my step."

"Just because he didn't," Peabody began, and Eve waved her off.

"I get it, Peabody, and it's a solid rundown. I think you're right about the feelings. Genuine or not, who knows, but definitely feelings there."

"But you still lean toward Barney?"

Eve stepped out into the garage.

"He's one of the Mr. All-Americans. Straight, white, male. Closing in on thirty, good-looking, solid job, sharp dresser. He's also pretty much gotten what he wants. The popular boy in high school and part of the shining couple. Quarterback—calls the plays. Team captain, and all that. Two siblings, younger sisters. So he's—potentially—the prince growing up."

She got in the car. "Like Lopez, he works, and like Lopez, works at a career of his choosing. His parents remain married to each other, live in a house in the burbs—the same house where he grew up. The same district where he, Shauna, Becca—and his younger siblings—all went to school."

"I don't understand how that applies."

"First, he's a big brother. Maybe he takes that role too seriously.

Second, he's a big brother in what reads like a very traditional family. He had—they call it a career, right?—an upscale sort of high school career. He was a kind of star—Becca said royalty. She said Shauna—and think Shaunbar—was high school royalty.

"And he did just fine in college—not royalty, but he did fine."

As she drove, she visualized it.

"Moves back—home first—works at a men's shop in a local, upscale again, shopping area. Then he moved into the city. But when I took a look at both, guess who moved to the city first?"

"Oh." Peabody pursed her lips. "Shauna?"

"Yeah, like about three months before him. And he not only moves to the city, gets a job in the men's shop where he manages now, but moves into the same building as Shauna."

"The same building?"

"At that time, yeah."

"I missed that. It's a pisser to have missed that."

"I don't know if either of us missed it before, or just didn't look at that timing. Becca was already in the city—zipped straight into her job after college. She was around the corner at the time, and she and Shauna reconnected. Then the three of them reconnected. Shauna's dating some-one else—and Barney hooks up with Becca."

"But you think he moved to the city, and where in the city, because of Shauna."

"I think it's possible. And now, what? She's dating another woman? She's engaged? She's getting freaking married?"

"An ego thing? Like what's wrong with my penis?"

"It's a solid point. That wasn't a damn pun."

"It would be a good one."

Eve pulled into the now familiar loading zone, flipped on her On Duty light.

"So his ego, led by his penis, decides Erin has to go," Eve continued.

"Or his big brother deal demands he has to go to save Shauna from making a mistake. A combination of both would work."

She considered as they hiked to the apartment building. "It's something to bounce off Mira. Both yours, and mine."

"But you think it's him."

"At this point, Peabody, it's a gut thing. It's the deli meat—'Let me make you a sandwich,' and Becca's casual 'Stop hovering.' Like he tends to do that. It's the walking home with her from work, and it's the timing when he moved here and where he moved."

At the building, she took out her master.

"And topping all of that? His face when he saw me in the hall. The way he shifted the box, the way he tried to pump me for info and kept tossing out the lowlife theory.

"And I didn't like the way he talked about Crack's place. Personal maybe, but I didn't like that, or how it slid just over the edge of victim shaming."

Inside, they hiked up the stairs.

"No proof," she added. "Nothing to hang that on but my gut. Nothing to hang it on Lopez but logic. We need enough to get one or both of them in the box. Just enough for that. It's a first kill, and if a kill can be planned and impulsive at once, this one was.

"We'd break him—or her. Killing's not who they are. Controlling is."

"Yeah, controlling," Peabody agreed. "Both of them. You're right on that. Maybe benign in Barney's case, but it's still a controlling nature."

"They shouldn't have left the case," Eve said as they came out on the fourth floor. "Whichever of them did it, they shouldn't have left the case, should've resisted the need to add pain onto pain for Shauna. We'd have almost nothing without that."

"I wish we had more than we do."

"Hope can suck you dry. Work instead. We won't be able to tell what Barney took—but we'll go through and see if anything strikes."

She mastered in.

After a quick scan of the living area, she gestured left, then to the side. "Photos gone, there and there. Of the two of them."

"She might've wanted those. I'd want those."

"Yeah, we'll see if we can find out. Art's still up."

She walked into the kitchen, checked the friggie. Not only empty, but spotless. Not a single spill in sight.

"AC's empty, too," Peabody said after a check.

They walked out. Peabody took the bedroom, Eve the office/studio.

"The wedding dresses—they're gone."

"Yeah, some of Shauna's shoes from in there."

"Same with the dresser, Dallas. Some of Shauna's stuff. It's the size, the style makes it easy to see what's hers, what was Erin's."

Eve moved in to the bedroom.

"There was another photo on the dresser—one of those e-frames that holds a bunch of photos and scrolls them when you want."

"Some of the jewelry's gone," Peabody told her. "I'm going to say Shauna's again—it's the style. Erin's stuff is more—I guess bold. Artistic."

Peabody moved into the bathroom. "Basic supplies missing. Hair, skin stuff, some makeup, OTC meds, like that."

"Okay. Okay. We've seen what we can see. I want to go by the gallery, speak to Frost, then we'll go to the memorial."

"Frost?"

"She'll know what's happening with the art. Let's find out."

Chapter Eighteen

GLENDA HAD JUST OPENED THE GALLERY WHEN THEY WALKED IN. EVE supposed she'd dressed for the memorial—or for work—which involved a slim back dress.

She stood with a man—early thirties, black suit, burnished blond hair in a small topknot—and held up a finger to Eve as a signal to give her a minute.

"Essie will prepare the Stenner watercolor for transport. Ms. Eglin's sending a messenger to pick it up around noon. Just make sure everything's ready. If Dale Wisebrenner brings in the bronze I approved after I leave, I want it placed in the south gallery."

"Glenda, you told me. We've got it. And I know to contact Mr. Gibbets about the pottery, and tag Wilfred if he doesn't show up by one. Don't worry, please don't worry. You've got enough on your mind."

"Nagging you helps take my mind off what's on it." She gave his arm a squeeze as she spoke. "Give me a second."

As she crossed to Eve and Peabody, the man discreetly moved through an alcove to give them the space.

"I hate memorials," she said. "I can't imagine anyone actually enjoys them, but I just hate them. Add I'm barely back from vacation and taking most of the day off. I'm dumping a lot on our team. Which is an excuse," she added, "not to think about how much I hate going to Erin's memorial. She's too young to be memorialized. She should've had decades more."

She brushed a hand over her perfectly styled hair. "And now I'm rambling. How can I help you?"

"I'm curious whether there are any plans for Erin's art. You mentioned you hoped to have a posthumous showing."

"Yes. Actually, Erin's mother contacted me yesterday. It seems the family, and Shauna, talked it over. They're going to choose some of Erin's paintings for themselves. They'd asked if I'd be willing to hold a showing in the fall. They want to start a scholarship in Erin's name for art students."

She squeezed her eyes shut. "Damn it. It gets to me. It's a generous idea, and Erin would love it. No question. I want to put together a proposal for the owners. They're in Florence at the moment. I want to waive or at least greatly reduce our percentage."

"So all her paintings—other than what she sold or gave as gifts, and whatever her family and Shauna want to keep."

"Exactly. None of them want to profit, and instead want to create something meaningful. She has a lot of work stored at the studio."

"Yeah, we saw it. Since they're planning this, there's a piece I'd like to pre-buy or bid on—whatever it is."

"Oh?"

"Pizza parlor, interior. A lot of color and movement, and a lone figure sitting at the window counter."

"Yes, I know the piece. It's good. Not her best, if you want my opinion—which was also hers. But it's good. Can I ask why you want it?"

"The place has a personal meaning for me."

Glenda smiled a little. "Which means I could double its price, but won't. In any case, if you find who killed Erin, they'll want to gift it to you."

"I couldn't accept that. Not how it's done."

"Understood. I'll speak to them. Personal meanings matter."

Glenda looked over toward the portrait of the old woman.

"It's all personal now."

"But you'll price the paintings you exhibit and sell?"

"Yes, that's my job."

"What about the paintings they keep?"

"I'll appraise them if they want, for insurance, or simply to have a record. They haven't asked about that."

"Has anyone else?"

"No." Her eyes narrowed. "You'd like me to let you know if anyone does."

"Yes."

"Then I will. If money was the reason, I hope you not only find them, catch them, but they live a long, miserable life in prison."

"When we find them, catch them, I expect they will. Thanks for your help."

They walked outside, headed for the car.

"It's not money," Eve said. "Maybe, maybe the killer realizes that's a handy side benefit, but it's not money."

"Money's not personal, and this was."

"This was, and is. But making some money off the dead artist? A sweet bonus."

When they reached the car, Eve slid behind the wheel. "We'll head over to the memorial."

"It's a little early."

"Yeah. This way we can watch people as they come in."

Eve couldn't claim to have a fondness for memorials, but God knew she'd been to more than her share.

The facility was quiet, dignified with its muted colors and subtly flower-scented air. Some light spilled through windows, but even that spilled subtly thanks to filters and privacy screens.

The second-floor room contrasted with the subtle, the muted, with vases and urns of boldly colored flowers, with more strewn on a long table of photographs of the memorialized. From childhood, Eve noted, to the end of her life.

On the other side of the room, another long table held finger foods, coffee, tea, more flowers.

What Eve assumed was a self-portrait stood on an easel at the front of the wide room. On the other side of a standing display of flowers stood another easel with an enlarged photo of Erin and Shauna, pressed cheek to cheek as they smiled out.

They hadn't arrived too early for all, Eve noted. She recognized Erin's family, and Shauna's, gathered together near that front display.

Shauna, wearing a severe black suit, her bright hair pulled back just as severely, stood with them. When she saw Eve and Peabody, she laid a hand on a woman's—Erin's mother's—arm, then stepped away to cross to them.

If she'd looked exhausted on the 'link screen earlier, now she looked nearly gray with fatigue. She'd done her best with makeup, but it showed through.

"Thank you for coming. I don't suppose you have anything to tell me."

"Not yet."

Shauna just nodded, looked around as if she'd forgotten where she stood. "Erin loved flowers. She liked vivid colors. We picked these for our wedding."

"They're lovely," Peabody said in her gentle way.

"We wanted what she'd want." She glanced up as music came on, soft but with a steady beat. And smiled a little. "No dirges for Erin. She liked vivid music, too. Would you come speak to her family, and mine?"

"Of course."

With Peabody, Eve walked down to the vivid flowers with their bold scents and spoke with the grieving.

"Is there nothing?" Erin's mother had given her daughter her eyes, and now they pleaded with Eve. "Nothing you can tell us?"

"I can tell you that Erin's our priority, and we're doing everything we can to find out who took her life, who took her from you."

"She was so bright." The mother looked toward the daughter's portrait. "So bright and full of life."

Her husband put his arm around her shoulders as they began to tremble. "Come on now. Let's sit down a minute. Let's sit down over here."

People began to sprinkle in, so Eve signaled Peabody. They'd stand in the back. And they'd watch.

Angie walked straight over to Erin's parents, embraced them both. And when Erin's mother broke down, embraced her again, and just held on.

Donna came in, tears already streaming, with Glenda holding her hand.

It didn't surprise her to see Crack and Rochelle come in, both in dark suits.

Becca came in, Greg's arm around her waist as they made their way to Shauna. He held them both in a three-person hug, then kissed Shauna's forehead.

He went to the refreshment table, poured two cups of tea, then walked back to them, urging them to take the cups.

Others came, a sprinkle, then a stream. Another older couple—Barney's parents, Eve identified. They went straight to Shauna, then to her parents.

Others she recognized from the party, some of them with other women or with men, some alone. Voices murmured over the music.

She spotted Lopez's grandmother, on the arm of a man with silver hair. And where was Lopez? she wondered.

"A lot of people," Peabody commented. "I don't recognize all of them."

"There's one who's not here."

"Yeah, I got that. Pretty strange if she doesn't at least make an appearance."

Marcus Stillwater rushed in, looked harassed. After a glance at Eve, he muttered, "Caught in traffic, damn it. Told them to leave without me, then got caught in traffic."

He hurried to Shauna, embraced her, then her family, then others. Crack and Rochelle made their way to the back and Eve.

"A lot of people cared about that girl," Crack said. "You're going to find the one who didn't."

"Working on it."

"The one who just came in? He's doing the eulogy. Shauna said she asked him, as she knew he'd handle it. She tried to write something out but worried she'd just break."

"Barely holding on now," Rochelle murmured. "I just can't imagine."

Stillwater pinned on a mic and stepped to the front of the center of the room.

His voice came clear and just loud enough to cut through the murmurs and still them.

"On behalf of Erin's family, Shauna and her family, thank you all for coming to remember Erin. I'm Marcus, and while I only knew Erin a little more than a year, she brought such light and love into my life."

He spoke, and spoke well, of her as a friend, a woman, an artist. His words brought tears, a little laughter, more tears, and Eve thought probably comfort.

When he finished, he invited anyone who wanted to say a few words, tell a story, share their thoughts.

Angie spoke of their long friendship; Donna of Erin's unshakable loyalty. Glenda added more about her talent and her verve.

Others shared personal stories.

Barney stood behind Becca and Shauna, a hand on each of their shoulders.

When Shauna stepped forward, he said something to her. But she shook his hand away and walked to the front.

"Erin changed my life," she began in a voice that trembled like the hands she clasped together. "She expanded my life and she brightened it. Who knew a pair of pink shoes could matter so damn much?"

A low ripple of laughter, and she managed a ghost of a smile.

"Without those shoes, she might never have shown me what love is, what it can be, what it needs to be. The sixteen months we had together opened my world, my mind, my heart."

As she spoke of love, Eve caught a movement out of the corner of her eye.

Lopez came in.

She wore red, stoplight, in-your-face red. A body-skimming dress that stopped at mid-thigh she'd paired with sky-high heels in the same bold color.

She moved through the crowd in a saunter that had Eve's instincts prickling.

"This won't end well," she muttered, and started to follow.

Lopez stopped a foot from Shauna, put a hand on one hip.

"This is bullshit."

Stillwater moved toward ChiChi, but Shauna shook her head.

"Leave her alone. What's bullshit, ChiChi?"

"This, you, all of it. You standing there with your teary eyes and in your shop clerk's black suit, talking about Erin like you knew her. You didn't! You knew what you wanted her to be. You know what you wanted out of her, and it's bullshit."

Lopez's grandmother spoke in low Spanish—Eve didn't need the language to recognize a harsh rebuke.

Lopez just flicked a hand.

"I knew her. I knew who she was. Not the boring doormat you turned her into. She had *life*, and you drained it right the hell out of her. You fucking killed her. You bitch, she's dead because of you."

People gasped, as expected. Stillwater moved forward again, but not before Lopez struck out with a slap that rang in the shocked silence.

And neither he nor Eve moved quite fast enough to stop Shauna when her fist jabbed out.

Good punch, Eve thought as Stillwater managed to catch Lopez before, eyes rolled up, she crumpled.

"She had that coming." Shauna heaved out a breath. Instead of gray-tinged fatigue, her face glowed with rage. Those dull eyes went brilliant with it. "I'm not sorry. She had that coming."

The grandparents stood. With dignity, the woman approached Shauna. "We apologize for ChiChi's behavior, her disrespect at such a time. We'll take her home."

"She's, ah, out." Stillwater looked up at Shauna with a mix of horror and admiration. "I can carry her out. I guess."

"Just out of the room," Eve told him. "If she needs medical attention, we'll call for it. Then she'll be charged with assault."

"Oh, but—" Shauna started to speak, then stopped at Eve's sharp, fierce look. "I hit back."

"Self-defense."

"She was overwrought," Ms. Lopez began.

"Yes, ma'am, she was. We'll give her time to settle down. She's coming around. If you could take her out so they can continue with the memorial, we'll take it from there."

"You'll make her pay a price." Ms. Lopez sighed. "Perhaps that's best. We should contact our lawyer. Should she have a lawyer?"

"That would be up to you. She's entitled to one. If you decide to bring one in, he can come to Cop Central. Peabody, go read Ms. Lopez her rights and ask if she wants medical assistance."

"Yes, sir."

The grandmother turned to Shauna. "I would apologize to you, Shauna, and to all who came to honor Erin on this solemn occasion."

"No, señora."

"Yes," she insisted. "Our very deep apologies. If you'll excuse us."

With considerable dignity, she took her husband's arm and walked out.

"I don't want to press charges," Shauna began.

"Yes, you do. Actions require consequences. If it all comes down to a slap, she'll get off with a slap."

"You think—"

"I'm going to find out. Leave this to us, and finish what you're here to do."

Eve glanced around the room, at the shocked faces, the fascinated ones, then left them all to it.

She walked to where Lopez sat on a sofa with her grandparents, and with Stillwater standing like a baffled and reluctant guard beside Peabody.

"Go back in, Marcus," Eve told him. "Drama's over."

"Sure. Okay. Wow."

"Ms. ChiChi Lopez states she doesn't require any medical assistance at this time."

"Fine. Did you inform her of her rights?"

"Just more bullshit," Lopez snapped. "But she rattled them off."

"ChiChi." For the first time, the grandfather spoke, and in tones of absolute authority. "Mind your tongue."

She set her bruised jaw, pressed her lips—the full bottom one split on the corner—together. And said nothing more.

"We'll forgo the cuffs," Eve told her, "unless you want more trouble."

"Go with them." Her grandmother patted Lopez's hand, then rose. "Behave sensibly. The lawyer will come if needed."

"I don't need a damn—" She broke off at her grandfather's cold stare. "Yes, *Abuela*, thank you."

Getting to her feet, Lopez walked between Eve and Peabody.

"It is bullshit." She snarled it once she was out of earshot. "And you know it. So I slapped the bitch. Big deal."

"Yeah, big deal known as assault. Add verbal assault for good measure, and let's kick in disturbing the peace just for the hell of it."

"You're enjoying this."

"Can't say otherwise. I'm also doing my job."

Outside, she put a hand on Lopez's head as she put her in the back of the car.

"We could throw in public drunkenness, couldn't we, Peabody?"

"Well, Lieutenant, she's definitely had more than a couple this morning."

"So I had a couple of drinks. I'm old enough, and someone I cared about is dead. Dead because of that stupid, whiny bitch."

Eve pulled out into traffic. "And how, exactly, is Erin dead because of Shauna?"

"Jesus, are you stupid?"

"Jesus, Peabody, am I stupid?"

"I would say the opposite of stupid. Especially when it comes to murder."

"Why, thank you, Peabody, for that vote of confidence. But, ChiChi, since you ask, why do you think I might be stupid?"

"Because it's freaking obvious." Wincing, she cradled her jaw as she snapped the words out. "If not for that prissy-ass bitch, Erin would still be alive."

Willing to play, and understanding the rules, Peabody shifted to look back. "So Shauna killed Erin?"

"Oh, for fuck's sake. Not just stupid, brain-dead. She wouldn't have the guts. She doesn't have the spine. Or the brains. Some second-rate shoe store manager playing at getting naked with another woman. For kicks. For adventure."

"Since they planned to get married this weekend, it sounds like more than playing. More than kicks and adventure."

"Maybe she'd have gone through with it for the splash, for the attention. But it wouldn't last anyway."

Eve pulled into the garage.

"How about we try this? Since you're so much smarter about this than we are, we'll go up, sit in Interview. You can tell us your thoughts. We'll put off processing you for the assault."

"I don't give a flying fuck about the assault."

"Then you shouldn't give one about a formal interview."

"I don't."

Peabody assisted Lopez out of the car, guided her to the elevator.

"Do you want some Sober-Up before said interview?" Eve asked her.

"I'm not drunk, for Christ's sake. I had a couple of drinks."

They flanked her in the elevator.

"Jaw's swollen," Eve commented.

"Fuck you."

"Back at you, but Detective Peabody will get you an ice pack."

When the doors opened for more cops, Eve edged Lopez back. For once, she'd ride all the way up.

And as she did, she watched some of the bravado erode.

"I got us Interview B, Lieutenant."

"That'll work."

"My family will take care of bail. I don't need this crap."

"Interview first, and maybe we can convince the injured party to drop the charges."

"I don't give a shit."

But she did, Eve thought. Now that the bravado, some of the Dutch courage wore thin, and the situation took hold, she gave more than a shit.

"Then, again, you shouldn't give one about an interview."

Taking Lopez by the arm, Eve led her out of the elevator on Homicide's level.

"Want something to drink?" she asked easily.

"Vodka martini, very dry, two olives."

"Yeah, we'll get that for you in about never. How about some water, Peabody, all around?"

"Yes, sir."

As Peabody peeled off, Lopez sneered. "Figures you'd go by 'sir,' like a man."

"Does it? Funny, I think of it as genderless respect, but it takes all kinds." She opened the door to Interview B. "Have a seat. Record on. Dallas, Lieutenant Eve, entering Interview with Lopez, ChiChi, on the matter of H-7823, and due to assault charges pending. Were you read your rights regarding those assault charges, Ms. Lopez?"

"Yeah, and assault's bullshit. You know it's bullshit."

"On the contrary, I personally witnessed your assault on Shauna Hunnicut roughly twenty minutes ago."

"So I slapped the bitch. She's earned worse."

"Note that the accused has admitted to said assault. Peabody, Detective Delia, entering Interview. And how has Ms. Hunnicut earned worse than a slap?"

"Erin's dead, isn't she?"

Teeth bared, she snarled it out.

"Are you accusing Ms. Hunnicut of killing Erin Albright?"

"Like she'd have the guts, or the spine, or the smarts."

Gingerly, Lopez pressed the ice pack Peabody offered against her jaw.

"But she's the reason," ChiChi continued. "It's her fault. It's all her fault."

Eve cracked her tube of water, took a casual sip. "Since we're all sitting here, how about you explain how Erin's death is Shauna's fault."

"You didn't know her, all right? You didn't know Erin."

"But you did," Peabody said, her voice as gentle as Lopez's was strident.

"You're goddamn right I knew her. She was bright and bold, really fearless. She had passion. Real passion. For her art, for life, for living life. Up for anything, that was Erin. Always on the go, always doing, looking, *being*. Shauna killed all that. She killed all of that before somebody finished the job."

"How?"

Those dark eyes bored into Eve's. "She manipulated her. Playing at the romance, all of it. Suddenly, Erin's staying home instead of partying. She's working on her art, sure, but she's not fucking living. Doesn't go out, starts hanging with those lame friends of Shauna's. It's all Shauna, Shauna, Shauna, all the damn time."

"And not you. Not after Shauna."

"Tells me to lay off Shauna. 'Oh, come on, ChiChi, don't be bitchy.' Says how happy she is, but bullshit. Laughs it off when I make a move on her, the way she used to like."

"That must've hurt." Peabody's eyes shined with sympathy.

"Fucking A, it hurt, but it showed me just how Shauna twisted her up. Like the two of us can't have sex anymore? Like she can't swing by the club for some laughs? No, oh no, they're saving money for a nice fucking sofa? Then, Jesus, they're getting married? What the serious fuck!"

"You resented all that," Eve said. "Who could blame you? You and Erin had something. Then Shauna got in the way."

"I'm telling you, she manipulated Erin. She dazzled her somehow. White dresses, a wedding? Maybe having kids down the road? That wasn't Erin."

"What did you do about it?" Eve asked her.

"I tried talking to her, but she wouldn't listen. I tried warning the bitch off, but she ignored me. I even tried talking to Angie, since she and Erin are tight, but she told me Erin was happy, in love, and I'd end up having her cut me off if I kept it up.

"And Donna." Lopez rolled her eyes. "She's useless. Whatever Erin wants is just perfect. Erin wants Shauna, so Shauna's perfect. They couldn't see what I could. None of them could see what I saw."

"Did you tell Erin you were in love with her, ChiChi?"

At Eve's words, Lopez's eyes filled. Tears fell in a flood. "She said she was sorry. *Sorry!* But she didn't feel that way about me. She couldn't feel that way. She loved Shauna. She was making a life with Shauna, and she was sorry."

"When did you tell her?"

"The morning of the goddamn party. The morning before she died. Died because she thought she loved Shauna. And she's spending the last morning of her life cleaning somebody's apartment."

"You went there."

"Yes, I went there. I went there to tell her. I went there to stop her from making this stupid mistake."

"Is that when she gave you the case, the case with the tickets to Hawaii?"

Like a child in a tantrum, she tossed the ice pack across the table.

"She didn't give me the goddamn case. She didn't tell me anything about Hawaii. I knew that was Shauna's thing. I knew how much Erin wanted to make it happen, but she didn't tell me. Because Shauna, always Shauna."

Now she laid her head down on the interview table and wept. "She'd be alive if it wasn't for Shauna. Why didn't they kill her? Stupid, second-rate shoe clerk with her boring friends and let's-stay-home lifestyle. Who'd miss the bitch? Erin was so much more. So much more."

"And feeling this way, you still went to the party that night?"

"I've got my pride, don't I? I'm not sitting at home alone. I'm not letting them all see how it hurts."

Straightening, she swiped at her face. Took a long moment to compose herself. The anger hadn't drained, Eve thought, not by a long shot. But when she spoke again, her voice was more controlled.

"I'd have made Erin happy. We could've had a real life together and not some pale, boring excuse for one. Now she's dead, and that pasty-faced redhead's standing up there talking about her like they had some love of a lifetime.

"She's lucky I just slapped her."

She took two deep breaths. "It wouldn't have lasted. Erin would've gotten tired of it, she'd have wanted to bust loose again, and that bitch would've wanted a dick again. But now Erin's dead, and it's over."

"Killing her, that's payback for rejection."

Eyes dry again, Lopez stared at Eve. "Look at me, for Christ's sake. She'd have come back to me, to the life, to the passions. I could wait. Yeah, I was pissed, but I could wait. Now, because of Shauna, there's nothing to wait for."

"Blaming Erin for wanting someone, something else makes more sense."

"You didn't know her," Lopez said again. "It wouldn't have lasted. She'd have come back. I could wait. Now she can't come back. And all because of Shauna's goddamn party. I don't give a fuck about the assault. Lock me up. Erin's still dead, so the fuck what?"

"What did you think when you saw Shauna stripping down onstage at the D&D?" Eve wondered.

"I thought, Jesus, Erin's giving up this"—Lopez skimmed her hands down her body—"for that? And I damn well knew she'd come back."

Looking into Lopez's eyes, Eve nodded.

"Yeah, I bet that's just what you thought. Peabody, take Ms. Lopez down to Booking. You can sit and think some more before your bail hearing."

Eve sat back. "I didn't know Erin, but I know her now. Knowing her's part of my job, and I'm damn good at my job. Only one person's responsible for her death, and that's the one who killed her. If it helps you sleep at night to blame the woman she loved and who loved her, that's your damage. But I'll do my job and see the person responsible's held responsible."

"Shauna's why she's dead. That's all I need to know."

"Get her out, Peabody. Interview end."

Chapter Nineteen

WHILE SHE WAITED FOR PEABODY, EVE WROTE UP HER REPORT, MADE more notes on the interview.

She heard someone coming toward her office—not Peabody. But she recognized the tread and got to her feet.

Commander Whitney filled the doorway, then her office. Broad-shouldered in his suit, the same color as the gray threaded through his close-cropped hair, he flicked a glance at her board.

Eve said, "Sir."

He gave an absent wave of his hand toward her desk chair, but she didn't sit.

"You arrested, interviewed, and are now booking a ChiChi Lopez."

"Yes, sir."

He nodded, and now his dark eyes flicked toward her AutoChef.

Eve didn't ask, simply programmed coffee, black, and offered it.

He nodded again. "On assault."

"Yes, sir. Also drunk and disorderly and disturbing the peace. Ms.

Lopez disrupted a memorial service, then verbally and physically as-saulted the fiancée of the deceased."

"I take it since you wouldn't waste your time interviewing this individ-ual over an assault while conducting a murder investigation, said individual is on your case board."

"She is."

"She is," he agreed. "I've received and reviewed copies of your re-ports. Also received a call from the mayor, who is a frequent patron of the family restaurant."

Politics, Eve thought, and struggled not to hiss. "The grandmother contacted the mayor?"

"The mother. Apparently there's a family disagreement on the issue. Due to the nature of the younger Ms. Lopez's career, the mayor would like to keep a low profile on any involvement."

"I bet. Sir."

Whitney's mouth twitched, just a little. "In any case, the mayor's office would like to see some leeway on the matter, due to the emotional state of all parties involved."

"I believe that will be up to the court, Commander."

"Agreed. I'm on my way out to a meeting or I wouldn't have inter-rupted you with this. While the mayor is also in agreement, the Lopezes' enchiladas are exceptional. And one of the younger Ms. Lopez's cousins works in the mayor's office."

Eve said nothing while he polished off his coffee, handed her back the mug. "So, I've done my duty, and have no doubt you'll do yours."

He started for the door, then stopped, turned back. "Is she your killer?"

"She has the nature and temperament for it, Commander. She's the center of her own world, and expects to be treated as such. A slap back by the court wouldn't hurt. But no, sir, I don't think she killed Erin Albright."

"I'm sure that will be a relief to the Lopez family, and the mayor. Have you got the scent?"

"I do."

"Then good hunting, Lieutenant."

When he left, Eve turned back to her board.

Yeah, she had the scent. What she didn't have was evidence. She believed, strongly, in following her gut. But without evidence, she couldn't make a case.

Now she heard Peabody coming.

"I saw Whitney as I was coming back. Is there a problem?"

"The mayor likes Abuela's enchiladas."

"Oh. Well, shit."

Eve shook her head. "No real interference there."

"Okay, good. Lopez is with her lawyer. The lawyer came in during booking. She was wearing Carminas."

"Carmina's what?"

"Shoes, Dallas. Carmina is a shoe designer, a goddess. These were a pale, pale blue. Stilettos with little cutouts on the sides shaped like butterflies. They're going to run like five grand, easy."

"I'm just thrilled to have a report on the lawyer's footwear."

"It's relevant," Peabody insisted. "If you can afford Carminas, and you're wearing a suit that looks like it came right off the runway in Milan, you're probably really good at your job."

"She'll probably bounce with community service and anger management."

"That seems . . . fair."

"It would be. Unless she pulls a judge who decides to dismiss the charges. There should be consequences, but that's not our department. We did our job."

"Yeah, but she didn't kill Erin Albright."

Eve gestured to the desk chair. "Take the chair, I'm not ready to sit yet." And she programmed coffee for both of them.

"Why didn't she kill Erin Albright?"

"Logistically," Peabody began, "it would've been tricky. Not impossible, but tricky. It feels like if she was going to do it, she'd have found a less tricky time and place."

Eve decided to counter, and make Peabody work for it.

"The time and place are part of the point of the killing. Ruining a celebration and destroying a dream at the same time."

"Yeah, but . . . Lopez is a hard-ass with a goddess complex. 'I'm so special, I'm so amazing. Look at me!' And I can see her shoving a sharp into somebody's throat. Or yeah, using a wire. But if she was going to do it, I think she'd have killed Shauna. And she'd have felt like she deserved to."

"It's Erin who rejected her. She probably hasn't heard a lot of nos in her life, and Erin gave her a big no. And Shauna pays. And pays. And pays."

Peabody frowned at her coffee, then frowned at the board. "Yeah, but . . . the way she broke down in Interview, what she said, how she said it. I really believe she loved Erin, or honestly thinks she did. And yeah, people kill what they love, and a lot, but this didn't feel like the way for her.

"She runs hot, Dallas, really hot. And there had to be a lot of cold to plan out and execute this killing. Maybe a hot motive—the passion—but a cold execution."

"Oh, she has plenty of cold in there."

Deflated, Peabody set down her coffee. "You think she did it."

"No, I don't."

Peabody looked up again, blinked. "You don't? Why?"

"For all the reasons you cited, and a couple more. If she killed Erin, where's the murder weapon? She didn't have it on her, it wasn't in the club. Sweepers went through dumpsters and recyclers, circled the block on that—which she'd have had to do if she had a bloody garrote on her."

"I forgot that one. I shouldn't have forgotten that one."

"She could've ditched it somehow. Snipped the wire to pieces, flushed. Had to have handles, but it's possible she found a way to destroy and dispose. Possible, but that's a lot of thought, and it would take more time. Then she's going to walk back into the club, slip in without notice, and keep partying?"

Eve shook her head. "I don't see her pulling it off. I can see her trying but failing. She's a performer, but that's her body, not so much her face. Something would've showed. If Crack didn't see something in her, Angie would have. She's got a sharp eye."

Eve wandered, drank coffee. "All of those points can, as I demonstrated, be countered. I hope she pays a price for what she did today, but she won't go down for murder."

"You think it's Greg Barney."

"I know it is now." Turning, Eve studied his face on her board.

Attractive, well-groomed, well-dressed, an easy, friendly smile.

"He smirked."

"Sorry? What? He smirked? At Lopez today?"

"No, not at Lopez, at Shauna. Between the slap and the punch. Lopez goes after Shauna verbally. Everybody's shocked, but he's fascinated. There were a couple more fascinated. And a couple of angry reactions. Angie, for instance, was pissed. Then the slap."

Certain of her ground, Eve turned back around. "You've got that split second, that—" Eve snapped her fingers. "Everybody's holy shit, or what the fuck. But he smirked. He's looking right at Shauna with that red blaze from Lopez's hand across her cheek, and he smirks. Like: Yeah, nice job. He covered it fast; he's got a good mask. But I saw it. Smirked, and you bet your ass he had to swallow a laugh."

"Um, are there counterpoints?"

"Oh, plenty. Involuntary reaction, nervous twitch." Eve shrugged. "But he enjoyed that moment. He enjoyed watching Shauna's emotional speech interrupted by a hostile drunk. And he seriously enjoyed the slap."

She tapped her lapel. "I turned on my recorder when Lopez started her rant."

"You recorded the smirk?"

"I had a decent angle. I'm going to have EDD enhance it. A smirk's not evidence, and we've got precious little. But I add that to the nerves outside the apartment, the way he handled the box. Add it to the no-alibi that was perfectly presented as alibi, the high school relationship, the hovering."

"You think he's in love with Shauna?"

"No, I don't think he loves anyone but himself."

She eased a hip on the side of her desk, then pushed off again. No, not ready to sit.

"He lost the Shaun part of Shaunbar. He'd been a star in high school, but part of that shine came from her, being coupled with her. Then they're back home after college, but she moved to the city. So he moves to the city, practically on top of her."

"The hovering."

"And the access to that shine. But she's not interested in going back to high school. So he starts up with her good friend and the self-identified high school wheeze. Gets some shine there. And Shauna's not really with anyone, or not with anyone for long."

"Until Erin."

"Until Erin."

"That changes everything," Peabody said, picking up the threads. "She's in her first real relationship since him."

"And she switched teams," Eve added.

Peabody frowned again. "Do you think that matters?"

"To him, yeah, it does. It matters to him. It's salt-in-the-wound time for someone like Barney. Look at his background, Peabody. His family is nearly universally straight, WASPy types. Any who aren't tend to move away. You hook up with someone of the opposite sex, eventually marry in that sector, preferably of the same race, culture, and likely creed if you've got one. You live a traditional, by those standards, life and produce a kid or possibly two. Divorce is frowned upon, so choose that life mate wisely."

"But he's not with Shauna, and hasn't been for years. Why would it matter so much, matter enough to kill?"

"Because she still belongs to him."

She tapped the board, Barney's photo, then Lopez's.

"They're a lot alike, these two. Self-important, the center of their own worlds, tight families where, I'd say, they're well loved, even admired."

They both fit the profile, she thought, because they were very much alike.

"Both of them used to getting their way. Instead of letting it play out, hire a fancy lawyer and let it play out, Lopez's mother whines to the mayor. The fucking mayor, when her daughter gets busted for being a raging, violent asshole. I'm betting if Barney hit any bumps along the way, his family found a way to smooth them, too."

"Appearances," Peabody said. "Looks, status—those are top priorities for them. Yeah." Thoughtfully, she nodded. "Yeah, both of them. And they were both sort of stars in high school, right? She had all those write-ups about her dancing, and he was part of The Couple."

"And neither of them had the same shine in college. Smaller fish, bigger pool. Still, they're entitled, both of them. She's got family money behind her, but he does well enough. They're both attractive and wouldn't have trouble with those hookups."

"Except for her, Erin," Peabody added, "and for him, Shauna."

"Exactly. For her, I don't think she realized how deep her feelings were for Erin until Erin was dead, so it starts with jealousy. With him? It's pride, not passion. If he wants Shauna back, it's not love, not lust, not passion. Straight pride. He may actually feel some of the love, lust, passion for Becca—she pretty well suits his needs. But he doesn't feel enough to let go of the shine."

Eve eased the hip on her desk again, and this time stayed, let out a breath.

"And none of that's evidence. None of that builds a solid case. So the question is?"

"How do we prove it?"

"How do we prove it?" Eve echoed. "I thought leaving the case was a mistake—panic or just stupidity—but I'm more convinced than ever that was deliberate, a part of it. Shauna had to pay, too, for bruising that pride."

She pointed at Peabody. "What do you want to bet Shauna shared that dream with Barney back in high school. Their dream honeymoon."

"No bet." Peabody scooped a hand through the air. "It slides right in."

"It's the salt in the wound again, for him. So he gives it right back to her. Fickle bitch won't be going to Maui now."

"It's just mean."

"Yeah, and again, the mean's part of the point. He had the motive, means, and opportunity. Erin gave him the perfect opportunity. Here's a difference between him and Lopez, as I see it. Lopez would've waited Erin out, sure the relationship, even tied up in marriage, wouldn't last. He couldn't wait."

"Because, for one thing, it's a personal insult."

Now Eve smiled. "There you go. He had that weapon ready, maybe planning to kill her before the wedding. Maybe at the damn wedding. But the Maui thing, that couldn't be tolerated, plus, perfect opportunity."

She pushed off the desk to pace again.

"Erin asks him to help her with the big surprise because she trusts him. Why wouldn't she? He's not so much part of the tribe, right, but of the circle. He's Shauna's good friend, he's Becca's cohab. He's not going to the party—girls only—so it'd be easy to get him the case, the swipe, give him what she thinks is the basic timing. 'Just come in the back way.'"

"And he's 'Okay, sure, no problem.' The good friend, the good guy, all happy to help."

"Slip in, do the kill. Need to take her 'link, as there's some communication on that, but he's going to stage a robbery anyway. Shouldn't have picked a place like the D&D—that's insulting, too. A sex club? That's not the place for Shauna. He covered himself well. Close the shop himself—so we have that security footage. Meet a mutual friend at a place he's known. Buy the damn flowers."

"Then go home, bide your time, turn on the screen." Peabody picked up the threads again. "Make sure it's programmed for something you can say you watched at the time of the murder."

"Take the case, the weapon, and have a short walk in the rain. He has to let her know he's there—send a quick text or get one—because he'd still have the swipe. She slips away, a little drunk, a lot excited. And he's right there. He has to move fast, the minute she shuts the door.

"It's easier than he thinks." She could see it. She could fucking see it. "Easier, quicker. It's horrible, all that blood, but it's done. Take the 'link, the little bit of jewelry, leave the swipe, and get out."

"He could've walked for blocks to ditch the weapon," Peabody added, "the 'link and jewelry, too."

"Not too far, but far enough. He has to be home when Becca tags him. He needs to be home so she can say he was home when the body's discovered and she tags him."

"You have to be right about the communication on the 'link. If we can just cobble together enough probable cause to look at his."

"If he's smart, and he is, he'd have destroyed it and gotten a new one. Contact Mira, see about getting me a consult. I want to run all this by her. I need to finish the report on Lopez and I want to swing up to EDD."

"EDD?"

"I want Feeney to take a look at the smirk. I'm not basing the investigation on that, but it was the capper. Meanwhile, do a search for people who graduated with him and the two women. Get impressions."

"Hey, that's a good angle. I'll be all over it."

Eve sat, finished the report. She spent a little more time on her notes, laying on her very circumstantial evidence against Greg Barney.

She took the glides to EDD—less crowded, more thinking time—then walked into the geek carnival of EDD.

Color, movement, sound. Everyone jiggled, pranced, or shook in their bibs and baggies with the stripes, checks, swirls thereon making constantly changing patterns.

E-speak rolled like a strange, foreign language.

She spotted McNab, airboots shuffling, bony hips ticktocking, red-streaked blond tail of hair swaying.

She turned to the brown and beige sanctuary of Feeney's office.

He sat, worn brown shoes crossed on his desk. With his explosion of ginger hair, wiry with threads of silver, a wild crown on his head, he tipped back in his wrinkled shit-brown suit, baggy eyes closed in his hangdog face.

Before she could step back, he held up a finger. "Thinking, not sleeping."

In about eight seconds, he nodded; a satisfied smile bloomed.

"Okay, got it." And opened his eyes. He got up, walked to his wall screen. He held up another finger—just wait—then changed the position of some lines of code or equations or whatever the hell she couldn't have translated with a stunner shoved in her ear.

"And there it is."

He swiped something else she could interpret as save, copy, send. Seconds later, someone in the bullpen shouted:

"Wee-oh! Dunked it! Wee-oh, Cap!"

"Fucking-A right." He stepped back, picked up the lopsided bowl his wife had made, and snagged some candied almonds before offering the bowl to Eve.

She started to shake her head, changed her mind, popped two.

"Whatcha after, kid?" Feeney asked her.

"I sent up a recording," she began.

"Yeah, yeah, got that right here. Had to deal with this one first."

He went back around behind his desk. Manually brought the recording on-screen where she'd cued it.

"The redhead's about to get clocked by the brunette," Feeney observed.

"Yeah. The guy, off to the left, behind the redhead, beside the blonde— reddish blonde . . ."

Strawberry blonde—essentially a redhead, she realized. He went from one redhead to another.

Interesting.

"That guy," she continued. "Watch him, okay? Run it to just after the slap and tell me what you see."

Eve turned to watch again herself without blocking Feeney's view.

Over the gasps and murmurs, the crack of flesh to flesh snapped.

"That one hurt. And he liked it."

He paused it where Shauna's head reared back and Lopez's open hand had just started to drop.

"Right? First, I want to enhance until it's as close to the four of them— slapper, slappee, smirker, and the blonde—as we can get."

Those basset hound eyes gave her a long look. "You know enough to do this."

"Yeah, and I did, but the angle's a little tricky."

He enhanced, zoomed, sharpened.

"Like that?"

"Yeah, slo-mo it back to right before she swings, then advance slow-mo to this point again. See? See how he puts his arm around the blonde's shoulders?"

"Looks like she was going to move in, maybe try to stop the brunette."

"And he stopped her. And then how he looks sort of shocked, but—"

"More like he's holding in a laugh."

"Yes!" Vindication had Eve mentally pumping her fist. "Yes, yes, then the brunette swings, connects, and what do you see?"

"Fucker's smirking."

"He's smirking. Now, if you're at a memorial for the fiancée of one of your oldest, closest friends, do you smirk when she gets clocked?"

"Hell no." Feeney zoomed out again, then ran it back. "See the guy on the right? He's pissed and moving in. If he'd gotten there before the brunette took that swing, she wouldn't've taken it."

"I need a copy of the zoom and enhance, then if you can do the same with his face. The smirking fucker."

Feeney nodded, worked his magic. "This the one who killed the fiancée?"

"I can't prove it, yet, but I'm damn sure of it."

"Good-looking face. All-American boy. When it smirks like that, it's punchable."

As Eve studied the enhanced close-up, Detective Callendar strolled in. "Hey, Cap— Sorry, Dallas, didn't see you. I'll swing back."

In her orange bibs and a tee that looked as if someone had tossed green paint on a white canvas, she started to step back.

"Hey, I know that dooser. Where do I know that dooser?"

Eve remembered the word—dick/loser—and sent Callendar a sharp look.

"You know him? Greg Barney?"

"Not the name, but that face. That asshole smirk. Check it!" she said, and lifted a hand. "Fancy men's shop guy, downtown shop."

"How do you know him?"

"Not know-know, but he's the one who gave me that same snarky look when I went in there."

She dug into one of the many pockets of her bags, pulled out a pack of gum. She offered it to Eve, who shook her head, then to Feeney, who took one before Callendar took one herself.

"My brother's twenty-first birthday, back several months, and what does he want but this fancy shirt from this fancy designer. Seems this place was having a sale, so I poke in. And this guy, he's watching me like I'm going to grab shit up and run for it."

She shrugged, tossed her short, streaky dark hair. "So okay, I don't look like most people who shop there. Then when I find the stupid shirt—it's just a freaking tee, but it's got the fancy guy's label on it, which means they can charge easy ten times as much—and I hold it up to check it out, he comes marching over. Tells me how they prefer people don't handle the merchandise. I say how I'm thinking of buying it and is it on sale?"

Snapping her gum, she slid her hands into hip pockets. "He gives me that look right there. Like I'm a bug and he's the boot that's going to really love squashing me. He says how that designer never goes on sale, and how I should try the L&W for a more affordable knock-off. He pissed me off so much I bought that damn shirt, full price. But my brother freaking loves it, and it was his twenty-first."

Callendar smirked back at the smirk. "Is he a vic or a suspect?"

"Suspect."

"Hope you nail him good and hard."

"That's the plan. Can you copy all that for me, Feeney, and send?"

"Already did. Thinking time," he told her. "Take some."

"Yeah, I'm going to. Soon as I can. Thanks. You, too, Callendar."

As she started out through the color, movement, and sound, her 'link signaled.

She pulled it out as she went, scanned the text from Peabody.

> Mira just got a window. She can give you about fifteen
> if you go now.

> On my way. Keep pushing on the high school
> angle. Move to college if possible. Back in twenty.

Movement, she thought as she hopped on a glide. Callendar had given her a new perspective of the man his friends described as a nice guy, a helpful guy, an average guy.

There would be other perspectives, too. Maybe enough when they put them all together, that would give her some buttons to push.

Chapter Twenty

THE DRAGON WHO GUARDED MIRA'S OFFICE DIDN'T LOOK VERY PLEASED when Eve strode in. But she tapped her earpiece.

"Dr. Mira, Lieutenant Dallas is here. Yes, I will. Go right in." She slanted Eve a look. "You're on the clock, Lieutenant."

"Understood."

Eve gave the door a quick knock, then stepped inside.

Mira already stood, programming what Eve knew would be tea. She wore a slim, plum-colored dress with a short white jacket, and heels that merged the two colors with tiny checks. A gold chain with little, flat pearly disks draped down the purple bodice. Even smaller pearly disks dangled with purple ones from her ears.

It never failed to amaze Eve how Mira managed it.

"I had a couple minutes to look over your report," Mira said as the flowery scent of the tea wafted into the air.

"I appreciate it."

"It's interesting. Have a seat."

Eve took one of Mira's two blue scoop chairs, accepted the tea in its fancy cup. Mira tucked a strand of mink-colored hair behind her ear and took the other.

"I found your side notes even more interesting. I sometimes wonder if you're bucking for my job."

"Not hardly."

Mira smiled. "You'd be good at it. But then part of being a good investigator is understanding who and what people are. ChiChi Lopez, definitely narcissistic tendencies, but much of her sense of self-worth is tied to her physicality, and more narrowly, her sexuality. A difficult woman who uses that physicality and sex to attain what she wants. Attention, approval, admiration."

Mira sipped some tea. "It may be different with her family, but in her other relationships, emotions, genuine emotions, have played little part. So when she finds herself with genuine feelings for Erin Albright, and these feelings aren't returned, her resentment, her anger, and her bafflement are aimed at the person Erin has feelings for."

"Not at Erin."

"That's not my read, no. Erin had to be misled, somehow deceived, as in every way Lopez—to her mind—is superior to her rival. Even that confident superiority isn't enough as time passes. The rival must become a trickster, a manipulator, a liar, a cheat, a user. And in the end, when Erin is killed, the rival must be responsible, must take the blame."

Mira paused, smiled again. "Which, clearly, you concluded yourself."

"More or less. If Albright had been killed with a handy blunt object, I'd narrow on her. Crime of passion, heat of the moment, I could see it. But to plan it out like this, execute it like this? If Hunnicut was the victim, again, I'd narrow on Lopez."

"I absolutely agree. So. Greg Barney."

"I'd like to add something I just learned, via Detective Callendar."

Eve relayed the story.

"Hearing that story didn't surprise you," Mira commented.

"No. You, either."

"No, but again, some of our work runs in the same lane of human behavior. He enjoys his social standing, again as he sees it. From a solidly, dependably upper-middle-class background, and a classically traditional one, he rose a bit above as a teenager. Class president, star athlete, and a pairing with a popular and attractive girl that made them both stars in that arena. I don't believe either of us will be surprised to find at least some—especially on lower rungs of the social ladder—of his former schoolmates won't remember him with particular fondness."

"He's a bully," Eve said, "but not an obvious one. He hovers, observes, insinuates, placates. He's ridden some on his looks, like Lopez. His job makes him a kind of boss, and in a shiny venue. Both are important to him. Appearances are important to him. I've seen Becca's high school pictures, and he wouldn't have looked twice at her back then. But since? She . . ."

"Blossomed?"

"Okay, that works. She found a style that suits her, developed confidence in herself, her looks, her work. But he didn't move to the city for Becca—even if he knew she already lived and worked here. He moved because of Shauna."

"Yet they remain friends."

"He found a worthy substitute. And, surfacely, she's a kind of redhead, too. If he follows his family pattern, he'll want to be married around thirty, and to a white woman, or at least not obviously mixed race. He'll expect to have a child within two or three years, and for the woman to take leave from her work and serve as professional mother for at least the first five years after that.

"It's like a template," Eve added. "And it's pretty rigid. Those who deviate tend to drift away."

"Then why kill Erin?" Mira lifted a hand, turned it palm up. "He has Becca to suit his lifestyle."

"Shauna was his—half of the whole. He may want her back, I'm not sure about that, but she was his, then she wasn't. Like with Lopez, her relationship with Erin might have triggered feelings. It was one thing, at least acceptable, since he had Becca, for Shauna to sleep with attractive men. But she deviated from the template."

"And whose fault is that?"

"Yeah, has to be Albright—manipulating, using, and so on. Not half of the famous Shaunbar. He manages. Not just the men's store, but people. And Shauna moves out of that scope—she can't be managed when she's marrying someone who doesn't fit the pattern. And what about the years they were together? What does it say about that, about him?"

"To him? She's made a terrible mistake. She'll not only ruin her life, but smear their history together. Diminish it—and him. It's very personal, as the murder was very personal."

Eve set the tea aside, then pulled out her 'link. She cued up the recording to the smirk.

"This is him, right as Lopez slapped Hunnicut."

Mira took the 'link, studied the screen. "An unguarded instant. A mean, satisfied smile. A derisive smirk. An approval of Hunnicut's come-uppance. His feelings for Hunnicut are very complicated, aren't they?"

Mira handed back the 'link. "He needs and holds on to what they were together, the glossy couple admired, envied, even revered by their peers. I believe he may have genuinely enjoyed their friendship—with him managing it—while he cemented a relationship with the old school-mate, and his former love's best friend."

"It says I've got someone, and—during that time—you don't. No one that sticks. Until Albright."

"Until," Mira echoed. "He may have been somewhat amused initially, then appalled when it became clear the relationship was serious. Undoubtedly alarmed by the idea of marriage, a future, when he began to disrespect, at the least, the woman who'd once been half of his whole due to what she became."

"And the last straw—Maui," Eve added. "How could he allow Albright to fulfill that dream? More, how dare she try to? And she has the nerve to ask him to help her pull it off?"

"You conclude Erin needed to die—the only clear way to stop the wedding, the mistake, the deviation. But Shauna had to be punished, had to suffer some consequences for her choices, for tainting what they'd been to each other, what they'd had together."

"That's the nutshell."

Now Mira set her tea aside. "I don't disagree."

"I need more."

"I think you're taking the right direction in speaking to former classmates. So much of his persona is still tied there. You might dig up some former staff. Current may not wish to speak frankly about his attitudes on the job."

"I'll do that."

"And when you interview him, when you're ready to, make him angry."

"I have a knack for that."

Mira's smile flashed, made her eyes sparkle. "You do. It's a gift. Insult that self-worth, the hidebound traditions, the high school hero status. You'll need to push for an unguarded moment, like that smirk. Pry that open? I'd be very surprised if the rest doesn't fall."

"You think he did it, too."

"I'm reading your reports and notes, and you certainly lean there. So that's a factor. But I believe he's earned his place as your prime suspect."

When Mira's personal 'link signaled, Eve started to rise. Mira gestured her down again as she took the 'link out of her jacket pocket.

"It's Dennis. One second. Hello, Professor."

"Dr. Mira."

Just his voice had Eve going soft inside. She could see him in her mind's eye, the sweet face, the soft green eyes and mussed gray hair.

"Say hello to Eve. She's with me at the moment."

"Hello, Eve. How are you?"

"I'm fine, thanks." Not just soft, she had to admit, but a little bit gooey inside. "I was just leaving."

"Oh, not on my account. I just wanted to let Charlie know I fixed the leak."

"Did you?" Mira's smile broke out again. "You're so clever, Dennis."

"No more dripping, and no need for a plumber. And since it's a good night for grilling, I'm marinating some ribs."

"That sounds perfect. I should be home on time."

"I'll be here, waiting. We'll have some wine, won't we? I just have to find the corkscrew. It's never where I think it is."

"Second drawer, right of the stovetop. See you soon."

"It's never soon enough. Goodbye, Eve, enjoy the rest of your day, and best to Roarke."

"Bye," Eve murmured.

Mira slipped the 'link away again. "Dennis gets a bit antsy toward the end of summer. He only teaches one class in the summer term. And he likes to think he's handy, with tools, around the house. Sometimes, surprisingly, he is. Other times?"

With a laugh, Mira rolled her eyes. "Oh, the chaos, the cursing. But the man's a genius with a marinade. It's lovely to know I'll go home to wine and a good meal."

"It is." Roarke might not be a genius with marinade—she didn't think either of them knew the first thing about marinade—but he always made sure she had a good meal.

"I need to get back to it. Thanks for the time, and the insight."

"I think you had more than enough of your own in this case."

"It helps to have some confirmation. I know he did it," she said as she rose. "I know how he did it, and if I don't have all the why, I have most of it. Make him angry," she repeated. "I don't think I'll have a problem there."

She started for the door, paused with her hand on the knob. "It's nice, being married."

This time Mira simply beamed. "Yes, it is. The right life partner makes all the difference. Wasn't it clever of both of us to choose so well?"

"I used to think I didn't choose so much as tripped into it."

"You don't trip, Eve."

"Well, not very often."

When she left, she got the gimlet eye from the admin that suggested she'd gone over her allotted time. Probably had, she considered as she kept right on going.

But it had been worth it.

Former staff—a good angle. Make him angry? She'd have done that anyway, but it was a solid tip to do that as quickly as possible.

When she walked back into Homicide, Jenkinson, his tie, and his partner were missing, as were Baxter and Trueheart. Santiago and Carmichael huddled at his desk. Eve hoped they consulted on a case and weren't making a bet that Santiago would surely lose.

Peabody signaled her.

"Jenkinson and Reineke caught one. Baxter and Trueheart are with a suspect in Interview A. And I talked to some former classmates. Actually three. Two were full of Shaunbar, and how Barney was such a star on the field and an inspiration otherwise. But then I got an earful from a . . . Julian Prowder."

"Fill my ear."

"Okay. He was careful at first. High school, who remembers, who cares. But then it turned out he remembered a lot and cared a bunch more. Let's see."

She pulled her notes, though Eve could tell she didn't need them.

"Puffed-up prick, stuck-up jerk with a stick up his ass. More than happy to narc on a fellow student for any infraction, but kept it down-low. Any guy who so much as looked at Shauna too close became a prime target for just that. He said Barney would wait and watch for a misstep, then pounce.

"Apparently Prowder wasn't among the best dressed in that era—family of three boys, and he was the youngest. So hand-me-down time. He said Barney liked to sneer and snark at him about his clothes, but again, down-low because he liked to pretend he was above the fray. And Shauna wasn't one for snarking that way."

"A different perspective. Keep at it. I'm going to dig up former employees at the men's shop. Let's see what they think about Barney's managerial style."

"That's a good one."

"More Mira's than mine, but yeah."

Then, she decided as she went to her office, she'd take another page from Feeney.

She'd put in some thinking time.

It took her awhile, but when she found one—a LeRoy Vic—she hit gold.

"Yeah, I can talk about Greg Barney, the fuck." Vic, age thirty-five, mixed race, sun-streaked brown hair, scowled on-screen. "I had an opportunity for a manager's position at Orlando's in Brooklyn. My wife was having a baby, and we wanted to move there to be closer to our families. It would've been a step up for me—a solid raise. I worked five years at On Trend, the last two as assistant manager under that prick. And what does he do? He gives me a crap eval. How my work ethic declined, I've taken too much time off, my customer service tended to be shoddy."

"You disagree with that evaluation?"

"Damn right. I always covered for Greg, or anybody, when they needed some time. Did I take some time, too? Sure. My wife had a real shaky first trimester, and she needed me. I had the time coming, and I took it. But my work was never, ever shoddy, and I had top sales six months running."

"Can you speculate why his evaluation was so poor?"

"I can tell you why. He didn't want me to get the job. I wouldn't have known about the eval, but the outgoing manager at Orlando's told me. He said how I'd aced the interview and so on, so I confronted Greg about it, and he said, like he's my keeper or something, how it was for my own good. How I couldn't handle that job, and was making a mistake taking on the responsibility when I had a kid coming."

"I see. What did you do about it?"

"I wanted to quit, but my wife talked me out of it. And she was right. What I did? I made copies of my sales records, and I contacted some of my regulars, asked for references. And I got them. I got passed over for the manager's slot, but I got a sales position, and I took it. Then I quit.

"That was two years ago. I'm manager now, so Greg Barney can kiss my ass. He had no right, no fucking right to do that, to decide what was best for me and my family. But he's the type who always thinks he knows best."

"I appreciate your input."

"You ought to talk to Sharlene Wilson. She was in sales, and he pushed her out. Maybe a year and a half ago."

"Would you have her contact?"

"Haven't talked to her in a few months, but yeah. Give me a second." Muttering to himself about Barney—asshole, prick, bullshit eval—he dug it up, gave it to Eve. "So, what did he do?"

"I'm just gathering information in an ongoing investigation."

"Well, I hope whatever it is, I read about it. Shoddy customer service, my ass."

"Thanks for your time, Mr. Vic."

"No problem."

She contacted Sharlene Wilson, left a voice mail.

Then she put her boots up, closed her eyes.

And took the thinking time.

Peabody said, "Um."

"I'm thinking." Though Eve had heard her coming, she stayed another moment as she was. "I reached Barney's former assistant manager, and have a voice mail into another former clerk. The former assistant manager shares your former classmate's opinion of Greg Barney."

Eve pointed to the AC, then opened her eyes. As Peabody programmed coffee, she relayed LeRoy Vic's statement.

"That's a crappy thing to do."

"It is, but more, it fits the 'I'm going to screw up your life for your own good' routine."

"I hit another who said he got the shit kicked out of him in high school, not by Barney, but because of him."

With her coffee, Peabody eased very, very carefully onto the ass-biting visitor's chair.

"One of Barney's teammates got suspended—from school and the team—when someone reported he had a couple Zoner joints in his locker. Since the teammate was going hard after Barney's team captain position, the guy figured Barney for the squealer, but Barney claimed he actually saw the other kid heading into the vice principal's office right before the teammate was called down and suspended."

Peabody shifted, again very, very carefully. "You have to figure the guy's got no reason to lie about it now. He says he never went to the vice principal, never said a damn thing, but got his ass kicked over it anyway. He figures Barney turned it on him because his locker was next to Zoner

Guy's and he was a member of the Clean Teens Club. They take an oath not to use illegals or drink alcohol, to eat only plant-based foods and abstain from sex."

Eve glanced up from her coffee. "Seriously?"

"I take it it's a pretty small club. Anyway, when Zoner Guy jumped Mr. Clean Teen—you're going to like this—he said Barney saw it go down. And he smirked."

"I bet he did. Oh yeah, he did. Gets rid of competition, covers his own ass, and gets to watch someone he probably considered an annoyance get tuned up."

Eve looked at the board, looked at Barney's easy, attractive smile. "You know, he'd have lived his life smoothly bullying and manipu-lating—a general asshole who'd probably have carved out the life he wanted. But then Shauna had to fall for someone he didn't approve of—and couldn't be smoothly manipulated out of it. So he turned to murder. He'd feel justified," she added. "In all cases, he'd feel justified."

She lifted her mug toward the board. "We're going to nail his ass, Peabody."

"I like to think so, but up till now the only real evidence we have, and that's still circumstantial, is he's an asshole."

"Next step." Thinking time had given her that. "We go through the victim's apartment again. With Shauna. Barney took something out with him in that damn box. She's the only one who'd know what's missing."

"That's going to be touchy."

"She'll stand up to it." Eve remembered the punch, the damn good punch. "I'm not going to hit her with it today. Not only too emotional, but she'll have too many people around her today. But tomorrow. You have to figure her friends need to go back to work—they can't surround her all day. So tomorrow, we go by where she's staying and convince her to go through the apartment with us."

"Okay, but if he took something she didn't even know was there—"

"She will. It's personal. Something he wanted for himself, or wanted back, or maybe some sort of trophy. It mattered to him enough to take it. If she notices later, well, it got lost in all the confusion, so sorry."

"It's worth a shot, but even with that—"

"It's the next step," Eve interrupted. "And it's going to lead to the one after. He's slick, Peabody. A first kill, yes, but he's been honing his skills in manipulation, ass-covering, that smooth bullying his whole life, so he's slick. We're slicker."

"I'd drink to that if I hadn't already finished my coffee."

"Go contact Shauna—you're just checking on her, letting her know we charged Lopez with assault. Lay on the sympathy and find out if she's still at Decker's for the next few days, blah blah. How you guess her friends have to get back to work. Don't mention tomorrow."

"Got it. Just confirm where she'll be, and if she'll be on her own."

"Then dig more into high school. I'll start on college. Let's build ourselves a pattern, Peabody. A profile of an asshole."

"You know, there are a lot of assholes in the world. Most of them don't kill people over bullshit."

Eve glanced back at the board. "This one did."

She gave it another hour, then ninety minutes when Sharlene Wilson tagged her back. Deciding her ears were full enough, for now, she called it.

She walked into the bullpen just as Baxter rose from his desk. A glance at the bullpen case board told her he and Trueheart had closed their current case.

"Wrapped it?" she said.

"In a bright, shiny bow. My esteemed partner and I are heading out for a celebrational brew. We just sent you the paperwork."

"I'll take a look from home."

"Wrapped ours, too," Santiago said from his desk as he continued to work his comp. "Just finishing up the eights. I'm in for a celebrational brew. Carmichael?"

"Twist my well-toned arm. Reineke?"

"We're waiting for the ME on ours. Gonna be accidental. Guy weighs in easy four-fifty. Decides he's going to sweat off the pounds and buys himself one of those hot boxes."

"Hot boxes?"

"Some fad, Loo," Jenkinson told her. "You buy this kit, put this box together with a temp control deal. Supposed to get a certified tech to do it, but this guy does it himself, puts on the suit that comes with it, goes in. Ends up baking himself, can't get out. Kit's got a fail-safe so it shuts off after like thirty minutes, but he didn't bother with that. So baked."

"Well, that sounds . . . ugly."

"Sure as hell was," Reineke confirmed. "I can meet you for one brew—I got time for one—after we clear this."

"I got a family thing," Jenkinson said. "Catch one next time."

"How about it, Peabody, Dallas?"

Eve shook her head at Baxter. "We didn't close ours. I've got work to do at home. Peabody, go home or go catch a brew."

"The Blue Line?" she asked. "I'll see if McNab's up for it, meet you if he is. Shauna's still at Decker's, Dallas, and everyone's got work tomorrow. She should be alone by nine-thirty."

"Then we'll go by after nine-thirty."

"I got a couple more statements."

"I'll read them at home. Take off. Good work," she added to the rest of the squad, and headed out.

She could see the steps toward closing out the case. But until that first step, the rest continued as speculation.

Right now, she wanted home. Some quiet. Some mind-clearing time.

A stupid murder, she thought, and found that single point infuriated her. Selfish, ugly, cruel, but she expected those elements in any murder. The stupidity of the motivation stuck in her craw.

And not over a high school girlfriend, she thought as she pushed through traffic. Not that, not really. It was more, and it was deeper than that. It came down to the need to direct others' choices, to open or block the life path of people connected to him.

An ordinary man, really, an average sort of guy with an average sort of background, income, lifestyle. Nothing particularly dark, nothing especially brilliant.

But in his way, he'd decided he was qualified to play God. He decided what suited, what didn't.

And in Erin Albright's case, who lived, who died.

Her advantage wasn't just that she knew it all, was as sure of it all as she'd been about any investigation in her career, but that Barney surely believed he'd gotten away with it.

She hoped by this time tomorrow, he'd learn differently.

As she swung through the gates, she felt her shoulders relax.

Just that easy, she realized. All it took was the sight of that castle-like house rising on that green ocean of lawn, the wild late summer blooms, the glint of window glass in the evening sun.

She'd update her board and her book, then maybe have that glass of wine with Roarke. Talk the whole thing over with him. Share a good meal, then maybe try to work some new angles, as the talking-things-over part often gave her that potential.

She parked, and didn't let the knowledge she'd need to go through the gamut of Summerset spoil the homecoming.

He loomed, of course, with his greeting partner Galahad beside him in the foyer where the cool air smelled, very subtly, of summer flowers.

"Yeah, yeah, I know," she began. "No blood again. Must be a record, since the anal keep track."

"Congratulations." He spoke dryly. "I'll be sure to mark it down on my event calendar. Roarke is upstairs in his office. He had a difficult day."

She'd bent down to stroke the cat, and looked up, straightened. As alarm bells rang in her head. "Is he hurt?"

"Not physically, no. He's brooding, which he's quite good at from time to time. I expect you'll deal with it. If not, I can cancel my plans for this evening."

"I'll deal with it." She started for the stairs.

"Fish and chips," Summerset added. "It's a comfort food for him."

"I've got it." She went up the stairs with the cat on her heels.

He didn't often need comfort, she thought. But she could figure it out.

Upstairs, she heard his voice—sharp and final, with a little more Irish leading the way. A sure sign of emotion—passion, anger, amusement. And in this case, anger.

"I said it's done, and handled as I choose. That's the bloody end of it."

She turned into the office just as he cut off whoever had been on the other end of the 'link.

He sat, hair tied back, jacket off, sleeves rolled. Work mode, she noted. But the cold blue fire in his eyes went dark and broody. Dark and broody enough he didn't sense her there.

The cat trotted over, leaped onto the desk.

"Not now, mate. Not now."

He started to lift the cat off, then spotted Eve.

"Ah. I didn't know you were home."

"Just got here. So, what was that about? On the 'link just now?"

"Nothing." He shrugged it off as he set the cat on the floor. "A work matter. It's handled. But I have a bit more to see to here."

Oh no, she thought, he didn't get off that easy.

"What kind of work matter?"

"It's handled," he repeated, and though the tone lacked the sharpness, it still held all the finality.

It clearly said: Butt out.

The tone would've pissed her off—if she hadn't seen the brooding under the temper.

But she knew how to light the match.

"When my work matters put me in a mood, you want to know why."

"Your moods are many," he muttered. "And it's not at all the same."

Okay, sometimes dealing with it meant pushing for a fight to burn off the brood, more with a torch than a match.

"Oh, because your work's so important and beyond my limited scope with me just being a cop and you being the great and powerful Roarke."

"Now she quotes from classic vids." He shoved up. It wasn't the icy fire in his eyes but all heat.

"I asked a simple question," she tossed back. "Instead of a simple answer, you lob insults."

"I stated a simple fact, but take it as you will. Now, for feck's sake, give me a bit of time. Christ knows I give you all you need there. Go deal with your board and scour your daily notes, and leave me to this."

She said, simply, "No."

The cat, who'd watched the exchange, decided to desert the field and jogged out the office door as Roarke rounded on her.

"This is my bloody space, for my bleeding business, so move on to yours. This has nothing to do with you, so go see to your own."

"You are my own."

With that, she watched the anger drain out of him as if she'd turned a tap.

"Ah, fuck it all."

When he dragged a hand through his hair, when it wasn't ice, or fire, or brooding in his eyes, but desolation, she stepped to him. Put her arms around him.

"Tell me."

He lowered his forehead to hers. "I had to fire someone today, some-one who's worked for me a decade."

"Who?"

"You know her a bit, I'd think. Alyce Avery."

Eve did a quick run through her mental files. "Okay, yeah, she's been to the holiday parties. Why did you have to fire her?"

"She stole from me—which is a haughty ledge for a thief to stand on."

"No, it's not—and former," she reminded him, laying a hand on his cheek.

"As if that wasn't enough, she tried to throw the blame on someone else to save herself. She could've come to me." He drew away to pace to the window and stare out. "Why didn't she come to me when she found herself in a squeeze?"

"What squeeze?"

"All that came out, didn't it, too late. Her son started gambling and got into considerable debt to the wrong sort. So she skimmed and shuffled—of course, intending to pay it all back. And when the skimming and shuffling came out, she tried to blame her assistant, which only made it that much worse, didn't it?"

He turned back. "I'd have helped her, but she broke trust between us, and would've let someone innocent pay the price. So now her life's in shambles."

"Are you pressing charges?"

The ice came back. "She'll pay it back. She'll have time, but she'll pay every penny back. That's my decision, and that's the end of it."

"Okay."

He lifted an eyebrow. "So the cop doesn't point out she broke the law?"

"No. Your wife points out you did what you had to do by firing her, and what you needed to do by giving her time to pay it back. And the son?"

"I had a word with him as well. I used the threat of his mother going to prison for embezzlement as motivation for him to enter rehab for gambling addiction. Likely not the way, but—"

"It's one way, especially if you were Scary Roarke."

He smiled, just a little. "I suppose I was at that. I was fair pissed enough to be. Others don't fully agree with my decision."

"Others aren't the boss of you. If it counts, I agree with it."

"It counts a great deal. Bugger it. It counts a very great deal. And I'm sorry for my vicious mood and slapping at you when you offered to listen."

"I'm not the only one whose moods are many."

He smiled again, just a little more. "I suppose you're not. I love you, Eve."

"It's a good thing I love you back. Enough that I'm going to take care of dinner, which we're going to eat on the patio. It's cooled off enough, and we could both use it."

"That sounds like a very fine idea. Thanks for it."

Chapter Twenty-one

SHE CHANGED INTO A BREEZY TANK AND SHORTS, AND HE INTO A T-SHIRT and casual pants. The August heat lurked under a sluggish breeze, but that, Eve decided, was summer.

The patio pots and planters appeared to agree, as they stood lush with color and scent while the sky held a bold and arrogant summer blue.

She figured if the alternative had been starving to death, she could figure out the grill. But under the circumstances, she took Summerset's advice.

She set out fish and chips, added some brown bread and butter, and switched out wine for Guinness.

Roarke took one look at the patio table and kissed her cheek. "Well now, this is perfect, isn't it?" He sat, lifted his glass to her. "Here's to you for knowing when and how to piss me off."

"It's a skill." She took his hand, squeezed it before she lifted her own glass. "And you're smart enough to know, when your head's clear again, you did her and her son a favor."

"A favor, is it?"

"You could've pressed charges, or you could have kept her on—made her pay the money back, but kept her on. You'd have considered both."

"I did, yes."

"But neither of those would've helped her, or her son. In her case, doing time wouldn't have accomplished much, and keeping her on? You'd never have trusted her again, and she'd know it. So she starts over from now. She fucked up and has to deal with the fallout."

"And that's a favor to her?"

"If you don't have to deal with the fallout, it's real easy to fuck up again, and it gets easier to fuck up on purpose, because why not?"

With a shrug, she rained salt on her chips. "She worked for you for a decade, you invited her into your home, so she's not an idiot or a career criminal. She'll remember what she did every time she makes a payment back to you. And unless the son's a complete dick, he'll remember how his actions affected his mother, which may—just may—help the rehab stick."

"She's not an idiot, no, and hardly one to make a career out of embezzlement. And rather than a complete dick, her son's young and foolish. Barely into his twenties, and if I'm a judge, sick at heart at what that foolishness cost his mother."

"You're a damn good judge."

"She raised him on her own—the father was out of the picture when I hired her. They're very close, so while I can't quite see the favor in it, I think they'll come around after a time.

"In any case, a brutal day, and I'm grateful to you for taking the edge off it."

Steam pumped out of the fish when she forked into it, and smelled pretty damn good. "I got to needle you, so that's a side benefit for me. Other than getting knocked on my ass by a piss-soaked junkie, it's about the only action I saw today."

"And how did a piss-soaked junkie knock you on your ass?"

"Couple of rooks hauled him into the elevator, which means I'm getting off because piss-soaked, and they let him slip. He rammed right into me. Jesus, the smell. I'm lucky it didn't have time to transfer."

"You meet such interesting people in the course of your day. And the memorial?"

It would take his mind off the brutal, Eve decided.

"I guess the highlight would be when Hunnicut's up there talking about Albright—heartfelt, touching—and Lopez comes in. Not altogether drunk, but definitely lit."

She ran it through—rant, slap, punch.

"I suppose that livened things up, so to speak."

"Shock, horror, fascination."

"And gave you a chance to take on Lopez in the box, I assume."

"Oh yeah."

She ran it through for him as they ate, and yes, she could see it took his mind off his own day.

"You don't think she killed Erin Albright."

"No. Do you?"

"She's impulsive, careless of others, hotheaded. And no. A moment's heat, an angry strike, then yes. But not the way this was done. It's far too cool and calculating."

"See, a good judge." She pulled her 'link out of her pocket. "Judge this. Greg Barney between slap and punch."

Roarke took the 'link, studied the screen. He looked at Eve and said, "Ah."

"Yeah, ah." After pocketing the 'link again, she ate more chips. "That's not the expression of a man, Mr. Nice Guy, watching his good friend and former sweetheart get clocked at her fiancée's memorial."

"So he's your man."

"Oh, he is. With any luck, I'll have him in the box tomorrow, and then in a cage."

"What else do you have?"

That single question, she had to admit, centered the problem.

"My gut, mostly, and personality. A kind of profile of an asshole."

She ran her day through for him as that day waned with softening light and quiet breezes.

"The last one I talked to, just before I left Central, worked under him at the shop. A woman, early forties, married, two kids. She worked there part-time, and said he made a habit of saying how she'd make more as a professional mother, and how much better off her kids would be if she stayed home."

"There's another ah from me."

"She'd say how she liked working, being out in the world, and her kids were fine. It irritated her some, but she didn't think much of it. He also wondered, out loud, why she wanted to work in a men's shop. Wouldn't she be more comfortable, if she insisted on working, putting in her time at a woman's boutique—shit like that."

She took the bread, slathered with butter, that Roarke offered, bit in.

"After a while, he started cutting her hours. Hired another part-timer—a man, naturally. She took off for a school function, with advance notice—but he wrote her up for it. Just continued to undermine her in little ways, claimed some customers complained about her attitude, her service, which she said was bullshit. And I believe her on that.

"Eventually, she quit—decided it wasn't worth the annoyance of dealing with him. And get this, he told her she was making the right choice for her family."

"More than a bit of a prick, isn't he then? And calculating."

"Exactly. He takes his time, maneuvers and manipulates. No problem lying to get his way, or using his position as a supervisor to bully staff. Because in his world, he's right, he knows best."

"And if Shauna—whom he'd consider part of his world—won't do what's best for her, won't live as he believes she should and must, well then, he'll simply remove the impediment. And she'll need to deal with the results of her poor choices, won't she? A dead love, a broken dream, a slap in the face."

Sipping her beer, Eve smiled at him. "It's nice eating fish and chips with someone who sees it like I do."

"I can certainly see why you don't like him on a personal level, and I can see why you do like him as Albright's killer. Why don't you help me see how you intend to get him into the box, then into a cage?"

"I can do that. Why don't we deal with these dishes, then I'll do that while we take a walk."

Now he reached for her hand. "Darling Eve. Are you making time for me?"

"For us. A few things—not case related. Did you know you're supposed to marinate ribs?"

"Whose ribs?"

She laughed, and polished off her beer. "The kind you eat smothered in barbecue sauce if you've got any sense."

"In that case, I didn't, no. Why?"

"Mr. Mira called when I was consulting with Mira. Apparently he fixed a leaky faucet or pipe or something." Considering him, she frowned. "Could you do that?"

"I could, actually, and have done."

"Good to know. During their brief conversation, he said he was marinating ribs, and they'd have wine if he could find the corkscrew. You know how he is."

"I do. Charming and wise."

"Yeah, he is. She told him where to find it, and it struck me like it did this morning. It's nice being married. So it's good to make time when we can.

"Then, as I'm about to leave Central, Baxter tells me he and Trueheart just closed one, and are heading out for a brew. Santiago and Carmichael are finishing up the paperwork on another, and are going to join. Jenkinson and Reineke are waiting for an ME report, and Reineke will meet them because Jenkinson has a family thing. Peabody's going to see if McNab's up for it. So they'll go hang some at the Blue Line, have a brew."

"You didn't want to join them?"

"Work on my mind." She shook her head. "And I just wanted to get home. But it made me think about the idea of Off Duty, and how it'll be good to have another place. Maybe you want more than a fake burger and a half-decent brew. Maybe you want some music and more variety after closing one, or when you've got a hard one and need a break."

"It's coming along well."

"Also good to know." She rose. "Let's get this stuff out of the way."

It felt good, that walk, as the sun slipped lower and some crazed bird sang to oncoming twilight. In the grove, peaches hung like rosy balls just waiting to be plucked.

Roarke did just that, handed it to her.

The first bite, so sweet, so fresh, had her taking another. "God, that's ridiculous. Nothing should taste that amazing."

"When I had them planted, years ago, I wanted the look and scent of them. As well as the magic Summerset can make with them. I never imagined walking here with you, enjoying them right off the branch."

"I sure as hell never saw myself eating a peach, or anything else, right off the tree." Since she was, she took another bite. "I'd never even seen a peach tree before these. Can you grow one from the seed or whatever it is?"

"I think it's a pit, and I suppose. How else would they get them?"

"How the hell would I know? Peabody would. We should give her some."

"Peaches or pits?"

"Well, if we give her some peaches, she'd have both."

"A fine idea. I'll see to it. Now. The box and the cage?"

"Barney took something from that apartment. I knew it at the time—nothing I could do about it, but I knew it. I'm more sure of it now. It fits his pattern, his profile."

"What sort of thing, do you think?"

"See, that's a question I've been playing with. Nothing big, nothing anyone else would notice. Family and a couple other friends have been in there getting things for Hunnicut, taking Albright's clothes and stuff, so nothing that stands out."

"Something tucked away then."

She pointed at him with what was left of her peach. "See that? That's cop thinking, and you just have to swallow it."

"I don't at all, because it's thief thinking as well. And there I have the foundation."

"Well, maybe." She'd allow it, she decided as they strolled toward the pond. "But even tucked away, not really something people would notice right off. They're bringing clothes and so on to her. And she was wearing earrings at the memorial. Not the ones she had on the night of the party, so someone brought those to her."

"Seems like something more between the two of them—Hunnicut and Barney."

"That's what makes the most sense. Something he wanted back because she didn't deserve it now. Maybe something he gave her at some point. And probably when they were a couple. That's what it feels like to me.

"'I gave you this when you were perfect, and now you're not. You can't keep it.'"

She sat on the bench by the pond, looked at the floating lilies. The tree with the flowing branches she and Roarke had planted seemed to have grown some. That struck her as an accidental triumph.

"I could be off there. Could be something else. A note he wrote her, a photograph. Maybe even something Albright gave her that burned his narrow-minded ass. Maybe something to do with the wedding the others hadn't removed yet."

She tossed the peach pit. "Wouldn't it be a kick in the ass if it grew a tree there?"

"I'd say more a minor miracle."

They sat a moment, enjoying the evening, the shine of the water as the sun dipped lower yet, the spread of the plants around the pond.

The worst edges of his day worn away, he laid a hand over hers.

"And how will you know what he took?"

"That's the sticky part. I have to convince Hunnicut—push her if it comes down to it—to go back to the apartment with me and Peabody. She hasn't been back since the murder, and she's made it clear she won't. But I have to get her to not only go back, but go through the place. To look in closets, in cupboards, in drawers. Then make absolutely sure she keeps her mouth shut about it."

Eve let out a breath. "She's used to sharing. It's her nature to tell things to her friends, her family. Possibly complete strangers. So the trick is, go back where she's staying in the morning, when we can be reasonably sure she's alone. Then convince her to go back, go through, and tell no one."

"She loved Albright. I don't think it'll be as sticky as you imagine to convince her to do this if she believes it will help."

"She's also used to trusting." As day slipped toward dusk, Eve tipped her head to Roarke's shoulder. "I have to make her trust me more than she does her tribe."

"She may not, but she'll respect your authority. She's a rule follower, isn't she? Wouldn't that be one of the reasons, besides her looks, why Barney was attracted to her, attached himself to her?"

"You're right about that. Hunnicut broke one of his rules, so she had to pay for it."

"How will that help you, if you find what he took?"

"By getting a search warrant for his place, finding what he took, charging him with theft, getting him into the box on it, then pushing the right buttons. I'm going to make it work. You took the edge off my day, too."

"Did it have one?"

"Mostly the edge of frustration. I know he did it, I know where to find him. I know how he did it—or close enough. Why, or close enough. But I can't just knock on his door and cuff him."

"But you like a challenge, Lieutenant."

"I guess I do. He's such a weak asshole, Roarke, the motive is so idiotic, it annoys me. He's so not worth it."

"So you remember Erin Albright is."

God, he understood her.

"So I remember Erin Albright is. It's small, annoying steps instead of a big takedown. But she's worth it."

She lifted her head, looked at him. "I forgot. I bought that painting—or will."

"Your first slice of New York."

"Yeah. I'll like having it for that. And to remind me that sometimes it takes a lot of small, annoying steps. I need to go in, take some more of them."

"All right."

"In a minute." She lowered her head to his shoulder again. "Just one more minute. I feel sorry for people who don't have a spot like this—not the big grand scope of all this. Just a quiet spot where they can sit, with someone who matters or alone, and smooth out the edges of the day."

She slid her hand into his, linked fingers. "I never imagined this, any more than eating a peach off the tree."

"We planted that one there."

"Sure as hell did. It's growing, right? It looks like it is to me."

"It's growing." He kissed the top of her head. "I suppose so are we."

They went back in, and up to Eve's office, where the cat lay sprawled in her sleep chair. He eyed them both as if to determine the need to retreat again.

Sensing the crisis had passed, he stretched, rolled, and sprawled in a different direction.

"Do you really have work to deal with?" Eve asked Roarke.

"Not really, no. I can get quite a bit done when pissed off, and did."

"Do you want an assignment?"

He slid a hand into his pocket, fingered the gray button. "Will I enjoy it?"

"You tell me. The first is to take a good look at Becca DiNuzio's family. I want to see how they fit in Barney's narrow worldview. The next is to check and see if Barney's insured any paintings since the murder. He'd have had time now if he thought to. And last, to look at his finances again."

"There now, we're getting to the enjoyment."

"Can you dig down into purchases, gift-type things, specifically for women? Girlfriend gift–type things, in the last three years."

"Ah, you want to see what he might buy for DiNuzio, as it may lead you to what he might have bought back in the day for Hunnicut. And taken back."

"Yeah. I want to see if he considers Becca—and her family—worthy enough, and if so, what he buys his girlfriend."

"All right. I'll enjoy that. Not such a small step, I'm thinking, as it may save you several others."

"That's the goal."

While he went into his office, she updated her board. Then set it aside to read over the paperwork from her other detectives, signed off. Good work there, she thought, all around.

Now it was her turn, so she programmed coffee and settled into it.

When Roarke came back, she frowned at him. "That didn't take long. No luck?"

"How easily you doubt me. First." He sat on the edge of her command center, drank what was left of her second cup of coffee. "DiNuzio's parents have been married thirty-one years. To each other. She's the oldest of three—I assume you ran her before so know the basics. Her mother's a mathematician, and took parental leave for each offspring. The father, an engineer, coached her younger brother's softball team. They've lived in the same house, the same neighborhood, for twenty-six years."

"Potentially worthy then, on his scale."

"And your instinct continues. He insured a painting, an Albright, only this morning, valued at forty-eight hundred. As for gifts, he strikes me as, again, very stagnant and very ordinary. Cross-reference DiNuzio's birthday, his mother's, his sisters' and it's easy to find. His mother, his sisters, a sweater, a scarf, that sort of thing. A girlfriend gets jewelry. The same holds for what I'd assume is Christmas, and as the date range matches for the last three years, what would likely be an anniversary. Add Valentine's Day."

"Jewelry."

"He tosses in a few other items for Christmas, but jewelry, yes, is the main thing. Nothing overly expensive, but not too cheap, either. He frequents the same jeweler on Fifth, or has for these purchases. Earrings are his go-to, but he's gone for a necklace, a bracelet now and then."

"She wore this necklace, linked hearts, played with it some in Interview."

"Linked hearts—a boyfriend gift, I'd say. And for her birthday last spring, a ring. Not an engagement type. A blue topaz flanked by citrines.

A blue stone," he explained, "with smaller yellow ones on each side. Set in silver."

"Yeah, I got it. She's had it on every time I've seen her. Okay, okay, it's jewelry. And it's probably jewelry he took."

She pushed up, paced. "Shauna got engaged. He's not ready for that yet, but he switches up and gives Becca a ring. Symbolic, maybe. It's always jewelry, so we'll try that first tomorrow. He's got a pattern, he has tradition. This makes sense. Thanks."

She glanced back at her command center where he sat still, looking so easily Roarke. Her coffee was gone, and she had nothing to do, not really, until the next morning.

As if reading her, he got up, slid his arms around her.

"Why don't you shut this down, and we go for a swim? We can smooth out the rest of each other's edges."

"You just want to get me wet and naked."

"I absolutely do." He kissed her, slow, long, deep, to prove it.

"Since that means I get you wet and naked, too, what are we waiting for? Close operations," she said, and kissed him back.

She woke in the morning with everything as smooth as it got.

And there, on the sofa, sat Roarke and the cat, so she began a day as well as she'd ended another.

She rolled out of bed and went straight for coffee.

"I'm so ready for today."

"Be ready for some rain as well," Roarke warned her. "We're likely in for a storm later."

"Before it's over, Greg Barney's going to find out I'm the goddamn storm."

When she went in to shower, Roarke looked at the cat. "She's not wrong about that, as we well know. Let's feed the storm, shall we?"

When she came out, he put his tablet aside. He enjoyed seeing her in a robe, which certainly explained why he couldn't resist buying them for her. This one was as close as he'd dared come to pink, with its deep rose tone, and in silk that shimmered, just a little.

He took off the domes as she sat, and found himself pleased when she gave the full Irish a nod and a narrow look.

"That's just right for today."

"You'll let me know, won't you, when you have him?"

"Sure. I want to take him at his shop. Mortify him." She shrugged as she crunched into bacon. "Not necessary, but it's a personal wish."

She glanced at him as she dug into her eggs. "You'll have a better day today."

"I will. What's done's done. I'll move along to what's next—as will you. Don't wear black today."

She paused as she cut into a fat sausage. "Oh, come on."

"Wear a strong color, but not black. He'll understand and respect the cut, the fabric. Add a strong color, and you'll intimidate, just a bit, along with it. A vest, once you're in the box, so your weapon's visible."

"I like that part," she mumbled.

"It wouldn't hurt, at least until he notices, to leave this out." He slid a hand over to lift the chain of the Giant's Tear diamond she wore under her shirts.

"I don't like to wear it out on the job. Cops don't wear big, fat diamonds."

"Exactly. This, the weapon, the clothes, the woman in charge? For his type, there'll be some confusion along with the intimidation. He won't like you and Peabody being in control. He manages people, and he's superior to women."

She considered as she ate. "Okay, those are solid points. And you've made it so fricking complicated I'm going to say you pick it all out. Which was your plan anyway."

"Consider it my contribution to helping him into a cage. I was there at the crime scene, Eve, and saw her in the room where you once were."

He settled on a jacket in a strong sharp blue and a vest in something like dark copper—but thankfully not shiny. The pants matched the jacket, but had a stripe of that something like dark copper down the sides.

And somehow she had a pair of boots in the same tone. He added a collared shirt in white. She studied herself in the shirt and vest and weapon, and decided, as usual, he'd been right.

"Take the diamond out."

When she did, she nodded. Okay, it made a statement, and a contrast. But she tucked it away again. "Maybe in the box, just for a few seconds."

"It's all you'll need." He rose when she swung the jacket on. He pulled her in and kissed her. "He doesn't stand a chance against you. But take care of my cop in any case." He patted her hip where he'd discovered a bruise the night before. "And watch out for piss-soaked junkies."

"You can bank on that one." She cupped his face, looked in his eyes. "Take care of my gazillionaire."

"I will. Don't worry."

She wouldn't—or not too much, she thought as she started down-stairs. She just found it . . . disconcerting when he lost his balance. But he'd found it again, so she wouldn't worry too much.

And she was about to take what she was determined would be the last steps in bringing down a killer.

She worked on her strategy—first in dealing with Shauna Hunni-cut—on the way downtown. She could leave any needed softening and stroking on that to Peabody. And the push she'd handle herself.

In the garage, she took the elevator halfway up before escaping the chaos of change of shift for the glides.

Since she'd beaten her squad in, she went straight to her office, then tagged Peabody.

ETA to Central?

Just got here, waiting for elevator.

My office as soon as you get here.

Knowing the elevator, Eve waited a couple of minutes before programming coffee. When she heard Peabody's clump, she sat. Then pointed to the mug of coffee and to the visitor's chair.

"Sit. I'll fill you in and tell you how I think it's going to go. It's going to be jewelry," she began as Peabody snagged the mug.

"You think he took some jewelry from the apartment?"

"Yeah, and here's why."

Chapter Twenty-two

WHEN SHAUNA OPENED THE DOOR OF ANGIE DECKER'S APARTMENT, SHE looked like someone recovering from a long, enervating illness. She stared at Eve with hope sparking in her deeply shadowed eyes.

"We don't have anything to report yet, and we're sorry to intrude. Could we have a minute?"

"Sure. Of course."

The apartment smelled of flowers—some of which, Eve noted, had been at the memorial. And the apartment felt empty but for the three of them.

"Is Ms. Decker here?"

"No. She had to go to work. People have to start living their lives again." She gestured toward a tablet on the table. "I'm starting an apartment search—trying to because it's hard to imagine . . ."

Tears swirled. Shauna pressed the heels of her hands against them as if to push them back. She won the struggle, dropped her hands.

"It's just hard. But I can't stay with Angie indefinitely. I—I had next week off anyway, so I'm hoping I can find a place, something in the same neighborhood, and start moving in.

"Is this about ChiChi?"

"Not directly. You should know she's agreed to plead guilty to the assault in exchange for mandatory community service and anger management training."

"Fine. It doesn't matter. It really doesn't matter. I'm sorry, let's sit down."

"Actually, I need to ask you for something."

"All right. Oh, the painting? Glenda told me you wanted to buy one of Erin's paintings. The one she did of the pizzeria. She thought it would cheer me up. It did, a little."

Sitting, she looked around blankly, like someone just waking from a hard sleep.

"Shauna, we need you to come with us, to go through your apartment with us."

"What?" Panic leapt into her eyes. "Why?"

"You're the only one who'll know, for certain, if anything's missing."

"But . . . Erin wasn't killed there. It wasn't a break-in. I don't understand."

"It's a loose end we need to tie up before we can move to the next stage of the investigation."

"What stage? What stage?" She pushed out of the chair. "We were supposed to be married on Saturday. Do you know what we should be doing today? We should be putting up decorations for the wedding. We should be laughing and arguing about what goes where. And checking with the florist—we didn't order a lot, but we each wanted bouquets, and flowers on the tables we'd set up. Now I have those."

She pointed at the flowers on the table.

"I have those, from her memorial. Now you want me to go back to the apartment where we lived together, made all these plans, where we had a life together?"

"Yes, I do."

"Do you think I killed her?" It wasn't anger, but absolute devastation. "Do you think I'll go there and break down and confess I killed the woman I loved?"

"No. You're not, nor have you ever been, a suspect."

"Then why? How could this possibly help you find who killed her?"

"Because if something's not there that should be, you'll know."

She dropped into a chair again, covered her pale face with her hands. "God, God. I know I'm being stupid about this. I know it's weak, but—"

"It's not stupid," Peabody corrected. "It's not weak. It's grief, and it's human and it's hard. We wouldn't ask if we didn't think it's important."

Dropping her hands, Shauna stared at Peabody. "Becca and Greg have gone in to get some of my things, to clean out the food stuff. And Donna and Angie helped Erin's family get some of her things."

"But you know what they removed," Eve said.

"Yes." Shauna closed her eyes, took a breath. When she opened them again, she looked at Eve. "You really think doing this will matter? Will help you find who killed her?"

"Yes."

"I need to get my purse."

When she walked away, Eve shook her head. "She doesn't believe me, doesn't believe this matters."

"But she's doing it. It's hard for her, but she'll do it."

"Yeah. She's tougher than she looks, but it's going to hurt. Let's make it as quick as possible."

Shauna said nothing as they drove the short distance from apartment building to apartment building. She broke her silence when Eve pulled into a loading zone.

"I bet delivery people hate when you do that."

Eve flipped on her On Duty light. "You win that bet."

Under the circumstances, Eve tolerated the elevator ride to four.

Outside the apartment door, Eve waited while Shauna hesitated.

Peabody laid a hand on Shauna's arm. "Maybe ask yourself what Erin would do."

"She'd go in, get it done."

Shauna unlocked the door, opened it.

"It looks so much like us," she murmured. "Who we were together. She used to say I had all the style, she had all the color, and how frosty it was we were each picking some of the other's up."

Slowly, she walked around the living area.

"I was going to sell the furniture. I'd keep her paintings, and maybe a few little things, but sell the rest. That was wrong. We bought most of this together, or brought it with us from our own spaces. I was going to sell it."

She brushed a hand over the back of the sofa. "But no, no, that's wrong. We'd sit here, watch a vid. We'd have takeaway and sit over there and talk and talk. I thought it would feel empty, but it doesn't. I know I can't live here anymore, but I can take some of what we shared with me."

She turned to Eve and Peabody. "I should've come back before."

"You weren't ready before," Peabody said.

"I didn't think I'd ever be." She wandered a bit more. "Everything's here that should be. Honestly, I don't know what I'm looking for, or why."

"Let's try the bedroom." Her eyes on Shauna, Eve gestured.

"Becca got clothes for me," she said as she walked to the bedroom door. "Toiletries and all that. She picked up what I'd need for making the arrangements, the memorial."

"Outfits, clothes, jewelry?"

"Yes."

"Why don't you start with the jewelry?"

"Fine, but it's not like I—either of us—have anything really valuable. It's mostly costume. We were going to exchange rings, so we—I—have those, but they weren't really expensive."

She opened a drawer. "Here they are," she murmured. "Right here." She opened the ring boxes, brushed a finger over each.

Then she slipped one on the ring finger of her left hand. "I have skinnier fingers." And put the other on the middle finger of her right. "It fits well enough there. Is it just whack that it makes me feel better wearing these?"

Eve said simply, "No."

"I'm going to wear them both. At least for a while, I'm going to wear them both. Okay." She breathed out. "I have these sapphire studs my parents gave me for my twenty-first. It's my birthstone. Most valuable I have, and they're right here."

She went through carefully, piece by piece. "Everything's here, except what Becca brought to me. Erin has more. She has more—not expensive—just more, and I know her parents took some pieces."

"But that's all your jewelry?"

"Yes. Oh, well, no, now that you mention it. I have some sentimental pieces. I don't wear them, but . . ."

She crouched down, opened the bottom drawer.

Then sitting back on her heels, frowned. "That's funny. Did I move the box?"

Eve cast her mind back to the search the morning after the murder.

"A small red box, hinged lid. A few pieces of jewelry inside."

"Yes, that's right. High school stuff. Nothing I've worn since, really, but—"

"Sentimental," Peabody finished after exchanging a look over Shauna's head with Eve.

"Yeah." She pushed through the other items in the drawer.

Gym clothes, Eve remembered, old sweats, and things you'd wear if you expected to get sweaty or dirty.

"I must've moved it. It's just a few things Greg gave me back in our day. A sweet little ring, some earrings, a necklace. Birthdays, Christmas, Valentine's Day, that kind of thing."

She rose. "I must've put them somewhere else. Maybe the closet."

"No, you didn't. I saw them in that drawer the day after the murder."

"I don't understand." Shauna went to the closet anyway. Rose on her toes to look at the top shelf. "I don't know why Becca would've moved . . ."

Trailing off, she turned. Color poured into her face. "You think Becca—that's ridiculous, and it's awful. She would never, never hurt Erin. Plus, for fuck's sake, she was onstage with me when . . . when it happened."

"Tell me who knew where you kept those pieces?"

"Well, I . . ." She ran a hand over her hair. "I guess everybody could have. I bought the little box years ago, because sentimental. I probably said how I liked looking at them once in a while and remembering those days. I know I said Erin didn't mind and I remember how Jon had. A lot. It was one of the reasons I knew we didn't fit."

As she spoke, she opened more drawers, pawed through.

"They're not worth anything, not really, to anyone but me."

"Peabody. Reo."

"On that." Peabody stepped out.

Her face set now, and with some color back in her cheeks, Shauna turned to Eve.

"You knew something would be missing, and there is. But I don't understand why."

"Shauna, I'm going to ask you some questions, but before I do, I need to trust you. Whatever we say here stays here. You can't and won't contact anyone, speak to anyone about what we say here."

Those blue eyes went hot, went sharp. "You know who killed her. You know." She gestured toward the bed in a gesture as hot and sharp as her eyes. "We slept there together. We didn't just have sex, we slept there, woke there, laughed there, made plans there. On Saturday, we'd have put on the white dresses we bought together, hung in that closet, and we'd have made promises to each other.

"You can trust me, Lieutenant, to not do anything, *anything* that will stop you from locking up whoever took her from me."

"I believe you. How did Greg react when you started dating Erin?"

Some of the fresh color faded from her cheeks. "You can't possibly—"

"He gave you those pieces," Eve pointed out. "He knew you kept them, correct?"

"Yes. Yes. I—I told him, God, I can't remember when, that I kept Shaunbar in a pretty red box in my bottom drawer. He—he thought it was sweet."

"And when you and Erin started dating, what did he think?"

She reached behind her until she felt the foot of the bed, then slowly sat. "He was surprised, and maybe a little . . . I don't know, disappointed? You have to understand, his family is very set. Man, woman, husband, wife." She chopped a hand in the air at each word. "They're not mean about it, just set. So he was surprised and maybe disappointed. But—"

"Angry."

Shauna rubbed a hand between her breasts. "I guess, a little. It was more like 'What the hell,' you know? He thought—at first, he thought—she was a kind of bad influence. I can't remember exactly what he said, but we had a little fight about it."

"You had a fight?"

"More a disagreement, and it was over a year ago. I told him what I did with my life, who I slept with, and so on wasn't any of his business. I was pretty harsh because I was already in love with her and he was so critical. But we made up, he apologized. And he and Erin got along fine. More than. You can't expect me to believe my oldest friend would have . . ."

"Who else could have taken the box, Shauna? Who else did that jewelry mean anything to?"

"I must've misplaced it. No, no, you said you saw it after . . . but—"

"Would Erin have trusted him? She wanted to surprise you with something you dreamed of, and Donna was out of town. Would she have trusted him?"

Her eyes went dead. "Yes."

"He knew about Maui. When you were together in high school, the two of you talked about it."

"Yes." Her voice sounded dead as well. "After college. We'd get married after college when we both had jobs. And we'd honeymoon in Maui because I'd wanted that since I was a little girl."

She didn't weep. Her eyes stayed dull and dead, and she didn't weep. "Why wouldn't she trust him? He was my oldest friend. I've known him since middle school."

"Dallas." Peabody spoke from the doorway, then nodded.

"Shauna, we're going to take you back to Angie's. I need you to stay there, and I need you to keep your word."

"Do you think I'd speak to him about this?" She got to her feet. "He knew where I kept the jewelry, and taking it was petty. He can be petty, but that's something you overlook in a friend. She would have trusted him. I trusted him. He always thinks he knows what I should do, what's best for me. I overlooked that, too, or ignored it. And if I got pissed about it, he'd back off, apologize. 'Just trying to look out for you, Shaunbar.' He'd call me that to make me laugh."

She laid a hand on her heart. "In here, I'm not ready to believe he could do anything like this. But in here?" She touched her other hand to the side of her head. "I can. Oh God, God, I can."

She dropped both hands. "I'll keep my word, but I need yours. You have to tell me, if you prove it's true, you have to tell me right away."

"You have my word."

When they dropped her off, Eve watched her walk inside.

"She won't contact anyone, least of all him. But let's make this as fast as possible, too."

"We got the search warrant for his apartment. When we find the box—and we have to hope like hell he didn't toss it all—"

"He wouldn't. Shaunbar's too important to him."

"Okay. When we find it, we'll get the arrest for robbery."

"Enough to take him in, sweat out the rest. He'll have excuses for taking the box," Eve continued as she drove. "He's going to be sure, at first, he can talk his way out of this. He sells, he manages, and we're just women, after all."

"Then this should be fun."

"Not for him," Eve said, and considered it a stroke of Roarke luck when she zipped into a place right outside the apartment building.

A third-floor unit, almost within shouting distance of where Shauna and Erin lived. No cams, crap security.

She mastered in, hit the stairs.

The soundproofing was better than Shauna's building, but not by much. This time instead of wailing, a baby laughed somewhere on the second floor.

Though she decided it was hard to tell the difference.

On three, she knocked first. "NYPSD, Lieutenant Dallas, Detective Peabody, record on. Please open the door."

When she got no response, she knocked a second time. "Dallas and Peabody entering premises by master for a duly warranted search and seizure."

She mastered in, looked around while Peabody secured the door behind them.

Not too dissimilar from the apartment they'd just been in. More stylish, Eve supposed, not as bold and bright, but a similar footprint.

One of Erin's paintings hung in the living area—a street scene showcasing Barney's men's shop. A gift, no doubt, and now insured for its increased value.

"No clutter," she observed. "No lived-in mess, and well-coordinated. Like a man's suit."

"You could say that," Peabody agreed. "Nothing out of place."

"He wouldn't keep it in a communal area. Bedroom, his space in there."

They took the short hallway, turned.

"Nice and neat, but you can see they've been busy and distracted for a few days—things a little jumbled on this dresser—hers—perfume bottle, little dish with stuff tossed in. This one's his, and that highboy, too, I'd wager. He'll have more than her. Got himself matching shoehorn, clothes brush."

Eve started to the highboy. "One closet, so communal. It won't be there."

"I've got his dresser."

Eve took the highboy. She opened the top drawer first. She had about four inches on Becca, and the drawer hit her about chin level.

Socks, folded, not rolled, and color coordinated in dividers.

She pulled it all the way out.

"Jesus, this was too easy."

"You're kidding!"

"Nope. He slid it in the back of the drawer, behind some red socks."

Eve took it out, opened it. "And here's Shaunbar. Ring, couple pair of earrings, necklace, two bracelets."

She bagged it, sealed, labeled.

"Would he keep the garrote? Hard to believe that, but since we're here."

A few minutes later, Peabody called out, "Not the garrote, but I've got piano wire." Peabody held up the package. "And funny, they don't have a piano."

"Bag it," Eve said, "and let's go bag him."

With, Eve thought when she double-parked in front of the men's shop, as much humiliation as possible.

Several horns blasted as she stepped onto the sidewalk. She ignored them.

The display window showed a couple of fake men. One wore a sharp charcoal suit with needle pinstripes that made her wonder if Baxter shopped there. The other, though it was sweltering August, wore a forest-green sweater with black leather pants.

It had a scarf in dull gold tossed jauntily around its neck.

She stepped in to cool air scented with something between pine and cedar.

Summer stuff—though sweltering August—was displayed on a sales rack or neatly folded on shelves.

Suits, hung in sections by designers, comprised most of one wall. Dress shirts, crisp and folded, were stacked in cubbies. Casual wear took the opposite side, and accessories—ties, cuff links, wallets, belts, and so on—had glass displays in the center.

It boosted her to see one of the staff with a customer while the other approached her with a smile.

"Good morning, ladies—nearly afternoon now! How can I be of service?"

"You can get the manager."

His young, slick, handsome face showed concern. "Oh, is there a problem?"

"Apparently. Where's Greg Barney?"

"He's in the dressing room area with a client. If I could assist—"

"You can, by getting him."

"Of course. Just one moment."

As he hurried off, the shop door opened.

Eve recognized Allisandra Charro, personal shopper, from a case they'd recently closed.

And Charro recognized her.

Beaming smiles, she stepped forward in red stilettos and offered a perfectly manicured hand. "Why, Lieutenant Dallas! We meet at last. I helped you identify a murderous teenager by his Stubens."

"I remember."

"Shopping for Roarke?"

"No. On duty."

"Really? How exciting. I'm just here to make some selections for a client—whom I assume has no murderous intent."

"Good luck with that."

As Barney came out, Eve walked toward him.

"Oh, Lieutenant, Detective. If I'd known— You've charged that terrible woman."

"Yeah, we did. And now it's your turn. Greg Barney, you're under arrest for robbery."

"What? What? That's insane. I've never stolen anything in my life!"

She sort of hoped he'd resist, but apparently he was too shocked to make a fuss as she cuffed him.

"You have the right to remain silent," she began as Peabody flanked him and they started out.

"This is some crazy mistake. Roderick, take over. I'll have this sorted out in no time."

"Bet you don't. You have the right to an attorney and/or legal representation," Eve continued as they walked him out.

"I'd absolutely *love* to dress you," Charro called out. "More than ever!"

"I take care of that all by myself." She continued the Revised Miranda, and Barney, flushed to the roots of his hair with mortification, continued to protest his innocence.

"This is outrageous!" he began to sputter when secured in the back of the car. "You've embarrassed me at my place of business."

Hope so, Eve thought as she got behind the wheel.

"I'm not a thief. What am I supposed to have stolen? How could you do something like this?"

"With a warrant."

"I don't believe you. I haven't stolen anything, so you can't have a warrant."

"Right here." Helpfully, Peabody held up the warrant she'd printed out on her PPC.

"I assumed the two of you were reasonably competent, but now I see why it took you days to arrest that stripper for Erin's murder."

Peabody started to speak, caught Eve's slight head shake, and let that ride.

"I told you it was some lowlife, and it was. Shauna should never have associated with someone like that, and wouldn't have except for Erin."

Keep talking, Eve thought. Record's on, rights read.

"Now you come into my shop, in front of clients and staff, and drag me out like a common criminal."

"I don't recall any dragging. Do you recall dragging, Peabody?"

"No, sir, I don't. And the record will show no dragging involved. He actually came along fairly meekly." She shifted to smile at him. "Thanks for your cooperation."

"It shows what happens when the flighty are given authority."

"Now we're flighty," Eve observed. "Peabody, we're incompetent, flighty draggers."

"Maybe. But he's the one in cuffs."

Pride swelled in Eve's chest as she pulled into the garage.

"And here we are, home again."

When they got him out of the back, he jutted out his chin.

"I can tolerate mistakes. People make mistakes. But there's no excuse for humiliating me at my workplace. There will be recompense."

"Counting on that," Eve said, and led him into the elevator. "Detective Peabody is going to process you, then we'll have a nice chat, the three of us, in Interview."

"The sooner this is sorted out, the better."

His chin continued to jut as the elevator stopped to let in more cops.

"And once we do, you *will* come to the shop, apologize to me in front of my staff, and you *will* contact Mr. Henrich and Ms. Charro and explain your mistake."

One of the cops in the car slid an amused glance in Eve's direction.

"Doesn't know you very well, does he?"

Eve just smiled. "Not yet. He's about to."

Chapter Twenty-three

SMARTER, EVE DECIDED AS SHE PREPPED FOR THE INTERVIEW, TO HAVE yelled lawyer right off the jump. But he considered himself in the clear on the murder, and as far as he was concerned hadn't stolen anything.

Add he considered himself smarter than a couple of female cops, and he'd decided to forgo that one. For now.

Tagging a lawyer also meant someone else knew about his arrest. He wouldn't want that.

She put the evidence bags in an evidence box, added some crime scene photos to a file. Then, checking the time, tagged Roarke.

His face filled the screen. "Lieutenant, you just caught me. Lunch meeting coming up."

"Well, bon appétit there. Just letting you know I'm bringing Barney into the box."

"For the murder."

"That'll be the end result. We're starting off with theft. What he took out of Shauna's apartment that day. I *knew* it. Now I know what. Some baubles he'd given her back in high school. She'd kept them in a box for sentiment. I guess he couldn't have that, so when he had the chance—alone in her place—he took the box. He hid it in his sock drawer."

"His sock drawer? Not very clever."

"Well, it's the top of one of those highboy things. He has his socks folded, in dividers, color coordinated. It's a red box, so with the red socks. Do you do that with yours? The folding, coordinating thing? I don't think I've ever been in your sock drawer."

"Why would you? But you're welcome to, as if I had anything to hide, I would be a great deal more clever. If I could postpone this meeting, I'd come down and watch you break him. Always an education."

Gone, she noted, was the sad, broody, angry Roarke of the night before. He looked like busy, in-charge Roarke now.

"We will break him, and I appreciate the assist in getting him this far."

"Anytime, Lieutenant. I'll expect to be fully briefed when I see you at home."

"Check it. Later."

She clicked off, then gathered her things for Interview A.

She sat as if studiously studying the file when Peabody led him in.

The Giant's Tear hung, flashing, outside her shirt.

"Record on. Have a seat, Greg. Dallas, Lieutenant Eve, and Peabody, Detective Delia, in Interview with Barney, Greg, in the matter of file number R/T-98721. Also of interest in this interview, file number H-7823.

"Mr. Barney, have you been read your rights?"

"You know very well I have." He fussed with his tie. "You recited them to me yourself after deliberately humiliating me at work."

"Well then, let's get started."

"I demand to know, right now, what I'm accused of. Just what are you deluded into believing I stole?"

"Why don't I show you?"

After opening the evidence box, she removed the evidence bag with the red trinket box.

He went very still, and his face went from annoyed to a cold, hard mask.

"Where did you get that?"

"Where you put it. Your sock drawer—lots of fancy socks, Greg. Red box, red socks. Found it in about ten seconds."

"And what gives you the right to go into my home, to paw through my personal belongings?"

"Peabody?"

"Why, that would be *this* warrant."

"Duly executed," Eve added. "This and what it contains are not your property, Greg. Hence, theft."

"I knew this was a ridiculous mistake." He huffed out a breath, leaned in a bit. "I gave what's in that box to Shauna."

"Gifts."

"Yes, yes, gifts."

"Are you aware that once you give a gift, it no longer belongs to you? Hence, I repeat, theft."

"I took them for safekeeping. Shauna's not been herself, as you should understand. She's had a trauma, and isn't thinking straight right now. She's talking about selling most of her things, and since I know she values those gifts, has kept them for years, I didn't want them to get somehow lost in the shuffle."

"So you took them, without asking her. Hence, I'm forced to repeat, theft."

"She would never think of it that way. People are going through her apartment. Friends and relatives of Erin. Who knows what they might take? I just wanted to keep them safe until she's feeling better."

"So, worried about thievery, you committed same."

"Oh, for God's sake." He waved that away. "Contact Shauna. She'll say it's fine."

"Yet, you hid this." She tapped the box.

"I didn't hide it. I placed it."

"In the back of your sock drawer. Without mentioning it to your cohab—that's Becca, isn't it? Also a good, concerned friend of Shauna's."

"I may have mentioned it. I don't recall."

"Peabody, why don't you step out and contact Becca DiNuzio, since Greg's memory is sketchy on it?"

"I probably didn't." He waved that away again. "We've been busy, distracted. A friend was murdered. Our closest friend is grieving."

"You took this, with its contents, from Shauna's apartment the evening you were there, ostensibly to remove items from the AC and the friggie."

"Nothing ostensibly about it. That's what I did. I thought of the box while I was clearing out. Maybe I acted impulsively." He shrugged at that. "But with what was best for Shauna in my heart and mind."

"You decide what's best for her?"

"She's grieving," he said with insulting patience. "She's hardly in the state of mind to make logical choices. This is a waste of time. A five-second 'link call to Shauna will straighten this out. And then, I damn well expect those apologies."

"Right. You didn't much like Erin Albright, did you, Greg?"

He managed to look shocked and insulted at once. "Of course I did! She was Shauna's fiancée. And I'm very grateful you, finally, caught her killer. But that doesn't excuse—"

"Yeah, we caught her killer." Eve tapped the box again, then, taking it out of the evidence bag, opened it. "What do you think, Peabody?"

"Sweet, pretty. Immature, but suitable for a high school girl."

"They're classic." He spoke coldly. "Timeless. Simple, yes, but classic, so used to dress up or dress down."

"Well, you're the fashion guy. Still, she kept them separate from her other jewelry. She didn't wear these anymore."

"She could have. Her choice."

"Yeah, hers. Like Erin was her choice. You were her choice once. Shaunbar."

"In high school. Happy memories, yes, and a strong bond between us. But I'm in a committed relationship with someone else."

"From high school."

His jaw tensed, then jutted again. "It's entirely different now, for all of us."

"It really is. Shauna was also in a committed relationship."

"I'm aware."

"And now you'll help her rebuild her life, move past the trauma."

"I'll certainly try."

"Because you look out for her. Making her sandwiches, walking her home from work when you can manage it, giving advice, doing favors."

His long sigh added a fresh layer to that insulting patience.

"Friends tend to do all of that. Good friends, *real* friends certainly do. Now, I'd like to leave. If you'd just contact Shauna—"

"We've talked to her already," Peabody said. "And she couldn't think of why you, or anyone, would take that box and the jewelry inside."

That concerned him, Eve noted, as his eyes darted away.

"Because you haven't let me talk to her, explain to her. As I think I've clearly explained to you."

"So you took it upon yourself to go into her bedroom—without her knowledge or permission—go through her dresser—without her knowledge or permission—remove a box containing jewelry—without her knowledge or permission. Then hid same in your own bedroom, in your own dresser. That's your explanation for stealing?"

She could actually see the muscles in his face tighten.

"You're being deliberately obtuse." His tone, deeply patronizing, carried an edge of ripe temper.

"Obtuse and flighty? I wonder what's next."

"I simply didn't want Shauna to do something she'd regret. And given her emotional state—"

"Are you her therapist, too?" Peabody widened her eyes. "A man of many facets."

"Oh, blow me."

When that edge went jagged, the smile Eve held inside was broad and fierce.

"Sorry," Peabody countered. "Performing sexual acts in Interview is frowned upon."

"This is bullshit. I was acting in the best interest of a friend who tends to act on impulse and emotion in the best of times. Which these clearly aren't. Now, I'm done with this. I'm leaving."

"Sit your ass down."

The whiplash in Eve's voice had him jerking.

"We're in charge here," she reminded him.

He sat, but eyed her with derision. "You won't be when this is over. Trust me on that."

"I'm a police lieutenant with a dozen years behind my badge. Do you think I'm afraid of some guy who sells overpriced ties? Some guy who steals some cheap jewelry from a friend and hides it in his sock drawer?"

"I manage a well-respected men's store that caters to a discerning clientele. And the jewelry I gave Shauna wasn't cheap. It may not compare to that rock around your neck, but it wasn't cheap. It was appropriate."

"This?" Deliberately, she lifted the diamond by its chain. "I just wear this for sentiment." Which was absolute truth, she thought as she dropped it under her shirt.

"So you stole and secreted this—appropriate—jewelry because you were looking out for your impulsive, emotional friend's best interest?"

"I removed them to safekeeping for Shauna's best interest, yes."

"You like to decide what's in others' best interest. Such as . . ." She opened the file. "LeRoy Vic, a former assistant manager at your place of employment. You decided it wasn't in his best interest to move to Brooklyn with his pregnant wife and take the manager's position at another store—and took steps to prevent that."

"What is this!" Outrage sizzled, and burned two spots of color in his cheeks. "You dug up a former employee—a classically disgruntled employee—to try to undermine me? He wasn't ready for the position and lacked the necessary leadership qualities to—"

"But served as your assistant manager?"

"*Assistant* is key," Barney snapped back. "I was doing my best to groom him, mentor him. A few more years under my supervision, and—"

"His sales were excellent, and his previous evaluations prior to this desired move? Also excellent."

"He wasn't ready." Barney did the chin-jut thing again, and this time folded his arms. "And what does my decision as a manager have to do with any of this?"

"In your capacity as manager, you also decided what was best for Sharlene Wilson."

"Oh, for God's sake."

"On several occasions you suggested Ms. Wilson should resign her part-time position and take professional parent status instead."

"She had children at home."

"I see. So in your opinion, women who choose to have a child or children shouldn't also choose to work outside the home?"

"If I recall correctly, Sharlene's professional mother stipend would have been more than her monthly pay from On Trend, where she worked, essentially, a handful of hours a week."

"Especially after you hired another part-time—male—employee and cut her hours."

346 J. D. Robb

"That was a managerial decision, and I don't have to explain it to you."

"No, you don't, mostly because it explains itself. You like to manage people. You get to decide what they should do, how they should do it. How they should live. What's best for them. Then you take the necessary steps to see they stay inside the lines you've drawn."

Eve studied him, tapped her fingers on the table. "It makes me wonder, Greg. What do you do when they refuse to stay inside those lines? How far would you go? Obviously, stealing isn't off the table."

"I've explained that. I'm not going to keep repeating myself. Shauna will understand, and will back me a hundred percent, so your intimidation tactics are a waste of time. If you had any common sense or any respect for the position you somehow found yourself holding, you'd let me speak with her and clear this up."

"I bet it pissed you off she put what you gave her in a box." Peabody drew his attention back to her. "And stuck the box in a drawer with her gym and slop clothes. Never wore what you gave her."

"You don't know the first thing about it."

"Tell us about it, Greg," Peabody urged. "Tell us how it felt to have Shauna put Shaunbar away, and live her life the way she chose. How even after college, she wasn't interested in taking Shaunbar out for another spin."

"That was a mutual decision. We'd both moved on."

"Speaking of moving," Eve picked up, "after college, after a brief adjustment period back in the old neighborhood, she moved to Manhattan. And you followed right along soon after, like a puppy. Even moved into the same building."

"For employment, and convenience to my employment."

"So the fact you took employment near hers, moved into the same apartment building had nothing to do with good old Shaunbar."

"Why shouldn't I move into the same building as a good friend?" he demanded, but looked away. "When it's convenient to my work."

"Then, lo and behold, you start dating another old schoolmate. And one Shauna's connected with, made good friends with. In fact, what they both consider best friends."

"What's strange about that? Becca and I began seeing each other, initially through Shauna. We fell in love."

"Did you? Or was she just second choice because Shauna didn't want you?"

"How dare you!" He slapped a fist on the table. "How dare you speak about the woman I'm going to marry that way."

"Oh, you're engaged." Peabody clapped her hands together. "Congratulations."

"Not yet. We will be."

"When you decide?" Eve asked. "When you decide it's the best time, it's best for her?"

"That's how it works!" As he had during the arrest, he sputtered. "When I feel it's right, I buy the ring, I pick the time, the place, and I propose."

"And naturally, she accepts. You decide when and where you'll get married, then if and when to procreate. And if you do procreate, she'll set aside her career until such time as you decide the offspring is old enough for her to pick it up again. If ever."

"Not that it's any of your business, but when I take a wife, I will be head of the household. When we have children, I will provide for them, and she will mother them. This is how strong families are built."

Take a wife, Eve thought. That was a good one.

"So parents who both opt to maintain a career aren't building strong families?"

"That's my personal opinion, to which I'm entitled."

"Sure you are. But what if both parents are men, or both are women? Who's the mom who stays home then?"

"The fact there's that question only demonstrates why such arrangements only foster confusion and difficult family dynamics. I want to speak to Shauna. Now!"

"But this conversation's so interesting. Aren't you interested, Pea-body?"

"Fascinated. You know, my aunts Gracie and Lottie have been married for . . . golly, I think it's forty-odd years. Three kids—grown now—I think it's six grandkids and counting. Gracie's a large animal vet—you know, horses, cows, like that. Lottie's a teacher—history, high school level. They're a pretty strong family."

"In your opinion," Barney commented.

"Yeah." Peabody just smiled. "Everybody's got opinions. Of course, I come from a Free-Ager background." Peabody caught the smirk and only smiled more brightly. "And we're big on tolerance and inclusion."

"And from my scan of your background, yours isn't in the Free-Ager area."

"Decidedly not. No offense," he said to Peabody.

"Oh, absolutely none taken."

"Given your background and stated opinions," Eve began, "what did you think when Shauna became involved with Erin?"

"That she was, again, acting on impulse and the emotion of the mo-ment. She'd dated men who'd disappointed her, or didn't suit her, so she experimented. Unwisely."

"How unwisely?"

He let out an impatient breath. "Aren't we sitting here right now due to that? Aren't I being interrogated and humiliated because of that? You've arrested the woman responsible for this upheaval in our lives. A person Shauna would never, ever have associated with prior to her involvement with a woman like Erin Albright."

"A woman like Erin?"

"A lesbian, for God's sake. A street artist, basically living hand to mouth, who counted strippers, trans people, gay people, people who con-stantly engaged in indiscriminate sex among her so-called friends. Freaks and losers."

"Clearly you didn't approve of the relationship."

Fury lived in his eyes as he leaned forward.

"I've known Shauna since we were ten. She comes from a strong, traditional family. She may have pushed some limits in college, that's almost expected. But she maintained her basic values."

"Which, you feel, mirror yours. Until Erin."

He spread his hands. "What happened to Erin is tragic. It's horrible, and only more so since she was killed by someone she believed was a friend."

"I completely agree."

Bolstered, he nodded. "How it affects Shauna is heartbreaking. As someone who basically grew up with her, who cares deeply about her, it breaks mine. In time, she'll move past it, and find herself again."

"Pick up those old values," Eve said, "and put away the lifestyle that was more . . ."

"Bohemian?" Peabody suggested.

"Bohemian. Good one. Is that accurate, Greg?"

"Yes."

"So as tragic, horrible, heartbreaking as it is, Erin's death cleared the way for Shauna to get back to where she belongs."

"I don't forgive ChiChi Lopez for what she did, but it does. Yes."

"Well." Eve looked at Peabody, nodded, looked at Barney, nodded again. "No wonder you had to kill her."

"What!" He surged up. "Are you out of your mind?"

"Sit down!"

"I will not listen to this."

"Sit down." Eve rose slowly. "Or I'll put you down. And believe me, I'll enjoy it."

"You have no right to treat me this way." But he sat. "No cause to say such things to me. You've got Erin's killer. You arrested her."

"We arrested Lopez for assault, on Shauna. Not for Erin's murder—

that was your assumption. And boy, did that fit right in for you. The stripper with the garrote in the sex club."

"Hey, like Clue! Love that game. But," Peabody pointed out, "it turns out to be the overbearing ex-boyfriend with the garrote in the sex club."

"Sure does. And when you add ex–high school boyfriend, it's only more pathetic."

"I take mementos for safekeeping, and suddenly I'm a killer?"

"That sure helped. You looked so damn guilty and twitchy when you walked into that hallway and saw me. I knew you'd taken something you shouldn't have. You should've left that alone and I might not have started focusing on you the way I did. That was weak, that was stupid, like it was stupid to try to push the lowlife stranger killer in the sex club on me. I'm a fucking professional."

"That only proves I care about my friend, not that I killed anyone. If you try to tell Shauna I did, I'll sue your lying ass off."

"Oh, she already knows. She knew when she couldn't find the red box with the cheap, high school jewelry. She's been over you for years, Greg. Now, she's done with you. No more Shaunbar."

"She'd never believe you. Never."

"Why? Because you're so good at playing the great guy, good friend? One who hovers, manipulates, and thinks he knows best? Who believes that, so deeply, he'll kill for it? For her? You killed Erin for her. You had to protect Shauna, whatever it took. Had to save her from making a terrible mistake. Save her before she married another woman, a bohemian—good word—who would and had led her astray."

"How could she love Erin," Peabody added, "when she'd been half of Shaunbar? How could she disrespect you, and what you are, by loving a woman?"

"She didn't love Erin, but that's beside the point."

"She was about to marry Erin," Eve pointed out.

"She was caught up, but beside the point."

"What is the point?"

"I didn't kill anyone, you idiot! In fact, I more than tolerated Erin. For fuck's sake, I have two of her substandard paintings in my apartment. It's obvious now you haven't been able to pin this on the stripper, so you're looking for a scapegoat. I will not be your scapegoat."

Eve tried on some insulting patience—and she believed she wore it better.

"Then you shouldn't have been stupid, Greg, and you were. So damn stupid." She rounded the table as his face splotched red with angry color, as she moved behind him. Leaned in, just a little.

"You shouldn't have left the case, the tickets, the note. You should've gotten rid of those. Nobody knew what was in that case but Erin, and you killed her. But you couldn't be sure, could you? Maybe Donna looked in it, because you sure as hell did."

Now she leaned close to his ear, lowered her voice. "And it burned you, burned hard. Maui? You couldn't take that insult. You were supposed to take Shauna there, on your honeymoon. That was the dream. How could you let this happen? Shauna had to suffer, too. She had to pay, too, for allowing it.

"But then"—she straightened, met his eyes in the mirror—"you always planned to kill Erin—remove that obstacle. I think you hoped to kill her right before the wedding, but the whole Maui thing opened another door."

"I'm with Becca."

"Maybe, maybe not. Either way, you couldn't be disrespected this way, couldn't have what you had smeared and defiled like this." She tapped the box as she walked around the table again. "You couldn't let this lesbian, this bohemian, this street artist who had sex with strippers lure Shauna into that life. You couldn't have Shaunbar defiled—would you take it to *defiled*? Yeah, you would. Defile what you were, what you are."

"And Shauna wouldn't listen." Peabody spoke quietly, in direct contrast to Eve. "She wouldn't be manipulated and maneuvered this time. No matter how you tried to influence her, she resisted. Because of Erin. Because she loved her."

"She did *not*! Erin manipulated her, maneuvered her, influenced her. Shauna in some sex club, dancing on a stage half-naked? Kissing another woman, and in public!"

"The horror," Peabody muttered.

"Playing house with another woman? None of that, none is who she is. Erin twisted something in her. Oh, she could be charismatic, no question. Exciting, adventurous. It was a fling, one that went too far, but a fling. It would never have lasted, so I had no reason to kill Erin."

"You did it for yourself." Eve sat back as she studied him. "It embarrassed you. It diminished you. And yeah, enraged you. Because you're a small, petty, stupid man."

"I'm a man!" He shouted it. "And you know nothing. Yes, their relationship embarrassed me. For Shauna. She was making a fool of herself. I actually said that to Becca once, and what did she say? She laughed, and said, 'A fool for love.'

"Women are so predictable. Love is the reason, the excuse, the fall guy for everything."

"You detested Erin."

"What if I did! She was ruining Shauna's future. She demeaned my past. We had something special, Shauna and I. Yes, we were young, but we had something special. We were something special, and what she was doing with Erin, what she intended to do with Erin despite all sense, demeaned what we had and what we were."

"You were never going to give Shauna back that jewelry."

"So what? So the fuck what? I gave it to her with an open heart. I took it back because she didn't deserve to have it."

"Because of Erin."

"Yes, because of fucking Erin. Maybe I'm not as sorry as you think

I should be that she's dead. But I didn't kill her. And you have nothing, absolutely nothing, to say I did."

"Actually, we have this one thing. Because you're a stupid man, Greg. A stupid man who thinks he's smart. A small-minded, stupid man who believes he's special. You're not special. You're pitifully ordinary."

"Fuck you. You have nothing."

"Well, we've got this." Eve reached in the evidence box, pulled out the piano wire. "Something else you should've ditched."

His face paled, then reddened again. "I've never seen that before."

"We found it in your drawer, Greg."

"Then you put it there. You've probably planted evidence countless times, cheating to get where you are so you can strut around with your stunner and your ridiculous diamond and harass innocent people."

"Every minute of the search is on record, and the recording is also in evidence."

"Then Becca must have put it there."

"Whoa." On a quick laugh, Eve sat back. "You're going to throw the woman you intend to marry under the maxibus." Eve shook her head. "Yeah, you're pitifully ordinary."

"And talk about predictable," Peabody added.

"Plus, more stupid." She tapped the package. "The name of the shop where you bought it's right here. And you weren't even smart enough to pay cash or go too far out of your own neighborhood to buy it. Then you fucking kept it. It took one goddamn 'link call to verify you bought it.

"What's below idiot, Peabody?"

"I think moron."

"That's you, Greg. You're a moron. Tell us, why do you have piano wire in your drawer when you don't own a piano?"

A light sweat sheened that all-American face. This time when he fussed with his tie, he loosened the knot.

"It's not against the law."

"Jesus, do you honestly think we can't match this to the wound you put on Erin Albright's throat? What's below a moron?"

"Maybe imbecile."

"He's getting there. A garrote's a mean way to kill, but she deserved it. So you bought the wire, and you looked up how to make a garrote. EDD's had time to go through your e's by now. Why don't you tag them up, Peabody, so we can close this out?"

"Stop it! Stop it! None of that proves anything."

"If there's something below imbecile," Peabody said, "I'm out."

"We'll just say Greg Barney. You have the wire, you have a search for the fashioning of a garrote on your e's. You detested her. She demeaned who you were, and she was leading Shauna into a deplorable—in your view—lifestyle.

"And."

She pulled the last bag out of evidence. "You kept your old 'link, Greg. We didn't need EDD to find your communications with Erin. She trusted you. She asked you for a favor, a favor she wanted so she could surprise Shauna. She didn't tell you what the surprise was—that was her big secret."

"And you agreed. It's all on there," Peabody told him. "When, you asked, where, and how. Such a good guy, such a good friend."

"The when? The day of the party, because she didn't want Donna feeling pressured to get back in time. The where? She'd bring it to you before you left for work—after Becca had already left. Then the how. She'd meet you when you took lunch, give you the swipe."

"I bet she told you not to peek, that she wanted Shauna to be the first to know. But you did, and that sealed Erin's fate."

"Hell, it's like she asked you to kill her. She handed you the perfect opportunity."

"If you had a friend who was hanging off the side of a cliff, would you

throw her a rope?" Barney demanded. "If you had a friend drowning because she'd swum out too far, would you do what you could to save her?"

"I would."

"That's all I did. And in time she'll understand."

"No, you did it for yourself, and you're glad she suffered, your good
friend Shauna. So you could hover, the loving friend. Offer to make her a
sandwich, offer to help get stuff out of her apartment, offer her a shoulder
to cry on.

"Then smirk," Eve added. "Yeah, I caught that. Smirk when she gets
her face slapped at her fiancée's memorial. What a thrill for you. Her
tears, her grief, a kind of payment for embarrassing you. For disrespect-
ing the shine of Shaunbar."

She shoved Erin's crime scene still across the table. "There's your
work. I bet you're proud of it."

"I took a life to save a life. And I want a deal."

"I bet you do. Let's go over your movements of that day, that night, so
we have all the details in place first."

Epilogue

IT TOOK TIME, AND TO HER AMAZEMENT, HE DIDN'T DEMAND A LAWYER until the end.

She'd given him too much credit for smarts.

He ended up with a public defender who huddled with him, who then huddled with Reo.

During the legal huddling, Eve dealt with the paperwork.

Then she closed her murder book and began to clear her murder board.

Then she huddled with Reo, and left satisfied, before she and Peabody went to deliver a different sort of notification.

Shauna deserved to know.

As a result, she drove through her home gates a little late. Not very, she decided, plus, she'd followed the Marriage Rules and tagged Roarke as requested.

She walked in, eyed Summerset, eyed the cat.

"Yeah, I'm late. And a stupid asshole of a murderer's in a cage."

"Then well done to you, Lieutenant."

"As well done as the law allows," she said, and headed upstairs with the cat.

When she walked into her office, Roarke was at her board, clearing it.

"You're clearing my board."

"You said it was done, so I thought I'd save you some time."

"It is, and it does. Thanks. Let's have some wine."

She walked over to grab a bottle herself. Hardly mattered which, as Roarke didn't stock anything that didn't meet his level. And that remained well above hers.

"He confessed?"

"He did. He's an idiot. No, wait, we decided he's a Greg Barney, which is below imbecile. You actually want to hear all this?"

"I do."

"Then let's sit over there, and I'll tell you."

She pointed toward the sofa, brought the wine and glasses herself. He'd opened the terrace doors to the breeze that approached a wind.

And it felt just fine.

She ran through the interview.

"And that was it, truly? He murdered a woman because her relationship with his high school sweetheart embarrassed him?"

"A lot of his self-worth's tied up in Shaunbar, and his incredibly rigid worldview. Shauna deviated from both, and he blamed Erin for it. His usual methods didn't work, so."

She shook her head, drank. "He'd have done it again."

"You think so?"

"I know it. If he'd gotten away with this, he'd have done it again. To Becca, maybe Shauna, a staff member who disrespected him. He'll get a shrink in prison, but I doubt they'll crack the wall of that worldview."

"Did he get a deal after all?"

"I wouldn't call it much of a deal. Life, on-planet. Possibility of parole at twenty-five in."

"You're satisfied with that."

"Yeah. He's in the system now, and he's not smart enough to work it inside. He's just not. He won't get parole at twenty-five."

She stretched out her legs, put her boots on the table as the cat joined them.

"Pushing his buttons turned out to be easier than I thought, and I didn't think it would be that difficult. Talking to Shauna, then Becca after? A lot harder."

"A kind of notification, isn't it?" He topped off both their glasses, then put his boots beside hers. "The center drops out of someone's world."

"Shauna'd had enough time to work through at least some of it. But Becca? She loved the guy, but the guy she loved doesn't exist. Shauna wanted to go with us, and Angie got home when we were there. So they both went with us."

"So Becca had a circle—some of her tribe."

"It helped. I guess it helped. When we left, they were packing up some of her things. She's going to stay at Angie's for a couple of days. I guess that helps, too."

"We need our mates, in good times and in bad."

"Yeah, I guess we do."

"Did you tell Crack?"

"Yeah, I felt he deserved to know. Which makes me think of Rochelle, and that leads to An Didean. Shauna understands I can't take that painting as a gift—and the money from the sales of Erin's paintings is going to a scholarship for artists. She asked if I'd find someone at An Didean for that particular amount."

"That's incredibly kind."

"She sees it as a way to pay me back, and she doesn't have to pay me back for doing my job. But—"

"It remains incredibly kind, and clever with it." He rubbed her thigh. "I'll speak to Rochelle, and she'll help you pick."

"I don't want to pick. Don't make me pick. It's too much pressure. Can't she just pick? It's sort of part of her job."

"That's right enough. That's the way we'll do it."

"Good. Whew. Feel the relief."

She laid her head on his shoulder, then tipped her face up to kiss his jaw. "Let's eat outside again."

"I could grill something."

"Would something be steak?"

"It could be."

"It should be. But let's sit here and finish this glass first. With the doors open, it's practically outside. And it feels good, just sitting here."

She linked her hand with his.

"It's nice being married," she said again.

"My idea, I'll remind you."

"I gotta give you that."

She sat sipping wine, the strong summer breeze blowing in, her hand linked with his, and the cat spread over both their laps.

Yes, she thought. It was pretty damn nice.

About the Author

J. D. Robb is the pseudonym for #1 *New York Times* bestselling author Nora Roberts. She is the author of more than 230 novels, including the futuristic suspense In Death series. There are more than 500 million copies of her books in print.